A SECRET,
A SAFARI,
A SECOND CHANCE

LIZ FIELDING

HOME TO
BLUE STALLION
RANCH

STELLA BAGWELL

MILLS & BOON

First Published in Great Britain 2019
by Mills & Boon, an imprint of HarperCollinsPublishers,
1 London Bridge Street, London, SE1 9GF

A Secret, A Safari, A Second Chance © 2019 Liz Fielding
Home to Blue Stallion Ranch © 2019 Stella Bagwell

ISBN: 978-0-263-27260-4

0919

MIX
Paper from
responsible sources
FSC C007454

Printed and bound in Spain
by CPI, Barcelona

A SECRET,
A SAFARI,
A SECOND CHANCE

LIZ FIELDING

For Donna, Barbara and Nina,
with whom I have shared great hugs,
both in cyberspace and in reality.
Forever friends.

PROLOGUE

'ARE YOU COLD, RED?'

Eve was shivering, but the Nantucket evening was balmy; the cold was coming from inside.

She'd been cajoled into joining this beach party by the older women in her family, who were worried about her and thought she needed to get out, assuring her kindly that some young company would 'cheer her up'.

Her cousins, given no choice in the matter, had done their best to include her, but these teenagers had known one another all their lives. She was twenty-one, in her last year at university; they all seemed so young, and her novelty value as 'the English cousin' was outweighed by the awkwardness of the fact that her mother had just died.

Bit of a downer, that.

She'd taken pity on them, pleading a headache to move away from the music and the bonfire to sit in the quiet shadow of the dunes, welcoming the chance to be on her own for a while, without having family fussing around her. Counting down the time until her grandmother would be in bed and she could slip back into the house, so that she wouldn't have to pretend to have had a good time.

So that her grandmother wouldn't have to pretend to care.

The last thing she needed was for someone to hit on her.

'If I lend you my sweater can I join your escape party?' She managed to stuff the little soft elephant she'd been cradling for comfort out of sight in her bag but, before she could tell the guy to get lost, he had draped a soft cashmere sweater across her shoulders and flopped down beside her on the sand. The sweater smelled not of woodsmoke but of the sea and, as her body relaxed into its soft warmth, she didn't shake it off but pulled it around her.

'Hi,' he said, offering a large, square hand. 'I'm Kit.' Years at an English boarding school had drummed in the automatic 'politeness' response but as she reached up to take it, her own name died in her throat.

She might only be an occasional summer visitor to her mother's birthplace, but everyone knew Kit Merchant. An island legend, he'd been a teenager when he'd brought home sailing gold from London and had been collecting trophies ever since.

Now in his mid-twenties, he was too old, and a lot too glamorous, to be hanging out at a teenage beach party.

'This isn't a party,' she said, but curiosity beat her irritation that he'd called her Red. Her hair, a gift from her mother's Scottish ancestors, had been an unending source of nicknames ever since she'd gone to school and it had got old. 'What are you escaping from?'

Without taking his eyes off her, or letting go of her hand, he waved in the general direction of the fun on the beach. 'It's my kid sister's birthday and I've been appointed the responsible adult.'

'Oh, bad luck.'

'Not that bad if I can sit it out with you?'

He had to be kidding but the guy was not only a legend, he was over-the-top gorgeous from his tousled hair to his long, bare feet. Suddenly, being on her own felt overrated.

'Is that what a responsible adult would do?' she asked.

'I've given them the "no booze, no sex" talk and, since they were polite enough not to laugh, I thought I'd retreat to a safe distance so that they can enjoy themselves.'

The flames of the bonfire were reflected in his eyes, dancing off his cheeks, adding golden highlights to his sun-silvered hair and she felt warmed, not just by his sweater, but his smile.

'In other words, no.'

'My responsibility extends to all my sister's guests, especially the ones sitting on their own looking sad. So, who are you? And why are you hiding out over here when you could be having fun drinking soda and toasting marshmallows?'

Despite the smile, there was an edge to 'having fun' that suggested he was having a bad evening, too. That neither of them wanted to be here.

'I hate soda,' she said, 'and my marshmallows always fall into the fire.'

Her name she kept to herself. Her mother's memorial service had been all over the local papers and if she told him that she was Genevieve Bliss, the flirtatious mood would shatter.

It felt like a lifetime since she'd smiled, since she'd been treated with anything other than kid gloves, let alone flirted with and, choosing not to be that 'poor girl' whose mother had died of a fever in a Central American jungle, she took her cue from him.

'Red is good enough and, like you, I'm too old for this party.'

He looked at her for a moment then with what might have been a shrug said, 'In that case, Red, can I tempt you to a decent bottle of wine and I'm sure to have something a little more substantial than marshmallows in the fridge?'

'You have a fridge?' She lifted a disbelieving brow and he laughed.

'I not only have a fridge,' he said, 'I have a cabin just down the beach.'

'What about the party?'

He looked across at the young people sitting around in groups, chatting, drinking soda. One or two were dancing to music that reached them as little more than a bass beat. He hesitated for a moment, then said, 'If they need me, they know where to find me.'

Could this be real? She was being invited by a world-famous yachtsman, a man whose face and ripped body had appeared on countless magazine covers, to have supper with him in a cabin on the beach?

Sensing her own hesitation, he said, 'I'm not hitting on you, Scout's honour.'

He sounded serious, but his eyes were telling a different story, his mouth was temptingly close and she was overwhelmed by a reckless need to be held, to be warm again.

'How disappointing,' she said, and his sweater slipped from her shoulders as she hooked her free hand around the back of his head. For a moment neither of them moved and then, as she closed her eyes, he kissed her.

CHAPTER ONE

Nearly four years later

'ARE YOU COLD, HONEY?'

Genevieve Bliss was shivering, but not with the cold. She had been on edge from the moment she'd arrived on Nantucket and tonight's charity dinner and auction to raise funds for an opioid clinic was not helping.

It wasn't the cause. She knew the clinic was desperately needed. It was the location. The Merchant Seafarer Resort was the last place she would have chosen to visit voluntarily, but her godmother, recovering from a hip replacement and pleading the need of her arm, was determined to bid at the auction.

'I'm fine,' she said, forcing herself to relax as they approached the impressive entrance.

It would be fine.

Kit Merchant, according to his team blog, was on the other side of the world putting a new multimillion-pound racing yacht through its paces. Even if he was here, he wouldn't recognise a girl who, for one unforgettable night, he'd called Red.

Not that she believed for one moment that it had been unforgettable for him. His playboy reputation was a gift to the gossip magazines and without the red hair to flag up a reminder, she would be lost in the crowd both literally and figuratively.

'I'm just a little overawed to be honest, Martha,' she said, as they made their way to the cloakroom. 'This place is way out of my comfort zone.'

'To be brutally frank, Eve, I'd say your comfort zone and your wardrobe are both overdue a serious shake-up.'

On the contrary, what she'd gone for was a shake-down.

Desperate to hide the red hair that could be seen from a mile away, just in case he made a flying trip home, she'd used a semi-permanent colour to tone it down. She'd been aiming for something approaching the glossy brunette on the carton; her hair had resisted the transformation and what she'd ended up with was a muddy brown.

It wasn't pretty, and it had been a shock to catch sight of herself in a mirror, but it was temporary, and she could live with it. Her dress was, she had to admit, not flattering.

She hadn't brought party clothes with her; it hadn't been that kind of visit. Even if there had been room in her bag after she'd packed for Hannah, she wouldn't have trusted the zipper on anything in her wardrobe.

Ghastly hair and the extra pounds were, she told herself, the perfect camouflage. If, by any chance, she was to pass Kit Merchant in the street, he wouldn't notice her, let alone take a second look.

If she were with Hannah on the other hand…

Far away in London, it had been easy to convince herself that she'd done the right thing. Here, where the Merchant name was everywhere, she wasn't so certain.

'Where on earth did you get that dress?' Martha asked, as she took off her coat.

'You really aren't helping my self-confidence, Martha,' she said as, attempting to make a joke of it, she struck a pose. 'This dress is a classic.' At her godmother's raised eyebrow, she said, 'Honest. I found it in Nana's wardrobe. She'd never even worn it. It still had the tags.'

Martha was not amused. 'The last time your grandmother bought a new dress Reagan was president.'

'It's lovely material.'

'It fits where it touches. At your age you should be shaking out the red curls Mother Nature gave you and wearing something outrageous to go with that tattoo you're so desperate to keep hidden.'

'A moment of graduation madness,' she said, turning around to try and catch a glimpse in the cloakroom mirror. 'I didn't realise it showed.' She tugged at the dress. 'I need to lose those last few pounds of baby weight before I wear anything likely to scare the horses.'

'Nonsense. Hidden beneath that shapeless sack of a dress you have a lovely figure.'

As Martha, unable to disguise her irritation, shook her own head, the pink streak in her sharply angled silver bob caught the light. A picture of elegance right down to her silver-topped Malacca cane, Eve's seventy-year-old godmother made her look like a dreary governess in some nineteenth-century novel.

'You were the loveliest girl, Eve, and somewhere, hiding beneath your grandmother's dress and a very bad hair colour, is a beautiful young woman. What on earth were you thinking?'

'The dress or the hair?'

She waved a dismissive hand. 'You can take off the dress and the sooner the better. Your hair is another matter altogether.'

'My hair was all anybody ever saw,' she said, capturing a wayward curl that no amount of hairspray could ever quite control, pinning it on automatic, implying that the change had happened long ago and had nothing to do with her visit to Nantucket. 'People didn't ask my name, they just called me Red.' Not true, only one person had ever called her Red, but there had been other names. Coppernob, Carrots, Clown. 'And I don't think the head of a prestigious boys' school would employ a science teacher who dressed outrageously.'

'Don't tell me you're planning to live with that look permanently if you get the job?'

She'd worn a conservative grey suit and pinned her hair up as tight as humanly possible for the interview and had somehow reached the shortlist. It had been the perfect excuse to keep her visit to her ailing grandmother as short as possible.

The best-laid plans...

'I had to call them when Nana died to let them know that I wouldn't be available for a second interview.'

'Surely, under the circumstances, they would have waited?'

'They could have held the post for another week, but the cottage was an unforeseen complication,' she said. 'Since I couldn't give them a date, I had to step down.'

'You weren't expecting to inherit your grandmother's cottage?' Martha asked, surprised.

After the way she'd left, she wouldn't have been surprised if Nana had left it to her cat. The creature was old, bad-tempered, and the rest of the family had, as one, taken a sharp step back when she'd raised the question of rehoming him.

'I didn't inherit it,' she pointed out. 'Nana left it, and everything in it, in trust for Hannah.'

The lawyers had made it plain that her plan to invite the family to help themselves to furniture and anything else they wanted, get a firm in to clear out what was left and leave it in the hands of a realtor, was not an option.

'I should probably sympathise with the lost opportunity,' Martha said, 'but good teachers are always in demand. You can't sell the cottage, but you and Hannah could live there. Stay on the island and let your hair grow out. Someone has to take care of that cat,' she added.

With the summer approaching, Eve had to admit that it did sound a lot more appealing than going back to supply teaching in London. Apart from the cat.

Unfortunately, Hannah's father wouldn't stay in the southern hemisphere for ever, forcing her to face the decision she'd been avoiding for so long that it now felt… impossible.

And she wouldn't be able to hide behind the muddy brown for ever.

She'd be for ever on edge, never knowing when she might turn a corner, with not just hers but Hannah's unmissable bright red curls blazing in the sunlight, and find herself face-to-face with the man who'd lived up to his reputation as a serial love 'em and leave 'em playboy.

'Once I've sorted out the family stuff and put it into storage I'm going to freshen up the cottage and put it on the rental market to build up a college fund for Hannah,' she said, aware that Kit Merchant wasn't the only one on the run.

'Or you could sublet your London flat and put that money in the bank,' Martha pointed out. 'Unless there's some pressing reason to return to London? You never talk about Hannah's father. Does he support her? Does she see him?'

'N-no—' It would have been the perfect excuse, but then she would have had to invent some man, a relationship that had gone off the rails. She'd told Hannah that she didn't see her father because he lived in another country but that he had been kind when her mama had been very sad.

Her best friend at preschool had a daddy who lived in Australia so she'd accepted it without question.

For now.

She knew that if Hannah was ever to know who her father was, she would have to tell Kit, but she was very afraid that he wouldn't want to know.

'He was there at a bad moment,' she told Martha. 'That's all.'

True, and less embarrassing than admitting that her precious daughter was the result of a one-night stand at a beach party with her mother's ashes barely in the ground.

Shame had sent her running back to England and then a pregnancy that would have caused gossip, raised eyebrows, a stain on her mother's memory, had kept her away.

Her daughter had turned three at the beginning of May, time enough, she hoped, for dates to have blurred.

'Did you ever tell him about Hannah?' Martha asked.

'I… No,' she admitted. 'He was long gone before she arrived.'

To say that Martha pulled a face would have been an exaggeration. There was the slightest movement of muscles, more than enough to show her disapproval. 'And now you're hiding out, afraid to get involved again.'

'It's simpler this way.'

'Men do tend to complicate life,' Martha agreed, 'but they add a little spice. You're a single mother, Eve, not a nun.'

'Martha! I'm shocked.'

'Are you?' Her godmother could write an essay with the lift of an eyebrow. 'Clearly you haven't heard the rumour that it was my generation that invented sex as a recreational pastime.'

It was perhaps as well that, having arrived at the entrance to the ballroom, Martha didn't wait for a response, but reached for a glass of champagne.

'This is stunning,' Eve said, following suit as she took in the magnificence of the ivory-and-gold ballroom.

She'd never been to the resort as a girl, although she'd instantly recognised Kit Merchant when he'd left the party to come and talk to her.

She hadn't wanted to talk, and she was pretty sure he hadn't followed her for the conversation. A local hero, he could probably have had any girl on the beach, but they were his kid sister's friends, pretty and no doubt keen to attract his attention. Trouble, in fact, which might have accounted for his eagerness to get away.

Normally, she'd have told him to get lost, but she'd been a mess. Her mother had just died, and her father hadn't felt the need to fly in to support her at the funeral. Her boyfriend had felt the same way, sticking to his plan to go backpacking around Europe during the spring break rather than fly to Nantucket, and she'd dumped him by text from the airport.

She'd been at the party because her cousins' arms had been twisted to take her with them and she had only gone to get away from another miserable night sitting in with Nana.

She had been desperate for someone, anyone, to put their arms around her, to hold her, and Kit had been in the wrong place at the wrong time.

Not that he'd failed her. Far from it. No doubt used to females throwing themselves at him, he had responded with some truly outstanding sex. Not the wham, bam, anonymous stuff she'd expected, had wanted right there on the beach to drive away the pain. Instead he'd grabbed her hand, racing with her to his beach hut where they'd had hot, mindless sex, as if they were both desperate to blot out the world. But then he had slowed everything down. They had drunk a rich red wine under a star-filled sky before making slow, sweet love; the kind that could break your heart. That you would never forget.

She swallowed, looking at the men in dinner jackets, the women in their beautiful clothes, and had a moment of regret for the head-turning red curls, wishing she were wearing something a little less…classic.

Wanting, just for a moment, to feel that alive again.

But only for a moment.

She'd been there and done that. She had Hannah, with her own Titian curls and Kit's bright blue eyes, as a constant reminder of the night she'd lost her head.

Her baby girl. The love of her life.

She knew she should tell him, that he had a right to know, but her world was complicated enough. She wasn't going to stick around and risk blundering into the man who'd made her laugh, made her cry, made love to her with a sweet passion that had changed everything in one starlit night.

The man who, at the fierce banging on his beach cabin door, the call that he was needed, had rolled out of bed, pulling on his jeans and grabbing his sweatshirt. All he'd said was, 'Stay out of sight…' on his way out.

She had waited until the first pink edge of dawn appeared on the horizon and then she had run back to her grandmother's house and thrown her things into a bag. Nana had been asleep, so she'd left a note, caught the first ferry back to the mainland and been back in London twenty-four hours later.

Had he waited, holding his breath, waiting for the call from one of the less glossy gossip mags asking for a comment on the story they were about to run?

My Night of Sex... Sex in the Sand... Abandoned After a Night of Sex...

There had been stories in the past and, even if some of them were pure fiction and others heavily embellished to make better headlines, he had clearly made the most of his youthful fame. There were still photographs of him with beautiful women, but these days no one was talking, and neither would she. Not even when, weeks later, after her finals were over, she'd had time to realise what was happening to her body and two pink lines had changed her life for ever.

She hadn't talked and she couldn't call Kit.

The news had been full of the start of the single-handed round-the-world yacht race, or maybe that was all she had been noticing because Kit was the skipper that every camera had been watching, the man already making the headlines after rumours that his entry had caused a rift with his family.

Calling him on the satellite link would have been a very public way to inform him that he was about to become a father. While the headlines would have cheered a newspaper man's heart and set Twitter alight, the trolls would have been out in force. She would have been mobbed by the press, her poor grandmother would have been under siege, and she would have had to go into hiding.

It had given her plenty of time to think. Time for her heart to stop when, two months into the race, his radio had gone silent after a storm. She'd hugged her belly protectively during the ten long days before he'd been spotted by search aircraft.

The photographs had shown that his damaged mast had been lashed back into place and the pundits had speculated with sickening detail how he must have climbed in heavy seas to repair it.

Worse, he'd signalled that his communication equipment had been smashed in the storm that hit his mast, but he was okay and was continuing with the race.

He'd finally limped home after more than four months in third place. A great feat of sailing, according to the yachting community.

Eve hadn't cared about the sailing or the press, she'd just been furious that he would recklessly endanger himself for a piece of silverware to stick on the mantelpiece.

Had he no feelings for his family and what they must have gone through?

She knew all about recklessness. Her mother had taken risks and died; she would protect the precious little girl growing inside her from that kind of pain.

'Kit? Where are you?'

'Sorry, sis. The ferry was late but we should be with you in about thirty minutes.'

'We could delay the start—'

'No, dinner won't wait so go ahead with the presentations. Lucy can speak after dinner before the serious bidding. How was Dad this evening?'

'Furious. Frustrated at not being able to remember stuff. To walk properly. To say what he's thinking.'

'That's probably a blessing.'

Laura laughed. 'Undoubtedly, but he's improving every day, even if the words aren't in any dictionary, so stand back to have your ears blasted.'

'Your grandmother and I used to come here all the time when we were growing up,' Martha said. 'Christmas parties, birthday treats, sailing. I missed her so much when she went off on her travels after college.'

'I didn't know Nana travelled. Where did she go?'

'Spain, France, Italy, Ireland. There are photographs. You'll find them as you sort through the cottage. Bring them over and I'll tell you who everyone is.' She sighed. 'The itchy-feet gene runs deep in your family. Your mother was away to Africa on some research trip the moment the ink was dry on her degree, met your father and never really came home again.'

'Nana wasn't...'

'Welcoming? Easy to live with?' Martha finished for her. 'She was such fun as a girl, but she was never the same after your grandfather died. We tried to involve her, but we didn't understand so much about depression back then and we were all so busy with our own families.' She shook her head. 'But that's not what kept your mother on the move. That's who she was. I've never been further than Boston, which is why she asked me to be your godmother. She wanted someone grounded in your life.'

Eve struggled for something to say but Martha rescued her.

'I thought you were going to follow in your parents' footsteps, Eve. I seem to recall that you were studying zoology?'

'I was.' She had dreamed of returning to Africa, to the scent of hot earth when the rains came, the thunder of hoofbeats as a million wildebeest migrated across the plains, velvet-black skies filled with stars. 'When I discovered I was pregnant I realised that fieldwork wasn't going to be an option, at least not for me, so I forgot about my Masters and I took a teaching diploma.'

'Pregnancy didn't slow your mother down.'

'She wasn't alone, not until Dad left her, but I'd never send Hannah to boarding school.'

Martha reached out and took her hand. 'Her death was

such a tragedy. I hope your little girl gives you some comfort.'

'She is a gift, Martha. My joy.'

'Well, let's hope this visit will be as blessed,' Martha said, innocently.

Eve realised that she'd underestimated her godmother's capacity for mental arithmetic, but she'd been away on a fishing trip when Eve had met Kit that summer. Martha might have put her swift departure together with Hannah's birthday and come up with a theory about where and when, but that was all it was. There was no way she could be certain that Hannah had been conceived on the island.

'People are beginning to sit down,' she said, changing the subject. 'Shall we go and find our table?'

Martha knew everyone at their table, mostly couples of her own generation who greeted her warmly before quietening to listen to Barbara Merchant welcome them and introduce the auction.

She had the same colouring as Kit, Eve thought; the same sun-streaked hair, the same vivid blue eyes. Lost in memories of that night, she heard little of her introduction to the cause for which the auction was being held.

'Let's go and check out the trips,' Martha said, when she was done.

Monitors showed film of the trips on offer at Merchant resorts and some of their partners, in fabulous locations.

There was whale watching off the west coast, trips to Europe—vineyards in France, culture in Italy, golfing and fishing in Scotland—but it was the last one, the wildlife safari, that brought a gasp to Eve's lips.

The Nymba Safari Lodge had been built high amongst the trees with viewing platforms where you could watch animals in a landscape that was painfully familiar. There was a glimpse of a giraffe at sunset, forelegs spreadeagled as it drank at the oxbow lake. There was the dusty green bark of fever trees, a family of warthogs snuffling through the grass.

'Eve?'

'Nymba… It was our home,' she said. 'It's where we lived…'

The cover of the brochure for the safari trip had a photograph of a mama elephant, trunk curled protectively around her calf, and Eve picked it up, instinctively hugging it to her.

Nymba…

It was what her mother had called their *boma*. The word meant home and for just a moment she could hear her mother's voice as she'd given her a hug before putting a small grey velvet elephant in her arms and sending her off to school.

'This little elephant's trunk is my arm, Evie. Hold onto it when you're lost…put it around you when you need a hug…'

She wished she could wind the clock back to those last few weeks with her.

'Excuse me? Can I get in there?'

The woman waited for her to move and Eve stepped back, forcing a smile as she turned to Martha.

'There are some really exciting trips on offer. Have you seen anything you like?' she asked.

'I was hoping for something a little more relaxing than zip-lining through a rainforest,' she said, 'but this one could have been made for you. Your grandmother left you some money and you could do with a break.'

'That's rainy-day money and, anyway, Hannah is too young to come with me.'

'The rule with an inheritance is to give ten per cent, save ten per cent and spend the rest,' Martha said. 'Serendipitously, if you were to make a winning bid for the safari, you'd be economising by giving and spending at the same time.'

Eve laughed at her logic but shook her head. 'Good try, but I couldn't leave Hannah.'

'It's only for ten days. I don't imagine you took her to lectures with you when she was a baby? Teaching practice?'

'Well, no. Obviously. She is in a wonderful day nursery, but I've never left her at night. She'd miss me.' And she knew everything there was to know about missing your mother.

'Mary would love to have her stay and Hannah would have a great time with her cousins.'

'You're very free with your daughter's hospitality.'

But Eve knew her godmother was right.

Mary was one of those women who wrapped you up in a hug and instantly made the world seem a better place. Older, she'd been married and living in New York when Eve's mother had died, or things might have been very different.

Now she and her husband were back on the island with their three children and a menagerie of pets, and Hannah adored, and was adored by, all of them. Every sentence seemed to begin with Cara and Jason and Lacey…

'Okay,' she admitted. 'I'd miss *her*.' Putting an end to the discussion, she turned to a rail journey across the US. 'This hits the less strenuous requirement,' she said. 'Or how about this camel trek across the desert? Camping out under the stars. You might meet a dark-eyed sheikh. Very romantic.'

'There is nothing in the least bit romantic about camels, Eve. They spit.'

'Okay… Is there anything here that you do fancy?'

'I'm rather taken with the idea of sailing down the Adriatic from Venice to the Greek islands in that classic nineteenth-century sailing yacht, and if Kit Merchant happened to be at the helm there would always be something attractive to look at.'

Eve felt her cheeks heat at the mention of his name. 'Isn't he estranged from his family?'

'There was a big row three or four years ago. Christopher didn't want him to take part in the round-the-world race. He said it was time to stop playing and concentrate on the business.'

'Sailing is his life.'

'The resort is his father's.'

Eve had to clear her throat, stop herself from looking around, although she suddenly felt as if she had a great big sign on her back saying 'HERE' before she could manage a bright, 'Maybe a brush with death will soften his father's attitude.'

'Maybe. Ah, now this is the one I've been looking for.' Martha picked up a pen, wrote her name and a substantial bid for a vacation at the Merchant Spa in Phuket. Then she held out the pen. 'Your turn.'

Eve looked back at the African trip.

'Just to show my support,' she said, raising a fairly modest bid that someone had already made.

She had only just put down the pen when a man picked it up and outbid her.

Martha had met someone she knew and, while she was talking, Eve checked by how much she'd been outbid. Five hundred dollars... It was still ridiculously cheap, and she placed another bid.

Just to help push up the price.

She straightened to find Martha, thoughtful, watching and guiltily put down the pen. 'It's going to go much higher.'

'They're starting to serve dinner,' she said. 'We should go back to our table.'

As they moved away someone else stepped up to make another bid. As Eve smothered a squeak of protest, Martha took her arm.

'Leave it until after dinner when we know what we're up against.'

'Yes… No!' Realising how quickly she'd been sucked in, she said, 'Wow, that's dangerous.'

'The trick is to decide on your top bid and not to get carried away. Well, not too much,' Martha added, smiling.

'Oh, no, I'm done,' Eve declared, but she couldn't stop herself from looking back, fingers twitching.

CHAPTER TWO

THE FOOD WAS EXCELLENT, the company—if more her god-mother's generation than her own—was interesting and the wine flowed freely enough that she was pleasantly relaxed by the time Barbara Merchant returned to the stage.

'Hi, yes, sorry it's me again but this is a charity dinner and you all knew you'd have to dig deep, right? Has everyone bought raffle tickets?' There was a murmur from the room and she said, 'Well, buy some more! We'll be drawing some amazing prizes very soon.' She paused a moment for the laughter to die down, then said, 'Before you all rush to spend money on a good cause, and to tell you why this fundraiser is so important, I'd like you to welcome my son, Kit, who, after his father's stroke, has come home to give us all his support.'

Eve was only half listening, her thoughts focussed on the past, and, not sure she'd heard right, she turned to look and there he was, standing beside his mother.

'Kit?'

The word was little more than a whisper but Martha leaned over and said, 'Word is that he's resigned as skipper of the Cup team.'

Before she could take that in, Barbara Merchant said, 'I'll leave Kit to introduce his friend and fellow sailor who has come all the way from New Zealand to tell you why this clinic is so desperately needed.'

This couldn't be happening. She'd checked the team's

blog before she left for Nantucket, just to be sure. There had been a photograph of him, taken less than a month ago, at the helm of the new yacht he and his team were putting through its paces in the Southern Ocean.

Even as her mind was rejecting the possibility that he was not simply in Nantucket but in this very room, Kit Merchant's low, baritone voice reached out across the space and touched her like a lover's caress.

'Ladies and gentlemen, friends...'

For a moment Eve couldn't breathe, couldn't move...

And then the reality of his mother's introduction, Martha's whispered comment, sank in. This wasn't a flying visit, Kit was back, if not for good, then for the foreseeable future.

'My mother has already thanked our generous partners throughout the world who have joined Merchant Resorts to offer thrilling, one-off experiences for this auction, but events such as this do not organise themselves...'

Every cell in her body was warning her to keep absolutely still; she was afraid that any movement would attract his attention, draw his gaze in her direction.

And then what?

From that distance all he would see was a badly dressed woman with mousy hair. The kind of woman who wouldn't hold his attention for a second.

She'd seen his face on a hundred magazine covers in the years since their encounter on the beach. She knew the exact shade of blue of his eyes, knew each line weathered into his face by sun, saltwater and wind, the shape of the close-trimmed beard that he'd grown. She knew the way his thick, sun-streaked hair stuck up as if he'd just dragged his hand through it. As if she had just dragged her hand through it.

It had been just one night, but she could still feel the

soft thickness of it beneath her own fingers, still knew the taste of his lips, the sweet murmur of his voice, the scent of sharp, clean sweat on his skin.

'…thank those of you who have given your time to help my mother and sister organise this amazing auction.'

She wanted to slide from her chair, curl up and hide beneath the table but she was frozen, unable to look away as, oblivious to her presence, he was turning to the lovely young woman standing beside him.

'Before you all rush to top up your bids,' he said, 'I want to introduce Lucy Grainger. Along with her brother Matt, she was a member of my crew. Matt was my first mate, my best mate, a friend, a brother from a different mother, who died last year. This auction is because of his death…'

As he stepped back Kit's eyes swept the room and for a moment, one brief shocking moment, they came to rest on her.

It was as if he could see through the brown dye to the red curls desperately trying to burst out of the clamped-down chignon. As if he could see through the boring dress to the body that she had once, desperately, thrown at him and which he had caught so deftly.

Relief came as he stepped back to leave Lucy in the spotlight and, as if released from some unseen force field, her breath could finally escape, allowing her body to sag as the tension left her.

'Eve? Are you okay?' Martha whispered.

'I'm a bit warm. The wine…' She shook her head when Martha suggested some fresh air, not wanting to draw attention to herself. She could slip away as soon as everyone made a move. 'I'll be fine.'

She sipped a glass of water as the young woman told the audience about her brother, Matt, a gifted international yachtsman like Kit, who'd hidden an injury so that he could continue competing and, as a result, had become addicted to painkillers. First prescription and then later, when they stopped working, to stronger and stronger drugs bought on the Internet and finally from the streets.

She was young, beautiful, there were tears in her eyes as she spoke of his kindness, his talent, and when she'd finished speaking Kit put his arms around her and held her, giving her a moment to recover before leading her from the stage.

She'd seen photographs of him with a dozen beautiful women, but this was different. There was a tenderness here that had been lacking in those posed shots. This girl was different.

It shouldn't matter.

He'd been her comfort in a bleak moment, in the wrong place at the wrong time. It wasn't just his recklessness, a complete disregard for his life, that had stopped her from calling him.

It had been a magical evening, a precious moment in a dark time, and she hadn't wanted to destroy that memory. It wasn't as if he was going to say, my bad, our child needs a father, marry me. No one did that any more and she'd read about too many cases in which the rich and famous had defended paternity suits through the courts, with every sordid detail aired for the world to salivate over.

She hadn't needed his money.

She'd had the London flat and divorce settlement, left to her in her mother's will. She'd had a career—science teachers were in short supply and she would never be short of a job. She and Hannah would be fine.

She'd thought it would be easy. She'd thought she would never see him again.

But there he was.

And it did matter.

'Give me a hand up, Eve,' Martha said. 'I've sat too long and seized up, but I'm determined not to be outbid.'

Grabbing the chance to escape, she said, 'Would you like me to bid for you?'

'And miss all the fun? Come on. Let's see how we're doing.'

There were more people around the bidding forms now, checking to see if they were in with a chance, making last-minute bids. Martha pulled a face and went higher.

'Is that your limit?' Eve asked, hoping to get away.

'My limit and more,' she admitted. 'Come on. It's your turn.'

There were half a dozen bids after hers and while she was looking up at the display someone took it up another two hundred and fifty dollars.

Nymba...

Home.

As she hesitated, torn between longing and reality, there was a movement at the far end of the table as Kit and Lucy arrived to chat to the bidders. There was a crush behind her and, boxed in, unable to escape, she took the pen that Martha was offering her and bent over the form, keeping her head down as she slowly wrote a fresh bid.

Behind her someone began to complain that she was taking too long, dragging it out to stop anyone else bidding. As if...

She surrendered the pen, but her apology was brushed aside as the man pushed past her. Taking a swift step back, she caught her heel in her hem and, stumbling, flung out an arm, groping for something to grab onto and stop herself from falling. There was nothing, she was going down, but then, out of nowhere, a hand grasped hers, catching her, steadying her.

She didn't have to look to see who had saved her. It was a hand she knew. A callused hand that had scraped over sensitive skin, waking up hitherto unexperienced heights of pleasure and, for a few brief hours, blocking all pain.

For a heartbeat that hand was all that was holding her up, but then a bell was rung for the end of the auction, jolting her back to reality and, as a cheer went up, she recovered her balance.

Keeping her head down, she muttered a hoarse, 'Thank you…'

No one heard. Kit had been enveloped in hugs, Martha was with friends and, finally, she was able to slip away.

Kit felt the woman's hand slip from his grasp in the crush but before he could go after her, make sure she was all right, he was being hugged by someone overjoyed at having made the winning bid for a trip.

He caught sight of her as she hurried away, presumably one of the unlucky ones who'd missed out at the last minute. Relieved that she was okay, he surrendered to the moment, congratulating the winners, all the while unable to shake the feeling that he'd seen something this evening, heard something. Missed something.

'Kit. It's good to see you, although not in these circumstances. How is your father?'

Martha Adams was one of his grandmother's oldest friends and he kissed her cheeks, introducing her to Lucy before answering her question.

'Frustrated. He's desperately trying to issue orders, but the words are eluding him.'

'The speech will come back, but it takes time. I imagine your mother has her hands full.'

'She's more than a match for him.'

'I'm glad to hear it. And how about you? How are you coping?'

'Brad is doing a great job and Laura is home, helping out. I'm trying to help but if I'm honest I'm just getting in everyone's way.' Getting in his brother's way. While he'd been chasing trophies, Brad had stepped into his shoes, buckling down to learn the business. Now his brother was convinced that Kit had returned to grab back his rightful place. 'Did you bid on anything tonight, ma'am?'

'I did,' she said. 'I'm going to your spa in Phuket and I couldn't be more excited. Have you been there?'

'I stopped over a couple of years ago when I was racing in that part of the world. It's beautiful and the staff are amazing. You'll have a wonderful time.'

Eve was sitting in the shadows on the terrace when Martha carefully lowered herself into the chair beside her with a contented sigh.

'I'm sorry to run out on you at the last moment, Martha,' she apologised. 'Did you win?'

'I did, thank you, but I saw that man push you out of the way. So rude. Are you all right?'

'The only harm was the hem of my dress and I'm sure you'd say that was a win. I just needed some fresh air.'

'Then you'd better take a big breath.' Martha handed her the folder she was holding. 'We're both going on a dream trip. You're going on safari.'

'What?' Eve's head was still reeling from the impact of the encounter with Kit. How close she'd come to being face-to-face with him and uncertain which would have been worse: the shock of recognition or the polite expression of a man who was being kind to a total stranger. 'No...' She was holding the glossy brochure, looking down at a photograph of the elephant and her baby. 'This can't be right. There was another bid. Right at the last moment…'

'The man who knocked you out of the way? So rude. He dashed off a bid but I managed to top it in the last seconds before the bell rang.' She hesitated, for a moment uncertain. 'I saw the longing on your face when you were looking at that photograph, Eve. If I was wrong, I have no doubt that your rival bidder would be happy to pay the extra hundred dollars and take it off your hands.'

Overwhelmed with such a rush of conflicting emotions, at that moment Eve couldn't have said which way was up but there was one thing she was certain about.

'No.' Clutching the folder tightly to her chest, she said it again. 'No,' she repeated. 'I'm going home.' She looked at Martha. 'There's only one problem. You've volunteered Mary to look after Hannah, but who is going to look after the cat?'

Martha rolled her eyes. 'I fed Mungo until you arrived, I suppose I can do it again.'

'It's the annual audit next month, Brad. You have to be here for that,' Laura said. With their mother fully occupied looking after their father, it was just Kit, Brad and his sister Laura at the family meeting. 'I can go to Nymba for the trust meeting. It's just a formality, showing a Merchant face once a year.'

'It's not just a formality.' Brad's temper was wearing thin. 'The Nymba Trust are major partners. But even if it was, sending a nineteen-year-old student to represent the company might be seen as a touch too casual.'

'I'll go,' Kit said.

Brad threw his hands up in the air. 'Break out the spinach! It's Popeye the Sailor Man to the rescue.'

'It takes more than spinach to put a world-beating yacht

in the water and win races,' Kit said, trying not to lose patience with his brother. He knew Brad had a lot on his plate. 'It takes teamwork, psychology and a great deal of diplomacy. This is me being diplomatic,' he added. 'You'll be a lot less stressed with me on a different continent.'

His brother's face twitched, but he was nowhere near ready to take the olive branch.

'This isn't just swanning around, graciously showing your face once in a blue moon at one of the resorts so that a bit of the Kit Merchant glamour rubs off on the business. Nymba Lodge is a major partner, that's why Dad always goes himself.'

'Dad always went himself because he loves Africa. He treated it as a holiday,' his little pot-stirring sister said, getting her own back for the 'student' put-down. 'I'm sure Kit can handle that.'

'Undoubtedly. We all saw the pictures of him having a good time in the Med last year with that French guy and Matt Grainger—'

He broke off, as Kit stood.

The holiday he and Matt had spent in Nice with Philippe d'Usay had been the last occasion they'd all been together before the accident that had led to Matt's opiate addiction and death.

'That was the last good time Matt had anywhere,' he said.

The last good time he'd had anywhere.

'I'm sorry. I didn't mean—'

'Forget it.'

It sometimes felt as if Brad had arrived in the world resentful that he wasn't the firstborn, but despite the fact that he sounded like a spoiled brat, and this time had strayed into dangerous territory, Kit had a certain amount of sympathy.

Guilt for not being there when Brad had needed him had never left him. Even when he could have come home and tried to mend fences with his father he'd made a conscious decision to give Brad a clear shot at succeeding their father as CEO.

His stroke should have been Brad's big moment to show the old man that he wasn't the second-best son. He was so wound up about it he'd convinced himself that his big brother—not content with gold-medal glory and a room full of trophies—had returned to steal his glory when nothing could be further from the truth.

His team were at the bottom of the world preparing for the biggest race in the yachting calendar and he should be with them.

He'd thought, once the crisis had passed, he would be able to make his peace and return to his team. Right now, with his father unable to talk in any way that was coherent, that was impossible, but it wouldn't hurt to start his peace initiative with his brother.

'Brad—'

Brad muttered something under his breath but lifted a hand in surrender. 'Make sure you read the files before you go.'

'Can I ask one favour?'

'You want us to polish your trophies while you're away?'

He ignored the jibe. 'Lucy has been through a rough time. I thought she could do with a break, so I asked her to stay for the summer. She doesn't know anyone here, and with Mom busy looking after the old man, I thought maybe you could find something for her to do?'

'Don't worry, we'll look after her,' Laura said, quickly, before Brad compounded the insult by suggesting she polish them. 'Won't we, Brad?'

'Sure. Don't feel you have to rush back,' he added. 'We're used to managing without you.'

'Will you try and get it through his thick skull that I don't want his job?' Kit said when Brad had gone, then shook his head. 'Sorry, it's not your problem. This is my fault.'

Laura didn't argue with him, just said, 'I'll book your flight.'

'Thanks.'

'At least you'll have some home company while you're there. The woman who won the auction will be at Nymba at the same time. Genevieve Bliss. Did you meet her?'

'I imagine so. I made a point of thanking everyone. I'll be sure to say hello.'

CHAPTER THREE

NYMBA SAFARI LODGE was breathtaking. Eve's suite, sheltered from the sun by the canopy of the trees, had an open-air shower, a roll-top star bath and the four-poster bed, draped in gauzy netting, could be wheeled out onto the deck if she preferred to sleep outside.

Who wouldn't?

She'd broken her journey in London, spending a week sorting out her flat, but the second, even longer flight to Kabila had left her exhausted. She could have easily curled up and gone to sleep right there and then but she resisted the temptation.

This trip was the most unexpected, most self-indulgent of pilgrimages and she wasn't going to waste a minute of it.

Once her personal butler, Michael, had assured himself that she knew where everything was and how it worked and left her to settle in, she stripped off her travel-crumpled clothes. It felt slightly wicked to be naked out in the open air, but she was visible only to birds, curious monkeys, a giraffe standing on the far bank of the river and, relishing the sense of freedom, she stepped under the shower and washed the long journey from her hair and skin.

First warm and then wake-up-cold.

Refreshed, she wrapped herself in a bathrobe, filled a glass from the water cooler and leaned against the deck rail, just soaking in the view.

Nymba.

The name hadn't been a coincidence. This really was the site of her parents' *boma*. It was where, after a morning at the village school, under the eyes of a girl called Ketty, she had played, done her homework and taken care of the orphaned animals that had found a home with them.

The air was dry, warm, rich with the familiar scents of woodsmoke, wild basil, long hot days that baked the earth. Thrumming with the sound of cicadas.

A glossy starling landed on the deck rail, with a flash of metallic green wings, looking for crumbs, then took off as, high in the treetops, a monkey shrieked an alarm.

It was taken up by others along the riverbank and she leaned over the rail to see what had caused the fuss.

A family of elephants splashing and rolling in the mud took no notice, but the zebras and impalas, edgier and ever alert to danger, had lifted their heads to sniff the wind.

After a moment the noise began to die down and the animals lowered their heads to the water. If a predator had been slinking through the shadows, it had moved on. Maybe.

Out in the river, a hippo emerged just sufficiently to show the rounded half-hoop of her eyes. A family of warthogs, tails erect, trotted by and there were birds, too. Egrets, several different kinds of starlings and little yellow weaver birds busy at their nests filled the trees around her. Eve could have watched for hours, but she didn't have time to linger.

She had been given the itinerary at Reception and it was time to go down for afternoon tea before being taken on the evening game ride.

Her hair had dried so quickly into natural curls that it would need serious time with the straighteners before she could wind it into a chignon, but she'd been happy to leave them behind. The semi-permanent colour was fading out, too. In the bright sunlight she could see the glint of red shining through.

It didn't matter.

Kit Merchant was seven thousand miles away and, after a couple of weeks of only leaving the cottage to shop for groceries, she could relax.

She applied copious amounts of the body lotion that her mother had sworn was a better insect repellent than anything on the market, and factor fifty to any bit of skin that would be exposed. Her hair might be temporarily brown, but she had the skin of a redhead and she took the extra precaution of adding a heavy zinc sunblock to her nose and cheekbones before dressing in a pair of the khaki pants and long-sleeved shirt that had once belonged to her mother.

She had found them washed, neatly pressed and layered with lavender, along with her broad-brimmed hat and ankle boots, when she'd been clearing cupboards in the cottage. The discovery had provoked tears, but they were standard bush clobber with useful pockets and fitted as if they had been made for her. Wearing them made her feel very close to her mother.

She swept her hair into a hairband, picked up her hat and headed across the walkway to the main building.

She'd already seen the thatched, open-sided central area where the reception and offices of the resort, along with a comfortable sitting area, were located.

The thatch extended over part of a stone terrace where tea was being served at a long table and a white-jacketed waiter drew back a seat for her.

She chose orange pekoe tea and, since the earlier arrivals were all staring at her, introduced herself.

'Hi, I'm Eve Bliss.'

They all responded with their names.

'You're American?' someone asked.

They were a mix of English, American and Japanese and in England everyone thought she was American. In America she easily slipped into her mother's New England accent but was often asked if she was English or Australian.

'My mother was American,' she said. She didn't talk about her English father, who had deserted them for a younger, less assertive assistant.

'And you speak the language,' someone else—Faye—said.

Was that why they were staring? Because she'd exchanged a few words with the waiter?

'It's not the local tribal language. Swahili is a lingua franca that's used all over east Africa. I picked it up when I lived here as a child. Have you been here long?' she asked. 'What have you seen?'

It was enough to turn the conversation away from her as they piled in with stories of their encounters with elephants, lions, a rare glimpse of a rhino. She listened with interest, making the appropriate noises as she tucked into the tiny sandwiches, scones and cakes that arrived on a tiered dish, along with a pot of tea.

Fortunately, she didn't have too much time to indulge her sweet tooth before they were collected for the evening game drive.

Eve didn't make it to dinner. Didn't see the stars from her sky bed or hear the cough of a lion. She didn't see or hear a thing until she opened her eyes to discover that the gauzy space she had fallen into was filled with a pearly pink predawn glow.

She lay there for a moment, putting together the where, the how…

Nymba. She was at Nymba and one sociable gin and tonic after the game drive had been enough for the jet lag she'd been fighting off all day to finally catch up with her.

She'd bailed on dinner—falling asleep with your face in your food was not a good look—and held herself together just long enough to tuck the mosquito netting around her bed before she closed her eyes and knew no more.

Right now she wanted nothing more than to take her time as the world awoke around her, but her itinerary started with an early morning river trip and she dragged her unwilling body under the shower. More or less awake, she tied back her still-damp hair and applied factor fifty to her skin and sunblock to her nose and cheekbones. Sunglasses usefully covered slightly puffy eyes and, hat in hand, she made her way along the treetop walk and down the steps to the terrace.

Breakfast wouldn't be served until after the early morning game viewing, but there was a buffet set up in the shade of the thatched roof, with pastries, juice, coffee and boiling water for tea.

She wasn't the only one desperate for a wake-up glass of orange juice. A man with the crumpled look of someone who had slept in his clothes drank down the glass he'd just poured and refilled it before realising there was someone behind him.

He turned, jug in hand, paused for a moment, no doubt startled by the picture she presented, before offering to fill the glass she'd picked up. 'Sorry, I'm hogging the juice…'

Eve felt the blood drain from her face.

It couldn't be.

Kit Merchant was supposed to be holding the fort in Nantucket.

Just as he'd been supposed to be aboard his yacht in the Southern Ocean.

Not.

As she hesitated, he gave her his full attention. 'Are you okay?'

Thanks to the sunglasses and thick white streaks of sunblock, he hadn't recognised her, which should have been off-the-scale okay, but she had the answer to the *Which would be worse?* question she'd asked herself back at the auction.

She knew it was wrong, that she should be relieved, glad even. To have him look at her the way he had that night... Well, that was the worst idea in the world.

He was waiting for an answer.

'Y...yes. Sorry. It's a bit early for the brain to be engaged.' She jammed her hat on her head, waiting for him to put down the jug and move away so that she could catch her breath. Fill her glass.

He hadn't recognised her. It was okay.

He wasn't ready to surrender the jug but turned to fill her glass. Unfortunately, her hand was shaking so much that he reached out to steady it.

His hand around hers did not help.

'Not to mention jet lag,' she added.

'Why don't you sit down?' he suggested. 'I'll bring this over for you.'

He didn't wait for a response, but deftly relieved her of the glass and led the way to a table set between two armchairs overlooking the river.

He set down her glass and, since her legs were not exactly cooperating, she sat down.

'Can I bring you anything else?' he asked.

No, no...

'I'm fine,' she said. And she would be. She just needed

a minute for her heart to stop dancing a crazy tango, for her breathing to recover. She'd thought she was safe. Hadn't brought a top-up hair rinse with her—she'd planned to do that in London on the way back.

What on earth was he doing here? How long would he stay?

She was just congratulating herself that he hadn't joined her, was beginning to recover from the shock, when a waiter arrived with a tray containing two large cups of coffee, pastries, plates and napkins.

'Have you got everything you need?' Kit asked, as he sank into the chair beside her.

Eve unglued her tongue from the roof of her mouth. 'Rather more than I can manage in five minutes.'

'Five minutes?'

'I have a canoe waiting.' Escape for a couple of hours while she figured out what she was going to do.

'That explains the warpaint,' he said and, just as he had once before, extended his hand and said, 'Kit Merchant.'

She'd had her minute. It wasn't nearly enough...

With no choice but to take it, she responded with what she hoped was the firm grasp of a woman in control of her limbs, if nothing else. 'Genevieve Bliss. Eve,' she added.

'Our very generous auction bidder. Laura asked me to look out for you.' He frowned. 'Why didn't we meet that night? I thought I'd thanked all the winning bidders personally and I wouldn't have forgotten you.'

Which had to be the very definition of irony...

'I tripped over the hem of my dress,' she said. 'You might remember catching me.'

'That was you? You rushed away before I could make sure you were all right.'

He was still holding her hand and she forced herself to let go and reach for her juice.

'I thought I'd been beaten at the last moment,' she said, hoping that the glass wouldn't rattle against her teeth as she took a sip.

'I hope you're glad that you won. Despite the jet lag,' he added, when she didn't immediately answer. 'That is one seriously tough journey.'

'It helps if you stay over in London for a day or two.'

'Is that what you did?' Kit reached for his coffee. 'I'm catching a touch of British in your accent.'

He'd said that, too. That night…

'I've been working there,' she said, without confirming her nationality one way or the other. 'I took a journey break to sort out a few things.'

A friend had suggested putting her flat on a rental site since she was going to be away longer than expected.

'Lucky you. This is a business trip and I didn't have time to indulge my love of London.'

Her stopover had mostly involved cleaning and packing away stuff to leave wardrobe and cupboard space free, arranging for a cleaner to come in between visitors, but she murmured her sympathy.

Kit rested his head against the back of the chair. 'This is so peaceful.'

If she'd thought about it, she would have assumed that the Merchant family were closely acquainted with all their resorts, but Kit hadn't been part of the business. 'You haven't been here before?'

The corner of his mouth lifted in a self-mocking smile. 'It's landlocked.'

He was inviting her to laugh at him, or maybe with him, it was hard to tell.

'There's a river,' she ventured.

'Are you suggesting I join you on your canoe trip?'

'N-no.' The last thing she wanted was for him to

think she was flirting with him. 'I'm sure it's full.' But he looked exhausted. He had looked tired at the auction… 'Maybe you could go this evening. We all need to slow down once in a while.'

He followed her gaze to look out across the still calm of the oxbow lake, reflecting the pink sky, but she suspected his thoughts were on a distant sea.

'How is your father?' she asked.

He came back from wherever he had been, lifted a shoulder. 'Stubborn, difficult, opinionated.'

'Getting better, then.'

The smile returned, this time deeper, provoking memories that she'd tried very hard to forget.

'He's recovering, but he's going to have to change his diet, take more exercise, avoid stress. My mother is going to be very busy.'

'And happy to be so, I'm sure.'

Martha had been full of the Merchants on the way home from the auction; they were one of those couples who had fallen in love in high school and never looked at another person.

'Yes,' he said. 'It's the kind of marriage you don't often see.' He glanced across at her. 'The kind built on friendship and respect, that is strong enough to endure the rough times. The kind that you hope for.'

CHAPTER FOUR

KIT, TALKING ABOUT his parents' love for one another, had spoken from the heart and Eve had to swallow down a large lump in her throat.

'I hope you find that for yourself,' she said, trying not to think about his tenderness towards Lucy. They had worked together, had an enduring bond in their love of sailing, of her brother, something solid on which to build a future…

A single night of passion, no matter how life-changing the result, was not a basis for any kind of relationship. In the lonely dark she might have longed for the touch of a man who had, no matter how briefly, lifted her heart, made her laugh, made her body sing, but with the dawn came reality…

Sitting beside him in the golden heat of an African dawn was something else entirely.

'How long do you think it will be before you can return to racing?' she asked.

Not an entirely disinterested question.

'It may never happen.'

'I'm sorry.' That wasn't a selfish 'sorry'. Sailing was his life. 'This must be so hard for you.'

He glanced at her. 'I've had a good run and now I'm needed at home. Needed here…'

'Is there a problem?' She shook her head. 'Sorry, it's none of my business.'

They were a couple of strangers having a polite conversation and if her pulse rate was unnaturally fast, she'd got over it once and would again.

If there was a problem, he'd be locked away with the staff while he was here and, needed at home, on his way in twenty-four or, at the most, forty-eight hours.

She just needed to keep her head down and her hat on in the meantime.

Kit leaned forward, picked up the plate of pastries and offered them to her. 'You should eat something, Eve. Breakfast is the most important meal of the day.'

She'd been struggling to lose the last of the weight that had clung on after she'd given birth to Hannah, finished breastfeeding, but her stomach gave a little gurgle of excitement at the sight of an almond croissant.

He heard and grinned. Blushing with embarrassment, she said, 'I missed dinner last night.'

'Then I must insist, in the cause of health and safety, that you eat something before you face the wildlife.'

Once it had become obvious that he didn't recognise her, she'd begun to relax a little. They had met as strangers and yet right from the first moment the connection had been so intense, so immediate. And it was still there.

While they'd been talking the rest of the guests had gathered, quickly downing juice, coffee and grabbing a pastry. Now they were beginning to disperse on their chosen method of game watching and it was time for her to move, too.

'If I don't go now my canoe will leave without me,' she said, 'but I'll take this to keep me going.' She picked up the croissant, biting into it as she forced herself to her feet, forced herself to walk away.

'Watch out for the crocodiles,' he said, rising with her, in an instinctive gesture of courtesy.

'It's a little-known fact,' she told him, gathering the pastry flakes from her lips and sucking them from her finger as she took a step back, 'that more people are killed by hippos than crocs.'

'Really. And you're going out there in a canoe?'

'It was on the itinerary I was given when I arrived. I've no doubt they would have changed it if I'd asked, but it's unbelievably peaceful on the water.'

'Peace and quiet sounds rather wonderful just now. Are you sure there isn't room on your canoe for a late arrival?'

Laughter reached them from the compound where guests were piling into the large four-by-four game-viewing vehicles. Relaxed, having fun, their only concern whether they had their cameras fully charged...

Kit had arrived tired and irritated, certain, with time to reflect on the long flight, that his brother had played him. The last thing Brad wanted was a reconciliation between Kit and their father and he'd used this meeting as a means of getting him out of the way.

He rubbed a hand over his face in an attempt to wake himself up, focus on why he was here, but it had been a bad few weeks and he felt drawn to the peace and quiet of Eve's canoe.

Or maybe it was just Eve.

She had taken a step back, distancing herself from him at his suggestion that he accompany her in the canoe. Not exactly a textbook reaction to an invitation from him. But then his invitations had always been rare; he was always the one creating the distance, but as Eve's tongue swept a stray crumb from her lower lip a kick of heat shot through him and he put the plate down before the rest of the pastries hit the floor.

'Jet lag,' she warned, and he would have been hard put to say whether it was sympathy or relief that he heard in her voice. 'Give breakfast a miss and take a nap.'

'Do I look that bad?' he asked.

'*Memsahib...*'

She said something in Swahili to the man waiting to escort her to her canoe before saying, 'You look exhausted. It will catch up with you sooner rather than later. Far better to be lying down when it does.'

She took another step back and, with a nod, turned to follow the man across the terrace, only hesitating when she reached the steps that led down to the dock to glance back. Almost, he thought, as if she regretted her decision.

Her face was shadowed by the brim of her hat and he wished he could see her eyes.

She'd chatted, been interested, thoughtful and yet he couldn't get a grip of what she was actually thinking. Whether she was just being charming to some poor bloke who looked like hell after travelling for twenty-four hours or... Or nothing.

He took a mental step back of his own.

Eve Bliss was wearing clothes chosen for comfort rather than style. Her hair, bundled up off her face, was mostly hidden beneath her hat, apart from a few wisps that had escaped. And she'd hidden her eyes, most of her face masked by a pair of large dark glasses and the white streaks of sunblock.

Pretty much all he could see of her had been her mouth, which would explain why it had been the sole focus of his attention from the moment she bit into that pastry. And yet that little lick of an admittedly luscious lip, the defensive lift of her chin, had tugged at some elusive memory.

It had been there from the moment he'd turned and seen her standing behind him. Nothing he could pin down. Nothing, despite the promise of a luscious body beneath the khaki clothes, and an intriguingly familiar accent, to have him thinking to hell with the jet lag, I want more of this, and following her to the canoe.

It had been there at the auction, too. Their only connection had been when he'd stopped her from falling, a quick glimpse of a very ordinary shade of brown hair, a plain black dress. He should be surprised that he remembered that much and yet, as he'd watched her hurry away, he'd felt what he could only describe as a disturbance in the atmosphere and later, as he'd rubbed the exhaustion from his face, there had been the scent of vanilla...

He shook his head. This was crazy.

He'd been tired that night. Even under stress he could sleep on a clothesline—it went with the job—but he'd been feeling guilty about Brad, who wanted this so much. Guilty about not wanting this when it meant so much to his father. Guilty about leaving his team at such a critical moment.

Everyone had been sympathetic to hear about the old man's stroke, but they'd expected Kit back within a week, two at the most.

Not one of them would understand why he'd apparently abandoned them at such a critical moment.

It hadn't taken the furious response from the sponsors to his resignation as skipper for him to understand that walking away at such a vital moment could well be the end of his career as an international yachtsman. But he'd made a promise, even though his father hadn't been listening, had turned his back, waved him away, that if, when, he was needed, he would be there.

He rubbed his hands briskly over his face, attempting to get his head in gear, trying to figure out what he was missing and there it was again.

Vanilla...

Who was she?

Eve's east coast accent was subtly layered with the kind of British accent spoken by women who hung around the yachting crowd. She'd said she worked in London, but she wasn't sharply enough turned out to be with one of the

PR teams or the gossip media that hung around the yachts hoping for photographs or stories.

Even on safari they wouldn't have been seen dead in a khaki shirt and pants with the washed-out look of long use that contrasted so starkly with the brand-new gear worn by the rest of the visitors.

They looked like tourists. She didn't.

Unlike the other guests, who had now dispersed on their game rides, hot-air-balloon trips, or whatever else was on offer, she seemed part of this place. She spoke the language, for heaven's sake. The staff had spoken to her in Swahili and she'd replied. Not just the standard 'hello' and 'thank you' that everyone picked up but in whole sentences.

He shook his head, dismissing the feeling that they had, somehow, met before. That couldn't be true; he knew to his cost that the slightest acquaintance was enough to have women clinging to him.

It wasn't vanity, it wasn't even about him; anyone with cover appeal would do and he had learned to avoid the worst of it.

The sponsors, however, wanted their money's worth.

Their yacht, their name, on front covers of the glossies and it was the PR team's job to make sure it got there. They threw the models and actresses in his direction and he was expected to catch them. His only memory of the occasion would be the sight of a magazine cover as he passed through an airport.

Eve, he thought, despite her understated wardrobe, wasn't a woman you'd forget.

'Mr Merchant, can I show you to your suite?'

He'd dumped his bag at Reception, desperate for coffee and to arrange to meet the Merchant partners so that he could leave as soon as possible, but Eve was right.

He'd been travelling for more than twenty-four hours,

was seven hours out of his time zone and he needed to at least take a shower before he met with anyone vital to the smooth running of their partnership.

Kit listened patiently while Patrick, his butler, gave him a tour of the suite, then said, 'Miss Bliss bid on a charity auction for her stay here. I hope she's being given the VIP treatment?'

'Yes, sir. As soon as our receptionist saw her name on the guest list she allocated her our very best suite.' He indicated a sky suite a little ahead of him to the right and just visible through the trees.

'Her name? You know her? She's a regular visitor?'

'No, sir. This is her very first visit to the Nymba Safari Lodge, but our receptionist, Ketty Ngei, knew her when she was a little girl and lived here with her parents. She was very much looking forward to greeting her, but her grandfather had to go to the hospital and she has accompanied him to the city.'

She'd lived here? Well, that explained a lot.

'Ketty Ngei? Is she related to Joshua Ngei?' He was the village elder who'd signed the original partnership agreement with his father. The man he'd come to meet.

'Mzee Ngei is her grandfather,' Patrick confirmed.

'Is he ill?'

'I'm sorry, sir, I couldn't say. Is there anything else I can bring you?'

'No, thank you.'

He set an alarm on his watch for lunchtime before he stripped off, took a shower and lay down under the cool of a stunningly wrought thatched roof. Would it be possible to have something like it on his beach cabin on Nantucket? They used thatch in England, but would it stand up to Atlantic gales?

His last thought, before sleep claimed him, was the memory of an extraordinary night he'd once spent there with an English girl who, like Cinderella, had vanished without trace, leaving behind not a glass slipper but a beloved grey velvet elephant to prove that it hadn't all been a dream.

Apart from the initial wobble with the glass, Eve thought she'd handled her unexpected encounter with Kit Merchant pretty well, all things considered.

In some ways it had been made easy for her. He knew that she'd been at the auction, so he expected her to know who he was and that he'd come home because his father was ill.

She'd even handled the suggestion that he might join her in the canoe without choking on her croissant.

But when she'd risked a glance back, she'd discovered that he was watching her. Had some small gesture, the way she moved her head, her mixed-up accent, triggered a memory, waking a synapse that was flickering but not quite making the connection? Like an old neon sign that was struggling to light.

She was the only one heading down to the waiting canoe and it would have been so easy to call out to him.

She would have insisted that he sit in front and then spent the entire trip looking at his wide shoulders, the lick of sun-bleached hair that settled in the nape of his neck, knowing exactly where he had a tattoo of a famous cartoon sailor and how his skin had tasted as she'd kissed it…

Her skin heated at the thought and a low ache settled in her womb as she closed her eyes, for a moment succumbing to the memory.

Madness…

Her breathing went to pot and she had to grip hold of her seat to stop her hands from shaking.

'You will be safe.' The man guiding the canoe through

the water, no doubt putting her nerves down to the sight of crocodiles basking on the far bank, attempted to reassure her.

'Yes. I know how skilled you are,' she replied before realising that the man had spoken to her not in Swahili but in the local dialect. And she had answered in the same language.

She turned in her seat to look at him and he grinned.

'Hello, Evie,' he said, in English. 'Long time, no see.'

She took off her dark glasses. 'Peter? Peter Ngei?' He'd been several years older than her and there had been a huge party before he'd left to study law at the same time as she'd been sent off to boarding school. 'Mom wrote to tell me that you'd got a first. What on earth are you doing paddling a tourist canoe? You should be a judge by now.'

He laughed. 'I'm getting there, but I was at home when Ketty told us you were coming to Nymba, so I volunteered to pick you up and bring you to the village. Unless you're only interested in the hippos? Maybe you're too grand for us now?'

'You have got to be kidding! My grandmother left me some money or I'd never have been able to afford this trip.'

'I'm sorry to hear that you have lost her. And your dear mother. The village wept when we received her bequest for equipment, books, for the school. Mzee Ngei put up a plaque in her honour.'

'She left money for the school?'

'You didn't know?'

She shook her head.

Her mother had made a number of charitable bequests, but she hadn't been able to stay in the room while the will was read.

It had been worth this trip just to hear that.

She blinked away the stinging sensation at the back of

her eyes and said, 'So tell me about you, Peter. What are you doing? Are you married?'

'I'm in the Attorney General's office, married to Maria and we have two boys.'

'Maria…?'

'It was always Maria,' he said.

'Of course it was.' They were another couple of childhood sweethearts… 'I'm so happy for you. Is she here?'

'No, she's working and the boys are in school, but it's Mzee's birthday next weekend and she's bringing the boys down for the party. What about you, Evie?'

'Nothing so grand. I'm an out-of-work teacher, not married,' she replied, 'with one little girl.'

'You didn't bring her with you?'

'She was three in May. Most safari lodges don't take children younger than six and Nymba doesn't take them at all.'

'Next time, come and stay in the village,' he said, neatly edging the canoe alongside a jetty. 'We take children of any age.'

As if to emphasise that fact, a dozen or more children ran down to meet them before stopping abruptly to stare at her as she stepped from the canoe.

'My grandmother has told them that your hair is redder than the setting sun,' Peter said. 'They can't wait to see it.'

'Oh, dear.'

'Problem?'

'For reasons far too complicated to go into, it's now a rather boring shade of brown.' She looked at the children. 'Maybe a picture of Hannah will do the job.'

She opened her bag and took out a leather folder, which contained photographs of her daughter. She took one out, folded herself up so that she was on their level, and held it up for them to see.

There was a collective gasp and when one, braver than

the rest, came closer to look, Eve handed it to her to pass around.

'You may have lost that,' Peter warned.

'I am a besotted mother. I never travel with less than six photographs of my baby. Plus the ones on my phone.'

She offered him the folder and he smiled. 'She is beautiful. The image of you as a child. Almost. I assume she got the blue eyes from her father. He's not with you?'

She barely hesitated before shaking her head. 'We are not together.' She raised an eyebrow. 'I've shown you mine…?' she prompted, to divert him.

He produced a phone and brought up pictures of the cheekiest-looking little boys.

'Oh, they are gorgeous, Peter.'

'They are a handful…' That was as far as he got before she was engulfed in hugs.

Kit was standing under a cold shower. He'd been dreaming. It was one of those recurring dreams that haunted you, where you were looking for someone, travelling down endless corridors until you woke in a sweat.

It hadn't happened in a while but, considering the way his life had been turned upside down, his disturbed sleep pattern, the fact that he'd been thinking about Red as he fell asleep, it wasn't surprising.

The sun was high now. Across the river, the savannah shimmered in a heat haze so that at one moment you were looking at a distant herd of zebra and the next they had vanished.

He raised the canvas sidings to let the air blow through and found himself looking into the huge, long-lashed eyes of a giraffe.

They stared at one another for a hold-your-breath moment and then the creature blinked and moved gracefully away to continue grazing on the trees.

A bird swooped past, a flash of blue and mauve, and as he followed it he found himself looking into the face of a small monkey. It bared its teeth at him, swung down on the rail beside him, leapt across the deck and grabbed an orange from a bowl of fruit.

And Kit laughed.

For the first time in weeks, he threw back his head and laughed. Eve would be back from her canoe trip and he couldn't wait to tell her.

She'd probably roll her eyes, tell him that it happened all the time, but he didn't care. She could roll her eyes all she wanted so long as she sat next to him at lunch and he could catch her scent.

CHAPTER FIVE

LUNCH WAS BEING served when he reached the terrace, but a glance along the table was enough for him to see that Eve was not there.

Disappointed and a little concerned, he crossed to Reception.

'Has Miss Bliss returned from her canoe trip?' he asked.

'No, sir, she won't be back until this evening. She is spending the day with friends in the village.'

She hadn't mentioned that when she was telling him how peaceful and quiet it would be on the river. No wonder she hadn't wanted company.

'Mr Lenku wondered if you would prefer to eat in the privacy of the staff dining room, sir?'

He nodded. 'Yes, thank you. Would you ask him to join me?'

He was here for a meeting, not to indulge his curiosity, indulge anything over a woman.

He'd met James Lenku briefly on his arrival. He was an experienced resort manager, and Kit was relying on him for a briefing before the meeting the next day.

'What time will it start?' he asked, when James arrived.

'I've just heard that the meeting will have to be put back for two or three days, Mr Merchant—'

'Kit.'

He nodded. 'Kit. Mzee Ngei had a hospital appointment today and they have decided to keep him there for some tests. His grandson, Peter Ngei, is now in control of the day-to-day running of the trust, but the annual meeting can't go ahead without Mzee present. Your father usually stayed for a week,' he added, 'so there is no problem over your accommodation.'

What had been Brad's parting shot? Don't hurry back...

'Is there anything we can do to make Mr... Mzee Ngei's stay more comfortable?'

'Ketty will take care of anything he needs. She'll let me know if she needs anything.'

'Do we have any idea how long it's likely to be? As you know my father is not well and I'm needed at home.'

'Not long. It's his birthday on Saturday and the village are throwing a big party. Nothing will keep him from that and in the meantime you have an opportunity to experience what Nymba Lodge has to offer the guests you send to us.'

He'd thought he was going to be doing something useful, but apparently this annual meeting was going to be more of a holiday, as it had been a holiday for his father, and he had to fill his time.

'Certainly. What would you suggest?'

'There are regular hot-air-balloon flights, river trips, fishing and walking with the elephants.'

'Walking with them? I thought African elephants were invariably dangerous.'

'These were orphans raised at Nymba by the behavioural biologist team who worked here. Rose and Jeremy Bliss. I believe you know Eve Bliss, their daughter?'

'We have met,' he confirmed. 'Were the elephants part of their work?'

'They were here studying the local population. I believe they rescued the babies after their mothers were killed by poachers. The trust has taken care of them since the project ended.'

'Will Eve be going on the walk?'

'I can check her itinerary and arrange for you to be in her party.'

That wasn't what he'd asked… Except why else would he have asked? 'Thank you.'

They paused while lunch was served and then Kit asked, 'What is likely to be raised at the meeting? It seems to be little more of an annual formality, but are you aware of any problems that might come up?'

'The relationship between the trust and Merchant is not something I'm involved in,' he said. 'Peter Ngei is the man you need to talk to. He'll be bringing Miss Bliss back to the lodge this evening. I'll send a message to ask if he can spare you some time then.'

Later, having checked the time difference to make sure that the Nantucket office would be open, he called to update Brad on the delay. Not that it would bother him. His sister answered.

'Hi, Kit, how was the flight?'

'Long. How's Dad?'

'Getting grouchier with every passing day, which I take to be a good sign. How's Africa?'

'So far I've had a face-to-face with a giraffe, a monkey stole an orange from my fruit bowl and the meeting with the trust is delayed because the main player is in hospital.'

'What can I say? Sit back and enjoy the view.'

'I have it covered. I do have a preliminary meeting with the guy who actually runs the Nymba Trust this evening. Can Brad spare a moment? If he's not too busy polishing my trophies.'

'He's not too busy with anything. He's taken Lucy over to the boathouse.'

'The boathouse? We are talking about Brad Merchant?'

'You asked us to look after her, so he took her to a Chamber of Commerce dinner last night.'

'Poor woman. I hope the food was good.'

'It's only around you that he's a grouch, Kit. Most of the time he's quite likeable. For a brother,' she added, pointedly. 'Anyway, they must have done more than eat because this morning, he was all about her starting a sailing class for the younger kids.'

'I'm speechless.'

'Always the perfect response.'

'Come on, Laura, we both know that Brad hasn't been near the boathouse since London,' he said.

'It's difficult having to live with always being second best, Kit. His way of handling it was not to compete. He turned to the business because it was something you didn't care about.'

And now he was back getting in his brother's way.

'He loved sailing, Laura. I should have been a better brother, been there when he needed me, when you both needed me.'

When Matt had needed him.

'You can't change the past, Kit. You have to live with it and move on. Have you called Lucy?' she asked.

'I called her when I had a layover in London and texted her when I arrived. I'll call her now.'

'Don't trouble yourself. Brad is doing a good job.'

'Brad… She's fragile, Laura. If Brad is making a play for her because he thinks it will hurt me…'

'You'll probably be surprised to hear this, Kit, but it's not all about you. Life doesn't stop when you're not around. Quite the contrary.'

'Laura—'

'How's our auction winner?' she said, abruptly changing the subject. 'Have you met her?'

His sister didn't give off the same hostile vibes as his brother, but she had blamed him for not being there when he was needed. He'd let them both down, but their feelings had been lost in the row with his father...

'Eve? Yes, I bumped into her at some unearthly hour this morning when she was going on a canoe trip.'

'Did she have a good time?'

'I don't know.'

'Maybe you'd better brush up on that diplomacy you were telling us about. I'll ask Brad to call you,' she said and cut the connection.

He stared at the phone in his hand for a long moment. It wasn't just with his father that he needed to build bridges. He was in need of a major construction programme.

He called his mother, who was kinder and reassured him that his father was 'progressing'. His call to Lucy went to voicemail—all he could do was leave a message to let her know that he was thinking of her. That she was loved.

'Thank you so much for a lovely day, Peter,' Eve said. 'It was a joy to meet everyone and catch up with all the news.'

The canoe had been ferried back to the lodge earlier and she had expected him to turn around after dropping her off but, having helped her down from the four-by-four, he escorted her into the lodge.

'Christopher Merchant sent a message asking if I could spare him a few minutes,' he explained. 'He's here for the Merchant annual meeting with the Nymba Trust.'

Christopher... She had never heard him called that but, of course, he must have been named for his father.

'That sounds serious.'

Of course it was serious. Kit wouldn't have flown out here in the middle of a family crisis to count the spoons. He had a lot more on his mind than a long-ago night spent with some girl who wouldn't even tell him her name.

Peter just smiled. 'I'll text you about the school project and the party, but you're welcome at any time.'

Peter kissed her cheeks, they exchanged a hug and, leaving him to his meeting, she headed across the lounge towards her suite.

'Hello, Eve.'

She jumped at the sound of Kit's voice. He'd been sitting, half hidden in a corner, and as she turned the light from his laptop threw his face into shadows, giving him an almost sinister look.

'I'm glad to see you've returned safely,' he said, rising to his feet. 'When you didn't come back this morning, I was sure a croc must have got you.'

Her morning disguise was gone. The zinc stripes had long since worn off her nose and cheekbones. She'd given her hairband to a child, her hat was in her hand and, with the sun dropping below the horizon, she'd propped her dark glasses on top of her head.

He was now looking straight into her eyes and she felt naked.

'Kit... As you see, I'm still in one piece.'

'I was all set to send out a search party,' he said, 'but James told me that you were having lunch with friends in the village.'

He'd actually checked?

'It was a totally unexpected treat. Peter took me completely by surprise this morning.'

'Peter?'

Kit was regarding her through narrowed eyes and, feeling utterly exposed, she turned to introduce them. 'Peter, may I introduce Kit Merchant? Kit, Peter Ngei.' Then, using her hat as a fan to hide her face, she said, 'If you'll excuse me, gentlemen, I'll leave you to your meeting.'

Kit took a step after her. This morning Eve's sunglasses had hidden her eyes. Green eyes, flecked with amber. Eyes that had haunted him for nearly four years.

'Mr Merchant?'

Red? Eve Bliss was Red? His boyishly slender Cinderella?

Even as he thought it, doubt set in. Eve's figure had a ripeness to it, her hair was the wrong colour. Could she be an older sister—?

'Where is Christopher Merchant?' Peter Ngei demanded.

'I'm Christopher Merchant,' he snapped, not looking around, but continuing to stare after Eve.

'But not the one I was expecting to meet.'

What?

'I'm sorry,' he said, apologising for his lack of attention. 'It was a long flight and my head feels as if it's still somewhere over the Sahara. I'm Christopher Merchant III,' he said, trying to put what he thought he'd seen out of his mind and focus on why he was here. 'My father is recovering from a stroke. It's going to take a while so I'm standing in for him. Everyone calls me Kit.'

The man gave him a long thoughtful look, glanced in the direction that Eve had taken and then back at him.

'I'm not everyone, Mr Merchant,' he replied, pointedly ignoring his outstretched hand.

Not a great start. Peter Ngei already thought he was dealing with the second team and his moment of inattention hadn't improved the situation.

It didn't help that, having seen the man hugging Eve, he wanted to punch him in the face.

Eve had to be Red.

You didn't feel that kind of intensity about someone with whom you'd spent no more than five minutes. Even this morning, behind dark glasses, the sunblock, the hat, he'd felt the connection.

He'd wrapped those wild curls around his fingers, looked into her eyes when the pupils were dilated with desire, knew that mouth and body intimately...

The moment he'd first set eyes on her that night on the beach, even before her hand had come into his, he'd recognised a life-changing moment.

He'd called her Red and she'd blazed into his life for one night, giving him everything and more. And then she'd vanished, not on the stroke of midnight, but just as effectively, leaving him with nothing but a toy elephant to prove that he hadn't dreamed the whole thing.

His sister, a self-absorbed teen besotted with the boy she was with that night, hadn't noticed her at the beach party, had no idea who she was or who she might have come with.

He'd roamed the island on his bike, the elephant in his backpack, hoping to catch a glimpse of flame-red hair until he'd left for France to prepare for the round-the-world yacht race.

'Mr Ngei. I didn't realise you'd arrived.' James emerged from the office in a flurry of concern. 'I see you have already met Mr Merchant. Shall we go through to the office? Kit?' he prompted.

Kit dragged his mind out of the past. He was here to represent his family and, so far, wasn't doing a great job.

Eve showered, washing off the dust of the day, wrapped herself in a towelling robe and took her laptop out to the deck. She talked to Hannah about her day, checked in with Martha to make sure she was coping with the cat and then found herself typing Kit's name into the search engine.

There were dozens of pictures of him at the helm of terrifying yachts, with trophies, with girls, but the most recent were of him at the funeral of his friend Matt Grainger. In all of them, he was with Lucy, his arm around her, supporting her. In one she had turned to sob into his shoulder and he was holding her as if he would never let her go…

She closed the laptop, put it down. While she'd been surfing, the sky had darkened to black, the stars had turned on their light show and the moon was rising, huge and white, silvering the landscape.

Below her, along the river, frogs began their nightly chorus. There were discrete splashes and plops as hippos emerged, the cries of nightjars, rustles through the treetops as small night creatures hunted for insects. The slightly disturbing sound of an infant crying that was made by a bushbaby.

All alien to anyone who lived in a city, or on an island off the east coast of the US, and yet, to her, so familiar…

There was a gentle tap on the gate to her suite and for a moment her heart stopped.

She couldn't be certain that Kit had recognised her, but there had been a reaction in that moment when, stripped of her mask, she had come face-to-face with him. Not so much recognition as confusion.

Peter's presence, their meeting, meant that he hadn't been able to do anything, say anything, ask the question, but she had been sitting in the African night, waiting for him to come.

Or not. She hadn't claimed a previous acquaintance and he had Lucy in his life now. Maybe he'd just leave it.

But if he did come?

She'd been sitting in the dark imagining what he'd say to her. What she'd say to him if he came, if he called her Red.

Just dismiss that night as a bit of fun, nothing to fuss about? He hadn't recognised her, and she hadn't wanted to embarrass him. Cue a few awkward moments, careful avoidance of one another until he left in a day or two. But then they'd both be in Nantucket, living in the same small town. They couldn't avoid one another for ever and it wasn't just her. One look at Hannah and he'd know...

Kit Merchant was Hannah's father. Hannah had a right to know who she was. Kit had the right to know that he had a daughter, to decide if he wanted to be a father.

It might be easier for her if he said thanks, but no thanks. Her father had never been interested in her or his grandchild. But it was Kit's choice to make, not hers.

'Memsahib?'

Her body sagged. It wasn't Kit at her gate. It was Michael.

'You missed dinner, Miss Eve. We wondered if you were too tired to come down. Or not feeling well. Is there something I can bring you?'

'I'm perfectly well, Michael. I had a rather large lunch at the village but thank you for your concern.'

'It is a long time until morning. I could bring something to put in your fridge in case you become hungry in the night?'

'Nothing to eat, but perhaps some tea?' she suggested. 'Camomile?'

'Shall I light the lamps for you?'

She shook her head. 'We never see this kind of dark in London, Michael. Never see stars so thick and bright.' So close that you could almost touch them.

* * *

Kit tapped on the gate that led to Eve's suite and, at her invitation to come in, crossed the deck and placed the tray on the table beside her.

'Is the resort so short of staff that they have had to draft in management for room service?' she asked, without turning around.

The lack of surprise, almost as if she'd been expecting him, the slight, almost undetectable shake in her voice was enough to confirm what he already knew.

Where to take it from here was something else.

Every instinct was to reach out, take her hand, just say, 'Hi, Red. I've been looking for you. I've missed you...' but he'd had a lot of time to think about how it would go if he ever found her.

To think about every second from the moment he'd seen her sitting on her own, the setting sun turning her hair into a fiery halo of curls.

She hadn't just distanced herself bodily from the party. She'd had the lost, slightly melancholy look of someone whose head was somewhere else and that would have taken him to her side even if she hadn't been strikingly beautiful.

In the cold light of day, faced with the reality of an empty cabin with not so much as a note with a phone number or pointed comment on his disappearance, the fact that she hadn't told him her name, it had seemed unlikely that there was no one in her life.

He'd kept his search low-key, afraid that what had happened between them had been a reaction to a row with a lover, partner, husband even and that, with daylight, she'd regretted her recklessness.

Were they still together?

She'd been at the auction, but it was obvious now that she'd avoided him so presumably had not been on her own.

She was alone here, however, and not wearing a ring of any kind, but had still acted as if they had never met when she'd seen him this morning, and again this evening. Maybe her response to the fact that he hadn't recognised her, but she could hardly blame him for that. She'd changed her hair colour and been covered up so completely that she could have been wearing a disguise.

Until he knew more, he would be content to have finally found her, to have a second chance of getting to know her, and leave it to her to decide when—if—she chose to acknowledge the night they had spent together.

'You have your eyes closed, Eve,' he said, putting the tray down on the table beside her. 'How did you know that I wasn't Michael?'

'He has a heavier footstep.'

'Then the next question has to be how did you know it was me?'

A little sigh escaped her. 'You bring an unexpected scent of the sea to the hot African dust.'

'The sea?' And this time it was his voice that was not quite steady. There was intimacy to scent. It involved touch, taste… For an age after they had made love, the scent of vanilla had clung to him. It had drawn him to bakeries. He had smelt it on his hands after the auction and he could smell it now. 'The nearest ocean has to be five hundred miles east.'

'Nearer seven hundred.' She opened her eyes and looked up at him. 'Maybe you have spent so much time being swept by saltwater spray that it has permeated your skin. Become a part of you.'

Now, he thought, she was going to say it now, but when the silence continued, he said, 'I waylaid Michael with your tray because I hoped you might spare me a little of your time.'

She glanced at the table. 'Really? Did you send him back for the pot of coffee? Not a good choice this late in the evening unless you're planning to stay up all night in the hope of seeing a leopard.'

'Is that likely?'

'The game wardens bait a tree on the other side of the river. Sit quietly and you may be lucky.'

There was the faint creak as, taking that as an invitation, he lowered himself into the cane armchair on the far side of the table.

'Can I pour your tea?' he asked.

'Michael would have added a Miss Eve to that.'

He began to relax.

He'd once, desperate to please, taken a girl to see some historical chick flick. At one point a pair of illicit lovers had met at a masked ball, pretending not to know one another, hiding their flirtation in full sight as they had danced together. He'd been fifteen, bored out of his mind, but he finally got the point of that scene.

Fifteen, he realised, knew nothing.

'You expect me to play butler?' he asked, managing to sound just a touch affronted.

'You brought the tray, you're about to pour the tea,' she pointed out.

The only light came from the soft glow of solar-powered lights around the edge of the deck, but the moon was full and huge, silvering her cheeks, creating a wild silhouette of curls that, in his head, was that extraordinary clear, bright red.

It had been weeks since he'd felt like smiling but he did his best to keep it out of his voice as he said, 'Would you care for honey with your tea, Miss Eve?'

'Yes, please. Just one spoonful.'

He added the honey, handed her the cup and then, done

with butlering, picked up his coffee and leaned back in his chair.

Eve hadn't asked why he was here, which suggested she knew, but there was no rush.

This was a good moment and he didn't want to spoil it by saying something stupid.

CHAPTER SIX

EVE STIRRED HER TEA, not at all sure what to make of this
turn of events.

The last few moments had felt very much like flirting.
In the darkness, the intimacy of the moment, she could
imagine spilling out the truth and that, somehow, it would
all be okay.

She glanced across at Kit. The shadows threw his face
in contrast, emphasising the hollows in his cheeks, the
dark smudges beneath his eyes. His life was in a chaos
and she knew what that felt like. He'd once seen that in
her, and he'd come to sit with her so that she was not alone.
Now she longed to go to him, kneel by his chair and stroke
his forehead, temples.

Now. Now was the moment…

'Kit—'

He started as she said his name. 'Sorry… Being your
butler has been the better part of my day. I asked for a few
minutes and I've overstayed that, but I need your help, Eve.'

What?

'I've seen how the people here respect you. How friendly
you are with Peter Ngei.'

The moment had turned in an instant from unspoken
intimacy to weird. Had she got it completely wrong?

'The respect is for my parents,' she said, hauling herself back from the brink of making a fool of herself. 'And
Peter and I go back a very long way.'

'James told me that your parents lived here. Before the lodge was built.'

'You were talking about me?' she demanded.

'I really was concerned when you didn't return from your canoe trip,' he said, 'but when I raised my concerns with James, he explained that the village had arranged a surprise for you.'

'Yes…' It had been a day for surprises. 'I had the shock of my life when I realised that it was Peter at the business end of the canoe.'

'He came for you himself?'

'You sound surprised.'

'Clearly I saw a different side of him.' It was true, he did need her help to smooth over the mess he'd made of his initial meeting with Peter Ngei. The fact that it gave him the perfect excuse to spend time with her was a bonus. 'James told me that you lived here when you were a girl. That the lodge was built on the site of your parents' *boma*.'

'You two did have a nice chat.'

'It wasn't… James and I were talking about the history of the place.'

'Did he tell you that it was my mother who called it Nymba?' she asked.

'No. What does it mean?'

Eve, who had anticipated a difficult conversation about the future, instead found herself drowning in memories. Not all of them happy.

She stirred the melted honey into her tea. 'It's a Swahili word for home.'

'It must have been a shock when you saw your home at the auction.'

'This wasn't my home,' she said. 'This is a hotel built where our house once stood. There was a thick thorn fence around it to keep out predators. We had a lot of orphaned animals.'

'James told me about the baby elephants your parents reared, that the guests can walk with.'

'Daisy and Buttercup.'

'They're names for cows.'

'They were cow elephants. My dad's idea of a joke.'

'They say elephants never forget. Do you think they'll remember you?'

'Come with me and you'll see,' she said, her smile so unexpected that for a moment it took his breath away. 'That's if you have time. I imagine this is a business visit? Here today, gone tomorrow?'

'That was the intention,' he said. 'I'm here for the annual meeting with the Nymba Trust, who are our partners here. Unfortunately, Joshua Ngei is in hospital and, although his grandson runs the trust now, it seems that the meeting can't go ahead without him.'

'Joshua is the senior village elder. It's a question of respect.'

'Stuff you know and I'm having to catch up with, but that's okay. It gives me a chance to get to know the place.' Get to know her. He took a mouthful of coffee, then said, 'James said that your parents were studying the local elephant population.'

'Yes. I had hoped to follow in their footsteps, but life got in the way.'

'Life has a way of doing that,' he said.

'There are compensations.'

'Are there?' He sounded doubtful. 'What do you do, Eve?'

'I teach biology to high school students.'

'And your parents? Where are they now?'

'My father left to head up a new project in Sumatra. My

mother stayed on here for a while. I came back that last summer and worked with her. I thought I'd be doing that until I joined her permanently, but then she left, too.' She looked at him. 'I had no intention of bidding at the auction, but when I saw Nymba on the screen it called to me.'

'Why did she leave? Your mother?'

Eve shook her head. 'My father had an affair with his research assistant. She went with him to Sumatra. This was his project and without him the money dried up. My mother moved to a new project in Central America. She was deep in the rainforest when she caught a fever and died before she reached the nearest hospital.'

'I'm sorry.'

'That goodbye has been said. This…'

He said nothing, waiting for her to find the words.

'When I left that last time, I thought I'd be returning at Christmas. Instead I stayed with my father's parents in England. I broke my leg just before Easter so I had to stay with them again. My mother was supposed to go to Nantucket that summer, so I went there, but she was setting up the project in Central America and was too busy.'

'What about your father? Why didn't you visit him?'

'He had a new research project and a new woman in his life. The last thing he needed was a stroppy teenager underfoot.'

'That must have been tough.'

'There were other girls at school who were going through the same thing.'

'That doesn't make it better.'

No. And it was why she'd given up her dreams and chosen teaching. To be there after school and during the holidays for Hannah.

'I'm sorry, Eve.'

She waved a hand. Today had been very emotional and this wasn't helping.

Kit had looked her in the face and, after all, hadn't recognised her. It should have been a relief but, having got what she wanted, she was suddenly, stupidly furious. With her mother for dying, for losing the home she'd loved, the life she had dreamed of, and with Kit for being so blinkered.

Brown hair? Was that all it took?

'Why are you here, Kit?' she demanded. 'What do you want from me?'

'I'm sorry. I just wanted…' He lifted a hand in apology, clearly taken aback by her fierceness. 'My dad loves this place. My parents stayed here, on a second-honeymoon trip. All our other resorts are on the coast, the sea is our business, but they fell in love with Nymba. The lodge was doing well and I can see why. The setting is magnificent. What the trust badly needed was a partner with investment capital so that they could not only expand, but upgrade to meet the expectations of the luxury end of the market.'

'A match made in heaven.'

'So it would seem. Dad comes every year for a week to have a meeting with the Nymba Lodge Trust and relax. This year, as you know, he can't come, my brother is up to his eyes in the annual audit, so I stepped in.'

'So, have your meeting and relax.'

'I thought it would be a good idea to talk to Peter Ngei before the meeting, to make sure there were no problems. James arranged for me to see him this evening and it all went downhill from there.'

Eve frowned. Peter had been full of his plans for the village, the school extension, Mzee's party, but hadn't mentioned anything about problems with Merchant.

'What happened?'

'I was distracted when he arrived and he was expecting to meet my father, not some playboy sailor.'

'Playboy sailor?' Eve, well aware that she had been the distraction, felt a stab of guilt. 'That's an outrageous thing to say.'

Except wasn't that how she'd always thought of Kit? Ignoring the dedication, the skill it must have taken to achieve so much in one of the world's toughest, most dangerous sports.

Judging him instead on the covers of gossip magazines.

'Did he really call you that?' she asked.

'A blue-eyed playboy sailor were his exact words.' He shrugged. 'It's water off a duck's back, Eve, but I've got to get this right. I've a lot of ground to make up with my family.'

'It's true, then, about the rift?' He glanced at her. 'It was all over the media just before you went on that round-the-world yacht race.'

'Dad was furious with me for entering. He said it was time I stopped messing about in boats and started using my name to support the business.'

'That was harsh. You must have already brought an enormous amount of publicity and prestige to the resort. I saw your gold medal beside your photograph in the entrance hall.'

'I gave it to him. I brought it back from London and gave it to him. He thought that was it, that I'd come home, go to college, join Merchant and wait for him to retire in twenty years…'

'Instead you did it again in Rio.'

'A two-hander that time, with Matt. After that there were other races, but when I announced I was taking part in the single-handed round-the-world yacht race he totally lost it.'

'Maybe he was scared for you,' Eve suggested, remembering how she'd felt watching the yachts put out to sea for the hardest race in the yachting calendar on the evening news. Up to sixteen weeks alone, not touching land, storms, whales, icebergs…

How she'd felt when he was missing.

'Imagine how you would have felt in his place,' she said.

'I had a taste when I got the phone call from Brad saying that Dad was seriously ill, but when you're young you think you're indestructible.' There was a long silence and she knew he was thinking about Matt Grainger. A year or two older than him, with everything to live for. Eventually he stirred, looked at her. 'I told my dad that I wasn't prepared to spend the rest of my life showing my face at resorts and shaking hands with the guests like some trophy he'd won.'

'No one can hurt you like family,' she said.

'You've been there?'

'Not quite like that. Your dad wanted you to be with him, mine didn't even bother to come to my mother's funeral. I know they weren't married any more, but I asked him to come. I needed him there.'

She'd needed someone.

What she'd got was Kit.

And Hannah.

'When he didn't come, I told him I no longer considered him my father and blocked my bank from accepting any more direct transfers from him.'

'What did he do?'

'Nothing that made any difference to me.'

'And your grandparents?'

'They moved to Spain.'

'In case you made a habit of breaking limbs?'

She smiled as she was meant to. 'Something like that. I'm so sorry you lost your friend, Kit.'

'He was my sailing brother. I should have seen what was happening to him. Instead I was on the other side of the world talking to race sponsors...' He was looking out into the darkness. 'Lucy went to give him a shout when he didn't turn up for training one morning. She found him lying on the floor, stone cold, a needle in his arm.'

'Poor woman,' Eve said, thinking of the tenderness with which he'd held Lucy... 'You are both doing a lot to raise awareness, raise funds. And you turned up when your family needed you.'

'And I'm still making a mess of it.'

'You're here when you'd rather be at the far end of the world at the helm of a multimillion-dollar racing yacht.' Winning another trophy.

Had her judgement been way off all round that summer? She hadn't been in the best place. Throwing herself into the arms of a total stranger had been totally out of character.

But then neither had he.

Forced to choose between his chosen career and his family business, he'd set off on that round-the-world race determined to prove something, even if it killed him. And it very nearly had.

There had been times when she'd wondered if it was just Kit's bad luck to be in her way when she'd lost it that night or whether any reasonably attractive man would have done.

She was about to turn his world on its head; the least she could do was try and help him.

'Peter is a decent man,' she said. 'Maybe you should suggest a fishing trip, sit quietly for a couple of hours, drink a couple of beers... You do know how to fish, don't you?'

'You put your toe in the water and wait for a bite?'

'Only if you're fishing for crocodiles.' She sighed. 'I'm not sure that I can help, Kit. The last time I saw Peter was the day my mother drove us both into the city. I was fourteen and going back to boarding school. He was just starting his second year at university. He was charming, glamorous and I had the world's biggest crush—'

There was a rattle of china as the teapot fell to the floor and smashed, and Kit let out an expletive.

'Sorry... I got a lapful of coffee.'

Eve leapt up to grab a towel from the pile stacked beside the bath, handing it to Kit as he abandoned the wet chair.

'Look out!'

His shout came too late as something that had been lurking beneath the towel leapt to her shoulder where, unless she turned to face it, all she could see was a dark shape.

She screamed as it brushed against her neck, her cheek, reduced in seconds from a grown woman who could handle anything to a gibbering wreck.

Kit knocked the creature away, sweeping it off the deck and out into the dark, and then gathered her in as she sagged, trembling, against him.

'Shh... It's okay...it's gone... I've got you...'

It had been seconds, it had felt like years, but his arms were around her, supporting her as she clung to him.

'Are you hurt?' he asked. 'Did it bite you?' She whimpered. 'Can I check?'

She nodded into his chest, not moving as he lifted her hair to examine her neck. 'I can't see any marks or swelling. Let's just...' He eased back her robe to expose her shoulder and went very still.

'What is it? Have you found something?'

'Yes,' he said, his thumb grazing her back a few inches

below her shoulder, 'but it's nothing to worry about. Just a butterfly.'

'Oh.' Her stomach clenched as she realised what he'd found, and she forgot all about the hairy-legged spider. 'The stupid things you do when you've had one glass of Prosecco too many…'

'Oh?'

'It was a post-graduation party. A group of us decided we should mark the occasion with a tattoo.'

'And did you all go for a visual pun?' he asked, 'or was that just you? Only that looks to me like a red—' he turned from his examination of her shoulder to look straight into her eyes '—admiral.'

'Kit…'

'Don't! Don't say a word… Not until I've done this.'

She thought he'd been holding her close, but this was a whole new level of intimacy and she knew she should stop it but, even as her brain was scrambling for the word she needed, his mouth came down on hers like lava on ice and the only word hammering in her head was *yes, yes, yes*…

CHAPTER SEVEN

RAIN AFTER DROUGHT, feast after fasting, wind after a flat calm…

Kit was going to wait, give Eve time to decide when, if, she ever acknowledged what had happened between them, but the butterfly changed everything.

She might have disappeared after their night together, but she had not forgotten. She did not want to forget, or why would she have had a permanent reminder inked into her skin?

And her response to him was not one of reluctance. It was everything he'd ever dreamed of during long nights alone because, despite the many lovely women he'd met, who'd smiled, saying yes with their eyes, no one else would ever do.

He'd lost count of the times he'd turned at the glimpse of red hair on a slender whip of a girl, but it was never that pure red. Never the right girl. And in the years that had passed since that unforgettable night in his cabin, she had matured into an infinitely desirable woman.

Was the woman as impetuous as the girl he'd met on the beach?

The first time had been frantic, clothes coming off as they'd raced up the steps to the cabin, already naked as he'd kicked the door shut, tearing open protection with his teeth.

They hadn't made it to the bedroom, let alone the bed. She'd been on him, desperate for raw physical contact, the primeval heat of a man inside her. It had been explosive, blow-your-mind sex that had left them breathless, staring at each other in stunned wonder.

And then he'd kissed her.

The second time had been dreamlike; a slow, sensually devastating exploration. Tasting, breathing in the scent of her skin, discovering where touch was rewarded with a moan of pleasure, how to bring that moan to screaming pitch.

He'd never felt so powerful or so humbled...

Sexually sated, they had turned to food, cooking pasta naked at the stove, dripping sauce on their bodies as they ate, licking it off each other, abandoning food for a deeper hunger.

They'd talked about nothing, music, films, books; no family. They'd laughed, made love again and some days he thought they might still have been there but for that damned beach party, the crashing knock on the door that could only mean trouble.

There was no landline at the cabin and he didn't have the number of her cell phone to let her know what had happened.

His one hope was that she knew who he was, would give him a chance to explain. But there had been no call. Never so much as a glimpse of the bright curls that were now tangled around his fingers. Of the woman he was holding so close that he could feel her heartbeat.

It was a kiss he never wanted to end because he had no idea what would come next and it was Eve who broke the connection. She pulled back to look at him and for a moment he saw everything he'd ever dreamed of in her eyes. Then, with the slightest shake of her head, she eased away.

His hand slipped from the curls to momentarily cup her cheek.

Her wrap, where he'd checked for a spider bite, had slipped down, exposing rather more than her shoulder. He longed to slide his hand around her breast, knowing that a touch to her nipple would bring a gasp to those sweet lips, bring her closer so that she would feel what he was feeling.

Instead, not taking his eyes from hers, he lifted her wrap back into place and took a step away.

For a moment neither of them moved, then Eve, having tightened her belt around her, got down on her knees and began to pick up the pieces of the broken teapot.

Which answered any question he cared to ask about her impetuosity.

It had been a hot kiss, the kind with only one destination, but, while her body had been with him, her brain was still engaged and, from the careless way she was picking up the broken china, she was angry. But not, he suspected, with him.

'Leave it. You'll cut yourself.'

She carried on and he joined her, picking up the smaller pieces and putting them into a saucer.

'Where did you go…?' He looked up. 'I want to call you Red, but you aren't red any more. Why have you covered up that gorgeous colour?'

'Maybe this is my real colour.'

'I think I would have noticed,' he said, and regretted it the minute her cheeks flooded with colour.

She abandoned the broken china and sat down as if her legs were about to give way. 'If we're talking about vanishing tricks, where did you disappear to, Kit?'

Attack being the strongest form of defence? But it was a fair question and his would wait.

'There was some trouble on the beach,' he said, finishing the job of clearing up. 'My brother and a couple of other boys turned up late and got into a fight over a girl.'

He placed the saucer on the table but remained on his feet. 'By the time I arrived there was an ambulance and a cop car at the scene and my brother was being read his rights.'

'Oh.' Her shoulders sagged a little. 'I'm sorry. That was my fault. If you'd been there—'

'If there's any blame to go around I think I'm second on that list. Right after Brad. He was lucky to get away with a black eye and community service.'

'Community service?'

'Brad and his friends had been drinking. They'd taken to their heels at the first sound of a siren. My idiot brother had been floored by a lucky punch. No one was prepared to give up names, including Brad.'

'Sit down, for goodness' sake, you're giving me a crick in the neck.' She waved impatiently at the seat beside her and, when he'd obeyed, said, 'It must have been hard, being the younger brother of someone who was world famous at sixteen.'

'He loved sailing, but he stopped when I was picked for the team.'

'Was he good?'

'We all learned to swim before we could walk and sail as soon as we could stand up in a boat.'

'But he was always playing catch up.'

'And I never slowed down to give him a chance.' He shook his head. 'I can't change the past, but he had the guts to change his future. He stopped being an ass, knuckled down to work. He knows the Merchant business inside out and it's obvious that he's been taking the strain for a while. He needed help and I should have been there.'

'How is your dad? Really?'

'His stroke was catastrophic. Not so much the loss of movement. That's distressing enough but gradually coming back. Speech is taking longer, although on the upside he can't tell me that he doesn't need me.'

'I'm so sorry.'

Eve reached out a hand to him in a sweet gesture of empathy. He desperately wanted to take it, hold it, but every instinct warned him her touch would be brief and quickly withdrawn.

'It's coming back, slowly,' he said, 'but he wasn't making a lot of sense and the lawyers produced his written instructions that I was to act as CEO in the event that he was ever incapacitated.'

'That's tough. On both of you.'

'Punishment may come late,' he agreed, 'but it comes.'

'That's how you see it? Not a statement of his trust in you?'

Kit stretched out his neck, easing out the tension, then shook his head.

'My sister reminded me when I spoke to her today that it's not all about me. He wrote the instruction right after Brad's court hearing; a threat to make him get his act together and it worked. I assumed he'd torn it up long ago. Brad is convinced that when Dad recovers sufficiently to make his wishes known, he'll choose me.'

'If he does, it's because he wants you home.'

He stared at her. She lifted her eyebrows, inviting him to think about it.

'I… It's not my life.'

'He won't be around for ever, Kit.' In the moonlight he saw her throat move as she swallowed, and her voice snagged a little as she said, 'You've had a great career, won every trophy going. What's left but to repeat yourself?'

His turn to swallow hard. 'I'm not…'

'What? Ready to play second fiddle to your brother?'

'Not cut out to sit behind a desk and run a resort business.'

'You're not sitting behind a desk now,' she pointed out. 'Have you given any thought about what you'll do when you retire from the sport?'

Retire? He wasn't thirty. He had years ahead of him. As soon as his dad was well enough to listen to reason…

'Why are we talking about this?' he demanded. He wanted to talk about her. About them. About Nymba Lodge, for heaven's sake!

'This *matters*.'

She said it with a fervour that made him wonder just how much it had hurt her to be sent away from the home she loved to the bleakness of boarding school.

'Boat design,' he said. 'Matt Grainger and I were talking about the three of us going into partnership.' One day. When they were old. Except Matt would never be old… 'There's some land on the far side of the Merchant Resort site that is perfect for a studio, workshops, a yard.'

'Three of you?'

'Matt, Lucy and myself.'

Lucy…

'She was in your crew as well.'

'She's as good a sailor as her brother. Matt's death has shaken her badly but she's started giving children sailing lessons at the Nantucket resort.'

'She's staying?'

Of course Lucy was staying. She hadn't flown all the way from New Zealand for a five-minute talk about her brother. She was not just beautiful, she shared his passion for sailing; she was everything that Kit could possibly want.

'Maybe the two of you should go ahead with the design business,' she said, before he could answer. 'If you told your father what you are thinking of doing, showed him plans, began to set things in motion so that he could see a day when you'd be there—'

'Slow down! That's years away.'

'Of course. I just thought…'

'You're making perfect sense and, yes, it matters but this, here and now, matters more. I looked for you, Eve, but I didn't know who you were, what your circumstances were, so I was discreet. I didn't want to cause trouble.'

'I'm sorry I misjudged you. I should have left a note but I ran away. You couldn't find me because I'd caught the early ferry back to the mainland and the first available flight back to London.'

'Because of me?'

'No, Kit, because of me. I was in a bad place. My mother had just died, no one knew what to say to me. My poor young cousins had their arms twisted to take me to that party.'

'I could see that there was something, but I swear I never meant—'

'I needed someone to hold me,' she said, cutting off his words. 'I'd never done anything like that before.'

'Nobody in the history of the world has ever done anything like that before, Eve. It was unforgettable.'

Unforgettable? For a moment the word filled her head before she managed, 'Maybe we were both in need of a hug that night.'

'Is that all it was? If it meant so little why did you pretend not to know me this morning? Did I imagine that kiss?'

'What did you expect me to say? Hi, Kit, remember me? We had a one-night stand about four years ago?' She ignored his reference to that kiss. It would never have happened but for a spider. And a butterfly.

'Is it Peter?' he asked. 'You seemed very close when you came back from the village.'

'Did we?'

Eve did her best to ignore the little heart flutter at the suggestion that Kit might be just a little bit jealous. She'd seen him holding Lucy with a tenderness that came from the heart rather than driven by the loins.

He might have kissed her as if one of them were going to war, but that was down to an adrenaline rush. A response to something that had happened a long time ago.

The first time had been magical, and now she knew why he'd disappeared, she wasn't going to destroy that memory with a mistake that they would both regret in the morning. Not when she still had to tell him about Hannah. Not when Lucy was waiting for him to start a new life with her.

'What does he do?' Kit asked.

'He's a lawyer in the Attorney General's office.'

'Still glamorous, then.'

'Oh, yes. Handsome, clever and one day he will be rich,' she agreed. 'He has it all. He's also thoughtful, kind, loves his family, adores his children—'

'He has children?'

'—and his lovely wife, Maria,' she added, finally. 'Peter might be a city lawyer, but the village will always be the home of his heart, which is why I know he'll do what's best for the Nymba Trust. That's why you're here,' she reminded him. 'To talk about the trust.'

'I knew who you were, Eve,' he said, ignoring her attempt to turn the conversation away from the past. 'Not at first. You covered yourself up pretty well.'

'Says the man who's grown a beard.'

He rubbed his hand across his chin. 'Maybe we're both hiding.'

He was getting too close and she needed daylight, distance and to be wearing more than a bathrobe when she told him about Hannah. 'I'm going to the village on Saturday for Mzee's party,' she said, rising to her feet, making it clear that it was time for him to go. 'You can come with me if you think that will help.'

'Thank you.' He lifted a hand, as if for a goodbye touch.

She didn't move. She didn't dare risk even that.

'Goodnight, Kit.'

He closed his hand, nodded as if he understood and walked away.

Eve waited until she heard the click of the gate before she released a long, shaky breath.

Ever since she'd arrived in Nantucket she'd felt as if she'd been holding her breath. Waiting for the other shoe to drop. Finally, it had.

When he'd turned up with the tea tray and it had seemed that his arrival had nothing to do with the past, she'd felt just a little bit peeved.

He hadn't recognised her? Really?

She'd put on a few pounds and had rather more to show in the boob department than before she'd given birth to Hannah, but had she changed that much?

The hair colour had been to stop her standing out in the street, and this morning she'd been able to hide behind her hat and dark glasses, but up close did it make that much difference?

No one she'd ever met in Nantucket—and they had all been at her grandmother's funeral—had been fooled.

And neither had he but if it hadn't been for a spider, and the momentary madness of a tattoo party, they might still be walking around the elephant in the room.

Whatever the truth of the matter, her mind was now clear.

Her grandmother's cottage needed a lot of work before it could be put on the holiday rental market, which meant staying in Nantucket for the summer. But Mary, like her mother, was urging her to stay on and she'd already had a call from the head of the local high school—no doubt prompted by Mary or Martha—inviting her to come and see him.

Her father was in Sumatra and her British grandparents had decamped to the warmth of Spain; she had no family in England.

Nantucket was where her mother had grown up, where they had spent a few precious holidays together. There was family she was growing increasingly fond of, cousins for Hannah and, despite having kept a profile so low that she was practically invisible, the island was beginning to feel very much like home.

Kit might or might not stay on the island, but it was her future and that meant telling him that he had a daughter.

Tonight there had been too much emotion, too much going on. Added to that was the fact that he would almost certainly be home before her, and she didn't know how he would react to the news that he had a daughter.

The Merchants were a powerful local family and it had to be wiser to wait until she was back in Nantucket and had the chance to consult a lawyer before she told him about Hannah. After that he could decide whether he wanted to be a part of her life.

Her decision made, she picked up her laptop but, as she had a video call with her baby, chatting away, telling her everything that she'd been doing in an accent that was rapidly taking on a local twang, she wondered what it would be like to do that with Kit beside her.

CHAPTER EIGHT

KIT SHOWERED, BUT HIS body clock was still off balance. He pulled on a bathrobe and leaned against the rail of his deck.

Somewhere below him on the riverbank, a creature grunted but his gaze was drawn to where Eve's sky suite was located. It had been carefully placed so that it was impossible for him to make out more than the faintest glow from the solar lights of the walkway but, amongst the other noises of the night, he thought he heard her laughing.

Was she calling home? Or talking to the faithful Peter Ngei?

He barely had time to wonder before his own phone, kept strictly on silent at the lodge, vibrated in his pocket.

'Brad…'

'I'm sorry I missed you this morning. How are things going?'

'Not particularly well. The man who actually runs the trust expected Dad and wasn't too pleased to get second best.'

'Wow, that must have stung.'

'Fortunately,' he continued, ignoring the jibe, 'our auction winner, Genevieve Bliss, used to live here. She knows everyone, speaks the language and she's taking me with her to a village party on Saturday. I'll do my best to make a good impression.'

'You know what, Kit? Right now, I don't care what you do, I just want Dad back, talking, even if he is giving me a hard time.'

'Maybe you should tell him that.'

'I did, but he wants to hear it from you.'

Kit expected Brad to end the call, but he didn't and, after a moment, he said, 'Laura told me that you took Lucy down to the boathouse this morning. How did that go?'

'Oh, yes. We were talking and she offered to run a class for beginners. Kids. She seems keen.'

'She needs to get back on the water, and the youngsters will be in good hands.' More silence. Clearly Brad had something he wanted to get off his chest, so he kept talking. 'When you have a moment, could you get that information on that piece of land I told you about before I left?'

'Why?' he asked, suspiciously.

'It's not urgent. I was just thinking about the future. Setting up a yacht design partnership.'

'Wasn't that something you were planning to do with Matt Grainger? Are you thinking of going ahead on your own?'

'With Matt and Lucy. I was thinking of asking Lucy if she'd be interested in just the two of us going ahead. She always had such great ideas and she doesn't have much to keep her in New Zealand.'

'You and Lucy?' he said.

'Is that a problem?

Brad's parting two words, one unprintable, one in the affirmative, suggested that it was. It had been a day of ups and downs, but Kit was grinning as he video-called his mother and asked her to put her tablet in front of his father so that he could talk to him.

* * *

It was still dark when Eve, late, swallowed a mouthful of coffee before going outside to where the balloon was being inflated.

'Did you oversleep, Eve?'

Kit. Of course he'd be there. He was everywhere.

There was no reason why he should have told her he was coming on this trip and she pushed away the thought that he had decided to come because of her. It was the last thing she wanted.

'It's still dark,' she hissed under her breath as one or two of the other passengers glanced their way. 'In no way can I be said to have overslept.'

'You're not a morning person, then?'

'While you are insufferably cheerful when you've got up before dawn.'

'Sailors catch sleep when they can. It means that I'm good for tea and toast in bed.'

'Only if you stick around,' she muttered.

'I thought we were over that.'

'Over and so done.'

'It doesn't sound like it.'

'I thought you were here on business,' she said, changing the subject.

'This is business. The delay in the meeting is giving me the opportunity to experience everything we have to offer our guests.' He nodded in the direction of the horizon. 'It's going to be spectacular.'

In the few moments that they had been standing there, the sky had taken on an imperceptibly paler edge and, while she was an owl rather than a lark, she gave a little sigh. 'It always is,' she said, turning away to listen to the pilot as he began briefing them on the flight, explaining what to expect while in the air, what they would see, how to stand for the landing.

That done, they climbed aboard, men first to help their partners into the basket, which meant that Kit was holding out his hands to steady her as she jumped down to join him.

The other women had managed it gracefully. Feet together, soft knees.

Still half asleep and, yes, definitely not feeling the love at such an early start, Eve caught her heel on the edge of the basket and she fell hard against Kit. He was rock steady, gathering her up, holding her so that her breasts were pressed against his chest, her face tilted up to his. Far too close.

Heat raced through her body, her lips felt hot and swollen and his eyes had the same darkness as the night she'd thrown caution to the winds, inviting his kiss and a whole lot more. The same darkness as when he had kissed her last night.

'Are you okay?' He was still holding her, his expression unreadable. The man should play poker.

'Y-yes. Sorry. You're right. I'm not great first thing in the morning. Or the evening, come to think of it. Heel in basket, foot in hem, boot in mouth... Thanks for catching me.' She managed a rather shaky laugh as she eased away from his body. 'You can let go now.'

'If you're sure?' His hands were holding the tops of her arms, still steadying her. 'You seem, a little shaky.'

'There was no one around to force-feed me a croissant.'

'I've got a Lifesaver...'

She took the candy he offered as flame roared upwards, heating the air in the balloon and, as it began to rise slowly from the ground, instead of letting go, he put his arm around her shoulders as they turned to look out across the top of the trees.

'It would ruin everyone's day if you fell out of the basket,' he said, before she could object.

'It would certainly ruin mine,' she agreed. 'It's good to see that you're taking an interest in Nymba, despite the lack of wind and tide.'

'Your enthusiasm is infectious,' Kit said, the basket rising above the trees just as the sun edged over the horizon, creating long shadows that stretched across the savannah, and turning the river into a winding shimmer of gold.

'Magic,' Eve murmured, allowing herself to relax against him, stealing a precious moment of closeness as they drifted silently above grazing zebra and antelope.

'Magic,' he agreed, but when she turned to smile up at him, hoping that he was feeling it, too, he wasn't looking at the world beneath them but at her.

Even as she registered the fact, he took the sunglasses hooked over his shirt pocket, flipped them open and put them on, leaving her with the impression that he was the one hiding.

Someone exclaimed at the sighting of three giraffe, moving majestically along the riverbank.

'I had a close encounter with one of those yesterday,' he said, not to her, but to the entire group. 'I opened the siding on my deck and it was right there. Have you any idea how long their eyelashes are?'

'Long enough to make an entire chorus line weep,' Faye said with a sigh and everyone laughed.

After that they all seemed to come together, bond in the experience, exclaiming as they rose high enough to see the curvature of the earth, catch a glimpse of the sun shining on a distant lake, see the range of hills between them and the capital in the west before the heat haze rose to obscure them.

'They're blue,' someone said. 'In England the hills are blue when it rains. Is it going to rain?'

The question had been addressed to Kit who, as a sailor, seemed most likely to know these things, but Eve said, 'In Africa the hills are always blue.'

Having established that she was the resident expert, they quizzed her on the animals they saw and she told them the local names: *twiga* for giraffe, *punda milia* for zebra, and then, as the balloon neared a rocky outcrop, *simba* for lion...

The others used a variety of equipment from heavy-weight camera gear to their phones to film the pride of lions lazing on the rocks, but Eve was content just to look and so, it seemed, was Kit.

The big cats were watching the herds of antelope grazing quietly below them, undisturbed by the balloon. The male gave a mighty yawn. The herd was safe enough for now.

At the pilot's urging they all reached out to grab a 'lucky' leaf as they swooped low along the river before landing gently an hour later.

The long wheel base four-by-four and trailer that had been following them arrived as they were all helping to gather in the deflated balloon. It had brought along a hamper with champagne and a picnic breakfast of smoked salmon, eggs, meat, cheese and pastries for breakfast.

Kit had been drawn into conversation with the men about yachting, leaving her with the women.

'You know Kit Merchant?' Faye asked, clearly impressed.

'I won a bid for this trip at a charity auction held at the Merchant Seafarer Resort in Nantucket that he was hosting. I had no idea he'd be here.'

'It's just coincidence?' Faye said, rolling her eyes. 'If you were to ask me, I'd say he has the look of a man who thinks he's the winner.'

'No,' she said, quickly, but knew she was blushing. 'He's here on business.'

'That would be Health and Safety.' The other woman,

Chrissie, smirked. 'Your health and safety.' And the pair of them laughed as they fanned their faces with their hands and mouthed, *Hot...*

Protesting further would only make things worse, Eve knew, but when they returned to the four-by-four the rest of the party scrambled into the two front seats leaving the rear vacant for the two of them. Kit stood back as she climbed, self-consciously, aboard.

'Have you got enough room up there?' he asked the others.

Having been assured that they did, he climbed up after her and, as they bounced back to the lodge on barely there tracks, said, 'Thank you, Eve.'

'What f-f-for...?' She yelped as the vehicle hit a particularly deep rut and she was thrown sideways. Kit caught her hand, then put his arm around her.

Faye glanced back, grinning as she mouthed, *Health and safety.*

Except that this didn't feel safe. Not at all.

'For this morning. For being here. This kind of thing is not much fun unless you're sharing it with someone.'

'I suppose so.'

She hadn't shared very much with anyone in the last three years. She met her uni mates from time to time, but her life was so different from theirs. While they were out clubbing, dating, living from one drama to the next, she was reading bedtime stories, watching natural history and cooking programmes and going to bed early to cope with an early-rising toddler.

Sharing even those things would make them special.

Eve was quiet for the rest of the ride back to the lodge, but that was fine. He was content to sit like this. To know that they had the rest of the morning ahead of them, then lunch.

He was fairly sure that an afternoon nap was the order of the day after that, a chance to catch up on the predawn wake-up call and prepare for the night-time game viewing, with the chance of spotting a leopard.

He refused to allow his mind to wander into the realms of siesta fantasy, but then another bump threw Eve against him. His hand brushed against her breast as he fielded her and he felt a quiver of awareness ripple through her that answered his own stirring arousal.

She pulled away, and as soon as the vehicle drew into the Nymba compound she jumped down without waiting for help.

'See you for coffee by the pool, Eve?' Chrissie called.

'Great,' she said. 'See you later.'

Kit was held by the necessity of helping down the other women, of being a good host, thanking everyone for their company, and all he could do was watch her go.

'Richard and I are going night-time fishing with the locals this evening,' one of the men said, claiming his attention. 'You're welcome to join us, Kit.'

'Don't be silly, Jeff. Kit has far more interesting things to do than go fishing.'

'Really?' He looked at his wife in surprise. 'What?'

'Clueless,' she muttered, shaking her head.

Jeff shrugged. 'Well, the offer is open.'

It was what Eve had suggested. He doubted that Peter Ngei would be in the party, but it would be a chance to prove to the village that, while he was not his old man, he was a fairly decent human being.

'I'd love to come along. Thanks, Jeff.'

'Men,' Kit heard Faye mutter to her friend as she walked away. 'They are all totally clueless.'

She was right, he thought. He was still wondering why Eve had acted as if they'd never met. He'd heard her reason, but she was a confident woman; if anything, he would have expected teasing. If it really hadn't meant anything. But she'd run away at the auction, too.

The attraction was still there, as hot and urgent as ever... He'd been thinking that kiss had been like the first time, but he was wrong. That had been all about discovery. This time, when he'd kissed her, it had felt like coming home after a long journey.

At least for him.

Eve had pulled away, but then she had no reason to think that he wanted anything other than a repeat performance. Wham, bam, see you in another four years.

At least this morning, once she'd got over her predawn snippiness, she'd relaxed in the calm of the balloon's gondola, leaning against him as if it was the most natural thing in the world while they'd wondered at the earth unfolding below them.

In the air, with other people around her, she'd felt safe.

Now they were back on the ground she wanted to put some distance between them.

He could wait.

He knew how to be patient, tacking against the wind, teasing his boat forward even in a flat calm. He'd waited four years to find his Red and the last thing he wanted was for her to cut and run again.

James was waiting to greet them back at the lodge with coffee, juice and water. 'How did you enjoy the balloon trip, Eve?'

With every cell in her body vibrating from the ride back with Kit, the ease with which she'd slipped into closeness, Eve had hoped to make a quick getaway and grab a little recovery time.

Caught, she said, 'It was wonderful. The sunrise was

spectacular, and we had a thrilling view of a pride of lions on an outcrop of rocks.'

'That's always good to hear. Photographs of the big cats on social media are good for business.'

As the rest of the party joined her she slipped away to her suite, tossed her hat aside and took a very cool shower. It didn't help and she sat for a while, her entire body shaking with need.

She'd leaned against Kit in the balloon and she'd wanted him to hold her, wanted to feel his skin against hers, to be touched. To assuage the ache to hold him within her body that had stayed with her in the months after she'd left Nantucket.

It had only eased in those early months of motherhood, when sleep had been reduced to snatched minutes and exhaustion had focussed all emotion on a small, demanding infant who'd looked at her with Kit's blue eyes.

She'd done everything she could to distance herself from the memory, only to be caught out by photographs on the covers of glossy magazines.

His kiss, long moments when the world had gone away and every barricade she'd erected had come tumbling down, leaving her weak with longing, had brought it all surging back.

Kit, with his hand close enough to a nipple throbbing for the stroke of his rough thumb, must have known that all it would have taken was one touch and it would have been that night on the beach all over again.

Instead he had covered her.

Not a playboy, but a *'parfit gentil knyght'*. A man who, when he'd looked for her, had taken care not to do anything that might embarrass her.

He was reckless, careless of his own safety, but he was a much better man than she'd given him credit for.

It wasn't Kit she was hiding from up here in her suite, it was herself.

This trip had been a chance to relive that last holiday with her mother, reach back to precious memories, but this wasn't the Nymba of her childhood. It wasn't even the Nymba of that last summer with her mother.

She had chosen to remember it as a magic time, and it had been, but her mother hadn't asked her to come, hadn't wanted her to come. Busy with what had later transpired to be the final details of the project and with papers to write, her mother had encouraged her to go and visit her grandparents in Spain.

It was she who'd insisted on coming, saying that she wanted to help.

Had her mother given in out of guilt for having sent her away? She could have come home after the Nymba project, they could have lived together in the London flat, done the things her friends did with their mothers. But she'd already chosen the dangers of the Central American rainforest rather than her only child.

Eve had, she realised, made a conscious decision not to be like her mother, and yet here she was chasing the past when she could be at home with her daughter, tucking her into bed, reading her stories.

She would have video-called her, just for a glimpse of her sweet face, but they would all be asleep in Nantucket. Instead she took out her photo wallet and vowed to her baby that she would never again be the mother who put her own desires, wishes, above those of her child.

CHAPTER NINE

KIT PULLED TWO loungers into a shady spot at the end of the infinity pool. With her colouring, Eve wouldn't want to be in the sun.

He sent a couple of texts—one to his dad telling him what he'd done that morning, what he'd seen; one to Lucy asking her if she wanted to stay in Nantucket and, if so, would she be interested in going ahead with the design partnership they'd talked about.

Then he opened a book and waited.

It was about twenty minutes before Eve finally arrived, a long beach wrap over her swimsuit, her face shaded by her hat, her eyes hidden behind dark glasses.

She looked around but all the other loungers were in the sun and Chrissie, clearly a sun-worshipper, called out, 'Kit sorted you out some shade.'

She waved an acknowledgement but took a breath that was as much mental as physical before joining him. 'I was concerned you'd get fried,' he said.

'That is very thoughtful.' She sat down, stretched out, produced an eReader from the bag she was carrying. 'I imagine it's a problem when you're at sea. What are you reading?'

He held up his book so that she could see the frozen ship on the cover and the title *Endurance*.

'Shackleton. The man who navigated across six hundred miles of the most dangerous sea in the world in an open boat. Just up your street.'

'You know about the expedition?'

'Our school houses were named after explorers. Stanhope, Kingsley, Shackleton and Livingstone. Two women and two men. They were hot on equality.'

'I'm glad to hear it,' he said, waving over a steward. 'What would you like to drink?'

'Iced coffee, please.'

'Two iced coffees, please, Jonah,' he said, then turned to her. 'So how was boarding school?'

'They did their best,' she said, 'but it was cold, it rained all the time, there was no freedom, no animals and no mother.'

'You hated it.'

'I hated not being here.'

'I don't suppose your parents had much choice.'

'I'm sure that's how they saw it. It's not one I'd ever make.' She stood up, slipped off her robe to reveal the stunning curves only hinted at beneath the shapeless bush gear she'd been wearing. 'I'm going to cool off.'

He watched her power up and down the pool for a few minutes before he joined her in the water, matching his speed to hers as he swam alongside her.

'Why are you so angry,' he asked as they reached the end of the pool.

She stopped. 'I thought sailors were superstitious about learning to swim.'

'A superstition they realised was bunkum the moment they fell overboard. Why are you so angry?' he repeated.

She propped her chin on her arms, looking at the heat haze dancing across the savannah. 'They say you should never go back.'

'You regret coming here?'

She sighed. 'I came here on a wave of nostalgia for

some golden past and it's great catching up with people I grew up with.'

'But?'

'Memory blurs the edges. I remember the animals, the freedom, those special moments with my mother.' She turned away from the view. 'She was adorable. Everyone loved her and there are sweet moments, but she was always busy, always working. Sometimes she and my father were gone for days. It was Ketty who took me to school, made sure I was fed, who was always there for me.' She dashed a tear from her cheek. 'The last holiday here with her is a precious memory, but even then her mind was on the future. All she could talk about was her new project. I was studying zoology so that I could be with her, be part of her life…'

He opened his arms and she came into them, laying her cheek against his shoulder. 'I miss her so much, Kit.'

Warm tears spilled against his skin as he held her and for a moment they were the only two people on the planet.

'I'm sorry,' she said, pulling away much too soon, wiping her face with her hand. 'I don't know where that came from.'

'I imagine that coming here has opened up feelings that you've been keeping bottled up for a long time. It's not easy to admit feeling angry with someone who's dead.'

She lifted her head to look at him, tears clumping her lashes together. 'Are you angry with Matt?'

'When I saw him, afterwards, I just wanted to grab hold of him, shake him for being so stupid. Demand to know why he hadn't trusted me…' He shook his head. 'The truth is that I was angry with myself for not being there, not seeing what was happening.'

'You're making a difference, Kit. People will live because of what you've done.'

'I hope so.' He looked down at her. 'Are you done punishing the water?'

She nodded, and they returned to the shade of their loungers.

'So what *are* you reading?' he asked, as she dried herself off and began to apply more suncream.

'Under the Sea Wind.' She looked up. 'Rachel Carson.'

'My grandmother knew her. She stayed at the beach cabin when she was on the island.' He nodded at the bottle of sun lotion. 'Do you want me to do your back?'

She hesitated a moment. 'If you wouldn't mind.'

He sat beside her.

'Does your interest in a local author mean that you're considering staying on the island?' he asked to distract her as he slipped the straps of her costume over her shoulder and began to smooth the cream across her shoulders and down the deep scoop of her costume.

'Nana died recently. I'm sorting out her cottage.'

'She left it to you?' Her skin shivered under the roughness of his touch. 'Sorry about my hands. Your friend Peter might think I'm a playboy but the calluses tell a different story.'

He offered her back the cream but as she took it she held onto his hand, stroking her thumb over two crooked fingers. 'Not just the calluses. These were the fingers you broke on a round-the-world race. You had to lash them together with gaffer tape until they mended.'

'You were watching?'

'The whole world was watching. You could have died, Kit.' She looked up, her eyes searching. 'You must have known you wouldn't win so why did you carry on?'

The temptation was to shrug, as if it weren't important, but this was Eve, who'd just opened herself up to him in the most intimate way. She deserved more than his usual casual brushing aside of the pain, hardship, loneliness of those months.

'It's the ultimate goal,' he said. 'Something I'd dreamed of since I was a kid. Sponsors want winners, or a story, and I knew that if I gave up, I might never have another chance.'

And that, he thought, was why Matt had hidden the pain he was suffering. Because if he was seen as damaged, a liability, he might never get another chance to crew the ultimate yacht.

'You gave them headlines they could only have dreamed of,' Eve said, breaking into the uncomfortable realisation that there wasn't a whisker between them... 'Would you do it again?'

His hesitation was answer enough and Eve let go of his hand, put on her sunglasses, picked up her reader and lay back in shade.

Would he?

Memory blurred the edges.

In his head he knew there was pain, exhaustion, the same boring food over and over, but there was the exhilaration of taking the worst the elements could throw at you and winning through.

He wouldn't do it now but maybe, ten years from now, in a yacht he'd designed himself...

'Are you hungry?'

Eve had been staring at the same page for what seemed like for ever. She had been warming to the idea that she had misjudged Kit. He was a kinder and more thoughtful man than she had given him credit for but, while he was home for now, he'd made it plain that he had no interest in the family business.

His business was with the sea. Sooner or later the siren

call of the ultimate challenge would be irresistible, and the next time Hannah would be old enough to understand.

Would she be watching and waiting for her daddy to come home with terror? Or would she be hooked?

It was a relief to look up and see that the pool had been deserted and guests were beginning to gather at the bar for pre-lunch drinks.

'I didn't realise it was so late.' She closed her reader and dropped it in her bag. 'I need to change.'

'You will come back?' he asked.

'Will you come and find me if I don't?' She'd meant it as a challenge, but it had come out sounding more like an invitation. She wasn't hungry, not a bit, but she said, 'Just give me ten minutes.'

She was halfway to the steps when she heard a splash.

'What have you done to that poor man?' Faye, perched on a barstool, asked as she passed.

'It's complicated,' she said, without thinking, as they watched Kit, his powerful, sun-bronzed shoulders gleaming as he drove through the water.

'On the contrary, that's the simplest feeling in the world, sweetie,' Faye said, with a little sigh.

She knew that. Had once surrendered to that most basic instinct without a thought. It was thinking that messed with your head.

It was too early to call home and talk to Hannah, but Eve took a photograph of a monkey in a nearby tree and sent it to her with a load of kisses. By the time she returned to the terrace twenty minutes later, Kit was sitting on a stool, hair damp, but wearing a short-sleeved shirt and a pair of chinos.

'What would you like to drink?' he asked.

'Just water,' she said.

'Still? Or will you risk a little fizz?' His face was poker-straight but she knew when she was being teased.

It had been so long since anyone had dared to tease her. Had held her. Had made her feel that she was not just Hannah's mother, but a woman, and she smiled despite her determination to keep her distance.

'I'll risk the fizz,' she said, but grabbed a vacant seat between Chrissie and a new arrival when they sat down to lunch. Kit raised an eyebrow but took a seat amongst the rest of the new arrivals and barely looked in her direction once.

He left before she did, touching her shoulder lightly as he passed, his fingers brushing over the butterfly hidden beneath her shirt, but saying nothing.

She watched him walk away but he didn't look back. She didn't see him again until, two hours later, he was waiting by the vehicle that would take them to the part of the reserve where they would walk with Buttercup and Daisy.

'It's just us?' she said.

'More than two and the elephants can get spooked. You have to book well in advance to have this privilege. Fortunately, it was part of the package you bid for,' he said, offering his hand to help her up in the seat.

'So how did you get lucky?'

'Everyone else came in pairs.'

The ranger who cared for the elephants had been at school with her and she hugged him, asked after his family, introduced him to Kit.

By then, Daisy, always the most curious, lowered her head and touched her gently with the tip of her trunk.

Eve put up her hand to rub it, murmuring softly as she rested her forehead on the great beast. Buttercup, not to be outdone, curled her trunk around her.

'Is she hugging you?' Kit asked.

'Elephants never forget,' Eve said, taking his hand, encouraging him to touch first Daisy and then Buttercup, telling them his name, reassuring them that he wouldn't hurt them.

They touched him, responding with happy little snorts.

'I think they can smell me on you,' she said.

'It's vanilla,' he said, looking at her, rather than the elephant. 'The memory of it stayed with me for weeks.'

For a moment Eve couldn't breathe, then she managed a slightly shaky, 'It's more likely that you got a blast every time you passed a bakery.'

'No, it was more complex than a cupcake.' He glanced at her. 'It was there after I caught you falling at the auction.'

'It's my perfume, Shalimar,' Eve confessed. 'My mother always wore it and she'd sometimes put a drop on my wrist. I bought a tiny bottle in the airport duty free on my way to school. I wasn't allowed to wear it, but I put it on my pillow. With you it's the sea that's become part of you. With me it's Shalimar.'

'And like the elephants, I have never forgotten it,' he said, taking her hand as they began to move off.

Eve skipped the early morning game drive and had a lie in, sitting up in bed on the deck, putting together pictures Kit had taken of her with the elephants, planning to send them to Hannah. Afterwards, he'd handed her phone to the ranger and asked him to take a photograph of the two of them.

They were standing with Daisy. She was making a fuss of Daisy and laughing, but Kit was looking at her in a way that brought a lump to her throat. In a way that she wouldn't want anyone else to see. She knew she should delete it, but then the phone rang, making her jump. An unknown number. Normally she would have let it go to voicemail, but it could be a call from home. Hannah…

'Eve Bliss.'

'I hope I didn't wake you.'

'I…' It was okay, no drama, just Kit. 'How did you get this number?'

'I sent a photograph of you with the elephants to my phone. We're going to put up a board with pictures showing everyone who won a bid at the auction having a good time. That one is going to be a winner.'

'What do you want, Kit?'

'I kept an almond croissant for you, but you didn't turn up for coffee this morning. I'm just being a good host and checking that you're okay.'

'I'm preserving my energy for the party. How was your evening? Did you catch any fish?'

'You doubt it?'

'Half a dozen men in a boat with a case of beer and basket of food. Oh, yes, I seriously doubt it. Was Peter there?'

'No. He went into the city to collect his grandfather, but he sent a message to say that we're having the trust meeting this afternoon, before the party.'

'Well, that's good news. You'll be able to go home tomorrow.'

'I could stretch to another day or two. I haven't had a canoe trip yet and I'm told there are waterfalls that shouldn't be missed. Would you like breakfast in your suite this morning?'

She sighed. 'You're outside my suite, aren't you?'

There was a tap on her gate. 'Service, Miss Eve.'

'Oh, for heaven's sake.'

She closed her phone as Kit carried a tray across the deck and laid it on the table.

'Coffee, orange juice, and since I wasn't sure what you'd like I brought eggs Benedict, pancakes, and avocado on toast with poached eggs.'

'That's a shocking waste!'

'I was hoping you'd say that. Will you come over here?' he asked. 'Or shall I join you over there?'

'Go!' she demanded. 'Now!'

'Can I take the eggs Benedict?'

If she'd had anything to hand, she'd have thrown it at him.

CHAPTER TEN

KIT, CHECKING IN to update Brad, got a call divert to his sister. Again.

'Hi, Laura. How's Dad?'

'He's still struggling to find the right words. The stuff he's coming out with is actually pretty funny. He and Mom are doing a lot of laughing.'

'Yes, I got that when I called on Skype yesterday.' Realising that she was struggling with tears, he said, 'You know recovery from stroke is really good these days.'

'It's going to take months, Kit. He may never get it all back.'

'Dad's a fighter.'

'I know. What are you up to?' she asked with determined brightness, and he didn't have to be there to see that she was making an effort to put on a smile. She was a fighter, too. 'Apart from ruining Brad's unusually good mood. Sitting around in the sun watching the wildlife?'

'Pretty much,' he said, looking down at a family of elephants playing in the river. 'Hot-air ballooning, fishing, walking with elephants and today it's the village elder's birthday and I've been invited to the party.'

'Working really hard, then.'

'You can come with Dad next year. What have I done to upset Brad? Where is he anyway? I thought he never left his desk but I've yet to find him there.'

Laura cleared her throat, meaningfully. 'Lucy wanted something in town.'

It took him a moment to process that. 'Are you telling me that he left his office to take her to the store?'

'When they came back from the boathouse she said, "Brad, I really need some of my special hand cream…"' Laura put on a breathy *I'm so helpless* voice that was so unlike Lucy that he laughed. 'You think I'm kidding? I'm telling you he was walking her to his car before I could ask him to bring me some chocolate.'

Actually, that wasn't funny. He didn't believe for a moment that the scene had gone down like that. Lucy might have said she was going to walk into town to get some hand cream, but that Brad had volunteered to take her bothered him.

'Do you want to hear the gossip about your Miss Bliss?' Laura asked, breaking into his thoughts.

'She's not my anything,' he said, shutting his mind firmly against the word *gossip*. He knew what that was worth.

He'd held this image of her in his head, his heart for so long and there had been a moment when he'd held her, kissed her, when it had seemed as if the wait was over.

Nothing could be further from the truth.

The falling-into-bed attraction was there, as strong as it had been that first night, but it was more than that. Just being with her was time well spent.

He'd missed her first thing. Her smile, the easy banter. She'd sent him away with a flea in his ear for his cheek when he'd taken up breakfast, but it had been worth it for the vision of her, mysterious behind the gauzy mosquito net, lying back against a pile of pillows. Her shoulders bare but for tiny straps that held up whatever she was wearing beneath the sheet, her hair a tumbled mass of curls.

Not his anything. But, if he was lucky, she might be his everything.

'I have to go,' he said. 'Give my love to Mom and Dad.'

* * *

Kit loaded his contribution to the party in the back of one of the lodge's vehicles and returned to Reception. Eve was standing in the reception area. She was chatting to James and she had her back half turned to him so she didn't see him stop dead in his tracks.

Her hair, a mass of loose curls, was glowing in a shaft of sunlight. It wasn't the clear bright red he remembered, but the colour she used was fading out, leaving it the soft shade of maple leaves in the fall. Make-up subtly enhanced her eyes, drew attention to her mouth and she'd abandoned the shapeless khaki bush gear for the party. The simple, elegant moss-coloured linen dress that reached her ankles would, he knew, exactly match the green in her eyes.

'Ready to go?' James asked, as he spotted him. She turned and for a split second, before she closed it down, he saw his own heart leap reflected back at him and it took him a moment to find his voice.

'Are these all yours?' he asked, indicating the large number of bags at her feet.

She lifted her shoulders fractionally in an apologetic shrug. 'I knew I'd be visiting the village, so I shopped for gifts before I travelled.'

'Is Peter here?' she asked, as he gathered them up in two hands. 'I didn't hear him arrive.'

'James has kindly loaned me one of the lodge vehicles so I sent him a message to say that we'd make our own way to the village.'

Eve raised an eyebrow. 'Grabbing back a little bit of control, Kit?'

Control? That was a joke. He was so out of control that, but for the touch-me-not force field around her, he'd be kissing the words right off her mouth.

His sexy Red had given him a night he'd never forgotten. Eve, he realised, had become so much more. Beneath the sexuality that she'd done her best to mask was an intelligent woman who'd seen through his motive as easily as through a pane of glass.

Eve, on the other hand, shimmered like a mirage…

'It's not about control,' he said, pushing the disturbing thought away as he stacked her bags on the back seat. 'It occurred to me that he wouldn't be able to relax and enjoy the party if he has to drive us back.'

'Actually,' she said, as she climbed up into the passenger seat, 'that's extremely thoughtful.' And his reward, as he started the engine, was to see the corner of her mouth lift in a smile. The real kind. She was fighting it, but she was losing.

Eve kept her eyes on the dirt road and Kit seemed unusually quiet. She'd sent him away this morning when having him stay, sharing breakfast with him, would have been a precious moment to remember.

Kit was going back to Lucy and, for Hannah's sake, they would need to be friends, or at least civil. The kiss could be excused as a response to the moment, but anything else could only lead to awkwardness, guilt.

He'd be gone tomorrow, giving her a few days to get her head straight, think about how she would tell him about Hannah. How she was going to tell Hannah.

The moment they arrived at the village the door was flung open and there was Ketty, older now, but arms open wide to embrace her as she jumped down.

The hug was a long shared moment, the silence filled with memories. Then, they were surrounded by excited children who she entrusted with most of the bags she'd brought. Two she kept.

'This is for you, Ketty. I'll go and give Mzee his birthday present, then I'll come and share out the rest.'

But Ketty was staring at Kit, who had opened up the rear of the vehicle and taken out a couple of cartons of beer.

'Ketty, this is Kit Merchant.'

'The young woman who took care of you when your mother was working?' Kit put down the beer. 'I've heard a lot about you, Ketty, from Eve and from James.'

'And I've heard much about you, Mr Merchant,' Ketty said before, with the briefest nod, she ushered the children away. 'I'll go and make tea.'

Eve, too shocked to hide her astonishment at such a cold reception, turned on him and said, 'What on earth have you done?'

He shook his head. 'I have no idea. Let's go and pay our respects to Joshua Ngei,' he said, reaching back into the vehicle for the box containing the bottle of whiskey he'd brought with him. 'If I survive that encounter maybe the frost will melt a little.'

The old man was sitting with his friends in the shade of a tree.

'Happy birthday, Mzee,' Eve said, placing her gift in his hands and kissing his cheeks, before wishing him a long life and good health. He opened the package and exclaimed with pleasure at the soft collarless cotton shirt she'd brought him. Then she turned to Kit, who had been standing back a little.

'Mzee, may I introduce my dear friend, Kit Merchant.'

He gave her a quizzical look before turning to Kit. 'I know your father,' he said. 'I am sorry to hear that he is not well.'

'He sends his warmest greetings with this,' he said, placing his gift of whiskey on the table beside the old man, 'and wishes he could be here to drink it with you.'

Then he offered his hand, holding his arm respectfully, bowing as he repeated a traditional greeting.

Mzee looked at her, as if to check her reaction. Puzzled, she nodded, smiled, put a hand on Kit's back as if to enclose him within the group.

'Send your father my prayers for his return to health, Mr Merchant,' he said, accepting Kit's hand, before he indicated with a gesture that he should sit beside him. 'We hope to see him here again very soon.'

Kit caught her hand as she let it drop and gave it a brief squeeze, acknowledging the 'dear friend', then took the seat vacated for him next to Joshua Ngei.

'I hear you are a great fisherman, Mr Merchant.'

'My father is Mr Merchant, sir, I am just Kit,' he said.

'Then open the bottle, Kit, and we will drink a toast to Christopher Merchant.'

Eve lifted her hand to her mouth.

She had lived with an image of him in her head for so long. The passionate and tender lover. The man who could make her laugh when laughing was something alien. The man who could make her feel when she was numb. The man who had seemingly abandoned her, but had looked for her.

The blue-eyed playboy sailor who regularly appeared on magazine covers, always with a glamorous woman at his side.

A man whose life was the sea.

The father of her child.

This skill as a statesman was yet another layer to this compelling man.

'Eve!'

She turned to see Ketty clutching the handbag she'd given her to her chest. 'It's so beautiful! Thank you.'

'I'm glad you like it,' she said, a little shakily, as they turned to walk across to where the rest of her gifts were waiting to be shared out, and she realised that all the women were looking at Kit.

'He is very pretty,' Maria said.

'He has a great ass,' one of the older women said. 'I'd be tempted.' They all laughed, everyone but Ketty, who just reached for her hand and squeezed it.

No one would let her help with the cooking, so she and Maria kept the younger children amused until the trust meeting was over. Kit gave her an almost imperceptible nod and she let out a breath she hadn't been aware she was holding.

'Did Peter tell you we're building a science lab for the school?' Maria asked.

'He said, but the workmen were there so it wasn't safe to go in. I'd like to take a photograph of the plaque you've erected to my mother.'

They were joined by several women who were home from the city for weekend celebrations who wanted to see how the extension was progressing and, having admired that, they all took a nostalgic tour of the classrooms.

'Oh, look,' one of the women said, looking at the pinboard with photographs of all the pupils in the class. 'They have a photograph of you when you were here, Eve.'

Maria took a closer look.

'That's not Eve. She has green eyes. This is her little girl. Peter said you'd given a picture of her to the children yesterday,' she said. 'She is very like you as a child.'

'It's just the hair.'

The scent of the sea had warned her of his presence a split second before Kit spoke. Before he reached over her head and took the picture down to look at it more closely.

'This child is the image of my sister at the same age.'

She turned, her mouth working, but no words coming out. She didn't have to say anything. One look and he'd known.

'What is her name?' he asked.

Her tongue was stuck to the roof of her mouth and it took a moment before she could say, 'Hannah Rose Merchant Bliss.'

He glanced at her, a nod acknowledging the inclusion of Merchant. 'She's beautiful.'

'Yes.'

'When were you going to tell me?' he asked, those blue eyes unreadable, his voice even, unemotional. 'Were you ever going to tell me?'

The others, at a signal from Maria, had melted away, leaving them alone.

'No,' she admitted. 'I only came back to Nantucket because my grandmother was sick.'

The sun, which had lit up the room just moments before, had sunk behind the trees and his face was all shadows. 'That's why you dyed your hair. You were hoping I wouldn't notice you.'

'Your team blog said you were in the Southern Ocean, but I couldn't take the risk.'

'You actually checked?' Even, unemotional, frighteningly calm.

'Yes, I checked. I should have been long gone by the time you returned, but Nana died and I had to stay and deal with the cottage.'

'Of course, you told me that she left you her cottage.'

'No.' She shook her head. 'She knew I'd sell it. She left it to Hannah.'

'Why, Eve? Why would you do this? Why didn't you tell me?'

'Why do you think?' she demanded. 'You meet a girl on a beach, have a one-night stand, then disappear.'

'I told you my name. All you had to do was pick up a phone.'

'And what? Ask for the money to take care of it?'

He took a step back as if she'd slapped him.

'You weren't hitting on me, remember? I jumped you and I chose to take responsibility for my own actions.'

'There were two of us in the room.'

'And then you left.'

He lifted a hand in a gesture at once helpless and exasperated. 'You know why!'

'Now I know. Then…' She shook her head, willing him to understand.

'Then you thought I'd had a good time and walked out on you.' She didn't want to tell him everything she'd thought. That was enough. 'Despite that, you chose to keep her,' he said, his voice softer.

'There was never any question about that, Kit. Hannah is my joy.'

'What about my joy?' he demanded. 'I have a child, a daughter, and you chose to keep her from me.'

Eve felt as if she was hanging onto reality by her fingernails. She'd been going to tell him, assure him that he didn't have to be involved, that he could walk away. That would have been better, but only marginally. She hadn't expected him to be angry. To feel cheated…

'I was going to tell you.'

'Why? Because I saw through your pathetic disguise?'

'Because I'm going to stay in Nantucket.'

'Too damn right you are,' he said, the cold calm finally breaking down.

'Kit… I was going to tell you, but not here. You're leaving before me—'

'And you thought I might take her?'

'I didn't know what you might do.'

CHAPTER ELEVEN

KIT BREATHED OUT an expletive and he sat on one of the class benches as if his legs could no longer hold him.

'She's my daughter, Eve, and I've missed so much of her life already. I didn't even get a say in her name.'

'I named her Hannah after my grandmother, Rose after my mother.'

'She had just died, hadn't she? Your mother. That's why you were in Nantucket. Why you looked so lost…' He shook his head. 'How on earth did you cope?'

'My mother got the London flat in a divorce settlement from my father. I lived there while I was at uni, and she left it to me, along with some money.'

'I didn't mean… How did you cope emotionally? With the pregnancy? The birth?'

'I was in the middle of my finals and I didn't realise I was pregnant until they were over.' She sat down on the bench opposite him. 'Truthfully, Kit? I was grieving for my mother, furious with my father and with my hormones shot to hell I might not have been entirely rational at the time, but the promise of a baby felt like a gift and for that I'll always be grateful to you.'

'Did you have anyone with you? At the birth?'

'The tattoo group rallied round. The one with the dragonfly is Hannah's godmother. They are scattered all over the world now, but they all considered themselves her honorary aunts and uncles.'

He took one last long look at the photograph and then slipped it in his pocket as he stood up.

'No,' she said. 'I gave that to the children. I have others you can have.'

'It finally explains the cold shoulder,' he said, as he pinned it back. 'Peter saw this photograph and when he brought you back to the lodge yesterday and saw us together, he guessed I was her father.'

'Because you both have blue eyes? That's a bit of a long shot.'

'He saw my shock when I recognised you and drew his own conclusions.'

'That jibe about the blue-eyed playboy.' She swallowed down a lump the size of a golf ball in her throat. 'I thought at the time it sounded personal. I'm sorry, Kit. I'll explain.'

'No need. It was plain enough for everyone to see what you'd done.'

'I didn't want a scandal, Kit. My mother's death was all over the local newspapers. Can you imagine the gossip? My mother was hardly cold in her grave and I was having sex with a stranger on the beach. I was so ashamed—'

'Ashamed?' For a moment he looked furious then dragged his hand over his face. 'I'm sorry. I can't begin to imagine what you were feeling.'

'I was sure you were on tenterhooks waiting for the story to appear in one of the gossip magazines.'

'It would have made a change for one of them to be true.'

'Are you saying they were all made up?'

'I was young and stupid but they were mostly spun out of a grain of truth. No one knows that I'm Hannah's father?' he asked. 'Adding "Merchant" to her name was a bit of a giveaway.'

'I was in London, Kit, and the registrar was too busy

to care what I called her. As far as the rest of the world is concerned, she is Hannah Bliss.'

'Not your family? Weren't your friends curious?'

'A secret shared is no longer a secret.'

'You told them you didn't know…'

She shrugged. 'A *Mamma Mia* moment.'

'That's the gossip my sister picked up. That you have a child whose father is something of a mystery.'

'You had your sister check up on me?'

'And chose not to hear what she'd discovered. More fool me. Not to worry, there's nothing like a wedding to gloss over the secrets of the bride.'

'What bride?' He didn't bother to answer. 'No,' she said. 'No way. I'm not… I won't…'

'I… I… I… This isn't about you any more, Eve. It's about putting Hannah first.'

'I do. I have,' she protested.

'And when she asked why she hadn't got a daddy? Or hadn't you thought that far ahead?'

She'd thought about it. She'd seen her baby's wrinkled forehead as she'd watched her cousins play with their father, the thought forming in her precious head.

'You can have all the access you want,' she said.

'You can bet your life I'll have access,' Kit said. 'Until the day you disappear back to London, taking her with you.'

'No!' she protested. 'I wouldn't do that.'

'You already did.'

'I told you, Kit, I'm going to stay on the island. I've got an interview for a job at the high school.'

'And who will look after Hannah while you're working? Who looked after her in London?'

'She went to an excellent day nursery. She loved it and I'm sure they have such things in Nantucket, so if you think you're going to marry me and I'll be a stay-at-home mom, think again.'

'Where are you living?'

'In Nana's cottage. Hannah's cottage.'

'I was looking for an address.'

'Oh. I see.' He waited and she said, 'Wisteria Cottage. It's in Paston Lane, just across—'

'I know where it is. It's been neglected.'

'It needs a coat of paint,' she admitted.

'It needs a complete renovation job. You can't stay there.'

'I have to. The cat won't move.'

'The cat?'

'Mungo. They tried to move him when Nana was in hospital, but he wouldn't eat.' He was clearly lost for words so she said, 'I'm working on it. I'm going to rent storage space so that I can clear out all the clutter and then—'

'Why don't you just get rid of it?'

'The cat?'

'The clutter.'

'The trustees have made it clear that it all belongs to Hannah. Nana and Grandpa's clothes. Cat-scratched furniture. Fifty years of paperwork…'

'That sounds like a fire hazard. We should get a ruling from the chief.'

'We…'

She pushed the temptation away. It was time to get real.

'You can't marry me, Kit. You're in love with Lucy.'

'What on earth are you talking about?'

'I saw you with her at the auction. I can recognise love when I see it. You're going into partnership with her, for heaven's sake.'

'You weren't thinking about Lucy when we kissed.'

'I wasn't thinking at all.'

The corner of his mouth lifted in a smile. 'That is the

effect one hopes to achieve. If it makes you feel better, my brain wasn't entirely engaged, either.'

'Kit...'

'Is that the only reason you're saying no?'

'It's a pretty big one, don't you think?'

'There's more than one kind of love, Eve. I've known Lucy since she was a sailing-mad kid. I love her, of course I do, but like a sister.'

Eve now had a lump the size of a mango in her throat and couldn't speak.

'Is there anything else?' Kit asked. 'Speak now or for ever hold your peace.'

She shook her head. 'Maybe we should fly to Vegas and do it on the way home,' she said, not entirely flippantly.

'You'd deny me that, too? And what about Hannah? Do you imagine our daughter will forgive us if she isn't a flower girl at our wedding?'

We... Our... They were such magic words...

'Our daughter is a little young to know that she's missing anything, but her cousins would be absolutely livid.'

He nodded as if it were settled. It wasn't. He'd had a shock, his emotions were in turmoil but once they were home, he'd begin to think straight.

'It's gone very quiet out there,' he said, standing up and offering her his hand. 'Perhaps we should put in an appearance before someone passes out from holding their breath.' She nodded. 'It would help if you could manage a smile. If they think I've made you unhappy they might feed me to the crocodiles.'

She laughed, as she was meant to and, with her hand firmly in his, he headed for the door. Outside there was a wide semicircle of people waiting.

'As you will all have realised, Eve has today surprised me with the greatest gift imaginable, that of a daughter.

In return I have asked her to marry me and she has made me the happiest of men by saying yes.' He turned to her, and, eyes hooded to hide his thoughts, and while she was still struggling with what had just happened, he kissed her.

It was brief, but emphatic and if, as a result, she clung to him just for a moment, while her knees remembered what they were for, it all added to the illusion that this was a happy-ever-after ending.

The announcement, the kiss, were greeted with a round of applause and then they were all heading back to the centre of the village where fairy lights had been strung in the trees, music was playing and, since it seemed to be expected, Kit took her in his arms and whirled her around the square.

It looked like one of those perfect moments. Lovers reunited, a wedding to plan, a new life waiting for them.

'Tears, Evie?' She did her best to blink them back as Ketty took her hand in both of hers. 'We are all thinking about your mother. She would be overjoyed to see you so happy.'

'Yes,' she said, and she reached into the very depths of her soul to dredge up a smile that would convince the world that it was the happiest day of her life.

It was late and the headlights piercing the darkness as they drove back to the lodge caught the reflections of eyes watching from the bush on either side of the track.

The party had been noisy and they'd left it in full swing, making the silence of the drive back to the lodge all the more intense.

'I have invited Peter and Maria to the wedding,' Kit said, at last. 'They'll stay at the Nantucket resort as my guests.'

'They needed convincing that you're doing the right thing?'

'A photograph would have done that.' He glanced at her. 'I thought you'd like to have them there.'

'I don't want anyone there.'

'You're still rooting for the Las Vegas option?'

'I'm rooting for the no wedding option.'

He stopped the four-by-four. 'You took a unilateral decision to deprive me of my child, Eve. The anticipation of waiting for her arrival, the anxiety of the scans, the joy of making a nursery, sharing the news, of being there when she was born.'

'I promise you, I wasn't feeling the joy,' she said, and immediately regretted it. The hours of discomfort, pain, had been forgotten in that first moment when she'd held her baby, seen the slightly puzzled look in those blue eyes, the surge of unconditional love. 'I… I thought I was doing the right thing for everyone.'

'I know, but it's a moment, a memory, I will never have. One of hundreds. Her first smile…'

'Her first projectile vomit,' she said.

'Her first step.'

'The panic of a temperature so high I called an ambulance, convinced she had meningitis.'

'Eve—'

'It was already going down by the time they arrived ten minutes later. She's had all her shots and is growing like a weed,' she said, reaching out to reassure him.

'I've never told her a bedtime story.'

'She didn't sleep for a year.'

'Her first Christmas.'

'She screamed the first time she saw Santa.'

'The first time she looked at me and said "Dada".'

Eve sighed. 'That's it. You win…'

'No, don't you see? I've lost and lost and lost. I don't even know her birthday. Early August so… May?'

'The fifth.'

'Tell me about her, Eve. What does she like?' he asked.

'Like?'

'What colour, what food, what toys…?'

As Kit listed the things he didn't know about Hannah, Eve put her head in her lap, covering it with her arms to block out his voice, overwhelmed by guilt as she accepted the reality of what she'd done.

She'd said sorry, but saying it a hundred, a thousand times could never undo this.

'Eve…?'

She shook her head, but he lifted her arms, pulling her up. 'Look at me,' he insisted and then, wiping tears from her cheek with his thumb, 'Talk to me.'

'My father wasn't there.' The words came from nowhere.

'Your father? But I thought, you said… He and your mother worked together?'

'Yes, but did you hear anyone mention him today? He never went to the village. He didn't take a bottle of whiskey to Mzee on his birthday. My mother did that, always with some plausible excuse why he couldn't come himself.'

'Your father was too busy?'

'It wasn't about how busy he was. He didn't know or care about such things.' She'd never thought about it before, not consciously, and pushed her hair back from her face with her fingers, as if that would make everything clearer. 'He's never remembered my birthday since he didn't have Mom to prompt him to say happy birthday. There was no room in his head for anything but his work.'

'There was enough room for him to notice his assistant.'

'He'd been offered a new research project, more money,

more prestige, and was ready to up sticks and leave. My
mother refused to leave their work at Nymba unfinished,
so he left her, taking a research student with him. Someone
to deal with the tedious stuff of life. Organise food, make
sure there were clean clothes, keep the records and type
up the notes. And, I imagine, anything else he wanted.'

'I'm not your father, Eve.'

'No, you have more humanity in your little finger than
he has in his entire body, but sailing is your life, Kit. It
has been since you could walk and to have achieved what
you've done takes the kind of a single-minded focus that
leaves no room for anything else.'

'That's why you asked me about the round-the-world
race.'

'And you couldn't give me an answer.'

For a moment there was only the *tick-tick-tick* of the
cooling engine and then Kit leaned forward, brought it
back to life and drove on, barely slowing, even when an
antelope burst through the bush and leapt across the track
in front of them.

They parted awkwardly when they arrived back at the
lodge.

'I'll book the first available flights,' he said, 'and let
you know when we'll be leaving.'

She nodded.

'No arguments?'

'I want to be home, too.'

It was only when she was back in her suite that she
remembered her promise to give Kit the photographs of
Hannah.

She took out her phone, found a little video she'd taken
of her putting together a puzzle. Hannah was chattering
to herself as she worked out how the pieces fitted together

and then, when she'd finished, she clapped and looked up with that great big smile and said, 'I won!'

'Go to Daddy,' she whispered as she hit send, and a few moments later, the words *I'm in love* came back.

The flight home was long and exhausting without the luxury of a break in London. Kit heard Eve give a sigh of relief as the lights of the harbour appeared out of the light sea mist and the ferry came into Nantucket.

Once they'd docked, he took her bag and headed for the taxi he'd called and, while the driver loaded her bag, asked, 'When can I see her?'

'It's late. She'll be in bed and first thing she'll only care about playing with her cousins. It will be more peaceful at the cottage.'

'When?'

'Come to lunch.'

'I'll bring it. What does she like?'

'Hannah loves a pizza. Just a simple one. Nothing spicy.'

'And what about you, Eve? I know you like pasta.'

'No…' Her blushes told him that she remembered how they had cooked it, how they had eaten it. One day, soon, they would do that again… 'A seafood pizza would be great. I'll make a salad.'

He opened the taxi door, watched her safely in and then closed it and stood back. She looked around as the car turned a corner and then was gone.

He hadn't told anyone he was coming home and he picked up his bag, slung it over his shoulder and began to walk. He'd just dropped his bag and fished out his keys when his phone pinged to let him know he had a message.

No words. Just a video of his daughter, stirring in her sleep, as if she sensed her mother's presence. He sat on the steps for a long time, playing it over and over, watching her breathe, watching Eve's hand as she smoothed back a curl and settled the comforter around their little girl.

'Martha? I'm sorry to call you so late—'

'Eve? Is anything wrong?'

'No. I'm home. I came back early.'

'Well, that's a shame. Wasn't the trip what you expected?'

'Oh, yes, absolutely. The lodge was lovely and I met so many people I hadn't seen since I was a child.'

'Including Hannah's father?'

'Martha—'

'I had lunch with his grandmother yesterday. She told me that Kit had gone out there for a meeting.'

'You knew?' Eve, who had retreated to the privacy of the veranda of Mary's home, sat down on the nearest chair.

'I guessed. Obviously something had happened to make you leave the way you did. You'd been to Laura Merchant's party and while either of the Merchant boys might have got lucky,' she said, 'what Brad was up to is a matter of public record.'

'Kit said she's the image of his sister as a child.'

'And that.'

'Why didn't you say anything?'

'You didn't want me to know, Eve, and I respected that.'

'I didn't want anyone to know,' she admitted, 'including Kit.'

'And now he does, I'm guessing. How does he feel about it?'

'He's furious with me for keeping her from him. He doesn't understand why I did that.'

'And what about you?' she asked. 'Do you know why?'

'I didn't. I was ashamed.' She sighed. 'I didn't want

my mother gossiped about and Kit wasn't to blame—I threw myself at him.'

'He didn't drop you.'

'No, but I assumed he was well-practised. By the time I realised I was pregnant he was taking part in the round-the-world race. I saw his single-minded focus and thought he was like my father. I loved him, Martha, but he gives nothing back.'

'Your father is completely self-obsessed. Ridiculously good-looking, of course, and your mother was very young when she met him. A fatal attraction.'

'I still wish she was here.'

'But she wouldn't be. She loved you, Eve, but she wasn't cut out to sit at home and be a grandmother. She would be in Central America, or Africa or Asia.'

'I know, but I could call her, talk to her.'

'I know. It's hard but Kit isn't like your father. He may be single-minded, laser focussed in a way that few of us can imagine, but he dropped everything when his father had a stroke and came home.'

'And he hates it. He wants to get married and play happy families right now, but how long will it be before he's missing the adrenaline rush? Looking out to sea with that thousand-yard stare? I don't care for myself, Martha, but I want more than that for Hannah.'

'Would not being married to him be any different? You'd still be watching and waiting, feeling the fear, but think of the joy when he comes home.'

'You think I should marry him?'

'If you love him.'

'I barely know him.' She shook her head. 'I'm sorry to burden you with this, Martha, but I had to talk to someone. Maybe I was hoping that you would wave your magic godmother wand and somehow make it all go away.'

'No wand, I'm afraid, but for now it's all about Kit and Hannah.' She gave a little sigh. 'There'll be media interest. It's going to be uncomfortable whatever you decide, but keep your mouth shut and a smile on your face and it will pass. I'm here for you. Whenever you need me.'

After more reassurances and a promise to call her after Kit's visit, Eve sat for a while, watching the video of her little girl sleeping, blissfully unaware that her young life was about to change for ever.

CHAPTER TWELVE

KIT WAS RIGHT. The cottage needed a lot more than a face-lift and, shut up for a week, it was also stale and covered in dust.

There was nothing to be done about the heavy dark furniture and faded curtains, but Eve had set her alarm and, leaving Hannah sleeping at Mary's, went to open the windows to let the sea air blow through. She fed the cat, who seemed unusually pleased to see her, and then went to town with hot water, furniture polish and the vacuum cleaner.

Once she had the place shining, she dashed to the market to pick up groceries and flowers, collecting her daughter, and a casserole Mary pressed on her, on the way home.

'Thanks so much for having Hannah. I can't tell you how grateful I am.'

'She's a sweetheart. I'll have her any time. I'm just sorry you cut your trip short…' The unasked question hung in the air.

'It's a long story and you'll have it all, I promise, but I have to go. I'm expecting someone.'

'An agent?'

'No. I've decided to stay.'

'Well, that's the best news I've heard this week,' she said, enveloping her in a hug, 'and you can leave this little one with us any time. We're going to miss her,' she said, as they walked to the door. 'Oh, and the children were thrilled with their presents, by the way. You will get thank-you letters.'

'They weren't disappointed that I didn't bring them a real lion cub?'

'I explained that mummy lions get really cross if you try to take their babies away. And the stuffed ones don't scratch or harbour bitey insects. The bitey insects seemed to sway it.'

'Bitey things with too many legs can cause all kinds of problems,' Eve said, with feeling.

It was still shy of twelve when she reached the cottage but there was a dashing classic Morgan two-seater parked in her driveway.

It was exactly the kind of car that, if she had ever thought about it, she could imagine Kit driving and, as she parked her rental alongside it, she saw him sitting on the porch steps waiting for them.

She lifted Hannah from her car seat, set her down and opened the trunk.

'Do you want to give me a hand with these?' she said, holding out a bag when Kit hung back.

'I know I'm early,' he said, taking it from her, 'but I couldn't wait.'

'Of course you couldn't,' she said, climbing the steps, unlocking the door, conscious that Hannah, clinging to one hand, was craning her head to look back at Kit as he followed them. 'I'd have been here earlier, but I had to get groceries. Take those through to the kitchen.'

'Yes, ma'am.'

'Take off your shoes, and put them away, sweetie.'

'Yes, Mama.'

Aware that Kit was watching Hannah like a child at Christmas, she said, 'Do you want to put that stuff in the fridge, while I find a jug for the flowers?'

'Yes. Yes, of course.'

He put away milk, cheese, eggs, not taking his eyes off Hannah, who was making a meal out of taking off her shoes, well aware that she was the centre of attention.

'She's noticed you, Kit. Give her a minute and she'll be climbing all over you.'

'I'm torn between awe and terror.'

She smiled. 'That's about right.' She found a pair of scissors and began to snip the stalks off the daisies she'd bought. 'How's your dad?'

'Still struggling with words, making them up as he goes along, having to count from one until he gets to the number he wants, but he's stronger. Walking better.'

'That's good news. And is everyone happy with your Nymba trip?'

'I came back with a bunch of new ideas put forward by the trust. All I need now is for Brad to pull off something amazing so that I can get my life back.'

She stopped snipping. 'Why don't you try living the life you have, Kit?'

He stared at her for a moment, but then Hannah, used to being the centre of attention, was tugging at the leg of his jeans.

'I'm Hannah,' she said. 'Who are you?'

Kit, taken aback by such a direct approach, looked across at her for help.

'Tell her, Kit.'

'Straight out?'

She'd lain awake half the night trying to think of some way to explain who this strange man was to her little girl. Now he was here, it seemed the simplest thing in the world.

'Straight out,' she said, and watched as he folded himself up so that he was on a level with Hannah.

'I know who you are, Hannah Rose Merchant Bliss. I am Christopher Harrison Merchant.'

'We have the same name.'

'That's because I'm your daddy.'

Hannah frowned. 'My daddy isn't here.'

The pain was fleeting. If she hadn't been watching so closely, desperate to monitor both Hannah's and Kit's reaction to this momentous first meeting, she would have missed it.

'I'm here now, Hannah,' Kit said.

It was Hannah's turn to look to her, seeking confirmation. 'It's true, Hannah. Your daddy has been living a long way away from us, out on the sea, but now he's come home.'

'Where on the sea?'

'In a boat,' he said.

'Are we going to live on a boat with you?'

'Would you like that?'

Eve uttered a slightly strangled, 'No...'

But Hannah, seeing only the practicalities, said, 'It would be a bit small and Mungo wouldn't like it, but you could live here. We have lots of rooms. Do you want to see?'

'I think we should ask your mama if that's okay.'

Too late for that...

'You can show Daddy around the cottage, Hannah.'

'Okay. Well, this is the kitchen. It's big, but it needs work,' she said, parroting the realtor who'd come to give her opinion.

He stood up, looked around, then back at Hannah and, picking up on the language said, 'It has a lot of potential.'

Eve gave him a congratulatory smile as Hannah, satisfied with his answer, took his hand and led him to the sunroom.

'This is where I play when it rains,' she said, taking

Kit's hand and pulling him into the enclosed sunroom on the back porch.

'You have a doll's house.'

'It was Nana's when she was a little girl.'

'It's very fine.'

Eve stood in the kitchen, putting the daisies, one by one, into a yellow jug, listening to the running commentary as Hannah gave Kit the grand tour.

'This is the living room. Mama says the carpet is...' She paused, trying to remember the word she'd used.

'Brown?' Kit suggested, helpfully. 'What colour do you think would look good in here?'

'Green. Like grass. With daisies.'

'Interesting. I like it.'

Eve swallowed down the lump in her throat. He was so good with her...

'This is the study. It's a nightmare.' Full stress on the word nightmare. 'There's stuff in here that should have been put on a bonfire years ago.'

Kit caught her eye as Hannah led him back across the hall. 'She's very...fluent.'

'I should have warned you. She was talking in sentences at eighteen months. Be careful what you say because it will come back to haunt you.'

'I'm getting that,' he said, clearly captivated.

He had yet to experience the kind of embarrassment bomb a small girl could drop when you least expected it, but she was glad that their first encounter was such a delight for both of them. And just a little bit terrified that he was going to steal her little girl's heart...

'Daddy!'

Eve pulled her lips back. Torn between laughter and tears. 'Pay attention, Daddy.'

Kit's poker face was history. He had the same, sandbagged look of raw love that she'd been wearing in the photographs her friends had taken when the newborn Hannah had been placed in her arms.

'The cloakroom is here,' Hannah said, 'but you don't want to see that.'

'I don't?'

'Mama is fixing it up, but she doesn't know what the heck she's doing. It's a mess.'

There you go, kiddo. Talk like that and your Merchant grandma is going to think I'm the world's worst mother. But she was laughing even as she wiped away a tear with the heel of her hand.

Hannah's voice, clear and carrying, continued to reach her as they went upstairs. 'This is Nana's bedroom. She died.'

'I'm sorry to hear that.'

'Did you know her?'

'I met her once,' he said. 'A long time ago when I was not much older than you.'

'Was she nice?'

'She gave me a cake. With icing.'

'She gave me her cottage,' Hannah said.

'Well, that's nice, too, but you can't eat a cottage.'

There was a moment of silence and Eve knew that Hannah would be frowning as she thought that through. Which was better, a cake or a cottage? A tricky decision when you were three years old. There would be questions later.

'I don't like it in here.'

'It's a bit gloomy,' he agreed.

'It's okay, Mama doesn't sleep in there.'

'Right.' He sounded bemused, but Eve was afraid she knew what was coming next and she didn't have to wait long.

'Cara and Jason and Lacey's mommy and daddy sleep in the same room, so you can share Mama's room.'

'It's very pretty.'

'The bathroom is an icky green but the other bathroom needs a plum.'

Eve covered her face with her hands. She really was going to have to start thinking before she opened her mouth. And never ever pass comment on other people's colour schemes.

'It's a bit early for plums. What colour is your bedroom, Hannah?'

'It's white, which is boring. Cara's daddy painted her bedroom pink. With a white trim.'

Eve didn't have to be in the room to know that she would be looking up at Kit with the sweetest smile. That child could work a room like an award-winning actress...

'Pink is lovely, but I think your pretty red hair needs a cool colour. Blue, maybe, to match your eyes. With a white trim,' he added when he didn't get immediate joy.

'Can I have a unicorn?'

'A real one?' he asked. 'Will there be room?'

Hannah giggled. 'Don't be silly. On the wall.'

'I think that could be arranged. And maybe a rainbow?'

Eve heard another delighted giggle.

'There is a room up some more stairs, but I'm not allowed to go up there.'

'Maybe your mama will show me later. Shall we go back down now? I need to order lunch and a little bird told me that you like pizza.'

'What little bird?'

'His name is Charlie. He lives on the beach.'

No...!

Kit had carried her downstairs and Hannah had her arms around his neck, looking straight into his eyes as she said, 'Can we go to the beach and look at your boat?'

'Lunch, then a nap, young lady,' Eve said, before he could answer.

Kit sat down, with her on his knee, and took out his phone, flipping through the menu, letting her look and guiding her choice.

'What shall we do until the pizzas arrive?' he asked.

'Can I play a game on your phone?'

'No, Hannah.'

Kit looked up, clearly about to say that she could do what the heck she liked with his phone, but thought better of it when he saw her *Don't you dare contradict me* face.

'Why don't you draw Daddy a picture?' she suggested.

'Of his boat?' She looked up at him and he obediently flipped through his phone until he found a picture of a small sailing dinghy.

Hannah drew the boat, then a family—mama, daddy and a little girl with red hair all holding hands—with a house in the background and a very large sandcastle.

She could see that Kit was desperate to take it, keep it, but Hannah thought that, like her cousins' daddy, Kit would come home every day so was fixing it to the fridge with a magnet.

Hannah chattered happily through the pizza, telling Kit about everything she'd been doing for the last week until, having talked herself to a standstill, went down for a nap without protest.

When she was asleep they stood, awkwardly, in the kitchen.

'You were great with her,' Eve said.

'I don't know which feeling is strongest right now,' Kit said. 'Gratitude that I have such a beautiful child, or anger that I've missed so much.'

Which pretty much mirrored her own feelings. Gratitude that he had been so wonderful with Hannah, that he had adored her on sight. Anger that he didn't understand how his little girl would feel when he disappeared back to his real life.

'You would have been away six months of the year,' she reminded him, briskly. 'The sea is your first love and you can't wait to get back to it.'

'You think that excuses what you did?'

'No, but I think you should take a reality check. It's not all pizza and unicorns.'

'I know that.'

'Do you? Your life does not, will never, resemble the picture Hannah drew.'

'I'm not going anywhere,' he declared and she was sure that, as he said it, he believed it. 'How long will she sleep?'

'For about an hour.'

'In that case I have time to go and pick up some paint.'

'Paint?'

'Hannah thinks white is boring.'

'I heard, but you don't have to paint her room. I'll get around to it.'

'You have your hands full with the cloakroom.' He paused at the door. 'Thank you for last night. The video.'

'You're welcome. Forget about marriage and you can have all the highlights without the boring or messy bits. Never be the parent saying no.'

'I've got a better idea. You give me a list of the stuff you don't think she should be allowed so that we can discuss it. Just remember that I have a say in that.'

'No phone, no tablet, no computer games.'

'I saw your face when she asked about my boat.'

She desperately wanted to say *no boats* but this was Nantucket and Hannah's father was a world-famous sailor.

'I'm sorry. This is hard…'

He came back, put his arms around her and drew her

to him. 'I'll follow your lead, Eve, but you're not on your own any more. From here on in it's the two of us.' He leaned back, looked down at her. 'I should have asked if you're happy with blue for her bedroom?'

She nodded, swallowed. 'Whatever makes Hannah happy.' She walked with him to the door, watched him drive away, then went back to the kitchen, took the picture down from the fridge and scanned it, putting the copy she'd printed out back on the fridge door. Then she opened up her laptop.

She had dozens of video clips of Hannah, from the moment of her birth until the one of her sleeping that she'd sent to Kit last night.

She couldn't give him back the time he'd lost, but she could give him a glimpse of some of those precious moments. And maybe one or two meltdown moments to remind him that it wasn't all unicorns and rainbows.

When Hannah saw the paint, she forgot all about boats. She wanted her room painted. Now.

'It's too late to start today, sweetheart,' Eve said. 'I'll have to move your bed.'

'Where do you want it?' Kit asked. 'She doesn't like Nana's room.'

'It's the big dark furniture and the smell of lavender polish. I didn't like it when I was little.' She pulled a face. 'To be honest, I don't like it now.'

'It's going to be a big bonfire.'

'I can't burn it! It's antique!' He grinned, she rolled her eyes, then laughed. The two of us, she realised, could be a lot more fun than do-it-yourself. 'You can take her bed into my room.'

The furniture moved, they were 'helped' by Hannah as they took down the curtains and ripped up the old carpet.

Hannah had scrambled eggs and toast soldiers for tea. Eve and Kit had Mary's casserole. The icky green bathroom, and everyone in it, got soaked when Kit introduced water fountain play at bath time and then he read his little girl a bedtime story before, having tucked her in, he set to work on her bedroom.

'I'll bet you didn't think you'd be filling dints and cracks in the plaster this evening,' Eve said, as she set about rubbing down the paintwork.

'I've done a lot today that I never imagined. I'd stay later, but I promised to give Mom a break tonight.'

'You should go. I can handle this.'

'No. I've got until ten. It's just in case he wakes up and needs something, or someone. He likes to be read to.'

After a couple of hours they stopped for a cup of tea, sitting side by side on the floor, backs to the wall.

'When did you get so good at DIY?' Eve asked.

'The resort, obviously, was decorated to the highest standard, but Dad didn't believe in paying union rates for the parts that were not on view. We were expected to pitch in and do what was needed in the offices, the storage units and outbuildings. Laura, too.'

'Equal opportunities child labour?'

'He said it was character-building. Maybe we should get Hannah painting tomorrow.'

'If you like, but you'll be in charge of cleaning up.'

'What about you?' he asked. 'It's not the first time you've sanded down a door.'

'When I moved into my mother's flat I was an eighteen-year-old student with a paintbrush and no one to stop me. I made a lot of mistakes—purple is not an easy colour to live with. The Internet taught me that preparation is all, and practice makes perfect.'

'But not, apparently, in the downstairs cloakroom.'

'It's my first attempt at tiling and the walls are not straight. I'm afraid I let my frustration show.'

'I've got a cure for that.'

Eve felt her cheeks grow hot.

'A spirit level?' he suggested, but his eyes were saying something else and his mouth was within an inch of hers when Hannah cried out.

'It's the strange room,' she said, ridiculously flustered. 'I'll go and settle her.'

But Hannah wanted her daddy.

He tucked her in, gave her a kiss and said, 'See you tomorrow, honeybun,' and she was asleep again before he left the room.

'She wanted to be sure you were still here,' Eve said.

'And you? Do you want me to stay?'

'It doesn't matter what I want. I know you'll leave.'

'You don't think a man can change course?' He dug in his jeans pocket and produced a small velvet ring box. 'If you don't like this, you can choose something else, but it's my promise that I'll always be there for Hannah. For both of you.'

CHAPTER THIRTEEN

KIT TOOK THE ring from the box but, while she'd given an involuntary gasp at a stunning diamond, flanked by rubies, that lay tucked into the velvet, Eve instinctively drew back.

'My hands are dirty,' she said. 'My nails are chipped.'

'If you want to get yourself gussied up, I'll take you out to dinner and go down on one knee,' he offered.

Startled, she dragged her gaze from the mesmerising sparkle to his face. 'You have got to be kidding.'

'Am I laughing?'

'Don't even think about it.'

He shrugged. 'If you're sure.'

'Sure? Kit, this is crazy. We barely know one another. Not in any way that matters,' she added, before he said something outrageous. 'I promise you don't need a wedding band, or a court order, to see Hannah. That you want to be a dad to her means more to me than I can begin to say, and I swear on everything that I hold dear that I will make our lives here. You can see Hannah as often as you wish. Pick her up from preschool, take her for ice cream, play on the beach—'

'Teach her to sail?'

She barely hesitated before she said, 'Teach her to sail. But marriage is a leap into the dark and the landing can be painful.'

'We can have a prenup,' he said. 'I'd hate for anyone to think I was after Hannah's cottage.'

'Oh, for heaven's sake…' Kit had made millions through sponsorship and endorsements. He was the one who needed to guard his fortune. 'Can you be serious for a moment?'

'I have never been more serious in my life.' His free hand was on her shoulder, the one with the butterfly. 'We both know that if you'd wanted money, you could have had it any time. The lawyers might have insisted on a DNA test but I would have known. You wouldn't have had to go to court.'

'How could I have been so wrong about you?'

'You didn't know me.'

'Yes… Yes, I did.'

'And I know that your promise is everything.'

'And yet there is a but coming.'

'I'm sorry, but… You said I needed a dose of reality and this is as real as it gets. I want my daughter to have my name, Eve. Not hidden away where no one ever sees it,' he said, before she could speak, 'but on the school register. I want to be there at bedtime not just for the stories, but to make sure she brushes her teeth. To feel the panic when she has a fever. I don't want to be the parent who swoops in with gifts, trips to theme parks, a puppy.'

'No puppy!'

'If I was an irresponsible father, with no conscience, I would put one in her arms and you wouldn't be able to do a thing about it.'

'But you're not and you wouldn't,' she said.

'I don't want to the part-time parent who is all about outings, toys, but never there when she's kicking off and being a brat.'

'You will so regret saying that when she's five going on fifteen.'

'I have a sister and, believe me, I have no illusions.'

'Seriously?'

'I don't want to be there just for the good stuff, I want to be there for all the stuff, and for that to happen, Eve, I need you. I checked the resort bookings this morning and there's space next Wednesday.'

He wasn't saying, I love you, will you marry me?

No pretence, no romance but she wouldn't have believed him if he had.

He was saying, I need you, you will marry me.

It wasn't romantic, but it was honest. And she hadn't said no. She'd said her hands were dirty and he believed he'd won.

'That's less than a week.'

'You were the one who mentioned the Las Vegas option.'

'I wasn't serious! I understand how you feel, Kit, but you've been hit by an emotional bombshell,' she said. 'You're not thinking rationally. Give it some time and you'll see I'm right.'

'Is there someone else?' he asked.

'What? No. No!' she repeated. 'There has never been anyone else since that night.'

'No one? You were never lonely?'

'I've steered clear of beaches since the night we made Hannah, Kit. She takes all my time.'

'I doubt you'll believe me but there has been no one else for me, either.' He put his head back against the wall, looking up at the ceiling, but she didn't think he was seeing much, except emptiness.

'No one?' she asked, with the same intensity as he'd asked that question.

'There were plenty of opportunities,' he admitted, 'but when you looked at me it was as if no one had ever seen me before. I searched for you all that summer, Eve, and since then, wherever in the world I was, I have turned at the sight of every redhead.' He grinned. 'Which was beginning to get embarrassing. But I never stopped looking, and that night at the auction... I didn't know you were there, but I felt something. You had marked me on your skin, Eve, and that night I caught the scent of vanilla and the air shimmered.' He was still holding her hand and this time she didn't pull back, allowing him to slip the ring onto her finger.

For a moment she was mesmerised by the rainbow flash of the diamond against her gritty hand and all she could think was that she really should have washed it first.

'Rubies? For a redhead?'

'The jeweller suggested emeralds but they seemed so cold. Rubies match your warmth, Eve, but if you'd prefer—'

'No. It's a bold choice, Kit. I love them.'

'You will always be Red to me. I have carried the scent of vanilla with me, carried you with me wherever I was in the world.'

'What...? How could you do that? You didn't know who I was.'

He reached for the battered leather backpack he always carried over one shoulder and from its depths he produced a small grey velvet elephant.

Its back and head were faded and, where it had been held by small fingers, hugged in sleep, the lush velvet pile was rubbed away, but there were still places in the folds where the legs met the body and where, hidden from the light, you still could feel the richness of the fabric.

'Ellie...' She breathed the word.

She looked so small in Kit's large, callused hands, but as she reached out, not quite able to believe her eyes, he placed the toy in her hands and she carried her to her cheek, her eyes closed, remembering the moment her mother had given the elephant to her.

'Where did you find her?' she asked.

'On the beach. It must have fallen out of your bag. Your Cinderella moment. It's not a glass slipper, but then I doubt a glass slipper would have survived what this little elephant has been through.'

'Not something you'd hug,' she admitted. 'But she's so worn, not even good enough to donate to Goodwill. Most men would have tossed her into the nearest bin.'

'She has the look of something long loved and I carried her with me all that summer so that when I found you, I could give it to you.'

Because he was not most men. She'd felt how special he was when he'd come to sit with her on the beach because she looked lost and unhappy…

'I only realised she was gone when I was in the departure lounge at the airport,' she said. 'It felt as if my mother had reached out from beyond the grave, so disappointed in me that she'd taken her back…'

'No!' He put his arms around her, drew her close. 'No. If she did anything, she plucked it out of your bag, leaving it for me to find. It wasn't a glass slipper, but it was all I had.'

With her face buried in his shoulder, the steady thud of his heartbeat bringing her own back down until it was riding in tandem with his, smothered in the scent of his body, his clothes, she knew that this was just comfort.

The beach all over again.

But she clung on long after the threatened tears had

evaporated, as long as she could without making a fool of herself.

Eventually, though, she drew back. 'Sorry. I…' She shook her head. 'It's just a shabby toy. I can't believe you've kept it all this time.'

'A fairy-tale prince would have carried that glass shoe with him and never stopped looking until he found the girl the shoe fitted.'

'By which time he would have a long white beard and she would be a wrinkled old crone. Real fairy tales tend to have a bitter twist to them,' she said, but she was laughing. 'Thankfully, you are no Prince Charming.'

'And you are no Cinderella. But your Ellie and I have become very close.'

'You really have carried her with you?'

'The early settlers in the west kept a grab-and-run bag by the door. Each night they'd put in their family Bible, the spindle from their spinning wheel, those things that were precious to them, that couldn't be replaced. Then they hung it on the door handle, ready to grab if there was fire, or an attack and they had to run for their lives and start again.'

'And…'

'This is my grab-and-run bag,' he said. 'The one that would go into the life raft with me if I had to abandon ship. It has been home to your little elephant since the day you left. She sailed around the world with me and we have kept each other safe.'

Eve held Ellie against her face for a moment, breathing in the scent of leather, the sea, the vanilla scent that her mother wore. Then she offered it back to him.

'Keep her. We all need something, someone to keep us safe. She is your mascot and my promise to you that wherever you go, Hannah will be here when you return.'

'But—'

'She is no longer lost and neither am I.'

He took it and, holding it in one hand, he reached out and cradled her cheek with the other.

'And you, Eve? Will you be here?'

For a moment he waited, not forcing it, waiting for her to come to him. Just one kiss. She wanted it so much, and they were so close that she could feel the heat of his mouth. She leaned her cheek into his hand, closed her eyes...

'Mama!'

His hand slipped to the nape of her neck and he rested his forehead against hers. 'You are never alone with a child,' she said, a little shakily. Then she drew back a little, kissed his forehead and went to see what Hannah wanted.

Kit leaned his head back against the wall. Nearly. So very nearly, but, despite her initial resistance, she was not only wearing his ring but had given him her own most precious possession. And they had been a breath away from a kiss. And not just any kiss. *The* kiss.

Today he had a daughter and a promise.

Tomorrow anything could happen.

'Have you told your family?'

'About Hannah?' Kit shook his head. They were standing on the porch, he had to go, but he'd never wanted to stay anywhere so desperately in all his life.

They'd had so little time and soon the world would crash in on them. He'd hoped that they would have been able to just sit and be together for a while. A few days, a week maybe, but he'd blown it.

'I thought we needed a little time before we had to face my family, but this afternoon I walked into a jeweller's in broad daylight.'

'On a small island like Nantucket? What on earth were you thinking?'

Eve was shaking her head, but smiling, and he took her hand, looked at the ring he'd placed on her finger. She'd taken it off to scrub away the dust, but she had put it back on.

'The truth, Eve? I haven't been thinking since you walked into the lodge with Peter Ngei and everything I'd been feeling since that morning made sense.'

'I…' She swallowed, for a moment floundering for a response. 'I've told my godmother, Martha Adams, that you are Hannah's father,' she said. 'I didn't want her to hear it as gossip.'

'I'm glad you did. I've known Martha all my life. She's a friend of my grandmother.'

'She won't say anything, but she had already guessed. And your car has been parked here all day in full view of anyone passing. I doubt there's another like it on the island.'

'I haven't exactly been discreet.'

'You never meant to be,' she said. 'You don't have to be.'

'So tomorrow, when I buy a family car with a state-of-the-art child seat, and the news is all over social media before the ink is dry on the receipt, you won't mind?'

'Your family need to know before your mother starts getting phone calls,' she said. 'And there are some people I have to tell before it becomes island gossip. The sooner the better.'

'Now?' He produced a phone from his pocket but she covered it with her hand.

'Face-to-face.'

'And the wedding? I know it's short notice, but we have someone who organises everything. I'll get her to call you—'

'Short notice? It's crazy. Your family will think you've lost your mind. Or that I've got your arm twisted up behind your back.'

'You could try.'

'Metaphorically.'

'No one forced me to do anything in my entire life, metaphorically or otherwise, but Nana's room doesn't scare me. If you're going to insist on a long engagement, I can move in tomorrow.'

'What? No!'

'Then stop playing hard to get, Eve, or I'll start demonstrating just how much I remember about you. So if you don't want to disturb the neighbours…' She gave an involuntary shiver, backing into the post supporting the porch roof. 'So easy,' he said, following her.

'It's just sex…' Her voice was no more than a hoarse whisper as his fingers slid into her hair.

'I know.' His kiss was teasing, a slow touch-and-go that had her treacherous body crumbling against him, demanding more, but he was the one playing hard to get, his lips barely touching hers, his body a tormenting distance. 'Fun, isn't it?'

Her only response was a low, desperate rumble in the back of her throat and for a moment he was with her, fingers tangled in her hair, his own raw need matching hers, lost in the depths of a shattering kiss that answered every midnight dream.

They were both breathing heavily when he drew back.

'Marry me, Eve. Once you have my ring on your finger, you can have all the fun you want.'

'Marriage is more than sex.' A final bid for common sense.

'It's a good start and we have a lifetime to work on the rest.' He stepped back, putting clear air between them.

'Be prepared to have my mother on your doorstep first thing tomorrow.'

'No.'

And beyond the teasing, she saw a flash of anguish as he raked his hand back through his hair. She still had her doubts but Martha had said this was 'meant'.

'Your father should be there, too,' she said, 'and since he can't come to us right now, Hannah and I will come to you.'

'You are…' He shook his head and this time when he took her in his arms it was something else, his kiss all tenderness. Gratitude. 'I should go.'

'Kit…'

Eve took a pen drive from her pocket. 'This is yours.'

'What is it?'

'A memory stick.' She leaned forward, kissed his cheek then stepped back inside and closed the door before she did something really stupid, like begging him to stay.

She leaned back on the door, holding her breath until she heard him cross the gravel, not moving until the sound of his engine was just an echo in her head.

CHAPTER FOURTEEN

KIT HAD SAT with his family that morning and told them about Eve and Hannah. His mother had wept, Laura had whooped, his father had been unreadable.

Afterwards Brad had sought him out.

'So that's where you were the night I was arrested,' he said. 'Making babies with Eve.'

'I'm sorry, Brad. I let you down.'

'We both know I let myself down, Kit, but it's easier to blame someone else. I'm glad you found her and your little girl.'

For an awkward moment they just looked at one another, then they were hugging.

'Hey, I'm an uncle,' Brad said. 'Can I tell Lucy?'

'You like her? I mean really like her?'

'Yes, I do. She's a woman you can talk to. Are you really going to set up a boat design business with her?'

'Have you a problem with that?'

'Not if it means she'll be staying here.'

'Just…'

'I'm not messing, Kit…'

His voice trailed away as a car pulled into the drive. Eve climbed out and lifted Hannah from her car seat and she reached out to him.

'Daddy!'

He took her from Eve. 'Do you want to meet your Uncle Brad?' he asked.

She looked over his shoulder and then back at him. 'Okay.'

'Eve, meet the brains of the family.'

'Hello, Brad,' she said, offering her hand.

He held it, shaking his head. 'My brother is one lucky man. As for you, young lady…' he said, turning to Hannah. 'Laura, but with red hair. You are going to be so much trouble.'

He'd imagined a slightly stiff meeting in the drawing room with his mother, but she was down the porch steps with Laura at her heels, stopping short, a hand to her mouth as she saw Hannah.

'Hannah Rose…' She took one little hand and held it for a moment while they looked at one another. 'You and I are going to have so much fun.' Then she smiled at Eve. 'Hello, Eve, I'm Barb and this is Laura, who is going to disappear right now so that we can get to know one another.'

'Don't worry,' Laura said. 'Mom isn't going to grill you. She's thrilled because it means Kit will be staying. Can I be a bridesmaid?' She didn't wait for Eve to answer before turning to him. 'Who is going to be your best man, Kit?'

'Brad,' he said.

She pulled a face. 'Well, that's no fun.'

'Kit,' his mother said, 'your father is on the deck waiting to meet his granddaughter.'

He took Eve's hand, kissed her cheek before turning to his mother. 'Do not show her baby photographs.'

His father was sitting on the deck, a rug around his knees. His mother had searched out some of the wooden puzzles that they'd had as kids to help his father and there was one on a small table at his side.

Kit put Hannah down and knelt beside her. 'This was

my puzzle when I was little,' he said. 'Grandpa's hands aren't working very well at the moment. Do you think you could help him put the pieces in the right place?'

Hannah looked up at his dad, picked up a piece and showed it to him. 'The chicken goes here...'

They both watched her for a moment as she slotted the farmyard animals into place and then his dad looked up at him and he smiled.

'Your family were so kind to me, Kit,' Eve said later, when they took Hannah home for a nap after a family lunch. 'And you were such a cute baby.'

He groaned, but was grinning. 'Hannah and Dad were great together. She chatted to him the way she does, and he was so gentle with her. He managed to say Han, and when he put all the pieces in the puzzle she clapped.'

'She's had a lot to take in, but you've all given her space, let her take the lead, so she hasn't felt overwhelmed.'

'She is adorable. We are all at her feet. You have done an amazing job, Eve. Dad smiled at me for the first time in years and when I took his hand, he squeezed it.'

'That's wonderful. I'm so happy for you.'

'There are no words.' He took her hands. 'I swear I will do everything I can to make you happy, Eve.'

She lifted a hand to his face, feeling the softness of his beard against her palm for a moment. 'Marriage is a partnership, Kit. We both have to work at it.'

'I can take a hint. I found some overalls—'

He stopped as she raised herself on her toes and touched her lips to his.

'Just working on it,' she said and then, because he didn't seem to know what to do next, 'Are you okay about living here?'

There was a plaintive *miaow* as Mungo, emerging from

his hiding place in the airing cupboard, curled himself around Kit's legs.

'That cat votes stay,' he said, and was rewarded with a purr when he bent to stroke him.

'Even with the icky green bathroom?' Eve said.

'It's nothing a coat of paint won't fix.' He looked up. 'When Hannah's had her nap we could go to the hardware store and pick out a colour.'

'A deep pink would match the rosebuds on the bedroom wallpaper.'

'About the flowers…'

'You're not keen?' She grinned. 'Better look at wallpaper samples, too. In fact, it might be easier to start at the top and work down. Do you want the top floor as a studio space? It's going to take a while to custom-build from scratch.'

'Eve…'

'Still working on it,' she said.

'Can I join in?'

'Help yourself,' she said, then felt her cheeks heat up as he grinned.

'I was going to suggest that while we're out we could call in at a dealership and choose a family car.'

The next day, Eve and Kit sat for a photograph that was issued by his agent with the announcement that Kit Merchant and Eve Bliss, who had a three-year-old daughter, were getting married in a private ceremony at the Merchant Resort in Nantucket. The media picked up on the fact he'd resigned as skipper for the racing season because his father had been seriously ill and connected the two events.

Lifestyle magazines immediately offered a seven-figure sum for the exclusive rights to cover the wedding.

Eve was horrified at the thought, but said, 'The money could go to the opioid clinic.'

'That is generous of you, but I'll donate the money myself before submitting my family and friends to that kind of intrusion.' He took out his phone and then looked at her. 'Are you okay with that?'

'Me?'

'I'm setting up a trust for Hannah, but if we're donating a million dollars to mark our wedding, you have a say.'

'I am lost for words.'

He grinned. 'I'll remember that if you ever get naggy.'

Kit might have imagined something small for the ceremony, but his mother and sister had other ideas. Fortunately, the Merchant wedding planner had everything under control. All Eve had to do was say yes.

Invitations were dispatched to Nymba, to the group who'd supported Eve at Hannah's birth, their family and Kit's friends who were coming from all over the world.

Laura and Lucy were both to be bridesmaids, along with Hannah and her cousins; Jason, bless his heart, flatly refused to be a page boy.

All she had to do was choose a dress and she had Martha, Mary and Hannah eager to help her with that.

It seemed as if everyone was giving the pair of them time to get to know one another. Kit worked on Hannah's room in the morning while Eve went shopping, or took her to see her grandparents, or to play with Mary's children.

They had lunch together and after Hannah's nap they spent the afternoon on the beach, or in the pool at the resort, where Hannah's early swimming lessons proved their worth.

'She's a little fish,' Laura said. 'She should join Lucy's Puddleduck sailing class.'

Eve stiffened. Hannah had been desperate to get on a boat since that first day, drew pictures of them all the time, but as she hesitated, Kit said, 'Why don't I take both of you out? You'll be able to see for yourself if she enjoys it.'

She knew she was being selfish, that sailing was part of life on the island, in the Merchant blood, but she didn't want Hannah to enjoy it.

Kit was waiting, not pushing her, but this was about learning to trust. For three years she'd had sole responsibility for this little bundle of joy and each small surrender was terrifying.

The first time she'd left him alone with Hannah was when she went shopping for a wedding dress. The first time she'd watched him drive away with her, just the two of them going for an ice cream. The first time he'd been the one she'd run to…

'I've never been in a sailing boat,' she said. 'I'd just be a liability. Hannah will let you know soon enough if she doesn't like it.'

Afterwards, when Hannah was in bed and they were alone, he said, 'The sailing thing. I know how hard that was for you.'

She shook her head. 'Maybe, when she's going out on her first date, you'll have some idea.'

'She is never going out on a date,' he said, then put his arms around her and drew her close, holding her as if he'd never let go. 'I'll take care of her, Eve.'

'I know you will.' She nodded. 'Nothing in the world will stop me from worrying until you're safely back on shore, but Hannah is as much yours as mine.'

'I'm scared witless by the responsibility.'

'Welcome to the club.'

'Thank you.' He brushed the curls back off her forehead. 'Now, on the subject of dates, I've been thinking that we should try that.'

'Dating?'

'Dinner somewhere. Or maybe there's something you'd enjoy at the arts centre?'

'You want to hold hands in the back row at a movie?'

'It's been a while but I'm sure I remember how that goes. We can have dinner afterwards.'

'I'll have to organise a babysitter.'

'Say the word and you'll be fighting them off. I'll check what's on.' His phone rang as he took it from his pocket. He glanced to see who was calling and then sent it to voicemail.

'You could have answered that.'

'It's nothing that won't wait. Okay, here we are,' he said. 'It's a live screening from the Met tomorrow. Opera?'

'Let's just have dinner. If you want to hold hands you can walk me home along the beach.'

'Tomorrow?'

'Tomorrow. Why don't you ask your mom if Hannah can have a sleepover?'

'You are a peach, but she'll think I'll be staying over.'

'Kit, she'll be babysitting our daughter so I don't imagine she'd be shocked, but if you think your macho reputation will be ruined if you go home, you are welcome to Nana's room. However, I'm sure Hannah would be thrilled to have you there when she wakes up.'

Cloud had blown in and there was rain in the air so they missed out the beach, but dinner overlooking the harbour had been lovely.

The food was doubtless perfect, but they'd talked so much that they'd scarcely noticed it. Even when Kit's phone had rung, he'd turned it off without even looking to see who had called.

He'd talked about his family, about being alone on the ocean, about his last holiday in France with Matt.

She had talked about her mother, about the kids she'd taught, about the chance of a prestigious job that she'd had to let go when her grandmother died.

'If she'd recovered,' he said, 'I would never have found you.'

'I would have found you,' she said. 'Hannah would have insisted.'

'Would it bother you if I said I would have liked you to have found me for you?'

'Maybe I'd been waiting for the excuse.'

Kit drove her home and walked her to her door. He took the keys from her, unlocked the door and Mungo strolled over and rubbed against Kit's legs.

'He likes you,' she said.

'He may change his mind when I bring home that puppy.' He looked up. 'No objections?'

'I've never had a dog.'

'We'll choose it together. Something with a soft mouth.'

She nodded. 'Are you coming in for coffee?'

'If I come in, I'll stay and I don't think you're ready for that. But I'll take a kiss.'

And he kissed her on the doorstep just as if it were an old-fashioned girl/boy date with her dad waiting on the other side of the door. Breathtakingly sweet and leaving her desperate for more.

The sea was quiet with the slightest breeze. It was very early when Kit took Hannah down to the dock before anyone was about.

Eve, having given him her trust, would have been on edge, transferring her nerves to their little girl.

He wanted her to experience that same thrill that he'd felt when his grandfather had taken him on the water for the first time. To have that same never to be forgotten moment of shared joy.

She was glowing with excitement as he smoothed sunblock on her face and hands, fitted her with a life jacket, talking her through what they were going to do, stressing on her the importance of listening to him and doing exactly what he said.

Half an hour later, as he brought the boat into the dock, Eve was standing on the dock, waiting for them.

She looked white, and when he lifted Hannah out of the boat and she ran to her exclaiming with excitement, she picked her up, kissed her.

'Did you enjoy that?' she asked, her voice perfectly calm, but she turned her back on him, walking away.

He lowered the sail, tidied everything away and went to face her wrath.

She was waiting on a bench and he sat beside her. 'I didn't expect you until after breakfast.'

'I found Hannah's toothbrush.'

'Bad timing.'

'No.' He saw her swallow and then she reached out and grabbed his hand. 'I'll be fine, just give me a minute.'

'The rest of my life.'

She leaned against him and he put his arm around her. 'My red hair, your seafarer's genes.'

'Our little girl. Where is she, by the way?'

'Gone to tell her grandpa how she's going to be a sailor like her daddy.'

CHAPTER FIFTEEN

LUCY SIGHED. 'You look stunning, Eve.'

The mirror reflected the image of a bride. Still, solemn, her hand against the scalloped lace necklace that settled just below her collarbone, the rubies on the ring Kit had given her a deeper shade of red than her hair.

'Mom said it's as if Kit had a piece missing for the last few years,' Laura said. 'Now he's found you and he's complete.'

Except they all knew he wasn't.

He had closed his phone half a dozen times when she'd walked into a room, as guilty as if he'd been texting with a secret lover and, in a way, he was.

Finally, she'd called him on it.

'You don't have to hide it from me, Kit. It's natural to want to know what's happening with your team. When do the yacht trials begin?'

'Next week.' He'd looked back at the screen. 'The weather is a concern.'

'They won't go out in bad weather, surely?'

'We're— They're behind. The keel wasn't performing as well as we'd hoped. I'd suggested adjustments to the design, but it hadn't been tested.'

'You should be there.'

'I'm needed here.'

There had been nothing she could say that wasn't a cliché; she'd just rested a hand on his arm.

'I don't suppose cake tasting would take your mind off it?'

He had covered his hand with her own, acknowledging her concern, but had said, 'Could you and Hannah handle that? The new carpet is coming for her room tomorrow and there's still stuff to finish up here. Unless you want to spend your wedding night in Nana's room?'

He'd been kidding—they would be spending the night at one of the resort guest cottages—but his eyebrow, lifted in a way that suggested all kinds of pleasure, hadn't convinced.

He was worried. Not about her or Hannah or his family, but about his yacht and his crew.

The wedding ceremony took place in a gauzy pergola sparkling with fairy lights. Hannah, Cara and Lacey led the way, sprinkling rose petals in her path.

Hannah, until this moment the centre of attention, looked up at Kit, expecting him to pick her up, tell her how clever she was, how pretty she looked, but Laura and Lucy shepherded the girls into their seats and then it was just the two of them. Kit looking at Eve as she walked on her own towards him. Given away by no one. Giving herself with a whole heart and a clear head.

He smiled as she reached him and, once she'd handed her bouquet to Lucy, took her hand, mouthing a silent *Thank you*. Not the usual greeting of a groom to his bride, but she knew his mind was elsewhere.

The sunset ceremony was simple, their vows the old, traditional ones in which Christopher Harrison Merchant and Genevieve Bliss promised before witnesses to love, comfort and honour one another for as long as they both should live.

Maybe they should have thought that through, written

promises that avoided that dangerous four-letter word. Too late now, but it was debatable which of their hands was shaking the most as they exchanged rings.

Kit, unusually clumsy, fumbled the moment when he slipped the plain gold band on her finger. Aware that it was badly done, he looked up and said, 'This is scarier than a force nine gale…' raising a laugh from their guests, and then lifted her hand to kiss it and there was an audible sigh.

Eve slipped the second ring on his finger and then took his hand and was still holding it as the minister pronounced them man and wife and invited Kit to kiss his bride.

He took her face in his hands and murmured something, but his words were lost in the mayhem of clapping as his lips touched hers.

Later, after they had cut the cake, kissed and been kissed by all their family and friends, Kit took her hand.

'Will you dance, Mrs Merchant?'

She hadn't thought about a first dance; the incredibly efficient woman who had planned the whole thing hadn't mentioned it. As she hesitated, a guitarist began to pick out a familiar melody and, as Kit took her in his arms, the man began to sing.

'How did you know that I love this song?' she said, laying her head on his shoulder as, oblivious to those who had formed a circle around them, they stood, holding one another, barely moving.

'I've been working to your playlist as I decorated Hannah's room and the words were so perfect. The first time I saw you, kissed you, felt your heart beat…' The music had finished and they were standing, looking at one another, but then Hannah raced over to them and Kit bent to pick her up.

'Hello,' he said. 'Who is this little princess?'

She giggled, then said, 'Uncle Brad says that Mama has to throw her flowers away. Right now.'

Kit looked at her and grinned. 'How good is your aim?'

'I will do my best.'

With her bouquet safely caught by a blushing Lucy, Eve placed her tiara on Hannah's head, told her to be good for Grandma, then kicked off her shoes, carrying them, her lace hem trailing in the sand as they walked along the beach to the guest cottage.

The stars were thick and bright over the sea. 'Sailors used to navigate by the stars,' Eve said. 'Can you do that?'

'Second star on the right and straight on until morning.'

'That's the way to Neverland,' she said, and shivered, as if a goose had walked over her grave.

'Hey, kidding. You do know that we use GPS these days?'

'But suppose it broke down? No radio, no satellite tracking device, far out in the ocean, out of sight of land. You would be back in the Dark Ages.'

'Fifteenth-century sailors travelled the globe,' he reminded her. 'Drake, Vasco da Gama… And you might have heard of an Italian guy called Columbus?'

'I'm being serious.'

'I'm sorry. I do know how to use a sextant,' he assured her. 'I could bring us home using the sun and the stars…' He stopped, looking south, for a moment lost to her but then the breeze whipped at her dress, bringing him back to her. 'Why did you want to know?'

'Just checking,' she said, as they moved on.

The veranda of the guest house was lit by candles in elegant glass jars. There was champagne in an ice bucket and the scent from a bank of creamy roses, mingled with the sea air.

Kit picked up the glasses and champagne bottle, holding them in one hand. The other he kept for her, leading her along the candlelit path to the bedroom.

'Did I tell you that you look beautiful, Eve?'

'Um, let me think…'

'You look so lovely in that dress that I can only think of one way in which you would look even more beautiful.'

'And how is that?'

'Turn around and I'll show you.' She turned. 'Lift your hair…'

She swept her hair up with one hand and he began to unfasten the hooks that held the lace together, kissing her nape and every exposed inch of her spine.

Hooks done, he took his time lowering the zip, continuing his kissing game, unclipping her bra when it impeded his progress, until the dress slid with a gentle sigh to the floor.

Kit stirred. Eve was sleeping, her face in the pillow, her hair a wild red tangle of curls across the pillow. For a moment he watched her; in a while he would wake her but even as he thought about how he would do that an alarm sounded, not on his phone, but on hers.

'You put in an alarm call?' he asked, grinning.

'I did and it's time you were up and in the shower.'

'If that's an invitation—'

'No. It's a fact.' She rolled out of bed, tugged on a robe and headed for the kitchen. 'I'll get the coffee on.'

'Hey. Don't I get to sleep in on my honeymoon?'

'No, you get a helicopter out of here in just under half an hour. You have a plane to catch.'

'What?'

'Lucy told me that the team director has been calling you repeatedly. That, despite the fact that you want more than anything to be with them, you've been saying no.'

'She shouldn't have done that. She knows I can't go. The wedding, Hannah, Dad—'

'The wedding is cake crumbs, Hannah has a whole new family, and Brad and I talked to your dad. He knows this is your life, Kit, and so do I. He was scared he'd die and you wouldn't be here, but you came when you were needed and he knows now that you'll come back, spend more time here.'

'I'll stay as long as he needs me.'

'I really hope it was true when you said you didn't want to sit behind a desk running a resort complex because he's going to name Brad CEO today. Not acting. The whole deal. You are free.'

'Once you have a child, freedom becomes an irrelevance.'

'I know that Hannah will bring you back like a bungee rope, but it's not a chain, Kit. Live the life you have. It's my wedding gift to you.'

'I don't know what to say.'

'You don't have time for speeches. Travel clothes are in the wardrobe. Your bag is packed. Your flight is booked, so get in the shower while I fix your breakfast.'

Ten minutes later his ride landed on the resort's helicopter pad and as he appeared, hair still wet from the shower, Eve put a travel mug of coffee in his hand and tucked a pastry into his jacket pocket.

'I'll call you when I get there,' he said, pausing for one last kiss before picking up the bag with his sailing clothes and the battered leather backpack that were waiting by the door. 'Tell Hannah I love her.'

Eve stood on the veranda, waiting for the helicopter to take off, watching until he was no more than a black spot in the sky heading towards the mainland, then she took a deep breath in and sat on the kitchen stool, clutching a mug of coffee.

She wouldn't cry. Tears never changed a thing.

It was what it was.

She was doing pretty well until her phone rang. She checked the caller and saw that it was her fellow conspirator.

'Hi, Lucy.'

'I saw the helicopter take off. Do you need company?'

'I'm going to pick up Hannah later and take her to the beach. I know Brad will be super busy, so if you'd like to join us, you're welcome.'

'That would be fun, although I was wondering how you feel about sailing lessons.'

'For me? Is that Kit's idea?'

'No, but it might help you deal with the fact that Hannah is daddy's little girl and it will give you something other than a missing bridegroom to think about.'

'I... Can you teach me how to use a sextant?'

'Kit is the expert,' she said, 'but I can explain the basics.'

Kit drank the coffee Eve had made for him, ate the pastry, still not quite believing that he was on his way to Australia. That her heart was that big...

Just this once, he told himself. Just this once and he would go home, be a husband, a dad, a son. For now, his entire focus had to be on the race.

It was going to be a long day, a long flight. It was now Saturday in Sydney, around three in the afternoon, and he was already texting the chief engineer for an update. For the first time in his life, though, sailing wasn't his entire life, and while his head was fully engaged, his heart was lagging far behind.

His phone still in his hand, he texted Eve.

I can't believe how lucky I am. Or how stupid I am. I had a gift for you but I was distracted. You'll find it in the pocket of my tux. x

The beep of an incoming message roused Eve. The words shimmered for a moment.

Lucky.

An adjective to join 'thank you' in the pantheon of the world's most underwhelming words from a lover…

She put down the mug, went into the bedroom and picked up their discarded clothes. She checked Kit's pockets, finding his keys and a package beautifully wrapped in red tissue paper and tied with gold ribbon.

She put them to one side, folded his tux and her dress to take to the dry cleaner, putting the rest of their clothes aside for the laundry.

The keys she tucked in the handbag that had been delivered, along with a change of clothes, to the cottage the previous day. The package she carried through to the kitchen, holding it to her, not sure what Kit would have thought appropriate. Afraid that whatever it was would be saying *Thank you* and *I'm lucky*…

She was still sitting there when Lucy tapped on the door. 'Eve? Can I come in? You sounded a bit…' She gave an awkward little shrug. 'I thought a warm pastry might help. There's buttered, chocolate, almond—oh, love…' she exclaimed, dropping the bag on the counter and scooping Eve into her arms. 'He'll be okay,' she said as Eve's tears soaked into her T-shirt. 'He'll be back in no time.'

A month…

It would be a month. She'd known that and had told herself she was fine with it.

'I'm so sorry. I promised myself I wouldn't cry but it was the almond croissant. So stupid.'

'No. It's the little things that get you.'

'I'm sorry, Lucy. After all you've been through, you must think me totally pathetic.'

'No. I think, we all think, that you are amazing.'

Lucy made coffee, chatting brightly, giving her a moment to pull herself together. 'It was such a lovely wedding, Eve. Your dress was stunning and I nearly died when Kit kissed your hand. I've never seen anything so romantic, except maybe the look in his eyes in that moment when he said, "I love you…"'

'What?'

'Sorry. It was a totally private moment, but it can be so noisy on board that you get really good at lip-reading.'

That was what he'd said before he'd kissed her? I love you?

'I…um…do you mind, Lucy? I need to take a shower, get dressed.'

'Sure. I was just, you know…' She bent and picked up Kit's present. 'You must have dropped this when I grabbed you for a hug. Red? Unusual for a bride gift.'

'Kit called me Red the very first time he spoke to me.'

'I can't think why,' Lucy said, grinning as she headed for the door. 'See you later.'

Eve held the package for a moment, then pulled the ribbon, tore off the tissue paper. Inside was a square velvet box, too big for a pendant, maybe a watch…? Which would be totally weird.

Not a watch, but a bracelet. A very simple open coil of gold like nothing she'd ever seen, and beautiful in its own right. But on the inside was inscribed the first verse of the song written by Ewan MacColl for the woman he loved. The song about all those special first times. The song that Kit had arranged for them to dance to at their wedding.

She took her phone, heart in her hands as she wrote,

Come home safe, Kit Merchant. There's something I have to tell you.

Kit didn't miss his phone until he reached to put it in the tray, along with his laptop, belt and wallet, at airport security.

There was no time to go back and look for it. His flight had already been called and he barely had time to pick up a new pay-as-you-go in duty free. As soon as he was on board he called Brad and asked him to text him Eve's number.

'You don't know it?'

'My phone knows it,' he said.

'Oh, boy. Talk about husband fail.'

'Just—'

'I'm afraid I have to ask you to switch to flight mode, Mr Merchant.'

'Now?'

'The announcement was made a couple of minutes ago.'

'Brad. Give Eve this number. Look after them…'

The stewardess was standing over him, sympathetic but emphatic. He didn't bother with flight mode, just switched it off and put it away because there was nothing to see.

There were no vids of his little girl, or pictures of her with his dad, or playing on the beach.

No picture of Eve with paint on her cheek, of the two of them with Daisy, or dancing at the Nymba party.

Forget GPS. This felt like the Dark Ages.

CHAPTER SIXTEEN

THEY WERE SEA TRIALS, not a race and so not newsworthy. Eve checked the blog at least twice a day, but all the teams were cagey about revealing their times, their strategies and the only big news was that Kit, having cut short his honeymoon, was back.

He'd lost his phone, hadn't got her text and so hadn't asked what it was she'd wanted to tell him, but that was fine. Some things should be said face-to-face. It would wait.

His phone had been handed in at the airport and returned to her, but he'd picked up a new one at the airport and, having asked her to send him some photographs, said to hang onto it.

He called every morning to talk to Hannah in what, for them, was the late afternoon.

And, because he knew that she worried, he texted her a GIF of a red admiral butterfly every evening—long before dawn in Nantucket—so that when she woke up, she would know that he was safely back in harbour.

She didn't wait until morning, of course. The beep of his text was enough to wake her. Then one night she just woke. There had been no beep, no butterfly. It wasn't yet time but, wide awake and full of apprehension, she checked the team blog, then the news.

She made tea, checked again and waited. The newsflash about a freak storm hitting the Southern Ocean began to scroll across the screen just after four and she knew, deep in her heart, that he was in the middle of it.

She called Kit's phone, but it went to straight to voice-mail and she was already throwing stuff into a bag when her own phone rang. It was a call from the team office, hoping to catch her before she saw on the news that Kit, putting the new keel through a test, had been caught by the storm.

It was only confirmation of what she'd known, but she still had to hang on to the wardrobe door, her body like ice, her teeth chattering as she said, 'Tell me you have contact?'

'Not at the moment, Mrs Merchant. The storm is in-terfering with the signals… The navy have dispatched a ship to the area. I'll call you as soon as I have more news.'

'No. I'm coming there… I'll be on the first available plane,' she said, cutting the woman off when she tried to suggest it would be better to wait. She needed to call Brad and warn him before his mother saw the news.

'Do you want to leave Hannah with us?' he asked.

'No, I want her to be the first thing Kit sees…' She broke off.

'He'll be okay, Eve,' he said, but he couldn't hide the shake in his own voice. 'I'll organise the flights and call you back.'

She monitored the news until she had to switch her phone to flight mode, checking again once they reached Boston, but there was nothing.

The journey seemed endless. They had a three-hour layover in Dubai, where there was still no news, and it was nearly thirty hours after they left Boston before they arrived in Sydney.

They were met at the gate and whisked through immi-gration and customs by airport staff and at the gate by a representative from the sponsor, who booked them into a hotel and then took them to the quayside office.

The staff did their best to keep the press away from them, but they had managed to get pictures of the wedding and the headlines were inevitable.

New Bride Waits for News...

They dredged up the drama of his round-the-world race, Kit's reputation for recklessness, everything she had ever dreaded. It read like an obituary, not just for him, but his team.

There were other families there. Partners, parents, children. They walked along the quay, eyes constantly scanning the horizon, drank so much coffee that they were all wired, ate food brought by the sponsors, all the time trying to ignore the press pack gathered to take photographs and stick microphones under their noses at the first sniff of disaster.

Needing some peace, Eve slipped away with Hannah, to choose an ice cream from a vendor who refused to take any money for it and found a quiet spot to sit for a while.

The clouds above them had been torn to shreds but Venus shone bright in the early evening sky. Kit could navigate by the stars, she told herself. He'd climbed a mast with broken fingers and lashed it together.

Men who could stand on a platform moving at fifty miles an hour were not mere mortals...

She heard someone running, calling her name. 'Eve! They're back!'

'What?'

And then she saw it, bent out of shape, the huge wing sail a tattered wreck, but moving under its own power towards the quay.

Everyone surged forward as the crew disembarked one

by one. Bruised, battered but grinning to be scooped up by family and friends.

Kit was the last to leave and as he stepped down everyone parted to let him through. He had a gash on his cheek, a massive bruise on his forearm, black hollows beneath his eyes, but he had never looked more perfect as he encircled her with his arms, picked her up and, without a word, kissed her.

There were flashes as the press filled their boots, clapping from everyone standing on the quay, his crew, their families, a chorus of hoots from craft in the harbour, saluting the man who had brought them all back safe.

'I can't believe you're here,' he said, when he'd set her down.

'I love you, Kit. Where else would I be?'

He drew her back into his arms. 'I swear I'll never put you through that again.'

She clung to him for a moment, but then pulled back, shook her head. 'I knew who you were when I married you, but there'll be no more long-distance phone calls or night-time texts. We'll stay while you get your yacht back up and running. While you race.' She put her hands on either side of his dear battered face and said, 'I love you, just as you are, Kit Merchant. All I ask is that you keep coming home safe.'

'Daddy…'

He looked at Eve for a long time.

'Daddy!' Hannah tugged on his pants and he finally glanced down.

'Hey, there, little Puddleduck.' He bent and picked her up in one arm, keeping the other around Eve. 'If you look in my bag you'll find Ellie.'

'Ellie?'

'She's a little elephant that belonged to your mama when she was a little girl.'

Hannah retrieved the grey velvet elephant and hugged her. 'She smells like Mama.'

'That's because she hugged her so much. She's very precious and I want you to look after her for me.'

'For always?'

'For always.' He turned back to Eve. 'I don't need her, any more.'

'Kit, no.'

'Eve, yes. Out there, imagining that I might never see you again, or Hannah, I finally experienced the visceral, mind-numbing fear that my family went through when I did the round-the-world race. That you went through because you were carrying my child. What you all must have been feeling for the last couple of days. You and all these people,' he said, looking at the families hugging his crew. 'The storm came out of nowhere, slammed into us, ripping away the communications, driving us out to sea. It's a miracle we didn't lose anyone overboard.'

'How did your keel hold up?' she asked.

'The keel saved us, but I could never race to the limit again, Eve. I have too much to lose. And if you can't there is no point. It's over.'

'I'm so sorry.'

'Don't be. It's the easiest decision ever, next to marrying you. But I should call my mother. What time is it in Nantucket?'

Eve swallowed. 'It makes no difference, Kit. She'll be awake.'

He called his mother, reassured her that he was fine, handed the phone to Eve so that she could reassure her again.

'He's bruised, battered and stinks. Apart from that he's

absolutely perfect.' She ended the call but didn't give him back the phone. Instead she put it in her pocket. 'You need a shower and ten hours' sleep.'

'Did I say I love you, Eve? Not just because you're Hannah's mom, but you.'

'You did just fine,' she said.

'Did I? It should have been the first thing I said. It was all I could think about saying when we were out there, but when I saw you waiting for me it was like that first day after winter, when the sun feels warm. I love you, Eve, more than I knew was possible. I didn't need Ellie out there. You were with me every minute, your smile, your warmth and I want all that, every day, and you beside me when I wake up for the rest of my life.'

'You've got it.'

He touched her face with gritty, filthy fingers and then he said, 'Who's looking after Mungo?'

'Lucy offered to move into the cottage while we're away.'

'So there's no need to rush back. Let's rent a place on the beach for a few weeks, just the three of us, and make the most of the Australian spring.'

'I'd like that. And then, when we go home, we'll start looking for a puppy.'

The opening of the Matthew Grainger Clinic was a very special occasion.

Matt's sister, Lucy, who made a moving speech about how easy it was for anyone to slip into opiate addiction, thanked everyone for their generous donations. The new diamond flashed on her finger as she unveiled a plaque to commemorate the opening.

'I felt like the Queen, swishing back that little curtain,' she said.

Brad hugged her. 'You are *my* queen.'

Eve, aware that Brad had waited until that weekend to propose in order to take her mind off today, said, 'Have you set a date for the wedding?'

'We thought Christmas,' Lucy said. 'Christmas weddings are so special but I'm going to need a little Christmas elf to help me through the day. I was hoping Hannah would be here so that I could ask if she could handle that.'

'She's having a sleepover with her cousins tonight, but I can confidently predict that she will be thrilled to be your elf.'

'And you, Eve. Will you be my matron of honour?'

'Oh, Lucy, bless your heart, I'd be so pleased to do that for you. Thank you for asking me. Is there anything I can do to help?'

'You can come dress shopping with me. Your dress was so perfect.'

'We'll take Martha with us. She's the one with the great taste.'

'That would be wonderful. My to-do list is shrinking by the minute,' she said, her eyes a touch too bright. 'I just wish Matt was here to give me away.'

Eve knew how tough it was to have that kind of gap at her wedding; she handed her a tissue, gave her a hug and said, 'Why don't you ask Kit?'

'Brad is going to want him as his best man.'

'Brad would give you the moon if it would make you happy.'

She smiled. 'I always wanted a big sister and you are just perfect, Eve. I'll go and find Brad and ask him.'

'What was that all about?' Kit asked, joining her.

'I've just volunteered you to give Lucy away. She's off to ask Brad to release you from best man duties.'

'I'm sure he'd rather have one of his own friends organise his stag.'

'I don't recall you having one,' she said. 'Or was it something so down and dirty that it was never to be spoken of?'

'Brad offered to lead me astray, but I told him I'd rather spend the time with you.'

She looked at him askance. 'Painting Hannah's bedroom?'

He grinned. 'Doing anything.' He took her arm. 'Have you seen the auction photographs Laura curated? We're up there with Daisy.'

'We?' She looked at the board. 'How did that happen? I gave her the one with just me and Daisy. That one is…'

'Me looking at you as if I want to eat you.'

'Yes, that,' she said. 'Besides you've no right to be there. You didn't bid on the auction.'

'Neither did Philippe d'Usay, an old friend of mine who hosted Jenna Brown on a trip to the South of France. From the look of this photograph I'd say they are very close.'

'And look at this one.' She checked the name. '"Maya Talbot, in a gondola with Vittorio Rameri."'

'He looks very happy.'

'And so does she.'

They looked at some of the other photographs and then Eve spotted another couple. '"Molly Quinn with fellow guest Eric Chambault, enjoying a moment together while whale-watching."'

'He actually bid on the auction,' Kit said. 'She beat him at the last moment but he decided to go anyway. I'm sure it was pure chance they went the same week.'

She laughed. 'Perhaps, but there must have been something in the air that night. Brad should organise another event, not on such an epic scale, but special evenings out in exciting locations with those extra touches that money can't buy. He could hold it on Valentine's Day.'

'It sounds like a great idea. He's always looking for new ideas, although he's still a man down and he might be pushed for someone to organise it.'

'What does it involve?'

'Finding people to donate the prizes is the biggest job. Mom did a great job with the opioid clinic auction, but she and Dad are planning a cruise early in the spring, Laura is back at uni and Lucy is completely absorbed in designing a boat adapted for teaching disabled kids to sail.'

'And organising her wedding. I do like her, Kit. I hope she and Brad will be happy.'

'He is wearing the glazed expression of a man who is head over heels. The same look I see in the mirror every morning.'

She leaned against him. He still smelled of the sea, but these days there were overtones of puppy.

'It's great to see you two comfortable together, too, but it occurs to me that if the resort is short a Merchant—in other words you,' she said, 'I should step into the breach. I'm only teaching two mornings a week so there's no reason why I can't organise a Valentine's Day auction.'

'I can think of one very good reason. The house is straight. We have a spare bedroom and I thought, since you have time to spare, that it might be fun to start working on a project that Hannah has her heart set on.'

'Oh? What's that?'

'We wrote a letter to Santa and she put a baby sister at the top of her list.'

'Oh.' She blushed then laughed. 'That would be fun, but you're forgetting something. I'm a woman—'

'No,' he said, his arms around her waist, drawing her close, 'I definitely haven't forgotten that.'

'I'm a woman and we can multitask, but even I can't

deliver a baby in time for Christmas. And she might have to take a brother.'

'She was adamant that it had to be a sister. We might have to keep working on it until we get it right.'

'I'm up for that. Shall we skip the buffet, go home and start working on it?'

* * * * *

HOME TO
BLUE STALLION
RANCH

STELLA BAGWELL

To all my horses,
for the love and happiness they've given me

Chapter One

Who the hell is that?

Holt Hollister pushed back the brim of his black cow-boy hat and squinted at the feminine shape framed by the open barn door. He didn't have the time or energy to deal with a woman this morning. Especially one who was pouting because he'd forgotten to call or send flowers.

Damn it!

Jerking off his gloves, he jammed them into the back pocket of his jeans and strode toward the shapely figure shaded by the overhang. Behind him the loud whinny of a randy stallion drowned out the sounds of nearby voices, rattling feed buckets, the whir of fans, and the muffled music from a radio.

As soon as the woman spotted his approach, she stepped forward and into a beam of sunlight slanting down from a skylight. The sight very nearly caused

Holt to stumble. This wasn't one of his girlfriends. This woman looked like she'd just stepped off an exotic beach and exchanged a bikini for some cowboy duds.

Petite, with white-blond hair that hung past her shoulders, she was dressed in a white shirt and tight blue jeans stuffed into a pair of black cowboy boots inlaid with turquoise and red thunderbirds. Everything about her said she didn't belong in his horse barn.

Frustration eating at him, he forced himself to march onward until the distance between them narrowed down to a mere arm's length and she was standing directly in front of him.

"Hello," she greeted. "Do you work here?"

Holt might forget where he'd placed his truck keys or whether he'd eaten in the past ten hours, but he didn't forget a woman. And he was quite certain he'd never laid eyes on this one before today. Even without a drop of makeup on her face, she was incredibly beautiful, with smooth, flawless skin, soft pink lips, and eyes that reminded him of blue velvet.

"It's the only place I've ever worked," he answered. "Are you looking for someone in particular?"

She flashed him a smile and at any other time or place, Holt would've been totally charmed. But not this morning. He'd spent a hellish night in the foaling barn and now another day had started without a chance for him to draw a good breath.

She said, "I am. I'm here to see Mr. Hollister. I was told by one of the ranch hands that I'd find him in this barn."

She was looking straight at him and for a brief second Holt was thrown off-kilter by her gaze. Not only direct, it was as cool as a mountain stream.

"Three Mr. Hollisters live on this ranch," he said bluntly. "You have a first name?"

"Holt. Mr. Holt Hollister."

He blew out a heavy breath. He might've guessed this greenhorn would be looking for him. Being the manager of the horse division of Three Rivers Ranch, he was often approached by horse-crazy women, who wanted permission to walk through the barn and pet the animals, as if he kept them around for entertainment.

"You're talking to him."

Those blue, blue eyes suddenly narrowed skeptically, as though she'd already decided he was nothing more than a stable hand. And he supposed he couldn't blame her. He'd not had time to shave this morning. Hell, he'd not even gone to bed at all last night. Added to that, the legs of his jeans were stained with afterbirth and smears of blood had dried to brown patches on his denim shirt.

"Oh. I'm Isabelle Townsend. Nice to meet you, Mr. Holt Hollister."

She extended her hand out to him and Holt wiped his palm against the hip of his jean before he wrapped it around hers.

"Is there something I can do for you, Ms. Townsend?" he asked, while wondering how such a soft little thing could have a grip like a vice.

She eased her hand from his. "I've been told you have nice breeding stock for sale. I'm looking to buy."

If Holt hadn't been so tired, he would've burst out laughing. She ought to be home painting her fingernails, or whatever it was that women like her did to amuse themselves, he thought. "Are you talking about cattle or horses? Or maybe you're looking for goats? If you are, I know a guy who has some beauties."

"Horses," she said flatly, while peering past his

shoulder at the rows of stalls lining both sides of the barn. "This is a horse barn, isn't it? Or are you in the goat business now?"

The sarcasm in her voice was the same tone he'd used on her. And though he deserved it, her response irked him. Usually pretty women smiled at him. This one was sneering.

"I'm in the business of horses. And at this time, Three Rivers isn't interested in selling any. You should drive down to Phoenix and try the livestock auction. If you're careful with your bidding, you can purchase some fairly decent animals there. Now if you'll excuse me, I'm very busy."

Not waiting to hear her reply, he walked off and didn't stop until he was out the opposite end of the barn and out of Isabelle Townsend's sight.

Furious and humiliated, Isabelle turned on her heel and stalked out of the barn. So much for all she'd heard about Three Rivers Ranch and its warm hospitality. Apparently, those glowing recommendations didn't include Holt Hollister.

Outside in the bright Arizona sunlight, she crossed a piece of hard-packed ground to where her truck was parked next to a tall Joshua tree.

Jerking open the door, she was about to climb into the cab when a male voice called out to her.

Wondering if Holt Hollister had decided he'd behaved like an ass and had come to apologize, she turned to see it wasn't the arrogant horseman who'd followed her. This man was slightly taller and perhaps a bit older than Holt Hollister, but she could see a faint resemblance to the man she'd just crossed words with.

"Hello," he said. "I'm Blake Hollister, manager of the ranch."

He extended his hand in a friendly manner and Isabelle complied.

"I'm Isabelle Townsend," she introduced herself, then added dryly, "It's nice meeting you. I think."

His brows disappeared beneath the brim of his gray hat. "I happened to see you go in the horse barn five minutes ago. If you're looking for someone in particular, I might be able to help."

"I was looking for the man who manages your horse division. Instead I found a first-class jerk!" She practically blasted the words at him, then promptly hated herself for the outburst. This man couldn't be held responsible for his relative's boorish behavior. "Excuse me. I didn't mean to sound so cross."

"Isabelle Townsend," he thoughtfully repeated, then snapped his fingers. "You must be our new neighbor who purchased the old Landry Ranch."

Since she'd only moved here six weeks ago, she was surprised this man had heard of her. News in a small place must travel fast, she thought.

"That's right. I was interested in purchasing a few horses from Three Rivers. But unfortunately, your brother or cousin or whatever he is to you isn't interested in selling. Or showing a visitor good manners."

"I'm sorry about this, Ms. Townsend."

The ranch manager cast a rueful glance in the direction of the horse barn and Isabelle got the impression it wasn't the first time he'd had to apologize for his brother's behavior.

"Frankly, Mr. Hollister, I had heard this ranch was the epitome of hospitality. But after this morning, I have my doubts about that."

"Trust me. It won't happen again." His smile was apologetic. "You caught my brother at a bad time. You see, it's foaling season and he's working virtually 24/7 right now. I promise if you'll come back to the ranch tomorrow, I'll make sure Holt is on his best behavior."

Isabelle didn't give a damn about the horse manager. As far as she was concerned, the man could ride off into the sunset and never return.

"Honestly, Mr. Hollister, I have no desire to do business with your brother. Exhaustion isn't an excuse for bad manners."

"No. And I agree that Holt can be insensitive at times. But you'll find that when it comes to horses, he's the best."

He might be the best, but would dealing with the man be worth it? If it would help make her dream come true, she could surely put up with Mr. Arrogant for a few minutes, she decided.

Shrugging, she said, "All right, Mr. Hollister. I'll be back tomorrow."

He helped her into the truck, then shut the truck door and stepped back. And as Isabelle drove away, she wondered why she'd agreed to meet the good-looking horseman with a tart tongue for a second time. Solely for the chance to buy a few mares? Or did she simply want the pleasure of giving him a piece of her mind?

The answer to that was probably a toss-up, she decided.

"Holt? Are you in there?"

The sound of Blake's loud voice booming through the open doorway penetrated Holt's sleep-addled brain. Groggily, he lifted his head just in time to see his older brother step into the messy room he called his office.

"I'm right here. What's the matter? Is Cocoa having trouble?" He leaned back in the desk chair and wiped a hand over his face.

"As far as I know, nothing is wrong with Cocoa. I saw her five minutes ago. She was standing and the baby was nursing."

"Thank God. I had to call Chandler back to the ranch to deal with her afterbirth. I was afraid she might be having complications," he explained, then squinted a look at Blake's dour expression. "What's the matter with you? You look like you've been eating green persimmons."

"That task would probably be easier than trying to fix your mess-ups," Blake retorted.

This wiped the cobwebs from Holt's brain. "My mess-ups? What are you talking about?"

Blake shoved a stack of papers to one side and eased a hip onto the corner of the desk. "Don't feign ignorance. You know damned good and well I'm talking about Isabelle Townsend. The blonde who left the horse barn with smoke pouring out of her ears. What the hell did you say to her anyway?"

Holt used both hands to scrub his face again. "Not much. I basically made it clear that I didn't have time for her. Which is hardly a lie. You know that."

Blake blew out a heavy breath. "Yes, I know it. But in this case, you should've made time. Or, at the very least, been polite to the woman."

Holt picked up a coffee cup and peered at the cold black liquid inside. He'd poured the drink about five hours earlier, but never found a chance to drink it. Now particles of dust were floating over the surface. "What is the big deal, Blake? It was very clear to me that the woman had no legitimate business here on the ranch. I seriously doubt she's ever straddled a horse in her entire life. We'll probably never see her again."

"Wrong. I invited her to return tomorrow. And I made a personal promise to her that you'd be behaving like a human being instead of a jackass."

Holt plunked the coffee cup back to the desktop. "Oh, hell, Blake, you have no idea how I behaved with Isabelle what's-her-name. You weren't there."

"I didn't have to be. I know how you are whenever you run out of patience. Like I said, a jackass."

"Okay, okay. I wasn't nice. I'll admit it. But I'm running on empty. And just looking at her rubbed me the wrong way."

Blake arched a brow at him. "Really? She was damned pretty. Since when has a pretty woman got your dander up? Unless—" His eyes narrowed with suspicion. "Dear Lord, I hope you didn't make a pass at her. Is that what really happened?"

"No! Not even close!" Holt rose from the chair and began to move restlessly around the jumbled room.

His mother often mentioned that he needed a nicer office, one that was fitting for a respected horse trainer, but Holt always balked at the idea. He liked the dust and the jumble. He liked having metal filing cabinets filled with papers instead of flash drives and computers with spreadsheets. If he wanted to throw a dirty saddle across the back of a chair, he did. If he wanted to toss a pile of headstalls and bridles into a corner of the room, he didn't worry about how it looked or smelled. He was in the business of horses. Not ostentatious surroundings. Or technical gadgets.

"Yeah, pretty women and I go hand in hand," he went on with a dose of sarcasm. "Except I don't like it when they pretend to be something they aren't."

"I don't get you, Holt. You don't know Isabelle Townsend. Why you've made this snap decision about her, I'll never understand. But I'm telling you, you've got it all wrong. She's purchased the old Landry Ranch and has intentions of turning it into a horse farm. And from what I hear about the woman, she has enough riding trophies to fill up this room."

Holt stopped in his tracks and stared at his brother. "Who says?"

"Emily-Ann for one. And working at Conchita's, you know she hears everything."

Holt sputtered. "Sure, Blake. Working at a coffee shop means she hears gossip."

"This is more than gossip," Blake countered. "Emily-Ann has become fairly good friends with the woman."

Holt looked away from his brother and down at the dusty planked floor. This part of the foaling barn had been built many years before Holt was born and the cypress boards, though durable, were a fire hazard. The floor actually needed to be ripped out and replaced with concrete, but like many parts of the century-and-a-half-old ranch, they remained as pieces of tradition.

"The old Landry Ranch, you say? That means she's our neighbor on the north boundary."

"Right," Blake replied. "And we don't need any kind of friction with a neighbor. So you think you can play nice in the morning?"

Holt grinned. "Sure. I'll be so sweet, she'll think she's covered in molasses."

Blake rolled his eyes. "I don't think you need to spread it on that thick, brother. Just be yourself. No. On second thought, that could be dangerous. Just be congenial."

Holt's weary chuckle was more like a groan. "Don't worry, Blake. I'll be on my best behavior."

By the time Isabelle reached the outskirts of Wickenburg, she'd managed to push her simmering frustration aside and set her thoughts on the breakfast she'd missed earlier this morning. Endless chores were waiting for her back at the ranch, and it would make more sense to go home and fix herself a plate of eggs and toast. But she was already close to town, and after that humiliating encounter with Holt Hollister, taking time for coffee and a pastry at Conchita's would be a treat she desperately needed.

After driving through the main part of Wickenburg, she turned onto a sleepy side street where the tiny coffee shop was located. Shaded by two old mesquite trees, the building's slab pine siding was weathered to a drab gray. Worn stepping stones led up to a small porch with a short overhang.

At the moment, the single wooden door stood open to the warm morning and Isabelle could hear the muted sounds of music. As she stepped inside the dim interior, she was met with the mouthwatering scents of fresh baked pastries and brewing coffee.

An elderly man with a cane was at the counter. Isabelle stood to one side and waited patiently while Emily-Ann sacked his order.

"Hi, Isabelle!" the waitress greeted. "I'll be right back as soon as I help Mr. Perez out with his things."

"Sure. Take your time. I'm in no hurry," Isabelle assured her.

The gentleman waved a dismissive hand at the young, auburn-haired woman and spoke something to her in rapid Spanish. Emily-Ann replied in the same language and made a shooing gesture toward the door.

"He insists he can carry his order out to the car on his own," she explained to Isabelle. "But I'm not going to let that happen."

While Emily-Ann assisted the customer, Isabelle stepped up to the glass cases holding a huge array of pastries and baked treats. She was still trying to decide between the brownies and the apple fritters when Emily-Ann returned and gave Isabelle a tight hug.

Laughing, Isabelle hugged her back. "You must have missed me!"

"I have!" Emily-Ann exclaimed, a wide smile lighting up her pretty freckled face. "You've not been in for a few days."

"I've been busy. So busy, in fact, that I missed breakfast this morning." Isabelle pointed to a top shelf. "Give me a brownie and an apple fritter. And a large regular coffee with cream."

Emily-Ann, who was the same age as Isabelle, looked at her in disbelief. "A brownie and an apple fritter? And you look like that? Do you know how frustrated that makes me? Just breathing the air in here makes me gain a pound!"

Isabelle shook her head. "You look lovely. I only wish I had your height. For the first fifteen years of my life, I was called shorty."

"That's better than being called freckles." Emily-Ann turned to a counter behind her and filled a cup with coffee. "Do you want this to go?"

"No. I don't want to gobble it down while I drive. I want to enjoy every bite."

"Great," she said. "The customers have let up for

the moment so I'll join you. That is, if you'd like the company."

"C'mon. I'd love your company."

The two women walked outside and sat down at one of the small wrought iron tables and chairs sitting in the shade of the mesquites.

"So what's been going on with you since I was here?" Isabelle asked as she broke off a piece of the brownie and popped it into her mouth.

Emily-Ann tilted her head from side to side in a nonchalant expression. "Nothing new. At this time of year, lots of snowbirds come in for coffee. Most of them are friendly and want to chat and ask questions about things to see and do around here. Honestly, Isabelle, when you've lived in one little town all your life, you don't really see things as a tourist. For example, that saguaro over there across the street. The tourists ooh and aah over it. To me, it's just a saguaro."

"That's because you see it every day." Isabelle sipped her coffee, hoping the caffeine would revive her from the long morning she started before daylight. "But think of it this way, one of those snowbirds that walk into the coffee shop might be your Mr. Right."

Emily-Ann grimaced. "I'm not sure I want to look for a Mr. Right anymore. The men I've dated have all turned out to be stinkers."

Isabelle shrugged. "At least you weren't like me and made the mistake of marrying the wrong man."

"From what you've told me, your ex would've been happy to stay married. And you did say that the two of you are still friends. Are you sure you don't regret getting a divorce?"

"Trevor was a good guy. A nice guy. But he—" He just hadn't loved her. Not with the deep, abiding love that Isabelle had craved. "Well, he was a great companion. Just not a husband."

Shaking her head, Emily-Ann sighed. "I'm not sure I get that. But as long as you think you're better off now, then that's all that really matters, I suppose."

Isabelle finished the brownie and unwrapped the square of wax paper from the fritter. "I am better off. I'm following my dreams."

Emily-Ann leaned back in her chair. "How is the ranch coming along? Have you found any horses to buy?"

Instead of blurting the curse word burning the tip of her tongue, Isabelle snorted. "Actually, I drove out to Three Rivers this morning to look at their horses, but I didn't get to first base."

"Oh, what happened? Out of all of the horses they have, surely you could find something that suited you."

"Ha! All I got to see was an arrogant cowboy and he promptly sent me on my way."

Emily-Ann's mouth fell open. "You mean Holt? *He* sent you packing?"

"He did. Emily-Ann, I thought you told me he was a charming guy and that he'd be easy to do business with. The guy is a first-class jerk!" Isabelle huffed out a breath and reached for her coffee.

Emily-Ann was perplexed. "I don't understand how that could've happened. But he's dreamy-looking. Right?"

Isabelle sipped the hot drink and tried not to think about the way Holt Hollister had looked standing there in front of her with his long legs parted and his arms folded against his broad chest. Dreamy? He'd looked rough around the edges and as tough as rawhide. "I'll admit he's sexy, but not the sort I dream about. I like manners and kindness in a man."

Emily-Ann batted a hand through the air. "Holt knows all about manners. Him sending you away— that's just not the man I know, and I've been friends with the whole family since I was a very little girl."

Isabelle shrugged, while trying not to take the man's behavior personally. "There must've been something about me that Holt didn't like. Or maybe something I said. Like hello," she added dryly. "No matter. Blake invited me to come back tomorrow and I'm going to take him up on the invitation."

Emily-Ann looked relieved. "Oh, so you met Blake. He's a real gentleman."

"I'll put it this way, he's nothing like his brother," Isabelle replied.

"So what did you think about Three Rivers? It's quite a place, isn't it?"

Nodding, Isabelle admitted, "Beautiful. But nothing like I was expecting. I thought the main ranch house would be a hacienda-type mansion surrounded by a stone wall with an elaborate gated entrance. Instead, it was a homey three-story house with wood siding and a front porch for sitting."

Emily-Ann sighed. "The Hollisters are a homey bunch. Guess that's why the family is so well liked. They're just regular folks. Even though they have oodles of money."

Isabelle's ex had also had oodles of money. Perhaps not as much as the Hollisters, but he'd had enough to give her a tidy fortune in the divorce settlement. Money was necessary, and Isabelle would be lying if she said she didn't appreciate the life it was allowing her to lead. Particularly with her plans to build a horse farm. But money wasn't everything. In the end, Trevor's money hadn't made up for his inability to love her.

"Well, if I don't meet a different Holt tomorrow, I'm going to suggest he drive up to the Grand Canyon and take a flying leap off the South Rim."

"Ouch. He must have really rubbed you the wrong way."

Just the thought of Holt Hollister rubbing her in any way sent a shiver down Isabelle's spine. Maybe the women around here went for the barbarian type, but she didn't.

Purposely focusing her attention on the apple fritter, Isabelle said, "Let's talk about something else, shall we? I don't want to ruin the rest of my day."

For the first night in the past ten nights, no foals were born and Holt managed to sleep until four thirty in the morning without being disturbed. Even so, the moment he opened his eyes, he jerked to a sitting position and stared around the bedroom, disoriented.

What was he doing in bed and what the heck had happened while he'd been asleep? Swinging his legs over the side of the mattress, he reached for the phone on the nightstand and punched the button for the direct line to the foaling barn. It rang six times before someone finally picked it up and by then Holt was wide-awake.

"Yep."

"Matt, is that you?" Matthew Waggoner was the ranch foreman and had been for several years. His job was mostly handling the cowhands, the cattle, and everything that entailed. He usually stayed away from the mares and foals.

"Yep, it's me. What's wrong?"

"Why are you in the foaling barn?" Holt asked. "Has something happened?"

"No. Everything is quiet. I'm spelling Leo. He's dead on his feet. Sounds like you are, too."

Holt raked a hand through his tumbled hair, then reached for the jeans he'd left lying on the floor by the bed. "When I woke up and realized I'd been in bed all night, it scared me."

Matthew chuckled. "That's a hell of a thing to be scared about. Hang up and go back to sleep. The mares in the paddock are all happy and the hands and I won't be leaving out of the ranch yard until six anyway."

"Thanks, Matt. But my sleep is over. I'll be down as soon as I grab something from the kitchen."

In the bathroom, he sluiced cold water onto his face, then ran a comb through his dark hair. The rusty brown whiskers on his face hadn't seen a razor in three days, but he wasn't going to bother shaving this morning. He had more important worries.

After he'd thrown a denim shirt over his jeans and tugged on a pair of worn cowboy boots, he hurried down to the kitchen, where Reeva was already shoving an iron skillet filled with buttermilk biscuits into the oven. The scents of frying bacon and chorizo filled the warm room.

"Got any tortillas warm yet, old woman?" Holt asked as he sneaked up behind the cook and pecked a kiss on her cheek.

Without batting an eye, she pointed to a platter stacked with breakfast tacos wrapped in aluminum foil. "The tacos are already made. What do you think I do around here anyway? Sit reading gossip magazines or lie in bed? Like you?"

In her early seventies, Reeva was a tall, thin woman

with straight, iron gray hair that was usually pulled into a ponytail or braid. She'd been working as the Hollister cook since before Holt had been born and now after all these years, she was a part of the family. Which was all for the best, he thought, since the little family she'd once had were all moved away and out of her life.

"Ha! I've seen you lounging around in the den reading gossip magazines and drinking coffee," Holt teased as he snatched up three of the tacos.

Reeva swatted the spatula at his hand. "Get out of here, you worthless saddle tramp."

"Don't worry, I'm going. As soon as I find my insulated cup."

"Right behind you. On the cabinet. And don't go out without your jacket. It's cold this morning."

"It's a good thing you're around to tell me what to do, Reeva. Otherwise, I'd be in a hell of a mess." He grabbed up the stainless steel cup and headed toward the door that led to the backyard.

"You stay in a mess even with my help," she said tartly, then added, "I'll send Jazelle down with some pastries later. And don't call me old woman."

Holt looked over his shoulder and winked at her. "Reeva, you look as fresh as a spring rose."

Reeva continued to flip the frying bacon. "You wouldn't know what a spring rose looked like. But I love you anyway."

"Right back at ya, old woman."

At the door, he levered on a gray Stetson and, to please Reeva, pulled on a Sherpa-lined jacket. After stuffing the tacos into one of the pockets to keep them warm on the long walk to the foaling barn, he stepped outside and was promptly slammed in the face with a cold north wind.

Ducking his head, he left the backyard and started toward the massive ranch yard in the distance. Along the way, he passed the bunkhouse where most of the single ranch hands lived. The scents of coffee and frying sausage drifted out from the log building and Holt figured the guys would be sitting down to breakfast any minute now, which was served at five on most mornings. Once in a while, he and Blake would join the group for the early meal, just to share a few casual minutes with the hardworking employees. But the bunkhouse cook was a crusty old fellow, who couldn't begin to match Reeva's kitchen skills.

At the cattle pens, there were already a half dozen cowboys spreading feed and hay. Dust billowed from the stirring hooves, a sign that so far the winter had been extremely dry. Grass on the range was getting as scarce as hen's teeth and Matthew had already warned Blake that the hay Three Rivers had baled back in the spring would soon be gone. As for the Timothy/alfalfa mix Holt fed the horses, he'd already been forced to get tons of it shipped in from northern Nevada.

At times like these, Holt figured Blake acquired a few more gray hairs at his temples. As manager of the ranch, his brother carried a load on his shoulders and he worried. But Holt didn't worry. Not about the solvency of the ranch. After a hundred and seventy-one years, he figured the place would keep on standing strong. No, the only thing he worried about was keeping the horses healthy. And his mother.

For the most part, Holt could control the well-being of the Three Rivers' remuda, but his mother was a different matter. Lately she was doing a good job of acting like she was happy. But Holt and his siblings weren't fooled. She was keeping something from the family.

Chandler wanted to think she'd fallen in love and was trying to hide it, but Holt didn't go along with his brother's idea. A woman in love had a look about her that was impossible to hide and his mother didn't have it.

When Holt reached the horse barn, the hands were already feeding the few mares that were stalled with their new foals. T.J., the barn manager, met Holt in the middle of the wide alleyway.

"Mornin', Holt," he greeted. "Everything is quiet. No problem with Ginger. She seems to have taken to her little boy. He's been standing and nursing and already looks stronger than he did two hours ago."

Holt wasn't surprised to hear T.J. had already been at the barn for two or three hours. He was a dedicated young man with an affinity for horses. He'd come to work for the ranch six years ago and since then had proved his worth over and over.

"That's happy news. I was afraid we might have to put him on a nurse mare." Grinning now, Holt patted his jacket pocket. "I have breakfast tacos. If you're hungry, I'll share."

"Thanks, Holt, but I promised William I'd eat at the bunkhouse this morning. Now that you're here, I'll mosey on over there."

"Better do more than mosey or there won't be anything left."

"Right. I'll be back in a few minutes." The barn manager turned on his heel and hurried out of the barn.

On the way to his office, Holt made a short detour to Ginger's stall. As T.J. had informed him, the colt was looking remarkably stronger since his birth yesterday. The fact that the first-time mare was now bonding with her baby was a huge relief and he smiled as he watched her lick the white star on the colt's forehead.

"He's a good-looking boy. Big boned, bright eyed and straight legs. By the time he's a weanling, he'll be strong and sturdy."

The unexpected female voice had him whirling around to see Isabelle Townsend had walked up behind him. The sight of her at any time of the day would've surprised him, but he doubted it was daylight yet. Blake had told him she'd probably return to the ranch today, but he'd not mentioned she might show up at five in the morning!

"Ms. Townsend," he said in the way of greeting. "You're out early."

To his surprise, she must've forgiven his nasty behavior yesterday. There wasn't anything sarcastic in the smile on her face. On the contrary. It was warm enough to chase away the chill in the barn.

"Yesterday you were too busy to deal with me. This morning I came early in hopes I'd catch you before that happened."

He had a thousand and one things to do, including eating the meager breakfast he was carrying in his pocket. He didn't have time for Isabelle Townsend. Not this morning, or any morning. But he'd promised Blake he'd be a gentleman and one thing Holt never wanted to do was break his word to his big brother.

"I was headed to my office. If you'd like to join me, we can talk there." He turned away from Ginger's stall. "Have you had breakfast?"

"No. But I'm fine. Sometimes I don't bother with that meal."

From the looks of her, she didn't bother with eating much at all. Yesterday he'd noticed she was petite. This morning, he could see she was even smaller than he remembered. Even with the heels of her cowboy boots adding to her height, he doubted the top of her head would reach the middle of his chest. The notion struck him that he could pick her up with one arm and never feel the strain.

But he had no plans to get that close to their pretty neighbor, Holt decided. Not unless she wanted him to.

Chapter Two

Walking to his office, Isabelle was careful to keep a respectable distance from Holt Hollister. She had no idea if Emily-Ann's remarks about him being a ladies' man were true or just rumors. Either way, she didn't want to give him the impression that she was interested in anything more than his horses.

"You must have assumed I start the day early," he said.

"All horse trainers start the day long before daylight," she replied. "That is, the good ones do."

He let out a dry chuckle. "Does that mean you put me in the company of the good ones?"

His voice was raspy, like he'd just lifted his head from the pillow after a long sleep. The sound shivered right through her.

"I've heard a lot about you, Mr. Hollister, but I don't go by hearsay. So I can't really answer your question—yet."

Her reply didn't appear to annoy him, rather he had an amused look on his face. "I've heard some things about you, too. But I don't rely on hearsay either."

Isabelle couldn't imagine what he might have heard about her. She doubted it could've been much, though. Since she'd moved here, she'd only made a few acquaintances around town.

At the end of the barn, he opened a door on the left and motioned for her to proceed him through it.

Isabelle stepped past him and into the small room that looked more like a tack room than an office. Jammed with a messy desk, two wooden chairs, and a row of file cabinets, it was also littered with bits and bridles, saddle blankets and pads, leather cinches and breast harnesses. In one corner, there was even a worn saddle thrown over a wooden sawhorse.

"Have a seat," he invited. "You might want to wipe the dust off first, though. We don't do much cleaning out here in the barn. It doesn't do much good."

"I'm used to dust." And mud. Rain and snow. Heat and cold. Early and late. In the horse business, a person had to get used to all those things and much, much more.

While she settled herself in one of the wooden chairs sitting in front of the desk, he placed the stainless steel vacuum cup he'd been carrying on the desktop, then walked over to a heater and adjusted the thermostat.

Back at the desk, he took a seat in a leather executive chair and picked up the receiver on a landline telephone. After punching a button, he promptly said, "Reeva, as soon as Jazelle shows up—oh, she has—that's good. Send her on with the pastries, would you? And more coffee." He paused. "That's right. The horse barn. Not the foaling barn. Thanks."

He hung up the phone, then leveled his attention directly on Isabelle. "My brother Blake tells me you've bought the old Landry ranch. Are you living there now?"

Isabelle nodded. "I am. The Landry family had been out of the house for a long time and it needed some repairs. Fortunately, I've gotten most of them done. At least to where the place is comfortable now. The barns and utility sheds were in far better shape than the house. There are still areas of the ranch that need plenty of work and changes made, but it's good enough for me to start adding horses to the ones I already have."

He looked somewhat surprised. "You already have horses?"

"That's right. Ten in all. Two geldings for work purposes and eight broodmares that are currently in foal to a stallion back in Albuquerque, New Mexico. I don't have a stallion of my own yet. But like I said yesterday, I'm looking to buy. Preferably a blue roan that's proven to throw color and produce hearty babies."

He suddenly grinned and Isabelle felt her breath catch in her throat. She could definitely see why the rumors of being a ladies' man followed him around. He was charming without even trying. But she'd been around men of his caliber before. They weren't meant to be taken seriously.

"We'd all like one of those, Ms. Townsend."

She shook her head. "Please call me Isabelle. After all, we're neighbors. Even if it is eighteen miles to my place."

"Okay, Isabelle. Since you seem determined to add to your workload, I'll show you a few mares I might be willing to part with. But I don't have a stallion I want to sell. Maybe in a year or two. But not now."

She shrugged one shoulder. "That's okay. I'll be happy to look at anything you have."

The room was getting nice and warm so Isabelle untied the fur-edged hood of her jacket and allowed it to slip to her back. As she shook her hair free, she noticed he was watching her as though he was trying to gauge what was beneath the surface. The idea was disturbing, but it didn't offend her. She was a complete stranger to the man. In his line of business, he had a right to wonder about her character and how she might care for the animals he sold her.

"You mentioned Albuquerque. Is that where you're from originally?"

She shook her head. "No. I was born in California and lived there all of my life until I, uh, married and moved with my husband to New Mexico."

Beneath the brim of his battered gray hat, she could see one of his dark brows quirk upward.

"Oh. You're married then?"

She felt like telling him that her marital status really had nothing to do with her buying horses. But she didn't want to irk him again. At least, not before she had a chance to do business with the man. Besides, her being a divorcée was hardly a secret, even if it was something that made her feel like a failure as a woman.

"No. I've been divorced for more than a year now. He still lives in New Mexico. I decided to move here." She gave him a wide smile to let him know she was feeling no regrets about her ex or the move to Arizona. "And so far I love it. The Landry Ranch was just what I was looking for."

He reached in the pocket of his jacket and pulled out three long items wrapped in aluminum foil and placed them on the desk. From the scents drifting her way, Isabelle guessed he'd been carrying around his breakfast.

"I imagine you've changed the ranch's name by now," he said.

Her smile grew wider. "I have. To Blue Stallion Ranch. I might not own him now. But I will make my dream come true one day."

"I see. Sounds like you've put a lot of thought into this."

"When a woman dreams for her future, she does put a lot of thought into it. And the dream of Blue Stallion Ranch is something I've had for a long time."

He started to say something, but a knock on the open door of the office interrupted him. Isabelle looked over her shoulder to see a tall blond woman about her own age entering the room carrying a large lunch bucket and a tall metal thermos.

"Breakfast is here," she announced cheerfully. "The pastries are fresh and the coffee is hot, so you'd better dig in."

"Jazelle, you're an angel in blue jeans," he told the woman. "I'll dance at your wedding with cowbells on."

Jazelle pushed aside a stack of papers and placed the containers on the desktop. "Ha! You won't be wearing cowbells or anything else to my wedding. 'Cause that ain't going to happen. And yes, I said *ain't*—so there!"

He responded to the woman's caustic reply with a loud laugh. "Sure, Jazelle. You and Camille have sworn off men for the rest of your lives. I've heard it all before, but I don't believe a word of it."

She glared at him. "Well, you'd better believe it, buddy! And if you had any sense, you'd swear off women, too."

He coughed awkwardly and Jazelle turned an apologetic look on Isabelle. "Sorry," she said, then shaking her head, she laughed. "Uh—Holt and I like to tease. We really love each other. Don't we, Holt?"

He grinned. "Just like brother and sister," he said, then gestured to Isabelle. "Jazelle, meet Isabelle. She's our new neighbor to the north. She's a horsewoman."

Isabelle rose and extended her hand to the other woman. "Nice to meet you, Jazelle. And thank you for bringing the breakfast. It smells heavenly."

Jazelle's handshake was hearty and sincere and Isabelle liked her immediately.

"The cook and I bake pastries every other day. These just came out of the oven." She continued to eye Isabelle. "I'm sorry I'm staring. But you're just too darn pretty to be a horsewoman."

Isabelle laughed. "And you're too kind."

Jazelle left the office and Isabelle looked around to see Holt had opened the lunch bucket and was in the process of filling two foam cups with coffee.

"Let's eat," he said. "There's creamer and sugar for your coffee if you want it. And take what pastries you want. I have three chorizo and egg tacos. You're welcome to one of them, too."

"No, thanks. One of these cinnamon rolls will be enough." She poured creamer into her coffee and with the cup and roll in hand, she sat back down in the chair.

Through the open doorway, Isabelle could hear the horses exchanging whinnies and the familiar clanking of gates as each stall door was opened and closed. Above those sounds was the faint hum of a radio and the noise of the workers as they called to each other.

Someday, she thought, her barn would sound like this. Look like this. With mares and foals everywhere and plenty of ranch hands taking care of the chores.

As much as Trevor had tried to make her happy, he'd never shared Isabelle's dream of having a horse farm. He'd only tolerated her obsession with equines because he'd been smart enough to know if he'd given her an ultimatum, she would've chosen the horses over him.

"Is working with horses something you've done for a while?" he asked. "Or is this a new venture for you?"

Isabelle swallowed a bite of the roll before she answered. "I first started riding when I was five years old. That's when my mom introduced me to a little brown pony named Albert. And I fell in love. By the time I got to be a teenager, I wanted to be a jockey, but Mom steered me away from that and into reining and cutting competitions. She considered being a jockey too dangerous."

He grunted with amusement. "Walking through the mare's paddock at feeding time is dangerous."

"That's true. But anyway, I got into the reining thing in a big way and eventually started training for breeders in southern California. After I moved to New Mexico, I began to acquire the mares."

"I see. So until now, you've not actually had a horse ranch?"

She sipped the coffee, then shook her head. "Believe it or not, my ex-husband was overly generous in the divorce settlement just so I'd have plenty to purchase the property and the horses."

The taco in his hand paused halfway to his mouth. "That's hard to fathom."

No. She didn't expect him to understand. Something about Holt Hollister said he was the sort who'd love with all his heart, or not at all. And whatever he possessed, he'd fight to keep. Whether that be a wife, or material assets.

"I realize it sounds a bit crazy," she said. "But we're still good friends. And he wants me to be happy. Add to that, the man has more money than he knows what to do with. That's the way with some folks in the oil industry. Money flows and things are acquired so easily that after a while everything loses its luster." She cleared her throat, confused and embarrassed that she'd shared such personal things with this man. "Anyway, Trevor is a good and generous man. And he's made it possible to invest in my dreams."

"Lucky you."

His quipped reply rankled her, but she carefully hid her reaction. "There was nothing lucky about it. I didn't ask for the money. Or the divorce."

His gaze dropped to the cup he was holding. "Sorry. I shouldn't have said that."

Was he really sorry? She doubted it. But then his opinion of her personal life hardly mattered. After today, she wouldn't be rubbing shoulders with the man.

"Forget it," she told him. "I have."

She might've already forgotten, but Holt hadn't. Damn it!

He didn't know how their conversation had turned to such personal issues. One minute they'd been talking about her connection to horses and the next she was telling him about her divorce.

Hell! He didn't care if she was married with five kids or devotedly single. He didn't care if she had a good and generous ex-husband. And he sure didn't care that she was the sexiest woman he'd ever laid eyes on. To Holt, she was horse buyer. Nothing more. Nothing less.

"Has your family always owned Three Rivers Ranch?"

Her question jerked Holt out of his reverie and he looked at her as he swallowed down the last bite of taco.

"The Hollisters first built this ranch back in 1847. Since then it's always been a family thing."

"Wow! That must go back through several generations," she said, then shrugged. "I can't remember the house my parents and I lived in when I entered middle school, much less know what sort of place they had when I was born. They were nomads. Still are."

"So you think you want to root down." He wished she'd quit talking about homes and family. She didn't look the sort and he was as far from a family man as Earth was from Mars.

"More than anything," she said with conviction.

Jazelle had brought a few little pecan tortes along with the cinnamon rolls. He gobbled down two of them and was finishing his coffee as fast as he could when she said, "I realize you're in a hurry to get me out of your hair, but at the pace you're eating, you're going to have stomach issues."

Dear Lord, was there nothing she missed? "I always eat fast. Otherwise, I might not have the chance to eat at all. If you're finished with your coffee, we'll go have a look at the horses."

Smiling faintly, she leaned forward and gracefully placed her cup on the edge of his desk. "I'm ready any time you are."

Rising from the desk chair, he pulled on his jacket and buttoned it up to his throat. By then, she'd gotten to her feet and fastened the hood over all that white-blond hair and pulled on a pair of fuzzy black mittens. She looked as sweet as Christmas candy and as fragile as a sparrow's wing. How could this woman ever manage to work a horse ranch?

That's none of your concern, Holt. All you need to do is keep your mind on your job and off the way Isabelle Townsend looks or sounds or smells. She's not your type. She never will be.

Shoving away the mocking reminder in his head, he gestured toward the door. "You're welcome to look at the mares and babies here in the barn, but none of them are for sale. Anything I might be willing to part with is outside."

"I'd love to take a leisurely look. But you're just as busy as I am. Let's just head on outside."

Her response should have pleased him. The quicker he could get this meeting over with, the better. Yet he had to admit a part of him had wanted to show her some of the fine babies his mares had delivered in the past few days. Like a proud dad, he would've enjoyed sticking out his chest and preening just a little. But she wasn't going to give him the chance.

"Fine," he said. "We'll exit the barn on this end."

Outside the building, she followed him over to a ten-acre patch surrounded by a tall board fence.

"This is where I keep the mares that have two or three weeks before foaling," he told her. "When they start getting to that point in their gestation, I like to keep a closer eye on them."

"Do you have a resident vet here on the ranch?"

"My older brother Chandler is the vet," he told her. "If something comes up that I can't handle, he'll come running."

"I'm just now putting two and two together," she said thoughtfully. "He must run the Hollister Animal Hospital. Does he live here on the ranch, too?"

Her question reminded Holt that he and his baby sister, Camille, were the only Hollister siblings left who didn't have a spouse and children. As for Camille, he couldn't speak for her wants and wishes, but on most days Holt was happy he was still footloose and fancy-free. There were too many women in the world to waste his life on just one.

"Yes, with his wife, Roslyn, and baby daughter, Evelyn."

A bright smile suddenly lit her face. "Oh, so there's a baby in the house. How nice."

"It's nice and noisy. There are three babies in the house. Blake has twins." Curious, in spite of himself, he glanced at her. "Do you have children?"

To his surprise, a pink blush appeared on her cheeks. "No. Trevor wasn't the type for fatherhood. But I'm hoping I'll be a mother someday. What about you—do you have children?"

He chuckled. "Not any that I know of."

She didn't reply, but the scornful expression on her face spoke volumes.

"I'm teasing," he felt inclined to say. "I don't have any children. And I don't plan on having any. I have plenty of four-legged babies to keep me happy."

She cut him another dry glance. "At least you know to stick to your calling."

If any other woman had said such a thing to him, he would've laughed. But hearing it from this blond beauty was altogether different. For some reason, it made him feel small and sleazy.

"At least I know my calling," he agreed. "Do you?"

"What is that supposed to mean?"

Suddenly Blake's voice was back in his head, reminding him to be nice to Isabelle. But damn it, Blake wasn't the one dealing with the woman. Holt was. And with each passing minute, she was getting deeper and deeper under his skin.

"I'm wondering if you've really thought about what you're taking on. Raising horses isn't an easy job."

"If it was easy, it wouldn't be rewarding, now would it?" she asked. "And I know all about hard work."

The sweetness in her voice was overlaid with conviction and Holt decided she was one of those stubborn females who'd rather die trying to prove a point than admit she might be wrong.

They reached the paddock and he opened a wide gate so the two of them could walk out to where the mares were munching hay from rows of mangers.

As they neared the horses, Holt pointed to one in particular. "I have one mare in this bunch that I'd be willing to part with and that's Blossom, the little chestnut over there with the star on her forehead and snip on her nose. She's made perfectly, I'd just prefer her to be a tad bigger. She was bred late—in May to be exact, so she should have a late April or early May baby."

"I'll go take a look."

They walked over to the mare and as she approached the horse for a closer look, Holt opened his mouth to remind her to be cautious, but instantly decided to keep the warning to himself. If Isabelle knew so much about horses, he shouldn't have to tell her a thing. This might be a good way to find out if she was the real deal or a woman with money and her head in the clouds.

Five minutes later, Holt had his answer. Blossom had not only forgotten the hay in front of her, she was nosing up to Isabelle as if they'd been friends forever. On top of that, the young mare had always been skittish about her feet, but Blossom had allowed Isabelle to pick up all four like she was a diva waiting for a manicure. It was amazing.

"She has a really nice eye and her teeth look good," she said as she dropped the mare's lip back in place.

"Chandler floats their teeth on a regular basis," he said, his green eyes dropping away from her hands and down to her rounded bottom encased in faded denim. Yesterday he'd been too tired and annoyed to notice Isabelle's perfect figure. This morning he was having trouble keeping his attention away from it.

She turned to face him and Holt jerked up his gaze before she caught him staring at her cute little butt.

"What sort of sire is this mare bred to?"

"The ranch's foundation stud. He's black and big boned. I'll show him to you after we look at the other mares."

She smiled and Holt's attention was drawn to the alluring sight of soft pink lips against white teeth. And suddenly he was wondering how she would look naked and lying next to him with her hair spilled over his shoulder.

"I look forward to seeing him," she said.

"So what do you think of Blossom?"

"She's nice. But I need to see the others before I make any kind of decision. Okay?"

Another smile softened her words and Holt felt his resistance crumbling like a shortbread cookie. Any man with half a brain could see she was a heartbreaker. But why should he let that put him off? He never made the mistake of letting a woman get near his heart. He enjoyed them for a while and then moved on. Isabelle was no different than the last beauty to warm his bed.

"Certainly," he answered. "Let's go find a truck and we'll drive out to the horse pasture."

* * *

Throughout the short trip to the pasture, Isabelle tried to ignore Holt's presence in the cab of the truck, but the more she tried to dismiss him, the more suffocated she felt. Back at the ranch yard, he'd wrapped a hand around her arm to assist her climb into the tall work truck, and even through the quilted thickness of her coat, the touch of his fingers had left a burning imprint.

But that was hardly a surprise. Everything about the man, from his sauntering walk to the growl in his voice, shouted sex. Or was he really no different than any other man she'd ever met? Could the long months of a cold, empty bed be causing her to see him in a different light?

Whatever the reason for her ridiculous reaction to the man, she needed to get over it and quick. There was no way she could make a smart business transaction when her mind was preoccupied with how he'd look with his shirt off, or wonder how it would feel to have those strong arms wrapped around her.

Damn it! She didn't need a man. Not now. And definitely not a Romeo in cowboy boots.

"I've not been here long enough to learn about your weather," she said, hoping to push her thoughts to a safer place. "Is it usually this cool in January? I was hoping that this part of the state was southern enough to miss the cold and snow."

"Other than a few rare flurries blowing in the wind, you won't see snow around here," he answered. "But it can get fairly cold. Especially at night. What little rain we do get comes in the winter months. I hope you have plenty of water sources on your ranch. Otherwise, when the dry months come, you're going to be in trouble."

Did the man think she'd gotten to Arizona on the back of a turnip truck? Or was he doubting her common sense because she was a woman? Either way, he seemed intent on insulting her intelligence.

But she was trying her best to ignore his remarks, the same way she was trying to dismiss the way his chin jutted slightly forward and the rusty stubble on his face had grown even longer since she'd seen him yesterday morning. Normally she had an aversion to men who didn't keep their faces clean-shaven. But there was something very earthy and sexy about the way the whiskers outlined his square jaw and firm lips.

She cleared her throat and said, "I made sure about the water supply before I purchased the property. And I've had enough firewood hauled in for the fireplace to last through the winter. I have fifty tons of Tifton/alfalfa in the hay barn and enough grain to last a month. In spite of what you might think of me, I do know how to make preparations."

He glanced at her and grinned. "I'm glad to hear you're prepared. And, by the way, how do you know what I'm thinking of you?"

She bit back a groan and decided the best way to deal with this man was to be forthright. Lifting her chin, she said, "It's fairly obvious you think I'm an idiot. I'm not sure why you've put me in that category, but you have. And I'm trying not to let it bother me. After all, I think you're a bit of an arrogant brute. So there—we're even."

Expecting him to be peeved with her, she was totally surprised when he let out a hearty laugh. "An arrogant brute, eh? I've been called plenty of things before, but never that one." He directed another lopsided grin in her direction. "And you have me all wrong, Isabelle. I hardly think you're an idiot. I merely think you might be biting off more than you can chew."

"Because I'm a woman?"

He shook his head. "No. Because you're clearly chasing a dream. Instead of facing the hard work in front of you."

She wanted to be angry with him. She wanted to tell him that a person without dreams wasn't really living. But she stifled both urges. There had already been too many personal exchanges between the two of them and it was beginning to make her feel uncomfortable. It was making her think of him as a man rather than a neighbor or horse trainer. And that was something that could only lead to trouble.

"I know all about hard work, Mr. Hollister," she said stiffly.

"Please call me Holt."

She rolled her eyes in his direction to see the grin on his face was still there. Five minutes with Holt Hollister was really too much for any woman to endure and hold on to her sanity, she decided.

He steered the truck off the beaten dirt track and braked it to a stop near a wide galvanized gate. Beyond the fence, Isabelle could see thirty or more head of horses milling around a cluster of long wooden feed troughs.

"Here we are," he announced. "And fortunately, the horses are still at their feed. I think there are thirty-five head in this herd."

Purposely keeping her gaze on the horses, she asked, "How many of these are for sale?"

"Four. I'll take a halter with me so you can take your time with each one."

"Thanks. I'd appreciate that."

They left the truck and after he collected a halter from the back, they walked over to the fence. While he slipped the latch on the gate, she said, "I thought you were in the business of selling horses. Why the limit of four or five?"

"This past year, we had to take several horses out of the working remuda for different reasons, such as lameness and age and so forth. And then Blake decided to add more cattle to our ranch down at Dragoon, so I've had to send more horses for the hands to use down there. Replacing them takes time and lots of training. So I'm actually running a bit short on older horses and somewhat short on the yearlings."

He followed her into the pasture and as Isabelle watched him carefully fasten the gate behind them, she realized that for once in her life, she was just as interested in looking at a man as she was a herd of horses.

"I see. I was thinking you might just limit the buyers who have their heads in the clouds."

He chuckled and Isabelle decided an arrogant brute who could laugh at himself couldn't be all bad.

"Not at all," he assured her. "I have special deals for those buyers."

Her laugh was shrewd. "I'll just bet you do."

Chapter Three

Over an hour later, Holt and Isabelle were back in the horse barn, where Holt had just finished showing her Hez A Rocket, the ranch's foundation stallion. She'd seemed very impressed with the animal, but Holt got the feeling she wasn't that enthralled with him.

And why would you want her to be, Holt? Right off the top of your head, you can probably think of four or five blond beauties who'd be happy to get a call from you. The last thing you need is a divorcée with a head full of dreams.

Holt purposely blocked out the voice of warning in his head as the two of them strolled in the general direction of his office. "Now that you've seen what I have to offer, are you ready to make a deal on one, or all?"

"Yes, I would. I—" She broke off as an ear-splitting whinny reverberated through the barn. "Wow! Someone wants attention. That sounds like another stallion."

Holt silently groaned. She'd told him her dream was to find a blue roan stallion and build her herd around him. Blue Midnight definitely fit her wishes, but Holt was grooming the young stud to replace Hez A Rocket in a few years. He'd never put the young stallion up for sale.

"That's Blue Midnight, one of my other stallions," he reluctantly admitted. "He can be quite a talker at times."

Her brows piqued with interest. "Blue? Is he a roan?"

With a resigned nod of his head, he said, "That's right. I was hoping to spare you from seeing him."

Confused by that, she asked, "Really? Why?"

"Because you're going to want him. And I'm going to have to say no and then you're going to be peeved at me—again."

"I really doubt that would ruin your day." She smiled and shrugged. "I've been told no plenty of times. I won't burst into tears—unless you refuse to let me see this super stud."

He shook his head. "You get a kick out of looking at a piece of pie even though you can't eat it?"

"I can always dream."

He should've seen that coming, Holt thought. "Ah, that's right," he said wryly. "You are fond of dreaming."

Taking her by the arm, he led her across the wide alleyway and past three empty stalls until they were standing in front of Blue Midnight's roomy compartment. Always eager for company, the horse hung his head over the top of the mesh iron gate and nickered softly at the two of them.

"Oh! Oh, Holt, he's gorgeous! Absolutely gorgeous! His hair is so slick and shiny! You must be keeping him blanketed."

Holt glanced over to see an incredible glow had come

over Isabelle's face. As though storm clouds had parted above her head and golden sunshine was pouring over her. He'd put some happy faces on a few women before, but none of those blissful looks compared to what he was seeing on Isabelle's lovely features.

"No blankets. Blue Midnight is naturally tight haired. He just turned four and I have to admit, he's my pride and joy."

"Most stallions bite. Does he?"

"Not this one. He's very sweet natured."

She stepped up to the gate and quickly made friends with the horse. As she gently stroked his nose, she glanced over her shoulder and gave Holt a beseeching smile.

"Are you sure you don't want to sell him?" she asked. "I'd give you top dollar. Just name your price. If I don't have enough money, I'll get the money."

From her rich ex-husband? The notion left a bitter taste in Holt's mouth and for one split second he wanted to tell her that if she'd keep smiling at him the way she was smiling right now, he'd give her the world and Blue Midnight with it. But thankfully, the urge only lasted a second before sanity stepped in and reminded him that pleasing a woman didn't require losing his mind and his best stallion with it.

"Sorry," he told her. "I have big plans for this guy and they're all right here on Three Rivers."

"Oh, I'm sorry, too." Disappointment chased all the lovely glow from her face and she turned back to Blue Midnight and rubbed her cheek against his. "You're such a pretty boy," she said to the horse. "I wish you could be mine. We'd be great buddies."

The interchange between her and the horse was

something so palpable and real that Holt felt like an outsider listening in on a very private conversation.

Clearing his throat, he stepped forward until he was standing at her side. Immediately, the sweet scent of her drifted to his nostrils and pushed away the smells of alfalfa, dust, and manure.

"Blue Midnight has a few babies coming later this spring. If one of them turns out to be a colt, I'll sell him to you."

She looked over at him and Holt was stunned to see a sheen of tears in her blue eyes. He realized he was denying this woman her most fervent wish, but mixing sentimentality with business never worked. Neither did getting dopey over a woman he'd just met.

"Is that a promise?" she asked, her gaze searching his.

Aside from his mother or sisters, Holt didn't make promises to women. But something about Isabelle's blue eyes was dissolving that rule.

"I wouldn't have said it if I hadn't meant it," he answered.

Her gaze turned back to Blue Midnight, who was gently nudging her shoulder for more attention.

"Thank you, Holt. I'll hold on to that promise."

After a couple more minutes with Blue Midnight, they returned to his office. A half hour later, she was using her phone to transfer money from her bank to a Three Rivers' account.

"You didn't have to take all five of them, Isabelle. Unless you really wanted to."

"I wanted to." She slipped the phone back into her handbag. "When will be a convenient time for me to come back with my trailer and pick them up?"

Holt wrote out a paper receipt, then went over to

one of the many file cabinets lined against the wall. "No need for that," he told her. "Myself or some of the hands will deliver them. After what you paid for the five mares, it's the least I can do."

He flipped through several folders before he finally found what he was looking for. Back at his desk, he signed the transfers and placed them, the receipt, and the registration papers in a long envelope and handed it to Isabelle.

"Here's all the paperwork. If you have any problems changing the ownership into your name, just let me know. I hope you'll be happy with the mares, Isabelle."

She stood and reached across the desktop to shake his hand. "Thank you, Holt. It's been a pleasure."

Holt rose and clasped his hand around hers. "A pleasure?" he asked wryly. "Dealing with an arrogant brute?"

A pretty pink color touched her cheeks and Holt was charmed even more by her modesty. He couldn't remember making any of his old girlfriends blush, but then none of them could be labeled modest.

"You made up for it. Especially with letting me meet Blue Midnight."

"Good. Because I'd like for us to be friends."

She pulled her hand from his and reached for her handbag on the floor. "I thought we'd already become friends."

He moved around the desk and stood in front of her. "We have. I only meant, uh, that I want us to be closer friends. The kind that have dinner together. What do you say?"

Her eyes wide with disbelief, she looked up at him. "Are you inviting me on a date?"

She made it sound like he was suggesting the two

of them make a lunar landing. "That's right. Nothing dangerous. Just a nice meal and some conversation."

Who are you trying to fool, Holt? For you, conversation with a woman is merely a means to an end. Just a step in the game of seduction. And once you do seduce Isabelle, then what? Is she the type you can brush aside like a pesky fly? You'd better think twice about this one, cowboy.

While he tried to ignore the taunting voice in his head, she said, "To be honest, I've not done any dating since my divorce. I'm not sure I'm ready to get back into that sort of thing."

That hardly sounded encouraging, Holt thought. But perhaps she meant dating in a serious way. If so, then the two of them would make a perfect couple. If there was one word in the dictionary that Holt tried his best to avoid in the presence of a woman, it was *serious*.

"Why?" he asked. "Is your heart too broken to enjoy an evening out with a man?"

She looked away from him and cleared her throat. "Do you think that's any of your business?"

She was his business. When and why he'd decided that, he didn't know. He only knew that at some point between eating pastries with her earlier this morning and making the final deal for the mares a few minutes ago, he'd become slightly infatuated with her.

"Probably not. But I'm a curious kind of guy. And I figured if I asked, you'd tell me."

She rolled her eyes and then her lips began to twitch as she fought off a smile. "Okay, since you asked, I'll tell you. I'm not carrying a torch for Trevor. My choice to stay away from dating is more about keeping myself on course with more important things."

"And having a man in your life isn't important?"

"No. And I'm not sure it will ever be important again. Not unless some incredible superman comes along. And I can't see that happening."

No. Holt couldn't see that happening either. The only superman he'd ever known was his father and he'd died several years ago.

"Sorry. Most of us guys do have faults," he said. "But I'll do my best to keep them to a minimum for one night. That is, if you're willing to spend an evening with me."

She laughed and Holt was surprised at how relieved he was to hear the sound. Normally, he didn't give a whit whether a woman turned him down. There was always another one waiting. But Isabelle was different.

"All right. I'll have dinner with you—sometime," she told him.

"Sometime? No. I'm talking about tomorrow night. I'll pick you up at six."

She placed the envelope filled with the horse papers into her handbag and pulled the strap onto her shoulder. "I might have something else to do tomorrow night."

He gave her a pointed grin. "Like feed the horses? You can let the hands do that."

She held up her hands. "These are the only hands I have."

"Oh. Then I'll come early and help you."

"Persistent, aren't you?"

"When something is important to me."

She looked at him for a long moment, then turned and started out of the office. Holt followed after her.

"Okay, I'll be ready. At six." At the door, she paused and looked back at him. "Goodbye, Holt. And thank you."

He clasped a hand around her elbow. "I'll walk you to your truck."

"That isn't necessary."

"I wasn't thinking it was a necessity. More like a pleasure."

Shaking her head, she said, "I have to say, when your older brother promised me you'd be in a better humor today, he wasn't kidding. What did he do? Give you some sort of nice pill this morning?"

Holt laughed as he ushered her through the doorway. "Isabelle, I have a feeling we're going to be more than just friends. We're going to be great friends."

The next morning Isabelle was out stretching barbed wire on a fence close to the barn when she heard the rattle of a livestock trailer.

Unfastening the stretcher from the wire, she allowed the heavy tool to fall to the ground, then turned and, shading her eyes, watched as a truck and trailer barreled up the dirt road that led to her ranch yard.

Was that Holt delivering her horses?

The mere thought that the driver of the big black ton truck might be the sexy horse trainer was enough to cause her pulse to quicken, but as she began walking in the direction of the barn, she determinedly kept her stride at a normal pace. If Holt was behind the wheel, she hardly wanted him to think she was eager to see him.

Still, she paused long enough to wipe her palms down the front of her jeans and smooth back the loose tendrils of hair that had escaped her ponytail. As for the long streak of grease on the front of her flannel shirt, there was nothing she could do about that.

However, by the time Isabelle reached the barn area, she realized all her preening had been for nothing. Instead of Holt climbing out of the truck, she spotted a pair of Three River Ranch hands. One was burly with red hair while his tall, lanky partner appeared to be much younger.

The older one of the pair was the first to introduce himself. "Hello, Ms. Townsend. I'm Pat," he said, then jerked a thumb toward the man standing next to him. "And this is Cott. We do day work for Three Rivers Ranch. Holt sent us over with your mares."

Disappointment rippled through her. Which was a totally silly reaction, she thought. He'd only suggested he might deliver the horses himself, he hadn't made it a promise. Still, it would've been kinda nice if he'd taken the time out of his busy morning to deliver the mares personally.

"Nice to meet you, Pat and Cott. Thanks for bringing the mares. If you'll follow me in the truck, I'll open the gates for you."

A few minutes later, the horses were bucking and running around the wooden corral, sending a huge cloud of dust billowing into the air. The sight of their excited antics caused Isabelle to laugh out loud.

"They're feeling good, Ms. Townsend," Pat said as he and Cott joined her outside the corral gate.

"I'm very happy to get them," she said, then politely offered, "Would you guys like something to drink? A cold bottle of water or lemonade? Sorry, but I don't have any beer."

"Thanks, but we're fine. We have water in the truck," Pat told her. "If you'll just show us where you want the feed unloaded, we'll be on our way."

Isabelle stared at him. "Excuse me? Did you say feed?"

Cott answered, "That's right. Two tons of horse feed. It's Three Rivers' special mix. Or I guess I should say

Holt's special mix. He's the one who originally concocted it."

She shook her head. "But I didn't purchase any feed from the ranch. Only the mares."

"No matter, Ms. Townsend," Cott replied. "Holt said to bring it to you and what he says goes."

Holt said. Holt said.

Just what was he trying to say to Isabelle? That much high-quality feed would be worth hundreds of dollars. Was he trying to butter her up?

She was being stupid. A man like him didn't need to score points with her, or any woman. She figured this was more about being concerned for the mares. Abruptly changing a horse's feed often caused serious health issues with their digestive track. Mixing the Three Rivers feed with hers would allow her to easily make the gradual change.

Realizing the men were waiting on her response, she gestured toward the far end of the big barn. "Okay. My feed room is around at the back of the barn. Follow me and I'll show you the way."

With the two men working in tandem, they had the stacks of fifty-pound sacks unloaded in no time. After Isabelle had thanked them and they'd driven away, she went straight to the house, where she'd left her cell phone on the kitchen counter.

A quick glance at the face told her she had two new text messages. One from her mother, who lived in San Diego, the other from Holt.

She punched Holt's open first and read: Sorry I couldn't make it with the mares. I'll see you tonight at six.

Tonight at six. The reminder caused her heart to thump hard in her chest.

What was the matter with her? Only two days before, she'd wanted Holt Hollister to jump off the rim of the Grand Canyon. How had she gone from that to agreeing to go on a date with the man? Sure, he'd been charming yesterday. But her failed marriage had left her emotionally drained. She had nothing to offer any man.

Deciding Holt's message didn't require a response, she opened the one from her mother.

I've managed to snag a showing at the Westside Gallery! Call me when you have a minute.

As far as Isabelle knew, Gabby Townsend had never had a one-minute conversation in her entire life. Especially when she got on the phone with her one and only child. But Isabelle hadn't talked with her mother in the past few days and now was just as good a time as later to call her.

Grabbing a bottle of water from the fridge, Isabelle downed a hefty drink, then sat down at the kitchen table with her phone.

"Issy, honey," her mother answered. "Can you believe my work is going to be shown at the Westside Gallery?"

The excitement in her mother's voice caused Isabelle to smile. "I absolutely can believe it. Your artwork is fabulous, Mom. It deserves to be shown to the public."

"That's what Carl said. Actually he was just as impressed with my charcoals as he was my oils, so both are going to be displayed. It's incredible!" Pausing, she let out a breathless little laugh. "I guess you can tell I'm walking on air."

"Just a bit," Isabelle said. "But you deserve to feel that way, Mom. Uh, who is this Carl? Do I know him?"

"I don't think so, dear. Carl Whitaker is the owner

of the gallery. I met him a couple of weeks ago at the Green Garden Winery. Caprice has a few of my paintings on her walls there and Carl spotted them. You remember the Green Garden, don't you? That's where that suave Italian businessman tried to pick you up."

Isabelle remembered, all right. He'd been good-looking and wealthy to boot. But she'd been turned off by his constant boasting and sleazy looks.

"You mean that snake wearing alligator shoes? I try to forget those kinds of encounters."

"If you'd cozied up to him, you might be relaxing in a Mediterranean villa about now," Gabby suggested slyly.

"I'd rather jump into quicksand with concrete blocks tied to my feet."

Gabby groaned, then said, "I don't want you to get involved with a creep, but I do wish you'd take an interest in men again. It just isn't right for you to be alone."

For some odd reason, her mother's remark caused Holt's rugged face to appear in front of her vision and she promptly tried to blink it away.

"You're alone, Mom."

"That's different," Gabby said. "I'm sixty-three. I've already done the marriage-baby thing. You have your whole life ahead of you."

Isabelle grimaced. "You're not exactly over the hill, Mom. And I've already gone through the marriage thing, too. Remember?"

Her mother's short sigh was full of frustration. "Issy, your marriage—"

After a long pause, Isabelle wanted to butt in and change the subject, but she'd learned long ago that trying to steer her mother was like trying to make a cat obey commands. The task was pretty much impossible.

Finally, Gabby said, "Yours wasn't a real marriage."

Bemused by that remark, Isabelle pulled the phone away from her ear and stared at it for a brief second before she slapped it back to the side of her head. "Excuse me, Mom, but it was real to me."

"If it was so real, then why did you divorce?"

Isabelle let out a long, weary breath. She'd not planned to get into this sort of conversation with her mother today. In fact, it had been ages since Gabby had brought up anything about Isabelle's divorce.

"Okay, Mom, let me rephrase that. It was real on my part. For Trevor, I was just an enjoyable companion."

"Oh, honey—well, at least you didn't have a baby."

Isabelle pressed a hand to her forehead and closed her eyes. "Thanks, Mom. That reminder makes me feel great."

"Isabelle, you know what I mean. It's terrible when a child is passed back and forth between parents—just because the parents can't cohabitate. Just look at your own parents. Look what it did to you."

Isabelle's parents had divorced while she'd been in middle school. And back then, she would've been lying if she said it hadn't upended her life. She'd loved her father dearly and when he'd moved out of the house, she'd felt like he'd deserted her and her mother. She'd been too young to fully understand that her parents had divorced because they'd been two different souls, both wanting and needing different things in life.

"It hurt for a while. But I think I turned out fairly normal."

Gabby said gently, "You're better than normal. Especially with having a pair of hippies for parents."

Isabelle chuckled. "You and Dad aren't hippies. You're free spirits."

"Aww, that's a sweet way of putting it, honey. Most of our friends would describe us as harebrained or worse."

"Who cares? As long as you're both happy."

"I'm certainly happy. And I think your father is, too. The last I talked with him, he was in New Orleans playing nightly on Bourbon Street."

Her father, Nolan, was an accomplished pianist. Twenty years ago, he'd helped to form a small jazz band. Since then, the group had traveled all over the country playing small venues. He'd made a decent living at his profession, but like Gabby, his craft was really all he cared about. As long as he was making music, he was happy.

"Hmm. A dream gig for him," Isabelle replied. "I haven't talked with him in a while. I'll give him a call soon."

"He'd like that."

Once again, Holt's image swaggered across her mind's eye and the unexpected distraction caused her to pause long enough to cause her mother concern.

"Issy, is something wrong? Have you quarreled with your father?"

"No. Nothing is wrong. Actually, I was thinking about someone," she admitted. "Believe it or not, I'm going on a date tonight."

Gabby reacted with a long stretch of silence.

"Mom, are you still there? Or have you fallen over in a dead faint?"

Gabby laughed softly. "I'm still conscious. Just a bit surprised."

Isabelle said, "I'm surprised at myself. I'm having dinner with the rancher that sold horses to me. It's just sort of a thank-you date on both sides. Him for selling and me for buying."

"Oh. Sure, I see. It's really a business dinner or… something like that."

Business? Isabelle could hardly look across the table at Holt and think business. In fact, she doubted she'd be able to think about much at all. But her mother didn't need to know her daughter was looking at any man in such an intimate way.

"I'm very happy for you, Mom. Maybe you'll sell a few things and you can book that trip to Hawaii you've been wanting to take."

"I'm not really worried so much about selling right now. I'm just happy to have my work exhibited in such a notable gallery. The rest will take care of itself," she said, then asked, "Will you be able to come down on the opening day? I'll be there to meet and greet and the gallery is supplying refreshments."

"When is this happening?"

"Two weeks from this coming Saturday. Don't worry. I'll remind you."

"I'll try. But I can't make any promises. It all depends if I can hire a couple of hands between now and then. Until someone is here to care for the horses, I can't leave the ranch for more than a few hours at a time."

"Have you advertised for help?"

"I don't want to go that route. I'm afraid I'd have all sorts of creeps coming out here to the ranch. Before I hire anyone, I'm going to ask around and get some recommendations."

"I understand. Don't worry about the showing. You have your hands full right now. We'll get together later on."

"I'd love that, Mom. Now, I've got to hang up and get back to my fence repairs."

Gabby let out a good-natured groan. "My beautiful

little girl out building fence instead of making use of her college degree."

"I'm happier now than I've ever been."

"You're just as much of a free spirit as your parents," she said gently. "And that's okay, too. Perhaps you can talk the rancher into helping you with the fence."

Holt Hollister stretching barbed wire? He was ranching royalty, a boss on one of the largest ranches in the state of Arizona. Isabelle seriously doubted he'd ever touched a posthole digger or a roll of wire.

"I can't talk that fast, Mom," Isabelle said with a laugh.

"Then add a little wink or two between words," Gabby suggested.

"Uh, if you knew what this guy looked like you wouldn't be giving me that kind of advice."

"Why? Ugly as sin?"

"No. Sinfully handsome."

"Oh," she drawled in a suggestive tone. "I need to hear more about this man."

Isabelle chuckled. "Bye, Mom. I'll call you soon."

"Isabelle—"

"Yes?"

"I'll keep my fingers crossed for you, honey."

Gabby ended the call and Isabelle put down the phone, but she didn't immediately leave the chair. Instead, she sat there thinking about Holt and their date tonight. She'd only agreed to go out with him so she could bend his ear about the horse breeding business, she told herself. And for no other reason.

Next time she talked to her mother, she'd explain the situation. For now it wouldn't hurt to let Gabby believe her daughter was interested in finding a man to love.

Chapter Four

Holt couldn't remember the last time he'd been any-where near the old Landry Ranch. Not since the fam-ily had moved to Idaho several years ago and put the property on the market. Holt had practically forgotten all about the deserted ranch. Until Isabelle had shown up on Three Rivers and Blake had informed him that she'd purchased the place.

Located about eighteen miles north of Three Riv-ers by way of a ten-mile stretch of narrow asphalt, plus eight more miles of rough, graveled road, the land butted up to only a half-mile section of Three Rivers' land. But that was enough for the Hollisters to consider the owner a neighbor.

Before he'd left home this evening, Holt had been about to step out the door when Blake had caught up to him. Seeing his brother had been curious as to where he was going on a weeknight, Holt had explained he was having dinner with Isabelle. In response, Blake had barely lifted an eyebrow.

I didn't figure you'd waste any time trying to get her into your bed, he'd said.

Ordinarily, Blake's coarse comment would've elicited a laugh from Holt. But Holt hadn't laughed. In fact, he'd felt strangely annoyed at his brother. Blake didn't really know Isabelle and to imply she was an easy girl had hardly been fair. But Holt figured his brother's remark had been more directed at him than at Isabelle.

The road he was traveling climbed a hill covered with agave and century plants, then curved abruptly to the right through spires of rock formation. After another curve in the opposite direction, the landscape opened up and far to his left he could see the house and the nearby cluster of barns and work sheds.

Holt remembered the ranch being in a beautiful area of Yavapai County, but until this moment he'd never really thought about how isolated the property was from neighbors or town. The idea of a tiny thing like Isabelle living out here alone left him uneasy. But then, she wasn't his responsibility. And how she chose to live was nobody's business but her own.

He'd barely had time to stop the truck in front of the hacienda-style house when he spotted Isabelle emerging from the front door. The sight of her jolted him and for a moment after he'd killed the motor, he sat there watching her walk to the edge of the porch.

She was wearing a black sweater dress that stopped just above her knees. The fabric clung to the curves of her body, while black dress boots outlined her shapely calves. Her blond hair was brushed to one side and waved against the side of her face. She looked sexy as hell and he wondered how he was supposed to eat a bite of food with that sort of temptation sitting across from him.

Collecting the flat box from the passenger seat, he left the truck and walked to the porch where she waited for him.

"Hello, Holt," she greeted. "I see you found the place."

The smile on her face was like sunshine on a spring day and it sent his spirit soaring.

"It wasn't hard. I've been here a few times. Back when the Landrys still lived here." He offered the box to her. "Here's a little something for you."

She took the fancy chocolates. "Thank you, Holt. This should keep up my energy."

He grinned. "I figured with all those extra horses you bought from me, you'd need it."

She gestured to the door behind her. "Would you like to come in and have a drink before we go?"

"That would be nice. We have plenty of time to make our dinner reservations."

She tossed him a wary glance before moving toward the front door. "You made reservations?"

"That's what I normally do when I go out to eat. Don't you?" he asked, as he followed her over the threshold and down a short, wide foyer decorated with potted succulents and a wooden parson's bench.

"No. I normally go to a fast-food joint. Or a café where you simply walk in and sit wherever you'd like."

They entered a long living area and Isabelle walked over and placed the box of chocolates on a dark oak coffee table.

"Well, I do that sort of thing with my buddies or my brothers," he admitted, then grinned at her. "If I took you out for a hot dog, you might think I was cheap."

She walked back over to where he stood and Holt was

once again staggered by the incredible smoothness of her skin, the vivid blue of her eyes. He'd heard the term *breathtaking* used many a time, but he'd never experienced it until he laid his eyes on Isabelle.

"As long as there's good conversation to go with the hot dog, I'd be happy."

Was she really that easy to please? She didn't look like a simple woman, he thought. But then, she didn't look like a hardworking horsewoman either. "I'll try to remember that."

An impish little smile played around her lips as she gestured to a long, moss green couch.

"Have a seat," she invited, "and I'll get the drinks. What would you like? Something alcoholic or a soft drink?"

Deciding he'd be able to breathe a bit better if he put some distance between them, he walked over and took a seat on the end of the couch, then crossed his boots out in front of him. "I'd really like a bourbon and Coke, but since I'm driving, a soft drink will do."

"I'll be right back," she told him.

She disappeared through an arched doorway and Holt glanced curiously around the long living room. He decided there was nothing frilly or overly feminine in Isabelle's taste. The furniture was solid and comfortable and all done in rich earth tones of greens and browns and yellows. Braided rugs added a splash of color to the dark hardwood floors. A TV filled one corner, while a tall bookshelf filled another, and though he was only guessing, Holt figured Isabelle reached for a book far more than she reached for the TV remote.

At the front of the room, a large picture window looked out at a distant cluster of hills dotted with cacti and rock formations. Since there were no curtains or blinds, Holt figured she either appreciated the view or enjoyed the sunshine streaming into the room or both.

The click of her high-heeled boots announced her return and he looked around to see her approaching with a glass of iced cola in each hand.

"Thank you," he said, taking the glass she offered.

"Would you like a chocolate to go with your soda?"

"No, thanks. I don't want to ruin my appetite."

She took a seat on the opposite end of the couch and carefully adjusted the hem of her dress toward her knees. The action drew Holt's attention to the shape of her legs and he found himself imagining what her thighs would feel like wrapped around his hips. Even though she was small, he had the feeling she'd be a strong lover. One that would look him boldly in the eye and dare him to thrill her.

"I'm glad I got this chance to talk with you before we left for dinner," she said.

Her voice jerked him out of the erotic daydreams and as he looked at her, he hoped to heck she couldn't read his mind.

"Pardon me, but what can we talk about here that we can't talk about later?"

"The feed you sent over with the mares. I need to pay you for it."

"The grain was a bonus that went with the mares. I won't accept pay for the feed."

She grimaced and looked away from him. "That makes me feel…very uncomfortable."

"Why? I've thrown in extras on other horse deals." Which was true, he thought. But he'd never given anyone else as much as he'd given her. The feed was something they mixed for their own use on Three Rivers. It wasn't sold or given to anyone. Until Holt had broken the rules this morning and sent her two tons of it. But she didn't need to know any of that. Nor did she need to know Blake had been a bit peeved at Holt's unusual generosity.

"I'm sorry you feel that way," he said. "It was meant to help you and the mares."

She leveled him with a pointed look. "And that's all?"

"What else?" he asked.

Through narrowed eyes, he watched her nervously lick her lips.

"Nothing, I suppose." She shrugged and glanced down at her drink. "I just don't like feeling beholden to anyone."

So she didn't want to owe him anything. Holt could understand her feelings. What he couldn't understand was how this woman affected him, how much he'd like for her to depend on him for advice and help and whatever else she needed. Which made no sense at all.

"That wasn't my intention," he said. "In case you hadn't noticed, I care deeply about my horses and even after they no longer belong to me, I want to know they're well taken care of. The feed was to help them make the transition from Three Rivers to here. It wasn't some sort of bribe for romantic favors. If that's what you were thinking."

The compression of her lips coupled with the bright pink color on her cheeks told Holt she was more than embarrassed; she was also annoyed.

"That wasn't what I was implying—well, not exactly," she said stiffly. "Anyway, I honestly doubt you need to play such silly games with the women you date."

Silly games? His sister Vivian had often accused him of playing women for fools. But that wasn't true. He never tried to manipulate a woman's feelings. That would be like trying to ride a horse without a bridle. It wasn't an impossible task, but it would take way more patience and time than he had.

He shook his head. "It's obvious you've already heard gossip about me. That I'm a playboy or worse."

The color on her face turned a deeper shade. "Believe me, Holt, whether you're a playboy or not means little to me. What you do with your private life is your business. You and I are just having dinner. That's all."

Just dinner. That's all he wanted, too, Holt thought. Having anything more to do with this woman would be inviting trouble. The kind he didn't need.

In spite of feeling oddly deflated, he smiled at her. "I'm glad we got all of that behind us. So if you're ready, I think we should be leaving. The drive to the restaurant takes a while."

Appearing relieved by his suggestion, she rose to her feet. "Certainly. Just let me get my bag and coat."

While she gathered her things from a nearby chair, Holt placed his empty glass on the coffee table and left the couch to join her. As he helped her slip into the coat, he was stuck by her flowery scent and small, vulnerable size. He could swing her into his arms without any effort at all. And with the silence of the house surrounding them, he could easily imagine himself carrying her to bed.

Dinner is what this evening is about, Holt. Remember? Not sex or drama or stifling strings or a broken heart.

And why the heck should his heart get involved if he took this woman to bed? He practically yelled the retort back at the negative voice going off in his head. He was thirty-three years old and he'd never made the mistake of falling in love. It wasn't going to happen to him. Not now. Not ever. He had nothing to worry about.

As Holt drove the two of them away from the ranch, Isabelle studied him from the corner of her eye. She couldn't deny he looked incredibly handsome tonight in a white shirt and dark Western-cut slacks. A bolo tie with a slide fashioned of onyx and silver was pushed almost to the top button, which had been left open. The black cowboy hat settled low on his forehead was made of incredibly smooth felt, the sort that cost a fortune. But the price of the hat was probably only a fraction of what he'd paid for the fish-skin boots.

The fact that Holt Hollister was rich should have been a total turnoff. Once her divorce to Trevor had become final, she'd made a silent vow to never waste her time or emotions on a rich man. From her experience, a man with stacks of money was rarely the homey sort.

He glanced in her direction. "Pat and Cott tell me you're looking to hire some day workers."

While the two men had been unloading the feed, she'd mentioned she needed to find a couple of dependable ranch hands. Apparently they'd relayed the information to Holt.

"That's right. I need help with the heavier chores. Right now I'm repairing fence and it's a rather hard job to do with only one pair of hands."

He shook his head. "Building fence without help is asking for trouble."

"The way I see it, working with a pair of creeps trying to take advantage of me is more dangerous than building fence alone."

"Hmm. You do have a point there."

She looked out at the passing landscape. "Trevor left

me pretty well set financially. But not well enough for me to pay two hefty salaries every month. I can't manage that until the ranch starts making a profit. Which won't be for a long time yet. Right now I'd be happy to find a pair of trustworthy wranglers willing to work a few hours a day."

"My family and I have plenty of connections. Maybe we can help you with that."

"I'd appreciate your help, Holt."

He glanced at her and grinned, and Isabelle thought how different he seemed now from that first day she'd walked up to him in the horse barn. He'd been cold and abrupt and anything but charming. The guy sitting next to her tonight had to be the one that Emily-Ann had called dreamy.

He asked, "Have you always been so adventurous?"

"What do you mean?"

"Other than my mother, I can't think of one woman who'd be brave enough or ambitious enough to take on the huge task of starting a horse ranch. The idea of living alone in an isolated area would be enough to put most women off."

She didn't know whether he was giving her a compliment or questioning her wisdom. But then, it didn't really matter what this man thought of her. Did it?

"I've never been the timid sort. My parents always taught me to follow my dreams, no matter how big or daunting."

"What do your parents think about this new endeavor of yours?"

"They're very supportive. Honestly, the idea of me failing at anything never crosses my father's mind. He, uh, sort of lives in his own little world. He's a musician, you see, and has played piano in a jazz band for more than twenty years. My mother believes in me, too. Except that sometimes she worries about me. She's a very open-minded person, but she has this old-fashioned notion that I'd be happier with a man in my life. Thankfully she'd doesn't pester me too much about it, though. With her being single herself, there's not much she can say."

He glanced curiously at her. "Your parents aren't together?"

"No. Not since I was a small girl. But they're still good friends."

"Hmm. Must be something that runs in your family."

"Divorce, you mean?"

"No. Being divorced friends. Like you and—what's his name?"

"Oh, like me and Trevor." She shrugged. "I guess in that way I'm like my parents. Except that they had a child together. Trevor and I didn't. Which is a blessing—that's what Gabby thinks."

"Gabby?"

"That's my mother's name. Her real name is Gabrielle, but no one ever calls her that."

His expression turned thoughtful. "So Gabby is relieved you didn't have a child with this Trevor guy. Are you?"

"Am I what?"

"Relieved that you don't share a child with your ex."

He was getting too personal, but then she'd practically asked for it with all this chattering she'd been doing. Darn it, she'd been talking way too much. Because she was nervous, she silently reasoned with herself. Not because she found this man easy to talk to.

Shifting around in the seat, she tugged the hem of her dress closer to her knees. "*Relieved* is the wrong word,

Holt. *Sad* is closer to it. I promised myself that whenever I had a child it would be with a man who loved me. Trevor didn't fall into that category."

A frown puckered his forehead. "You can tell me to mind my own business, but why did you marry him if you believed he didn't love you?"

He couldn't begin to know how many times she'd called herself a fool, or how often she'd questioned her hasty decision to marry. "We had a whirlwind courtship and when Trevor whisked me off to a wedding chapel in Las Vegas, it was all so romantic. It felt like love. Later on I learned differently."

"I see."

How could he see? He'd never been married. And from the vibes she'd been getting from him, she seriously doubted he'd ever been in love.

"You do?" she asked quietly.

"Sure. Your ex mostly wanted a pretty woman on his arm and in his bed. Now you want a real husband and children. But you aren't interested in dating. How's that going to work out?"

Her short laugh was a cynical sound. "I'm only twenty-eight. I have a few years before my childbearing days are over."

His only reaction to her answer was the slight arch of one brow, and Isabelle figured he was probably thinking she was impulsive and silly and not the sort of woman he'd ever want to get involved with. Well, that was good, she told herself. Because he was the sort of man who would never fit into her future plans.

Twenty miles and just as many minutes later, darkness had settled across the desert landscape and Holt turned off the main highway and onto a narrow asphalt

road. As the truck began to climb into a forested mountain, Isabelle grew increasingly curious.

"Excuse me, Holt, but are you sure we're going to
dinner? This looks more like we're on the road to a
hunting cabin. I'm getting the feeling that our food is
hanging from a hook and you're going to cook it over
an open fire."

He laughed. "What little I can cook, you wouldn't
want to eat. Trust me. We're going to have a regular
sit-down dinner with glass plates and silverware. No
throwaway plastic."

"Do you always go this far out of town to eat? Or
are you just driving this far to avoid being seen with
me in Wickenburg?"

He laughed again and the sexy sound slid down her
backbone like the warm tip of a finger.

"Now, why wouldn't I want to be seen with you?"

"You might have lady friends there who wouldn't appreciate seeing you with me," she said shrewdly.

"That would be their problem, not mine," he said,
then added, "Actually, I'm driving this far because the
place is unique and I thought you might enjoy it. Plus
the food is delicious. Their specialty is Italian, but they
have American dishes on the menu, too."

"I'm not hard to please," she told him. "I would probably even eat whatever you cooked over the fire."

He chuckled. "Maybe I'll practice up and put you to
the test sometime."

Holt had been right when he'd said the restaurant was
unique. The gray stone structure resembled an English
manor and was perched high on the edge of a mountain.
Footlights were strategically placed on the grounds to

illuminate the planked board entrance and a beautiful lawn that was canopied with tall pines and spruce.

"This is like a forested fairyland, Holt. It's... completely enchanting!"

"I'm glad you approve."

He helped her out of the truck, then tossed the keys to a waiting valet. Then curving an arm against her back, he urged her toward the main entrance.

Once inside, they were greeted by a young hostess. She promptly ushered them to a small, square table near a wall of plate glass.

After they were seated and the hostess had disappeared, Isabelle looked around in fascination at the sea of linen-covered tables, tall beamed ceilings, and intricate tiled floor. As Holt had suggested, it was unique and very special.

"Beyond the glass wall, there's a balcony with tables. Usually in the winter, they keep a fire going in the firepit. It's a nice place to have after-dinner coffee—if you'd like," he suggested.

"Sounds wonderful," she agreed, then asked, "What do you usually eat when you come here?"

"Steak." Chuckling, he attempted to defend his mundane choice. "What can I say? I'm a rancher. But I do usually get ravioli or spaghetti with it. That gets me a bit out of the box, doesn't it?"

She laughed. "The spaghetti alone puts you way out of the box."

A young waiter arrived with menus and Holt ordered a bottle of sparkling red wine. While they sipped and waited for the first course of their meal to be served, Isabelle did her best to keep the conversation on the safest subject she could think of, which in their case was raising horses. But after a while, she found herself wanting to know more about Holt Hollister the man, rather than the successful horse breeder.

Throughout the delicious dinner, she managed to tamp down the personal questions, but after they moved to a table on the balcony, her guard began to relax and before she knew it, she was encouraging him to talk about himself and his family.

"So you got your love of horses from your father?" she asked, as they enjoyed cups of rich, dark coffee.

Behind her, the crackling heat from the firepit warmed her back and cast an orange gold glow over Holt's rugged features. Nearby, in a ballroom attached to the balcony, music had begun to play and the occasional sound of laughter drifted out to them. The atmosphere was decidedly romantic, Isabelle thought, but she was trying hard not to focus on that part of the evening.

He nodded. "The first time Dad put me on a horse I was too small to walk. Mom said I screamed to the top of my lungs when the ride ended. Dad was a great horseman and I always wanted to be just like him."

"You must have achieved your goal. From what people around Wickenburg have told me, you're a regular horse whisperer."

Smiling modestly, he shook his head. "I might be good with horses, but I'll never be the man that Dad was."

She frowned. "You keep saying was. Isn't your father still living?"

For the first time since she'd met Holt, she saw an unmistakable look of sadness on his face.

"Dad—his name was Joel—died over six years ago. An incident with a horse. He was found with his boot hung in the stirrup. He'd been dragged—for a long distance."

She gasped. "Oh, how tragic, Holt. To lose him that way—I mean, to have his death connected to a horse—something he dearly loved. Something you dearly love. It's horrible."

He cleared his throat, then took a sip of coffee before he finally replied, "A horse didn't kill Dad."

Totally confused by his remark, she stared at him. "What?"

His gaze left her face and settled on the shadows beyond the balcony. "I shouldn't have said that. We—don't really know what happened to Dad. But we're pretty damned sure the horse didn't have anything to do with his death."

The tightness of his features told her there was much more to this story, more than he wanted to talk about. And it suddenly dawned on her that Holt Hollister might've been born into wealth, but his life hadn't been without heartache.

"Oh," she said. "Then you're thinking he must have had a heart attack or stroke or some sudden medical problem while he was out riding."

"That would be the logical deduction, but you're wrong. The autopsy showed no sign of any medical issue. Dad was in great health." He looked at her, his expression both bleak and frustrated. "At that time, the Yavapai County sheriff was a close friend of ours. He ruled Dad's death as an accident. Only because he didn't have enough evidence to prove otherwise. He passed away a few years ago from lung disease, or he would still be working on the case."

In spite of the fire behind her, she felt chilled. "Evidence? You mean—that someone—purposely harmed your father?"

He nodded. "That's what I'm saying. My brothers

and I have been searching for answers all these years. We think we're getting close to finding out what really happened, but we need a few more pieces to put the whole puzzle together."

"I'm so sorry, Holt. I didn't realize your father was gone, much less that anything so—horrible had occurred. I'm sure it's not something you want to talk about."

He shrugged. "Sometimes it helps to talk about things that hurt."

Yes, like having a husband who hadn't loved her. Like desperately wanting children and not having any. Yes, she'd experienced things that hurt.

"What happened with the horse your father was riding?"

"Major Bob is still on the ranch," he said fondly. "Still being used in the working remuda. That's the way Dad would've wanted it. And once Major Bob grows old and dies, he'll be buried on the ranch next to Dad. They were great buddies."

"Like me and Albert." Tears suddenly filled her eyes and she blinked rapidly and reached for her coffee in an effort to hide them. "I'd like to see Major Bob and the rest of the remuda sometime. If that's possible." She gave him a wry smile. "I'm sure you've already come to the conclusion that I'm horse crazy. Or maybe just crazy in general."

"Not yet." He grinned and gestured toward her cup. "If you've had enough of coffee, let's walk over to the ballroom. It has a really nice dance floor."

Isabelle loved to dance. But she wasn't at all sure about taking a spin around the dance floor in Holt's arms. No. That wouldn't be smart, at all.

"I, uh, think I'd better pass on the dancing."

His eyes narrowed with speculation. "Why? Scared you might miss a step and crush my toes?"

She purposely straightened her shoulders. "No. I'm not scared of missing a step. Anyway, I'm not heavy enough to crush your toes."

Laughing, he rose to his feet and reached for her hand. "Then I don't have a thing to worry about. And neither do you."

Deciding it would look silly to protest too much, she allowed him to pull her to her feet and lead her across the balcony.

As they entered the ballroom, the band began playing a slow ballad and Isabelle didn't have time to ready herself. He quickly pulled her into his arms and guided her among the group of dancers circling the floor.

Even if she'd had hours to brace herself, she wouldn't have been prepared for the onslaught of sensations rushing through her. Having his strong arm against her back and her hand clasped tightly in his was enough to cause her breathing to go haywire. But to have the front of his rock-hard body pressed to hers was totally shattering her senses.

"This is nice," he said. "Very nice."

His voice wasn't far from her ear and she knew if she turned her head slightly to the right, she'd be looking him square in the face. The thought of what that would do to her put a freeze on her neck muscles and kept her gaze fixed on a point of his shoulder.

"I've not danced in a long time," she admitted, hoping the sound of the music hid the husky tone of her voice. "I'm a little rusty."

He moved his hand ever so slightly against her back and she momentarily closed her eyes against the heat that was slowly and surely beginning to spread through her body.

"It's just like riding a horse," he murmured. "You get in rhythm and the rest comes naturally."

The man was undoubtedly a master at the art of seduction and if she didn't do something and fast, she was going to become his next victim.

"I'm beginning to think I should have worn my boots and spurs," she said.

His fingers tightened around hers and she wondered why the touch of his hand felt so good against hers.

"You know what I'm beginning to think?" he asked.

"I won't try to guess."

"You're scared of me."

That was all it took to repair the paralysis in her neck and she turned her head until her gaze was locked with his.

Lifting her chin to a challenging angle, she said, "I'm not scared of anyone."

The corners of his lips tilted ever so slightly. "You think that's wise?"

Nothing about being with this man was wise. But it was darned thrilling. And every woman needed to be thrilled once in a while, she decided.

She said, "I'd rather be brave than wise. Besides, I'm beginning to think you might just be a little afraid of me."

Amused by her remark, he grinned and Isabelle forced her gaze to remain boldly locked onto his.

"And why would I be afraid of you?" he asked.

She could feel her heart beating way too fast and hard. But with Holt's arms fastened around her, there was no way she could make her pulse settle back to a normal rhythm.

"You might get to liking me so much you'll decide to sell Blue Midnight to me," she answered.

Laughing, he pulled her even tighter against him. "Oh, Isabelle, this evening is turning out to be better than I could've ever imagined."

Her resistance a crumbling mess, Isabelle rested her cheek against his shoulder and promised herself that she had nothing to worry about. This was just one dance, Holt was just like any other man, and tomorrow when she was back to stretching barbed wire, this magical night would be nothing more than a pleasant memory.

Chapter Five

The next morning Holt was up early enough to make his rounds at the barn and get back to the house for breakfast, which Reeva normally served at five thirty.

When he entered the dining room, the dishes of food were just starting to make their way around the long oak table. The scent of warm tortillas and chorizo made his stomach growl with hunger.

Blake, who always sat at the end of the table next to their father's empty chair, looked up as Holt sat down next to his sister-in-law Roslyn.

"Good morning, Holt," he said. "I thought you were probably sleeping in."

Evelyn, his baby niece, was sitting on her mother's lap and Holt leaned over and kissed the top of her little head before he glanced down the table at Blake.

Holt smirked at him. "You know I've never slept past six o'clock in my life. Even on my sick days."

Sitting on the opposite side of Roslyn, his brother Chandler let out an amused grunt. "What sick days? You've never so much as had a sore throat."

At that moment, Jazelle leaned over Holt's shoulder to fill his cup with steaming hot coffee. He gave the maid a wink before he replied to his brother's comment.

"It's all my clean living," Holt told him. "Keeps me healthy and fit."

Everyone at the table let out good-natured groans.

"Sure, Holt," Chandler said. "If only we could all be as straitlaced as you, we'd live to be a hundred or more."

"Where's Nick and the twins?" he directed the question to his sister-in-law Katherine while he filled his plate with eggs.

"Upstairs," she told him. "The twins are still asleep and Nick volunteered to watch them while his mom has breakfast with the rest of the family."

Holt nodded knowingly. "Nick is like me. Thoughtful."

Blake and Chandler groaned. Katherine said, "Nick is thoughtful. But he's also wise. He wants to go to the res this weekend and ride horses with Hannah."

"See, the boy is like me," Holt reiterated.

Blake rolled his eyes, then asked, "So how did your date with our new little neighbor go last night?"

Chandler glanced around the group at the table. "What new little neighbor?"

"She bought the old Landry Ranch," Blake explained. "And she's just Holt's type—young, beautiful, and single."

"What other type should I have?" Holt asked as he shook a heavy hand of black pepper over his food. "Homely and married?"

Holt had directed the question at Blake, but Chandler was the one to answer.

"I'm beginning to think you shouldn't be looking at any type," he said. "It's damned annoying to have your jilted girlfriends come into the clinic wanting me to give you nasty messages."

"Sorry," Holt told him. "The next time that happens just give her a worm pill and send her on her way."

"You're a worm all right," Blake retorted. "You worm right out of every relationship you've ever started."

Frowning, Holt picked up his coffee cup. Normally, he would simply laugh off his brothers' remarks, but this morning he wasn't feeling amused. True, after years of playing the field, he deserved a few negative comments from his family. But Blake and Chandler were already assuming that Isabelle would end up being just another jilted lover. They had no inkling that Isabelle was different. And that he had no intentions of treating her like a disposable toy.

Really, Holt? Last night when you took her home, you were practically panting for her to ask you in for a nightcap. All you could think about was creating a chance to make love to her. And if she'd given you one, you wouldn't have turned it down. So don't be thinking Isabelle is any different. That you want to be a different man with her. You can't change, Holt. You're a cheater, a user. You'd never be able to exist as a one-woman man. So get over these soft feelings you're having toward the woman.

Hating the taunting voice in his head, Holt sipped his coffee and did his best to ignore it.

"What is this?" he asked. "Be mean to Holt morning?"

"I'm with Holt," Roslyn said. "You two are being

mean to your brother. Just because you both decided to become married men doesn't mean that Holt wants to go down that same path. He has a right to date who and when he wants."

"Thank you, Ros," Holt told her. "I'm glad someone around here is willing to stand up for me. And by the way, where is Mom? She's never late to the breakfast table. Has she already eaten?"

Katherine was the one to answer. "She gulped down a cup of coffee and a doughnut. She's in a hurry to go to Phoenix this morning."

Holt exchanged a concerned look with Chandler. "Phoenix? Again?"

Chandler gave him a clueless shrug, while Blake said, "She's going to some sort of meeting for Arizona ranching women. Frankly, I think she just needs to get away for a few hours. And God knows she deserves some free time. We all know she works too hard."

A stretch of silence passed before Chandler said, "Maybe she's going to see Uncle Gil, too."

Holt stabbed his fork into the mound of eggs on his plate. For the past few months, everyone in the family had noticed a change in Maureen. At times she appeared preoccupied and even depressed. They all understood that she missed their late father. But this was something different. It was almost like she was hiding something from the family.

"Yeah. I'd make a bet she meets with Gil," Holt said flatly.

Gil was Joel's younger brother. He'd worked on the Phoenix police force for more than thirty years and had never married. Everyone in the family had been expecting the man to soon retire, but so far he'd made no sign of giving up his career as a detective.

Holt could feel Blake's skeptical gaze boring into him. "And what's wrong with her seeing Uncle Gil?" Blake asked. "They've always been close."

"Nothing is wrong." Holt wished he hadn't said anything. Now everyone was looking at him as though he some sort of inside information. Which he didn't.

The group around the table suddenly went silent. Except for little Evelyn. The baby began to fuss and reach her arms out for Holt to take her.

Happy for the diversion, Holt gathered the girl from Roslyn and with his arm safely around her waist, stood her on his thigh. She immediately began to laugh and tug on his ear. He tickled her belly and as she giggled with delight, Isabelle drifted through his thoughts.

I've always wanted children.

Her revelation hadn't surprised Holt. At some point in their lives, most women did want to become mothers. And yet, hearing her voice her wishes had been a reminder that she was off-limits to him. That sometime soon, he'd have to step aside and allow her to find a man who'd give her children. A man who could give her that real love she'd talked about.

For some inexplicable reason, the idea saddened him, but he wasn't going to allow himself to dwell on the situation. Isabelle was sweet and lovely and a joy to be around. It wouldn't hurt anything to date her a few more times before he told her goodbye. And by then, he was certain he'd be ready to move on to the next pretty face.

Later that afternoon, after riding fence line for more than two hours, Isabelle returned to the ranch yard and was unsaddling her horse when an old red Ford truck barreled up the long drive and pulled to a stop a few feet away from the barn.

The vehicle wasn't Holt's and Emily-Ann drove a car. Since those were the only two people she knew well enough to make the long drive out here, she couldn't imagine who this might be.

Swinging the saddle onto the top board of the corral, she walked toward the vehicle. She was halfway there when two men climbed to the ground, wearing stained straw hats, kerchiefs around their necks, and Sherpa-lined jean jackets that had seen better days.

The taller of the two lifted a hand in greeting. "Are you Ms. Townsend?"

She walked across the hard-packed dirt to join them. "I'm Isabelle Townsend," she said a bit cautiously. "This place is a far distance from town. Are you guys lost?"

"We probably look like we're lost, but we aren't. We know this whole county like the back of our hand," the shorter one said with a wide grin. "My name is Ollie and my partner here is Sol."

Ollie had a stocky build with mousy brown hair and a mouth full of crooked teeth. His partner was as thin as a reed and what little she could see of his hair beneath the bent hat was snow-white. Isabelle gauged both men to be somewhere in their early sixties, but since the Arizona climate was rough on a person, they could've been younger.

"Nice to meet you. Is there something I can do for you?"

Sol decided it was his turn to speak. "We heard you needed ranch hands. We're here for the job."

Isabelle studied both men as her mind whirled with questions. The only people she'd talked with about hiring help was Holt, and the men who'd delivered her mares. So how did this pair know she was thinking about hiring?

"I haven't advertised for help. Who sent you here?" she asked.

Ollie cast a cagey look at his partner. "Reckon we might as well tell her, Sol. She has to know."

"Tell me what?" Isabelle asked, then decided to voice her suspicions out loud. "Did Holt Hollister send you over here?"

"Well, he didn't exactly send us," Ollie said a bit sheepishly. "It was like this, we were in the Broken Spur having a cup of coffee and he just happened to stroll in. The subject of work was brought up and he told us about you needing an honest pair of men to help you."

"And that's us, Ms. Townsend," Sol added. "Honest as the day is long. Just ask the Hollisters. We've done day work at Three Rivers for close to thirty years now."

Ollie nodded. "That's right, Ms. Townsend. And we can do about anything you might need. Sol's a damned good farrier, too. He can save you lots of money."

Isabelle didn't know what to say, much less think. These two were just the sort she needed here on the ranch. Older, polite, and experienced with ranch work. She wouldn't have to waste time showing them every little thing that needed to be done.

"You men aren't working anywhere right now?"

The two cowboys glanced at each other again as though neither one of them knew how to answer her question.

"Uh—no," Ollie told her.

Sol shook his head. "Not steady. But we can be steady for you, Ms. Townsend. We're ready to go to work right now. Got our gear in the truck."

"Well, I'm going to have to think about this," she told them. "I do need help. But there's no way I can match the wages that Three Rivers pays you. And I can only afford to use you a few hours a day. You guys are probably looking for full-time work."

Again, the two men looked at each other and Isabelle decided the pair were like twins; one didn't make a move without the other.

"Oh, no. We aren't worried about wages, Ms. Townsend," Ollie assured her. "We're happy with whatever you can pay us."

Sol added, "We're all set to work every day. We don't have anything better to do. If you got some place we can bunk, we'll be as happy as a bear in a tree full of honey."

Isabelle stared at the two men in disbelief. "I must have missed something," she said. "You two are willing to bunk here and work full-time for part-time wages?"

Sol grinned. "Why sure. That way we can sorta be your bodyguards. It's not safe for a woman like you to be living out here alone. Any kind of riffraff could wander up here at night."

Shaking her head, she said, "I don't know what to say about any of this."

"No need to say anything," Ollie told her. "Except you might show us where we can put our saddles and our horses. We have two mares and two geldings between us. They're in the trailer waiting to be unloaded. So you won't have to worry about mounting us on working horses."

Ever since Isabelle had moved onto the ranch, she'd been worrying and wondering how she was going to hire good, reliable help. The idea that it had practically fallen into her lap had left her a little dazed and a whole lot suspicious.

"I think—" Before she could go on, the cell phone in her shirt pocket began to ring. Annoyed with the interruption, she said, "Excuse me, guys."

"You go right ahead, Ms. Townsend," Sol said. "We'll go unload our horses."

The men walked away to tend to their horses and Isabelle tugged the phone from her shirt pocket. To her surprise, the caller was Holt.

"Hello, Holt. I wasn't expecting to hear from you today."

His raspy chuckle immediately took her back to last night when he'd held her in his arms on the dance floor. She still hadn't recovered her shattered senses.

"I couldn't wait to hear your voice again," he said.

He was teasing and she took his words in that manner. "Is that why you called me? Just to hear my voice?"

He chuckled again. "Partly. I also wanted to see if Ollie and Sol have shown up yet. I thought you might be concerned and want a reference."

She looked toward the old red Ford and faded white trailer hooked behind it. The men had already unloaded one horse and Ollie was tying the bay to a hitching ring. The men were the real deal and would be a great help. But she couldn't afford them and, furthermore, Holt knew it.

"You sent them out here, didn't you?"

"They needed something to do. Presently, Three Rivers is a little crowded with help and I thought this would be a solution for all three of you."

Crowded with help? Maybe. But she had the feeling that he'd more than nudged them in her direction.

She said, "That's hard to believe. Calves start to drop in January. It's a busy time for cattle ranches."

He paused, then said, "I didn't know you knew about cattle."

"I'm hardly an expert," she admitted. "But I'm not green on the subject either. As for Ollie and Sol, they have the crazy idea that they're going to stay here on the ranch. I can't afford to pay them like round-the-clock ranch hands. I tried to make that clear to them, but they're not listening to me. I think I'd better put one of them on the phone and let you explain the situation before it gets out of hand."

"You really shouldn't concern yourself about that, Isabelle. Ollie and Sol are just happy to be helping out. They're not the type to worry about money. As long as they have a horse, a roof over their head, and something to eat, they're happy."

Isabelle was far from convinced. "What about their families? How do they support them?"

"Both men are widowers. No kids either."

The information tugged on her heartstrings. "That's sad. But it doesn't change the fact that I can only use them for three or four hours a day. Would you please make that clear to one of them?"

"Okay, put Sol on the phone. I'll set him straight."

"Thanks, Holt."

Isabelle walked over and handed the phone to Sol, then waited a few steps away while the man did more listening than talking.

Finally, Sol said, "Yeah. I understand, Holt…No. No problems here. We'll handle everything…Sure. You can count on us. I'm giving her back the phone right now."

The skinny, old cowboy handed her the phone, then without a word to her, went back to work unloading the last of the horses.

Shaking her head, Isabelle put the phone back to her ear. "Holt, I don't think you got the message across. Sol is unloading the last of the horses."

"Sol knows what he's doing. Don't argue, Isabelle.

You needed good help and now you have it. Just quit asking questions and be happy."

"I am happy. But—"

"Good. Then maybe you'll invite me over soon and show me some of your cooking skills."

Totally caught off guard by the abrupt change of subject, she tried to assemble some sort of logical response. "You're asking me to cook for you?"

He chuckled. "When I say cook, I mean just give me something to eat. A sandwich will do. I'd like to come over and see the mares you shipped down from New Mexico."

Last night, when he'd brought her home, she'd very nearly made the mistake of asking him in for coffee. A part of her hadn't wanted the time with him to end. But thankfully, common sense had won over and instead of inviting him in, she'd given him a quick kiss on the cheek and rushed into the house.

"Isabelle, are you still there?"

She mentally shook herself. "Uh—yes, I was just thinking. It's foaling season. Aren't you terribly busy right now?"

"I figure I'll have a few days of peace until the next moon change. It comes on Monday. What are you doing tomorrow night?"

"Aren't you being a bit pushy? We just went out last night."

"And it was very nice, wasn't it?"

Too nice, Isabelle thought. Now every little nuance about the man seemed stuck in her head.

"Yes," she agreed. "It was enjoyable."

"Then why shouldn't we see each other again?"

Isabelle was smart enough to recognize that if she continued to see the man, she'd soon wind up in bed with him. And no matter how sexy or pleasant his company was, an affair with a playboy wouldn't be a smart choice. Now or ever.

And yet, she was starting a new life here in Yavapai County. It was nice and helpful to have a fellow horse trainer to talk with.

"No reason," she answered, then before she could change her mind added impishly, "I suppose I could manage to put some cold cuts between two slices of bread. Would that be enough cooking for you?"

He chuckled. "Sounds perfect. I'll be there before dark."

"I'll see you then."

Not giving him time to say more, she ended the call and dropped the phone back into her pocket. Tomorrow would be soon enough to worry about having Holt over for dinner. Right now she had to make two old ranch hands understand she couldn't use them on a full-time basis.

The next afternoon, after finishing several chores in Wickenburg, Isabelle decided to treat herself to a short break. When she dropped by Conchita's coffee shop for an espresso and frosted doughnut, Emily-Ann greeted her with a huge hug.

"If you hadn't shown up soon, I was going to file a missing person report," Emily-Ann said as the two women sat outside at one of the little wrought iron tables. "I haven't seen or heard from you since the morning you went to Three Rivers and had it out with Holt."

Isabelle carefully sipped the hot espresso, then lowered the cup back to the table. "The next day I went back to Three Rivers and things went far better with Holt. I ended up buying five mares from him."

Emily-Ann smiled brightly and Isabelle decided the young woman looked extra pretty today wearing a canary yellow sweater with her red hair braided over one shoulder.

"Now that's more like it," she said with approval. "I was going to be truly surprised if he didn't come through with a good deal for you."

"The mares are exceptional. Their babies should fetch a good price," Isabelle told her. "I'm thrilled to get them."

Emily-Ann leaned eagerly toward her. "Forget the horses. I want to hear how you got on with Holt? You were mighty angry with him."

Isabelle could feel her cheeks growing warm. "We, uh, got on fine. Actually, we went on a date—to dinner."

Emily-Ann's mouth fell open. "You're kidding, right?"

"It was against my better judgment, but I did go," Isabelle admitted. "And frankly, I had a lovely time. It was nice to be out and away from all the work on the ranch for a few hours."

"Wowee!" Emily-Ann exclaimed. "You actually went on a date with Holt! I'm stunned. Not that Holt asked you out. But that you agreed to go!"

Isabelle shrugged. "I couldn't very well refuse. From what he told me, he had no intentions of selling any more mares this year. I was fortunate that he agreed to part with those five. The least I could do was show him my appreciation."

Emily-Ann giggled. "Sure, Isabelle."

Frowning, Isabelle picked up her espresso. "You act as though he's some sort of rock star in a cowboy hat."

Emily-Ann shrugged. "I admit I sound silly. But he's one of the most eligible bachelors around here. Doesn't it make you feel special that he's interested—in you? It would me. But then nobody of his caliber is ever going to take a second glance at me."

The frown on Isabelle's face deepened. "This isn't the first time I've heard you putting yourself down, Emily-Ann, and I want you to stop it. You're a bright, lovely woman. You're just as good as me or Holt or any person."

She smiled wanly. "If you say so."

"I do say so." Isabelle popped the last of the doughnut into her mouth and savored the taste before she swallowed it down. "I've got to be going. I have the truck loaded down with groceries. Oh, I almost forgot—I have two hired hands now. Ollie Sanders and Sol Reynolds. Do you know them?"

Emily-Ann shook her head. "I'm not familiar with either name, but I might recognize them if I saw them. Are they the sort to stop by here for coffee?"

Isabelle laughed at the image. "No. This pair is a little rough around the edges for Conchita's."

Bemused, Emily-Ann gestured to the small building behind them and the simple outdoor tables. "This place is hardly fancy. What kind of guys are they?"

"The sort that drink plain coffee at the Broken Spur. Ollie's sixty-one and Sol is sixty-three. Neither has a family and ranch work is the only job they've ever had."

Emily-Ann frowned. "Are you sure you can trust these guys? Where did you find them anyway?"

"Holt sent them over. They normally work at Three Rivers. Now they're staying on Blue Stallion with me. I'm helping them turn one of the feed rooms into a little bunkhouse so they'll have a comfortable place to stay. I already had a hot plate for them to use and today I bought a small fridge. Next I need to purchase a couple of single beds and some linen. Last night they slept on cots and sleeping bags."

Emily-Ann frowned thoughtfully. "Are you sure these guys are going to be worth the extra money they're costing you?"

Isabelle nodded. "They've already done more in one day than I could do in ten. And don't get the idea that they're too old to be useful. Both of them could work circles around a man in his thirties."

"Sounds like you're happy with these guys," Emily-Ann remarked.

"I couldn't be more pleased," Isabelle told her. "But there is something nagging at me. When I told them the amount I'd be able to pay for a monthly wage, I expected them to turn tail and leave. Instead they seemed indifferent. It's weird."

Emily-Ann drummed her fingers thoughtfully against the tabletop. "Interesting that Holt sent them over. If I didn't know better, it sounds like he's trying to take care of you."

Isabelle reacted with a sound that was something between a grunt and a laugh. "That's ridiculous. Holt is only being a helpful neighbor."

The smirk on her Emily-Ann's lips said exactly what she thought about Isabelle's explanation. "None of my neighbors have ever been *that* helpful."

Isabelle didn't want to get annoyed with Emily-Ann. She was the closest friend she had here in Wickenburg and she genuinely liked her. Even though she did get these silly notions.

"Look, Emily-Ann, I'm sure you'd be the first person to advise me against getting serious about Holt Hollister," Isabelle told her. "So let me assure you. He's a friend and that's all he'll ever be to me."

Emily-Ann rolled her eyes. "How funny, Isabelle. Me giving you advice about a man. But I happen to think it would be fitting if you'd give Mr. Holt Hollister some of the same love 'em and leave 'em medicine he's dished out over the years."

Isabelle crumpled the wax paper that her doughnut had been wrapped in and dropped it in her empty cup. Thank goodness she hadn't mentioned to Emily-Ann that Holt was coming over to the ranch this evening. She'd really be having a field day with that tidbit of information.

"I thought he was an old family friend of yours," Isabelle remarked.

"He is. But it's past time he met his match." She smiled cleverly. "And I happen to think you're it."

"Oh, no. Not me." Isabelle rose to her feet just as a customer pulled into the parking area of the coffee shop. "Time for me to go. See you, Emily-Ann."

Emily-Ann waggled her fingers. "Drop by soon. I can't wait to hear what you'll have to tell me then."

Rolling her eyes, Isabelle pulled the strap of her purse onto her shoulder. "The next time I stop by for coffee, you're not going to hear one thing about Holt Hollister. And that's a promise."

Emily-Ann laughed. "You know what they say about promises. They're made to be broken."

Chapter Six

Sundown was still more than an hour away when Holt arrived on Blue Stallion Ranch. As he parked the truck a short distance from the house and climbed to the ground, he noticed a cloud of brown dust rising near the barn area.

Squinting against the lingering rays of sunlight, Holt spotted Isabelle in a large round pen riding a little bay mare with a white blaze down her face. Ollie and Sol were perched on a rail of the fence, watching their new boss in action.

As Holt approached the two men, Ollie threw up a hand in greeting. "Hey, Holt. Come have a seat and watch the show. Isabelle's got the little mare spinning on a dime."

Holt leaned a shoulder against the fence and peered through the wooden rails as Isabelle continued to put the mare through a series of maneuvers.

Sol said, "I never thought I'd see anyone ride as well as you, Holt, but Isabelle comes pretty damned close."

Holt glanced up at the older man. "Aww, come on, now, Sol," he joked. "You think that just because she's a lot prettier than me."

Ollie chuckled. "Well, I wouldn't argue that point. But she sure knows how to handle horses. Surprised the heck out of me and Sol, that's for sure."

Holt turned his attention back to the pen just in time to see Isabelle rein the mare to a skidding stop. He couldn't argue that she sat the saddle in fine form. Loose and relaxed while being in total control, it was easy to see she was a very experienced rider. She was also the sexiest thing that Holt had ever laid eyes on.

Maybe that was why he couldn't stay away from the woman, he silently reasoned. It wasn't like him to take time away from the ranch when foals were coming right and left. But this evening when he'd made his rounds through the barns, the mares he'd put on foal watch had all seemed settled and happy. And if by chance one did decide to suddenly go into labor, Holt knew he could depend on T.J. and Chandler to handle the situation.

For the past few years, Holt's family had been urging him to ease his workload and spend more time away from the horse barn. Preferably finding himself a good wife and growing a family. Hell, why would he want to fence himself in like that? Even with a woman like Isabelle.

He was pushing the question aside when she suddenly spotted him and trotted the mare over to where he was standing near the fence.

"Hi, Holt. I wasn't expecting you this early," she said with an easy smile. "I haven't made those sandwiches I promised you yet."

He smiled back at her and wondered why seeing her made him feel like he was standing on a golden cloud with bright blue sky all around him.

"I'm not worried. I doubt you're going to let me starve."

Isabelle dismounted and led the mare out of a gate and around the fence to where Holt was standing.

Before she reached him, Ollie and Sol climbed to the ground and she handed the sweaty mare over to the two men.

"We'll take care of her," Ollie told Isabelle. "You go on with your visit."

"Thank you, guys."

The two men left with the horse in tow and Holt turned his attention to Isabelle. Her perfect little curves were covered with a pair of faded jeans and a yellow-and-brown-striped shirt. A dark brown cowboy hat covered her white-blond hair, while spurs jingled on the heels of her boots.

To him, she looked just as pretty in her work clothes as she had in the clingy black dress she'd worn to dinner, and Holt decided just looking at her made him feel happier than he'd felt in years.

"I noticed you didn't give the men any instructions about the mare," he said.

She shook her head. "I don't have to tell them anything. They know exactly what to do. But you knew that when you sent them over here."

So she'd figured that out. "Aren't you glad I did?"

She pondered his question for only a second. "I'm very glad. And if I haven't said thank you, I'm saying it now."

"No thanks needed," he replied, while telling himself there was no need for her to ever find out the whole deal about Ollie and Sol. Sure, he'd sent them over here, and that was all she needed to know.

She swiped the back of her sleeve against her cheeks and said, "Sorry I look such a mess. We've been repairing a bunch of feed troughs this afternoon and then I decided to give Pin-Up Girl a little exercise."

"No need to apologize. You look as pretty as Pin-Up Girl," he said.

She laughed and he realized he liked that about her, too. That she could laugh at him and herself.

"Thank you, Holt. Before we head to the house, would you like to walk on down to the barn and take a look at my horses?"

"I would like that," he told her. "And by the way, your little Pin-Up Girl looks great. Did you train her?"

She stepped up to his side and as they began to amble in the direction of the big weathered barn, Holt had to fight the urge to curl his arm around the back of her waist.

"Thank you. Yes, I did train her," she answered. "She's only three. She was born to one of my mares shortly after I moved to Albuquerque. It's only been these past few months that I've had a chance to work with her on a regular basis."

Albuquerque. He was beginning to hate the mention of that city. Not that he had anything against it. But he did resent the reminder of her ex and the married life she'd had with the man. Which was stupid of him, Holt realized. He'd dated divorced women before and nothing about their exes had bothered him in the least. He had no right or reason to be jealous or possessive of Isabelle.

"I'll be honest," he said, "When I saw you that first day you came to Three Rivers, I thought—"

Intrigued, she prodded, "You thought what?"

Right now he figured he looked as sheepish as the day Reeva had caught him digging into a pie she'd made especially for his sister Vivian's birthday party. Thankfully his sister had always forgiven him anything. He wasn't sure that Isabelle would be so forgiving, though.

He said, "That you looked like you spent most of your time on a tropical beach. That you were probably one of those women who wanted to try a new hobby every few months. And this month just happened to be horses."

Her laugh was deep and genuine. "What a wonderful impression you had of me. Is that why you gave me the cold shoulder?"

What was wrong with him? Nothing embarrassed him, or so he thought. But now that he was beginning to know Isabelle, he wanted her to think highly of him.

"I'm sorry about that, Isabelle. I was being a real ass that morning. But you see, I have a problem with women."

"Yes, I've heard that."

Her deadpan response had him laughing. "I'm sure you've heard plenty of things. What I meant was I have problems with women showing up at the barn as though it's a petting zoo. Most of them don't understand that horses can be very dangerous. Especially to a greenhorn. Then there's the loss of time and work it takes for one of the hands to escort the woman around the barn. It's worse than annoying. It's like I said—a problem."

"I see. You thought the only kind of horse I'd ever ridden was the kind where you drop a quarter in the slot." Her smile was playful. "I forgive you. After all, you'd never met me. But that should teach you not to make assumptions just by appearances."

"That's a lesson our mother tried to drive in all of us kids. I guess it didn't stick with me."

She chuckled. "Well, I wouldn't worry, Holt. You're still very young. You have plenty of time to learn."

Shadows were stretching across the ranch yard and the warmth of the springlike day had begun to cool when Isabelle and Holt finally walked to the house.

"I do hope you're hungry," Isabelle told him as they entered a door on the back porch. "I have a surprise for you."

He followed her into the kitchen. "Let me guess. You got more than one kind of lunch meat. Bologna, I hope. That's my favorite."

"I do have bologna. But I—"

She paused as she turned to see him sniffing the air.

"Something is cooking and it doesn't smell like sandwiches."

She walked over to a large gas range and switched off the oven. "No. I decided to take pity on you and give you something besides bread and cold cuts. But don't get too excited until you do a taste test. This dish is one of the few things I can cook and it doesn't always turn out right. If we dig in and it tastes awful, I'll drag out the bologna."

"With an offer like that, I can't lose." He held up his hands. "If you'll show me where I can wash up, I'll help you get things ready."

"Follow me. The bathroom is just down the hall," she told him.

They left the kitchen and started down a narrow hallway. Isabelle could feel his presence following close behind her and she wondered what would happen if she suddenly stopped and turned to face him? Would he want to kiss her? Had the thought of kissing her ever crossed his mind?

Stop it, Isabelle! You're a fool for thinking about such things! You just got out of a loveless marriage. Why would you want to enter into a loveless affair? Just so you could feel a man's strong arms around you? Forget it.

Shutting her mind off to the silent warning, she hurried ahead of him and opened the bathroom door. "Here it is," she said. "Help yourself and I'll, uh, see you back in the kitchen."

"Thanks."

As soon as he disappeared into the bathroom, Isabelle rushed to her bedroom and threw off her hat. After dashing a hairbrush through her hair, she swiped on pink lipstick, sighed helplessly at the dusty image in the mirror, and hurried back to the kitchen.

She'd barely had time to take the casserole out of the oven when Holt returned to the room and sidled up to her at the gas range.

"That really smells good, Isabelle," he said. "But you've made me feel awful. I honestly didn't expect you to cook."

There were plenty of things about Holt that Isabelle hadn't expected, she thought. After their dinner date a couple of nights ago, she hadn't figured on seeing him again. At least, not this soon or in such an intimate setting. And from all she'd heard about his womanizing, she'd expected him to be making all kinds of sexual advances. So far she'd been all wrong about the man.

She cast him a droll look. "That is what you suggested on the phone."

"Yes, but I was only using that as an excuse to invite myself over."

She couldn't stop a playful smile from tugging at her lips. "I know that."

He grinned. "And you cooked for me anyway. That's sweet, Isabelle."

His eyes were twinkling as a grin spread slowly across his face. The tempting sight jumped her heart into overdrive and she knew if she didn't move away from him, she was going to say or do something stupid. Like rest her palm against his chest and tilt her lips toward his.

Drawing in a shaky breath, she turned and moved down the cabinets to where the dishes were stored.

"Just don't let it go to your head," she said. "And if you want to make yourself useful, you might fill some glasses with ice while I set the table."

"Ice? No wine?"

"Sorry. I'm out of wine. I have tea, soda, or water."

"I should've brought a bottle, but I thought we were having sandwiches. Water is plenty fine for me, though." He found the glasses and was filling them with crushed ice when he suddenly snapped his fingers. "Oh, I nearly forgot! I have something for us in the truck. I'll be right back."

He hurried out the back door of the kitchen and while he was gone, Isabelle set the table in the dining room, then added the food and drinks. She was lighting a tall yellow candle when he walked in carrying a round plastic container.

"This is nice, Isabelle." Standing next to her, he slowly surveyed the long room. "I love all the arched windows. You can see all the way to the barn from here."

"Yes and the mountains beyond. This is one of my favorite rooms in the house." She gestured behind them to the table and matching china hutch. "One of these days, I'm going to get more furniture. Like a longer dining table and a buffet to go with it. But since it's just me and I don't do any entertaining, there isn't much need for me to rush into furniture shopping. Actually, if you weren't here tonight, I'd be eating in the kitchen."

"Nothing wrong with that. I do it quite often because I'm usually late coming in from the barn. And sometimes I just want to have Reeva for company."

She pointed to the plastic container he was holding. "Is that something to eat?"

He grinned. "Pie. Blueberry with double crust. I asked Reeva to make it especially for us. I hope you like blueberries."

"I love them and what a treat to have a homemade pie." Isabelle took the container from him and set it on the table alongside the casserole, then motioned for him to take a seat. "Everything is ready. Let's eat."

"Not until the hostess is seated." He pulled out her chair and made a sweeping gesture with his arm. "For you, my lady."

She laughed softly. "What am I? Cinderella in dusty blue jeans?"

"Of course you are. And I'm the prince in cowboy boots. But I wasn't thinking. I should've brought you a glass slipper instead of a blueberry pie."

He pushed her and the chair forward and once she was comfortably positioned, she expected him to move on around to the other side of the table. Instead, he lingered there with his hands on the back of the chair and Isabelle held her breath, waiting and wondering if his hands were going to slide onto her shoulders.

But they didn't and when he finally stepped away, she expelled a breath of relief. Or was that disappointment she was feeling? Oh, Lord, the man shook her like nothing ever had. And he'd not so much as kissed her or even touched her in a romantic way. She must be losing her grip, she thought.

"No need to worry," she said. "I threw the other glass slipper away a long time ago."

He took the seat across from her, then leaned his forearms against the edge of the table and looked at her. "I think you meant that as a joke, but you didn't exactly sound like you were teasing."

"If I sounded cynical, I didn't mean to," she said. "It's just that sometimes I get to thinking about—" She paused and shook her head. "You don't want to hear this kind of stuff. Let's eat. You go first."

She picked up a large serving spoon and handed it to him.

He filled his plate with a large portion of the Mexican-type casserole, then reached for a basket of tortilla chips. "I do want to hear. What is it that puts you in a pessimistic mood?"

She shrugged, while wishing she'd never said anything. "Okay, I get to thinking about all the time I wasted trying to make things be the way I wanted them to be."

He frowned. "You're very young, Isabelle. You have plenty of time to make your life's dreams come true."

Dreams. Yes, she'd always had those. But only one of them was coming true. Her dream of Blue Stallion Ranch. And that's the one she needed to focus on. Not on a man to hold her tight or put a ring on her finger or give her children.

She gave him the cheeriest smile she could muster and began to fill her plate. "You're right, Holt. I have my whole life ahead of me. I might just go buy myself a new pair of glass slippers and kick up my heels."

"Now that's more like it."

He reached across the table for her hand and as his fingers wrapped warmly around hers, she arched a questioning brow at him.

"What's wrong?" she asked impishly. "You think I'm going to run away from the table and leave you with all the mess?"

His thumb gently rubbed the back of her hand. The soft touch caused a layer of goose bumps to cover her arms. Thankfully, with her arms hidden by long sleeves, he couldn't see just how much he was affecting her.

"No. I was just thinking how pretty you look and how much I'm enjoying being here with you like this."

Her cheeks grew warm and she figured they had turned a telltale pink. "You're flirting now," she murmured accusingly.

"A little," he admitted. "But I'm also telling the truth. You can't know what it's like being in a big family with three-fourths of us living under the same roof. It can get loud. And it takes work to find any sort of privacy."

Before she melted right there in her chair, she eased her hand from his and picked up her fork. "But it must be nice having brothers and sisters. I've always thought having siblings would be wonderful."

"It is. And I'm very close to all of them. It's just that sometimes I want to be alone and keep my thoughts to myself."

She nodded, then smiled. "Or perhaps just talk to the cook."

"Yes, thank God for Reeva. I can say what I really think to her. She gets me. How she does, I don't know.

The woman is seventy-one. Nearly forty years older than me."

He took a bite of the food and Isabelle could tell from the look on his face that he liked it. The fact sent a ridiculous spurt of joy through her.

"Age isn't what makes two people click. It's being on the same plane and having the right chemistry mix and a lot of other things."

He looked up from his plate and Isabelle felt a jolt as his gaze met hers.

"You sound like my sister Viv. She's always telling me that one of these days I'll find a woman who I'll click with. One I'll want to be with the rest of my life."

"And what do you say to her?"

"I mostly laugh."

"Why? Because you want to change women like you change shirts?"

"Ouch! If that's how you think of me, then why did you invite me here tonight?"

That was a good question, Isabelle thought. Just why exactly was she spending time with Holt when she knew there was no future in it?

"You invited yourself, remember? And I agreed to it."

"Because?"

The smile she gave him came from deep inside her. "I like you, Holt. And I like your company. And I'm not expecting anything more from you than friendship. That's why I agreed to see you again."

He studied her face for long moments and Isabelle was struck by the look in his eyes. It was almost like she was seeing hurt or disappointment, yet that couldn't be right, she thought. Holt was a guy who was just out for a good time. He wasn't wanting anything from her, unless it was sex. And so far, he'd not given her any sign that he wanted even that.

"Hmm. That's fair enough. And being your friend would be special for me. I've never had a female friend before."

No, she thought dismally, he most likely considered them lovers rather than friends. "You have Reeva," she told him.

"She's like a second mom."

"What about Jazelle? The blond woman who brought the pastries to your office?"

He nodded. "Jazelle is like family, too. She's been with us for a long time."

"Really? She looks very young."

He ate a few bites of the casserole before he commented. "She is. But she came to work for us when she was only in her teens, so we've all known her for a long time. She's a single mother of a little boy. He's probably four or five now. Sometimes she brings him out to the ranch, but mostly her mother watches him while Jazelle works."

A single mother. Isabelle hadn't ended up being one of those, but sometimes she wished Trevor had given her a child. Even though he hadn't loved her, a child would've been something more than his money could buy. With a child, she wouldn't be so alone now. She'd have a real purpose and reason to build her ranch. And most of all, she'd have someone to give her love to. But he'd kept putting her desire to have a baby on the something-to-do-later list, like many years later.

Shoving those miserable thoughts aside, she asked, "What about your siblings? Do they have children?"

He laughed. "Lots of them. Blake and Kat have a son, Nick. He's getting close to thirteen. And then they have twin toddlers, Abagail and Andrew. Chandler and his wife, Roslyn, have a baby girl, Evelyn. Viv has a fourteen-year-old daughter, Hannah, and she recently learned the baby she's carrying is actually twins. Joseph, my youngest brother, has a three-year-old boy, Little Joe, and they're expecting again, too."

"Sounds like the Hollister family is growing fast. So you're the only one who isn't married with children?"

"No. My baby sister, Camille, is still single. She lives at our other ranch, Red Bluff. And before you ask," he added with a little laugh, "none of the horses down there are for sale."

She laughed with him. "Well, it never hurts to try."

When Holt finally pushed his plate to one side, the casserole dish was nearly empty and the corn chips were little more than a pile of crumbs in the bottom of the basket.

"You were telling a fib when you said you couldn't cook, Isabelle. That was delicious."

"Thanks, I'm glad you liked it." She stood and began to gather dishes. "Don't forget we have Reeva's pie for dessert. I'll carry these things to the kitchen and get some coffee going."

"I'll help you." Rising from the chair, he collected his dirty plate and silverware and followed her out of the dining room.

"Actually, there's something other than the dishes that you could help me with," she said. "Do you know how to build a fire?"

His gaze instinctively dropped to the sway of her shapely little butt. "What kind of fire are you talking about?"

Glancing over her shoulder, she pulled a playful face

at him. "I'm not asking you to be an arsonist, if that's what you're thinking. I'm talking about the fireplace."

He'd forgotten she even had a fireplace. His mind was too preoccupied with the bedroom. Damn it! He must be developing some sort of personality disorder. What else would explain his uncharacteristic behavior? Where women were concerned, he'd always had one objective. Until the morning Isabelle sat in his office looking like a breath of spring. From that day on, something had tilted in his head. Now he wanted Isabelle more than any woman he'd ever known, but he was hesitant to even allow himself to touch her. What the heck was he doing here anyway?

Seeing that she'd paused to look at him, he mentally shook himself and tried to sound normal. "The fireplace," he repeated inanely. "Sure, I'm great at building fires."

The faint curve of her lips told Holt she'd also been thinking about another kind of fire. The notion not only surprised him, it rattled him right down to his boots. Making love to Isabelle might prove to be fatal to his common sense. That was something he needed to remember.

"I thought you would be."

Holt kept his mouth shut as he followed her into the kitchen and, after depositing the dishes in the sink, he went to deal with the fire.

In the living room, he found wood and kindling stacked on the left side of the fireplace and matches lying near a poker stand. In a few short minutes, he was standing with his back to the flames, soaking up the heat while he waited for Isabelle to appear.

When she finally entered the room, carrying a tray

with the pie and coffee, she glanced appreciatively at the blazing fire.

"That's nice, Holt." She walked over and placed the tray on the coffee table in front of the couch. "I can feel the heat all the way over here."

So could he, Holt thought, and it had nothing to do with the burning mesquite logs.

"Come on over," she invited as she took a seat on the long green couch.

Holt left the fireplace to join her and took a seat more than two feet away from her, all the while his brothers' mocking laughter sounded in his ears. If they could see him now, they'd never believe it, he thought wryly.

"Help yourself, Holt," she said. "I brought the whole pie so that you could cut the size you want."

"I'll do yours first," he told her.

After he handed her a dish of the pie and cut a hefty portion for himself, she said, "If you like, I can turn on the TV. I have satellite so the reception is good and there's plenty of channels to choose from."

"I don't necessarily need it, unless you'd like to watch." He settled back with the desert and tried to forget that the two of them were alone. That fire was warm and she'd be even warmer in his arms.

"It must be a horse trainer thing," she commented between bites of pie. "I don't watch either. After a day in the saddle, I don't have the time or desire to watch."

"Once I grew past cartoon age, I forgot all about TV."

She slanted an amused glance at him and he chuckled.

"What's wrong?" he asked. "You can't imagine me watching Looney Tunes?"

"I can see you rooting for that nasty coyote," she teased. "He's just your type. Fast and wily."

"I'll tell you one thing, I can't see you as the little helpless heroine tied to the railroad track yelling for help," he replied, then arched a questioning brow in her direction. "Do you ever yell for help?"

"Things have to get pretty desperate before I yell," she admitted. "But we all need a helping hand sometimes. And being too proud to accept it is really stupid."

And she was far from stupid, Holt thought. In fact, he'd never dated any woman who was ambitious and hardworking enough to build a ranch on her own. Was that why he was feeling so different about Isabelle? Because he admired and respected all those things about her? He wished he knew the answers. Maybe then he wouldn't be feeling like he'd lost all control of his faculties.

"I'm glad you accepted Ollie's and Sol's help," he said. "I won't be worrying about you so much."

She frowned and reached for her coffee. "Worrying about me? You shouldn't be doing that."

She was right. He had no right or reason to be fretting about her well-being. But something about Isabelle brought out the protector in him.

"Anything could happen to you out here. If a horse bucked you off and the fall broke your leg—" He paused and shook his head. "Well, it's just better that the men are here with you."

A gentle smile crossed her face and Holt noticed that even with her lipstick gone, her lips were still a soft pink. The color reminded him of cotton candy and he figured she'd taste just as sweet as the delicate treat.

"I'm glad the men are here, too," she said. "I like their company. I'm learning Ollie is the more talkative of the two and can be very funny at times. Sol is more solemn and serious, but just as nice."

She leaned forward to place her cup on the coffee table and Holt watched her silky hair slide forward to drape against her cheek. He didn't have to be told the color was natural. The texture was too smooth and the shades too varied to be anything but what she'd been born with. Which made the pale color even more amazing.

He was fighting the urge to reach out and touch the strands when she suddenly took away the opportunity by straightening from the coffee table and settling back in her seat.

A pent-up breath rushed out of him and he quickly decided he needed to leave before he lost control and allowed himself to do something that might ruin their relationship.

Relationship, hell! What are you thinking, Holt? You don't have any kind of connection to this woman! And even if you did, what good would it do? The Holt Hollister you once were is gone. He's turned into some sort of mushy cream puff. Since when did you ever worry about pulling a woman into your arms and kissing her?

Since he'd met Isabelle, that's when, he silently shouted back at the cynical voice revolving around in his head.

Suddenly feeling trapped, he started to rise and cross to the fireplace. At the same time she chose that moment to shift around on the couch so that she was facing him and Holt stayed where he was.

She asked, "Have you ever had any serious horse injuries?"

Grateful for the momentary distraction, he scooped up the last of his pie and placed the small dessert plate onto the coffee table.

"If I start listing all my injuries, you're going to think I'd be lucky to ride a tricycle."

She laughed. "Not hardly. I've taken plenty of spills and bites and kicks. It just goes with the job."

He nodded. "I've had black eyes and a lost tooth. A broken ankle that required surgery to repair. A cracked wrist and ribs. Oh, yeah, and a dislocated shoulder. I've had a few concussions, too. Which my siblings say I've never fully recovered from."

"That's mean of them."

"They like to tease me."

Her gaze dropped away from his. "I do, too," she murmured. "I like how you're such a good sport about it."

His mocking conscience had been wrong, Holt thought ruefully. He wasn't even a cream puff anymore. She'd just turned him into a melted marshmallow.

"Is that all you like—about me?" he asked.

She looked up at him and Holt was fascinated with the way the corners of her lips tilted upward.

"I like that you laugh about certain things instead of whine and complain."

There she went again, touching a spot in him that he'd thought was long dead. "Dad always taught his sons that real men don't whine, they fix."

"Sounds like your father was a wise and fair man," she said.

"He was all that and more. It's no wonder that Mom—" He broke off, surprised that he'd been about to share more personal details about his family with her. He didn't do that with other women. Why did it just automatically seem to come out when he was with Isabelle? "Right now she's going through a rough patch emotionally."

"We all go through those." Her gaze slid earnestly over his face. "Are you worried about her?"

She wasn't just mouthing a question. She really cared, he thought. The idea pierced something deep inside his chest.

"No," he said, then shrugged. "Well, perhaps a little. But she's a trouper. Eventually she'll get smoothed out. I'm sure of that."

She nodded and Holt told himself it was beyond time for him to go home. Even if the evening was still early, he was asking for trouble to keep staying.

He was about to push himself up from the couch and announce he was leaving, but then he heard her sigh. The sound prompted him to look at her and all at once his intentions of fleeing were forgotten.

"The fire is so lovely," she murmured. "It's especially nice when it's quiet like this and you can hear the logs crackling."

What he found lovely was the way the glow of the flames was turning her smooth skin to a pale gold and lit her blue eyes with soft yellow lights.

"Do you ever get lonely here, Isabelle?"

Her head turned toward his and his heart skipped a beat as he watched her lips slowly spread into a smile.

"I'm not lonely now. You're here," she said simply.

Something in him snapped and before he could stop himself, he was sliding over to her and wrapping his hands over the tops of shoulders.

"Isabelle, I—" He paused unsure of what he wanted or needed to say.

When he failed to go on, she shook her head. "I thought you didn't want me—like this. Do you?"

The doubt in her voice was so opposite of the yearning inside him that he groaned with frustration. "You can't imagine how much I want you, Isabelle. How much I want to do this."

He didn't give her, or himself, time to think about anything. He lowered his head until their foreheads were touching and his lips were lightly brushing against hers. She tasted soft and sweet and as tantalizing as a hot drink on a frigid night.

"I've thought too much about you," she whispered. "About how much I wanted this to happen."

Her last words tore away the safety he'd tried to erect between them and the next thing he knew, his lips were moving over hers like a thirsty man who'd finally found an oasis.

This wasn't a kiss, he thought. It was a wild collision. A wreck of his senses.

After a few seconds, he recognized he was in deep trouble. He needed to put on the brakes and lever some space between them before he lost all control. But how was he supposed to stop something that felt so incredibly good? Why would he ever want to end this delicious connection? He'd never felt so thrilled, or had so many emotions humming through his veins.

Her arms slipped around his neck and then the front of her body was pressing tightly against his. Desire exploded in his head and shot a burning arrow straight to his loins.

The assault on his senses very nearly paralyzed him and even though he was silently shouting at himself to pull back, he did just the opposite and deepened the kiss.

It wasn't until she broke the contact of their lips and began to press tiny kisses along his jaw that a scrap of sanity hit his brain.

"Isabelle, this isn't good," he whispered, then groaned.

"I mean—it is good—so good, but not the, uh, right thing for us."

That was enough to snap her head back and she stared at him in dazed wonder. "Oh. I—thought. I don't understand, Holt."

"Neither do I," he said gruffly, then quickly jumped to his feet before he had the chance to change his mind and pull her back into his arms. "I really like you, Isabelle. I like you too much for this. So I—have to leave. Now."

He turned and hurried out to the kitchen to collect his hat from the end of the cabinet. By the time he'd skewered it onto his head and reached the back door, Isabelle had caught up to him.

"You're leaving now?"

The confusion in her voice intensified his determination to keep a space of sanity between them.

"Yes. I'm sorry, Isabelle. But I—don't want to ruin things with us."

She marched over to where he stood with his hand already clutching the doorknob.

"Ruin things? How do you mean? You kissed me and realized you didn't like it? Well, all you have to do is tell me so, Holt. You don't have to hightail it out of here to avoid being tortured again!"

Tortured? Yes, that was the perfect word for it, Holt thought. But not in the way she'd meant.

Spurred by her ridiculous remark, he snatched a hold on her upper arm and tugged her forward. She stumbled awkwardly against him and Holt was quick to take advantage by once again latching his lips over hers.

This time the kiss was just as deep, but he managed to end it before it turned into something neither of them was ready for.

"Good night, Isabelle. And thanks for the dinner."

She didn't reply. Or if she did, Holt didn't stay around to hear it. He left the house and hurried to his truck before he lost the last shred of decency he possessed. Before she had a chance to see the real Holt Hollister. The one who gobbled up sweet little things like her and moved on to the next one.

Chapter Seven

Two days later, Holt entered Blake's office, located at the north end of the main cattle barn. A few years ago, his older brother had worked out of the study where their father had always dealt with all the ranch's official business. But as Three Rivers had continued to grow, Blake and the rest of the family had agreed it would be best to have the flow of ranch clients away from the house.

With Holt's office still a cubbyhole that had once been a tack room, he often teased his older brother about having the fancy digs to work in, while he had to deal with barn dust and pack rats. But in truth, Blake deserved the comfortable office, along with a devoted secretary, who helped him carry the heavy load of managing Three Rivers Ranch.

"Good morning, Flo," he said to the older woman sitting behind a large cherry wood desk.

She peered at him over the tops of her bifocals and as Holt took in her short red hair and matching lipstick, he figured in her younger years she'd been a raving beauty. Now, toward the end of her sixties, she was sporting some wrinkles. But there was still a shrewd gleam in her brown eyes that told Holt she'd dealt with men like him before and had always come out the winner.

"Morning, Holt. You have work for me today?"

There were times when he got behind on his paperwork and Flo was always charitable enough to do it for him.

"No. I'll need some registrations done on the new babies soon, but that can wait. I need to talk with Blake for a few minutes."

She jerked her thumb toward the closed door to Blake's portion of the office. "He's in there and your mother is with him."

"Good. I'll hit her up to give you a raise. You deserve one for putting up with Blake, don't you?"

"Ha!" She snorted. "I deserve a huge one for putting up with you."

Laughing, he patted the secretary's cheek before he crossed the room and entered Blake's office.

"What's going on in here? A family powwow?" He walked over to where his mother was standing at the window and smacked a kiss on her cheek. "Hi, Mom. You look beautiful this morning."

She wrapped her arm around his waist and gave him a little hug. "Okay, what are you wanting? Blake has already told you we're not getting an equine pool. At least, not yet."

"I'm not worried about a pool. But just think what a great tax write-off it would be," he said, slanting a pointed look at Blake, who was sitting casually at his desk. "Probably save the ranch a few thousand."

"We need another well drilled if we're going to turn that range over by Juniper Ridge into a hay meadow. And you know that isn't going to come cheap."

"Maybe we ought to just get more hay shipped in," Holt suggested. "The Timothy/alfalfa mix we get from Nevada is great."

"And very expensive." Maureen spoke up. "We have the climate and the machinery to grow and bale our own. All we need is water and it isn't going to fall from the sky, unfortunately."

"Sometimes it does. If you'd open those blinds and look outside right now, you might see otherwise," Holt told her.

She peeked through the slatted blinds and gasped. "It is raining! Oh, and I left my horse hitched in the arena and he's wearing my favorite saddle! I'd better run!"

Maureen raced out of the office and Holt walked over and sank into the chair in front of Blake's desk. "The rain started about ten minutes ago. Mom's saddle is probably already soaked."

"Some of the hands will oil it for her," Blake said, then leaning back in his chair, he crossed his arms over his chest and looked at Holt. "What are you up to this morning? I thought you needed to go into town for something."

Holt shook his head. "I decided that could wait. I wanted to talk to you about the horse sale coming up this weekend at Tucson."

"I wasn't aware there was one. Why? Are you planning on going?"

"It's been on my mind. There's about six head in the

catalog that interest me. And I'd like to replace those five mares I sold to Isabelle."

"Fine with me," Blake told him. "You know you don't have to ask me before you spend Three Rivers' money."

Holt chuckled. "Until it comes to an equine pool."

Blake groaned. "You're never going to hush about that, are you?"

"Probably not. I can always use it to irritate you."

A sly grin crossed Blake's face. "Speaking of Isabelle, I haven't had a chance to talk to you about this, but Matthew tells me that you sent Ollie and Sol over to Isabelle's ranch to work for her."

"That's right. I figured it would be easier for us to find day workers than it would be for Isabelle. She only knows a handful of people around here. And that ranch of hers is so isolated I didn't want riffraff out there with her."

Blake shrugged. "Well, I don't have any beef about them working for her. But they're still on the payroll here at Three Rivers and—"

"Uh, I'd like for you to keep it that way, Blake. I promised the men they'd keep getting their Three Rivers' paycheck—because Isabelle can only afford part-time help right now."

Blake leaned forward and stared at his brother. "I'm not sure I got this straight," he said. "Ollie and Sol are working for Isabelle, but we're paying them? And she went along with it?"

Grimacing, Holt shook his head. "Isabelle knows nothing about this setup, Blake. And I don't want her to know. She'd have a fit and send the men packing."

"I don't get this—or you, Holt! I—"

"Don't get all het up about this, Blake. Just take the

amount of their pay out of my monthly salary. I'll never miss it."

Blake's mouth fell open and he studied Holt for long moments before he finally let out a heavy sigh of surrender. "Okay. Whatever you do with your money is none of my business. But—"

"But what? Go ahead and say it, brother," Holt muttered in a sardonic voice. "You think I've lost my mind or worse."

"What could be worse than losing your mind?" Blake shot the question at him.

Falling in love, Holt thought. But he wasn't doing that. No. Not by a long shot. He simply wanted Isabelle to be protected. He wanted someone there to help her. He wanted her to achieve her dreams and not be hurt along the way. That's all there was to it.

"Well, getting tangled up with a woman."

Blake's brows arched upward. "Are you getting tangled up with Isabelle?" he asked, then with a shake of his head, he rose to his feet and crossed the room to where a utility table was loaded with a coffee machine and all kinds of snacks. As he poured himself a cup of coffee, he went on, "Don't bother to answer that, Holt. You've already told me that you're more than tangled."

"I have? How so? Just because I sent Ollie and Sol over to help her?" Holt snorted. "Can't a man help a woman out without sex or love or anything like that being involved?"

"With you, Holt, we can safely rule out the love. But the sex is another matter and I—"

Annoyed that Blake was assuming he'd already been sleeping in Isabelle's bed, he barked back at him, "You what? I really don't have time for a lecture on women this morning, Blake. Besides, who are you to give me advice about women? You were lucky enough to literally run into your wife on the sidewalk. You didn't have to date dozens and dozens of women to find Katherine. You didn't have to wonder if she was marrying you for the Hollister money, or just because she liked having sex with you!"

Blake coughed loudly. "You're taking my concern all wrong, brother. I don't want you to get hurt, that's all."

"Since when has a woman ever hurt me?" Holt countered with the question. "Not once. And it's not going to happen this time. I'm just trying to help Isabelle. She's a fellow horse trainer and I admire her ambition and courage. I like her. That's all."

Blake rolled his eyes toward the ceiling, then looked at Holt and grunted with amusement. "You like her enough to pay her ranch hands' wages. I'd hate to see what you'd spend on her if you really loved her."

If he really loved her. Holt didn't know about love. Other than the kind he felt for his mother and siblings. He wasn't sure he'd recognize the emotion if it whammed him in the face.

"Don't worry, Blake, I'm not going to make the foolish mistake of falling in love with Isabelle. Be pretty hard to do anyway, for a man without a heart."

"Who says you don't have a heart?"

Holt wiped a hand over his face in an effort to swipe away the image of Isabelle's face when he'd left her house two nights ago. She'd looked angry, hurt, and shocked all at once. He figured right about now she'd be the first one to say he was a heartless man.

To answer Blake's question, he made a point of looking at his watch. "I'm not sure I have enough time to go down the list."

Blake shook his head and walked over to the window to peer out at the rain.

"So what was Mom doing in here?" Holt asked. "Didn't you talk to her at breakfast?"

"No. I missed breakfast. Kat needed help with the twins while she was getting ready for work." He pulled the cord to the blinds until the large window was uncovered. "Mom stopped by to discuss the cost of replacing a bull down at Red Bluff. He's getting too old to service the cows, but you know Mom. She doesn't want to sell him. He's going to be put out to pasture for the rest of his life."

"Oh. I thought she might've mentioned her trip to Phoenix the other day. Or Dad's case."

Blake glanced over his shoulder at Holt. "She didn't mention the trip. And you know good and well that she stopped talking about dad's case a long time ago. And I have no intention of bringing up the subject."

"I'm worried about her."

Blake shrugged, then walked over to his desk and eased a hip onto one corner. "I'm trying not to be. Whatever is going on in Mom's head will straighten itself out eventually. Our mother is a wise woman, Holt. We have to trust the choices she makes."

Holt wasn't too good at trusting. Especially when it involved women.

"What about Joe?" Holt asked. "Is he going out searching this week?"

At least one day a week, their brother Joseph came over to the ranch to ride the area where they believed their father had initially met his demise. Usually Blake rode with him, but sometimes Holt went instead. So far they'd found several pieces of evidence. Joel's spur rowel, a silver belt tip, and a small tattered piece of the shirt he'd been wearing that fateful day.

"He'll be over this afternoon. This rain won't last more than ten minutes anyway."

"Do you want me to ride with him this time?" Holt offered. "I can spare a few hours. And I only have about five two-year-olds to ride today."

Blake shook his head. "Thanks, Holt. But I'll go. Flo will take care of things here. And it gives me a chance to get on the back of a horse. I kinda get tired of being in an executive chair for most of the day."

Holt rose from the chair and started to the door. "I'd hate to think I had to trade that chair for a saddle."

Blake said, "Holt, about the sale, buy as many horses as you want. I trust your judgment completely."

Blake trusted his judgment with horses, just not with women, Holt thought wryly. Well, that hardly mattered. One of these days, his family was finally going to accept that he wasn't cut out to be a family man.

"Thanks, Blake. I'll keep the buying within reason. Good luck this afternoon on the search. Maybe this time you'll unearth something definitive."

"I pray you're right, little brother."

That afternoon on Blue Stallion Ranch, Isabelle picked up a lame gelding's front foot and used the handle of the hoof pick to gently peck on the sole. When the animal flinched on a certain spot, she examined it closer but failed to see anything out of the ordinary.

"This seems to be the area that's bothering her," she said as Ollie and Sol peered closely over her shoulder. "What does it look like to you guys?"

Ollie was the first to answer. "Don't see a thing, Isabelle."

"Could be a stone bruise," Sol added his thoughts on the matter.

"Can I be of help?"

The sound of Holt's voice momentarily stunned her. She'd not seen or heard from him since the other night when he'd hightailed it off the ranch like a demon was after him.

Slowly, she lowered the horse's foot back to the stall floor, while the men turned to greet their visitor.

"Hello, Holt," Ollie said. "You couldn't have shown up at a better time."

"Yeah, Isabelle's gelding is lame," Sol added. "Maybe you can figure out the problem."

Isabelle cleared her throat. "Holt isn't the vet at Three Rivers, his brother Chandler is. I'll load the horse in the trailer and take him to the Hollister Animal Hospital," she told the two men.

Holt entered the stall and shouldered his way between Ollie and Sol to stand next to Isabelle. She forced herself to look up at him and as soon as her gaze clashed with, her heart lurched into a rapid thud. Every moment of the past two days had been haunted by the memory of his kiss and how incredible it had felt to be in his arms. Now, she could only wonder how long he'd be here before the urge to run hit him again.

"Let me take a look first," Holt suggested. "I might be able to figure out the problem."

A part of her wanted to tell him to get lost, while the other part was jumping for joy at the sight of him. Dear Lord, the man had turned her into a bundle of contradictions.

"If you don't mind," she said. "Any help is appreciated."

She stepped to one side to give him room to work.

Behind her, Ollie and Sol moved backward until they were both resting their shoulders against the wall of the stall.

"Did this come on the horse all of a sudden or did it start out barely noticeable and progress into a full-blown limp?" he asked.

"I'm not sure," she told him. "The last day I rode him, which was three days ago, he was fine. Then I turned him out to pasture with a few of the mares. When I got him up today to ride him, he could barely walk."

"Hmm. So you've not ridden him in the past few days?"

"No. And he's never had laminitis or arthritis or anything like that."

Holt picked up the gelding's foot and began to put pressure on the outside wall of the hoof. When he hit a certain spot, the horse tried to jerk away from Holt's tight grip.

"It's okay, boy. You're going to be all right." He lowered the animal's foot back to the floor and gently stroked his neck before he turned to Isabelle. "Like you said, I'm not a vet, but Chandler will tell you that I can doctor horses. This one is developing an abscess. Either a small foreign particle has entered his foot through the sole or it's been bruised or injured by striking it against something hard."

"So what happens now? Do I need to take him into your brother's clinic for treatment?"

"Maybe not. You might be able to treat him yourself. Do you have any soaking salts?"

"Yes."

"What about oral painkiller for horses?"

She nodded. "I always keep it on supply."

"Great," he said. "We'll start out by giving him a

dose of painkiller and then his foot needs to be soaked for at least twenty minutes twice a day. Eventually, a spot near the hairline will burst open. But don't worry. That's a good thing. It relieves the pressure of the abscess and whatever is inside will run out."

Wanting to believe it was that simple of a problem, but still doubting, she asked, "You really think that's what it is?"

"I'd bet every dollar I own," he told her, then gave her a reassuring wink. "I have a supply of antibiotics in the truck you can give him to help with the infection. In a few days, he'll be fine."

"Don't worry, Isabelle." Ollie spoke up. "Holt knows what he's doing. He's an expert on horses."

"You stay here with Holt," Sol added. "We'll go fetch everything from the tack room."

The two men left to gather what was needed to treat the horse and Isabelle took a cautious step back from Holt.

"I think I'll go help Ollie and Sol," she said. "They might not be able to find the phenylbutazone."

She started to leave the stall, but he quickly reached out and caught her by the forearm. "Wait, Isabelle. I want to talk to you before the men return."

Her nostrils flared as she looked down at the strong fingers encircling her arm. "Look, I'm grateful for your help with my horse, Holt. But I'm not sure I want to talk with you about anything personal. That's over! Not that it ever started," she said in a brittle voice.

His fingers eased on her arm and Isabelle forced herself to lift her gaze up to his. The dark, bewildered look in his green eyes confused her.

He said, "I thought by now that you'd be wanting to thank me for leaving when I did."

"What is that supposed to mean?" she asked flatly.

He made a sound of frustration as he stepped closer. Isabelle told herself she really should pull away from him and run to the tack room and the safety of Ollie's and Sol's company. But something about Holt mesmerized her and chipped away the anger and hurt she'd been carrying around with her the past two days.

"It means that whatever was happening between us was getting out of hand—really fast. I wanted you to have time to take a breath and think about me and you. I wanted to give myself time to think about what was happening."

His voice was like the low, soft purr of a cat and the sound slowly and surely lured her to him. Closing her eyes, she rested her palms against his chest. "You're right. It was a quick explosion. But I—wished you had stayed long enough to explain. Running off like that was—not good."

His hands gently wrapped around her upper arms. "I'm sorry, Isabelle. I realize it probably made me look like a jackass. But if I'd stayed a second longer, I couldn't have stopped kissing you or—anything else. Don't you understand? For once in my life, I was trying to be a gentleman."

How could she stay annoyed with him when the simple touch of his hands was melting every cell inside of her? She couldn't. No more than she could resist the urge to be near him.

"I didn't know that, Holt. And why has it taken you this long to explain?"

His expression rueful, he shook his head. "Saying I'm sorry doesn't come easy for me, Isabelle. And when I do apologize, it never comes out sounding right. If you want the truth, I had to work up my courage to come over here."

Suddenly tears were stinging the backs of her eyes and she turned her back to him and swallowed hard. Something about his words and the way he'd said them had struck her in a deep, vulnerable spot.

She sniffed and said, "If you want the truth, I'm glad you're here. I just—"

"You felt like you needed to take me to task a bit," he finished for her. "I understand. I don't blame you."

Smiling now, she turned to face him. "It doesn't matter. I forgive you. And hopefully you've forgiven me."

Surprise arched his brows. "For what?"

Her cheeks felt as though they were flaming. "For acting like that kiss of ours was—something more than just a pleasant, physical connection."

His green gaze made a slow survey of her face. "Is that what you think it was? Just a physical reaction?"

Actually, Isabelle still wasn't sure what had happened between them or how they'd gone from a simple kiss to an explosion of passion. To her, it had been like nothing she'd ever experienced with any man. But she'd never admit such a thing to him.

Making love to a woman was second nature to Holt. He knew exactly how to make her feel special. Even loved. Isabelle wasn't going to be so stupid as to think Holt could ever have a serious thought about her. With him, everything was physical and that's all she was going to allow herself to feel about him.

"I'm positive it was," she answered.

He let out a long breath and Isabelle figured it was a sign of great relief.

"I see," he said. "Well, that's good. Because neither of us want strings between us."

Foolish pain squeezed the middle of her chest, but she smiled in spite of it. "No. No strings. I believe we can enjoy each other's company without any of those, don't you?"

Surprise, or something like it, flickered in his eyes and then he smiled back at her. "Absolutely."

There, she thought. She'd fixed everything. He believed that kiss had meant nothing more to her than a few moments of physical pleasure. Now, all she had to do was convince herself.

A half hour later, with the gelding treated and turned out to a small lot near the barn, Holt and Isabelle stood outside the fence observing the horse as he walked gingerly toward a hay manger.

The rain had cleared and bright sunshine was warming the muddy ground around the ranch yard. It was turning into a beautiful day, Holt thought. Especially now that Isabelle was smiling at him again.

She asked, "Would you like to walk to the house and have a cup of coffee? I'd offer you what was left of the blueberry pie, but I gave it to Ollie and Sol. I do have brownies, though. That's the least I can do for your vet services."

He put a finger to his lips and made a shushing noise. "Don't say that out loud. Chandler will have my hide for practicing without a license."

Isabelle laughed. "I'm sure," she said drolly. "He's probably grateful for the help."

"He does have too much to do," Holt agreed. "And I do, too. As much as I'd like the coffee, I'd better head on back to town. I actually need to stop by the clinic and pick up a few things we need at the ranch."

She rested her back against the board fence and

jammed her hands in the pockets of her brown work jacket. In dress clothes, she looked like a glamour girl, yet she'd chosen a very unglamorous job for herself. She was such a paradox and he had to admit that everything about the woman fascinated him.

"You know, I do have a cell phone," she said. "You could've called to apologize."

There was an impish curve to her lips that made Holt want to snatch her into his arms and kiss her. But now was hardly the time when Ollie or Sol could walk up on them at any moment.

"I thought you said you were glad I came."

"I am," she replied. "I'm just wondering why you took the time to drive all the way out here."

He casually rested one shoulder next to hers. "It's always better to be face-to-face when you tell someone you're sorry for being a jerk. But I also have something else on my mind to talk to you about."

Her blue eyes widened a fraction, but she didn't bother to look at him. Instead she kept her gaze on the open land stretching away from the barn area. He wondered if that far-off look had anything to do with him or if she was simply thinking about this ranch and all that she wanted it to be.

Blue Stallion Ranch. She hadn't found her blue stallion yet, but she was already building her dream around him, he thought. Holt hadn't forgotten how she'd practically begged him to sell his roan colt, Blue Midnight, to her. Nor had he forgotten the instant bond she'd made with the stallion. If it had been any colt but that one, he would have been more than happy to sell to her. But his future was wrapped around that horse. He couldn't give him up just to make Isabelle happy.

"What is it you wanted to talk to me about?" she

asked, breaking into his thoughts. "You want me to cook for you again?"

He laughed. "No. I wanted to invite you to take a trip with me. There's a horse sale going on at Tucson this coming Saturday. The horses are all registered and cataloged. I thought you might enjoy it. You might even want to purchase something."

That turned her head in his direction and she pondered his face for long moments before she finally replied, "I would enjoy it. Does it take very long to drive down there?"

"From Wickenburg, it takes about three hours or a little over. But it's a nice drive and if you've never seen the Tucson area, it's very pretty."

"I've not been to that part of the state before. I'd love to see it. And I suppose I could take my checkbook. Just in case I saw a horse I like. Who knows, I might even find that blue stallion I want," she added with a clever smile.

"Did you ever see a horse you didn't like?" he teased.

She laughed. "I think you're beginning to know me, Holt."

And he was beginning to like her more and more, he thought. Asking her to join him on the trip to Tucson was like inviting trouble to walk right up and sock him in the jaw. But he'd never been one to take the safe route. Not even where a woman was concerned.

"So can I plan on you going?"

"Sure. How could I possibly refuse a day of horses and—you?"

Holt wasn't sure whether she was being serious or sardonic. Either way, it didn't matter. The playful twinkle in her blue eyes was enough for him.

"Great. The sale starts at ten so I thought we might

meet at Chandler's clinic around six and leave from there. That way we'll have about an hour to look over the horses before the auction begins."

She pushed away from the fence. "I'll be there."

"See you then." Smiling, he bent and placed a swift kiss on her cheek.

"Saturday. Six o'clock. Don't leave without me," she said.

Feeling like he'd just stepped onto a cloud, Holt laughed and started the short walk to his truck. "Not a chance," he called back to her.

Chapter Eight

That night, after a long shower and a plate of leftovers, Isabelle carried her phone and a cup of coffee to the couch in the living room and punched her mother's number.

Gabby didn't answer and Isabelle hung up, thinking she'd probably already gone to bed for the night. But after a couple of minutes, the phone rang with her mother's returning call.

"Did I wake you?" Isabelle asked. "I didn't realize it was getting so late."

"You didn't wake me. I just got back in the apartment. I was over at the Green Garden going over some things with Carl about the showing."

"How's that working out? Is everything still on go?"

"Yes! I'm really getting revved up about this, Issy. I'm thinking this might give me a giant step forward."

Isabelle felt a pang of guilt, but only a small one.

"Well, the showing is what I'm calling about. I was planning on flying down this weekend, but I've had something else come up."

Her mother paused, then groaned. "All at once, you've managed to make me happy and sad. I'm thrilled that you were coming and sad that you aren't. I hope that whatever has come up is important."

Isabelle had to be honest. "I don't know about being important, but it's something I want to do. I'm going to a horse sale down at Tucson—with a friend."

"A friend? Male or female?"

Isabelle drew her legs up beneath her while wondering what her mother would think about Holt if she actually met him. That her daughter was playing with fire? She wouldn't be wrong, Isabelle thought.

"A man. The rancher I went to dinner with. The one who sold the mares to me. Remember?"

"Yes. I remember. I think you said his name was Holt something or other."

"Hollister. They own half this county and more."

Gabby was slow to reply and when she did Isabelle noticed a thread of concern in her voice. "Issy, I've been praying you'd find someone else. But I honestly can't say I'm getting good vibes about you seeing this man. Trevor had too much money and it sounds like this one does, too. Don't you think you'd be happier if you found a poor ole Joe? One that would focus on you instead of padding his bank account?"

"I don't think Holt's that way about making money. Yes, when it comes to his horses, he's a workaholic. But I don't think wealth is all that important to him. And anyway, I'm not getting serious about him, Mom. He's just a man that I enjoy being with."

"That's the worst kind. You get to enjoying it so much you never want to be without him."

Isabelle wasn't going to let herself get that attached to Holt Hollister. When she did finally open her heart and allow a man to step inside, it was going to be one who was yearning for the same things that she was longing for. A home and children together. Their old age spent together.

"That isn't going to happen, Mom. He's not the serious type. And after what I went through with Trevor, that's just the kind I need right now."

There was another long pause from her mother and then she said, "Okay, you're a grown woman and I'm not going to try to run your love life. I am curious about one thing, though. You said you were planning on flying down—what about the horses? Have you finally hired some ranch hands?"

Isabelle told her all about Ollie and Sol and what a great help they'd been to her, then ended with describing the bunkroom she'd helped them construct in the barn.

"Oh, so the men are staying on the ranch full time. That's great, honey. I can stop worrying about you living out there alone now."

I won't be worrying about you so much.

Holt's comment had taken Isabelle by complete surprise. It had almost made him sound like he cared about her.

Don't start going there, Isabelle. Holt only cares about himself and his family. And you're not a part of the Hollister family. You never will be.

"Isabelle? Are you still there?"

Her mother's question pushed away the warring voices in Isabelle's head. "Yes, Mom. I'm here. I was just thinking—you never mentioned that you worried about me."

"You've had enough to deal with these past few months without listening to a whiny mother. But sometimes I—wish you would've decided to stay here with me in San Diego. It would've been a cinch for you to have gotten your old job back with the energy company. You made a humongous salary there. And the stables where you boarded your horses weren't all that expensive. You had a nice life here until—"

For some reason, Isabelle looked over at the cushion where Holt had sat next to her. Just having him here with her in front of the warm fire, listening to his voice, and watching the subtle expressions play across his face had been so nice and special. Then when he'd reached for her, she'd been shocked and thrilled. In a matter of moments, she'd wanted to take him by the hand and lead him straight to her bed.

Shaking her head, she tried to focus on her mother's remarks. "Until I met Trevor. Isn't that what you were going to say?"

"Yes, but—forget I said any of that. It's just that I miss you."

"I made a foolish choice when I married Trevor. But as for me ever moving back to San Diego—that isn't going to happen. I love my ranch, my land. Someday it's going to be the home I always wanted."

"Complete with horses and children," Gabby said, her voice tender. "That's really all I want for you, honey, to be happy and loved by a man. God knows your father never really loved me. Not as much as he did his piano. But that's okay. He gave me you. And that's a priceless gift."

A lump of emotion was suddenly burning Isabelle's

throat. "Oh, Mom, you're making me cry. I'm hanging up—I'll call you later."

"Good night, Issy. And have a nice time with your rancher."

Isabelle ended the call, then left the couch and walked over to the picture window. From this angle, she could see a portion of the main barn and a light burning in the small window of Ollie and Sol's bunkroom.

Knowing the men were there was a comfort to her. Yet they couldn't fill up the emptiness in the house or in her heart.

To be happy and loved by a man, that's what her mother wished for her. And that was all Isabelle had ever really wanted. Not money or travels or a glamorous social life. Just a loving, caring man at her side. But would she ever find that man?

Not with Holt, she thought sadly.

But that didn't mean she couldn't enjoy his company. And that was exactly what she intended to do.

At half past eleven that night, Holt was still in the foaling barn, carefully watching the newly born filly wobble to her feet and begin to nose her mother's flank. Eventually, she found one of the warm teats and he smiled with satisfaction as the baby latched on and began to nurse hungrily.

He was still watching the pair when Chandler's voice suddenly broke the quietness of the barn. "I ran in to T.J. heading to the bunkhouse. He told me you were in here."

Holt glanced over his shoulder to see his brother entering the large stall. "What the hell are you doing down here at this hour? You should be in bed with Roslyn," he scolded.

Shaking his head, Chandler came to stand next to him. "I couldn't sleep. I didn't want my tossing to disturb Roslyn and I was a little concerned that you might need me to help with the mare. You've been out here at the barn too long."

"The mare seemed to make it okay. But from my records, I think she's delivered a bit early. Maybe that's a good thing, though. Look how big the foal is. Mama might have had real trouble if she'd carried it any longer."

Chandler carefully moved closer to the bay mare and matching filly. "The baby looks good and strong, Holt. No matter about the due dates. Mother Nature always knows best. Since I'm here anyway, do you want me to check them over? Just to make sure?"

"I'd feel better if you would," Holt told him.

Chandler approached the new mother and daughter and went to work examining both. Once he was satisfied with his findings, he folded the stethoscope he'd carried with him and jammed it back into the pocket on his jacket.

"Both of them are fit as fiddles," he pronounced.

Holt slapped a hand on Chandler's broad shoulder. "Thanks, brother. Now get back to the house and go to bed."

"I'm not ready for bed."

"Hell, it's almost midnight. And you have a busy day tomorrow." Holt took a second look at his brother's taut features and decided there had to be more to his showing up here at the foaling barn at such a late hour. "Okay, what's wrong?"

Chandler patted the mare's neck, then moved to the opposite side of the stall. "Nothing is wrong. Well, not exactly," he mumbled. "Hell, I'm not sure what I'm feeling right now."

"There's a crease in the middle of your forehead as a big as the Grand Canyon." Holt gestured to the stall door. "Let's go to my office. I think there's some coffee still on the hot plate. You can tell me what's on your mind."

Chandler nodded. "I'll pass on your syrupy coffee, but there is something we need to talk about."

The two brothers left the foaling barn and entered the end of the main horse barn where Holt's office was located. After both men were seated and Holt was nursing a cup of the strong coffee, Chandler closed his eyes and passed a hand over his forehead.

"Man, you must really be down about something," Holt commented as he carefully studied his brother's miserable expression. "Are you and Roslyn having problems? Has her father been making waves?"

"No. It's nothing about Roslyn. And miracle of miracles, Martin seems to be getting softer as time goes by. He's already talking about coming out for another visit this spring."

Holt let out a humorous snort. "Maybe you'd better prescribe yourself some horse calmer before he arrives."

Chandler grunted. "My father-in-law won't give me any problems. Anyway, it's the Hollister family that's worrying me now. Joseph just left the house a few minutes ago."

Totally puzzled, Holt leaned forward. "Joe went home earlier this afternoon—after he and Blake got back from their ride. I heard Joe say they didn't find anything. He came back over here tonight? For what?"

Chandler pulled off his hat and raked both hands

through his hair. Since he rarely showed signs of stress, his unusual behavior was making Holt uneasy.

"When Joe got back to the Bar X, he found Tessa in one of her cleaning moods and asked him to carry some boxes down from the attic. She's slowly been trying to sift through all the things that Ray had stored up there before he died."

"So what happened?"

Chandler clapped his hat back on his head. "The two of them were digging through some old papers and correspondence and happened to run into a notebook filled with logs about Dad's case."

Holt's jaw dropped. "Seriously? This sounds too far out to be real, Chandler."

"I can assure you it is real. Joe brought the notebook over and showed it to me and Blake."

"Hell, I leave the house for three hours and all of this happens," Holt muttered. "So what did it say? We've been hoping and praying for a break in uncovering the truth. Is there anything in there that's going to help?"

Chandler shook his head again. "We don't know. Maybe. One thing is for sure, if the evidence gets out, it's going to cause a hell of a storm."

Stunned, Holt stared at him. As sheriff of Yavapai County, Ray Maddox had ruled, for lack of evidence, Joel's death an accident. But their old friend had never actually quit investigating the incident.

"Evidence? I thought we had everything Ray had gathered."

"I shouldn't have called it evidence. It's not that exactly," Chandler told him. "It's more like a break that might lead to solving the case. Ray kept some things to himself."

"Why would he do such a thing? Ray and Dad were

like brothers. He wanted to expose the truth about Dad's death just as much as we do."

Chandler heaved out a long breath. "We suppose he hid the info because he couldn't connect it with anything. And given the nature of it, he probably figured it would cause more harm than good. But damn it, he should have told us. Mom didn't have to know then. And she sure as hell isn't going to know now. Not unless we put two and two together and come up with a feasible explanation."

"I'm in the dark here, Chandler. Maybe you'd better tell me exactly what you found in these notes of Ray's."

Chandler glanced away from Holt and swallowed as though he was trying to get down a handful of roofing nails. "From Ray's notes, he believed that Dad was meeting a woman on a regular basis at the stockyards in Phoenix."

Holt couldn't have felt more dazed if the ceiling of the barn had crashed in on his head. "What?"

"That's right. The same finding was entered several times in the notebook. More than once, Joel had been observed in the company of a blond woman. Petite in build and about the same age as him. Whoever gave Ray this information must not have known the status of their relationship, because Ray didn't mention any of that. Ray scribbled down a list of dates with the word *Phoenix* written out to the side. One of the dates was a day after Dad's death."

Holt's mind was racing with a thousand questions and just as many possible answers. "The stockyards. A day after Dad's death," he mused out loud. "Chandler, a year or so ago, Mom found that old agenda book of Dad's. There's a note in it, saying he was to meet a man at the stockyards on that day. Joe researched the man's name and learned the name was phony. Maybe it wasn't a man Dad was planning on meeting that day, but rather the blond woman?"

"It's possible. But why would Dad have been so deceitful about it? Why would he put down a man's name if it had been a woman he was meeting? Mother never was the jealous kind. If he'd been meeting a woman for a business lunch or something of that sort, she wouldn't have cared."

Holt felt sick inside, then immediately felt guilty for even doubting his father's fidelity for one minute. "I don't know what you and Joe and Blake think. But as far as I'm concerned, I don't believe there was any sort of romantic involvement between Dad and this woman. Yes, he probably was seeing her and what that reason might have been is a big question mark. But he wasn't cheating on Mom. Dad wasn't made like that. He was an honorable man. A family man. And he loved Mom more than anything on this earth. Even more than Three Rivers and that's saying a lot."

Chandler blew out another heavy breath. "Yeah, that's what I think, too. I'm not sure what Blake thinks. You know how he is, he keeps most of his thoughts to himself. The important ones, at least. Joe is different, he sees things as a lawman. He weighs the evidence in an analytical way. And during his tenure as a deputy, Joe has witnessed some shocking things. I don't think he'd be that surprised to discover our father had been having an affair. After all, think how stunned everyone one was when we learned that Ray was really Tessa's father."

Holt swigged down a mouthful of the gritty coffee. "That's true. But Ray's wife was wheelchair bound. They had no children. That was no excuse for him having an affair, but I can kind of see why it happened. But

Dad had a beautiful, vibrant wife with six children. He had no reason to have an affair."

Chandler eyed him for several pointed moments. "I'm surprised to hear you say that. You love women. I thought you didn't have to have a reason to have an affair. Other than lust."

"Damn it, Chandler, that's a low, low blow."

"Oh, come off it, Holt. Righteousness doesn't fit you."

"Thanks. Being noble was never my goal in life," he said sarcastically. "Just give me faster horses and more women and I'll die a happy man."

He tossed the remainder of his coffee into a trash basket and replaced the glass cup next to the coffee maker.

Behind him, Chandler groaned. "Okay, that was a low blow. I'm sorry."

"Forget it. I can admit that I'll never be like my brothers. I'm not cut out for it, Chandler. But that doesn't mean I'm a tomcat with no feelings or discretion." He wiped a hand over his face as Isabelle's image tried to push itself to the front of his brain. "Oh, God, brother, what if we're wrong about Dad? What if he was cheating on our mother and an enraged husband or boyfriend killed him? Mom would be—well, I don't want to think of what that might do to her."

Chandler looked resolute. "Listen, none of us are going to breathe a word of this to Mom. She's already been having too many melancholy moods. This might send her into a tailspin."

"What does Joe intend to do with this bit of information?" Holt asked. "You suggested it might be a break in the case. But how? It's been years since Dad died. It would be miraculous if anyone remembers anything."

"Joe is going to keep asking questions. He believes he'll eventually find a cattle buyer or worker at the stockyards who might remember something about Dad and the woman."

Holt's stomach gave another sickening lurch. "I understand now why Mom doesn't want to search for the cause or reason of Dad's death. The truth might make everything worse."

His expression grim, Chandler rose to his feet. "If we find that Dad was living a secret life, we're going to bury the facts. No one will know except us four brothers."

Holt couldn't believe Chandler was even considering the possibility that Ray's speculations could be true, much less that they should hide the truth from their sisters. "And not tell Viv and Camille? Chandler, your thinking is all mixed up!"

"If I'm confused, then so are Blake and Joe, because they think the same thing. Viv and Camille adored Dad. He was their hero. Nothing good would come from crushing their ideals and memories."

Their father had been Holt's hero, too. He'd gotten his love of horses from Joel and his ability to laugh at the challenges that training them presented. Had he also inherited a straying eye for the ladies from his father?

No! Until Holt's dying day, he'd always believe Joel Hollister was a true husband and father.

Isabelle gazed out the passenger window of Holt's truck at the desert hills covered with tall saguaros and areas of thick chaparral and slab rock. In the past few minutes, the sun had dipped behind a ridge of mountains to the west and shadows were painting the rugged landscape. It was a lovely sight, she thought. A fitting close to the beautiful day she'd spent in Holt's company.

"Are you sure you didn't mind leaving the auction early?"

Holt's question broke into her pleasant thoughts and she glanced over to where he sat behind the steering wheel, driving them toward Wickenburg. Throughout the day, he'd never left her side and during all that time, their hands had brushed, their shoulders rubbed. The touches had been incidental, but to Isabelle they'd felt like the sizzling contact of a branding iron.

Now, with each passing minute, she felt a connection growing between them. Whether the link was emotional, sexual, or something in between, she couldn't determine. And she wasn't going to ruin the remainder of their trip trying to figure it out.

"I didn't mind at all. Each of us already purchased two mares," she said pointedly, then chuckled. "And leaving when we did probably saved me a few thousand dollars. I would've probably gotten into a bidding war for that buckskin colt that caught my eye."

"Just about every horse at the auction caught your eye," he said.

"I'm guilty. I confess. Mom always said I never saw a horse I didn't love."

"I'm curious about your mother," he replied. "Where did she get her knowledge about horses?"

"From her parents—my grandparents. They owned a small ranch near Bishop and Granddad was an excellent horseman."

"Are your grandparents still living?"

"No. Granddad died from complications of diabetes. When he passed, Grandmother was in still in fairly good shape, but losing him took a toll on her. They'd been married for more than fifty-five years and she wasn't the same with Granddad gone. She died about a year after he did." She glanced at him. "What about your grandparents, Holt? I don't think I've heard you mention them."

He shook his head. "Both sets are gone now. My Hollister grandparents lived and worked on the ranch all their lives. They both died of different ailments when I was in elementary school. My mom's parents lived in another state and we didn't see them very often. Her father passed away from a stroke and her mother died from a car accident. It was just a little fender bender, but she wasn't wearing her seat belt and her head hit the windshield." He reached over and slipped a forefinger beneath her belt and gave it a tug. "That's why I want you to promise me that you'll always buckle up."

Did he really care about her safety that much? No. She couldn't let herself go down that path. No serious strings. No thinking about love or the future, she scolded herself.

She forced a little laugh past her throat. "I promise. But we don't have safety belts on our saddles."

"No, we just have to hang on tighter." The grin on his face disappeared as he slanted her another glance. "I'm sorry you didn't find a blue stallion for your ranch, Isabelle. I was hoping you would."

He honestly seemed to care about her dreams and wishes. Something that Trevor never bothered to do. Oh, he'd wanted her to be happy, but he was never interested in the things that were most important to her. He'd thought handing her a check to a limitless bank account was enough to make up for his indifference. Maybe that should have been enough for her, but it hadn't been. She'd felt like an afterthought, something to be petted and admired and placed back on a shelf.

"That's okay," she told him. "Blue roans are not that plentiful. That's one of the reasons why they're so sought after and expensive. The two that we watched go through the ring weren't that great. I'll find my stallion someday."

"There's always a chance Blue Midnight will throw some nice colts. I won't forget I promised you a shot to buy one."

She smiled at him. "That's a long time off, but I'll hold you to your promise."

He didn't reply and for the next few miles Isabelle could see he was deep in thought about something. Was it her, the horses, or something too personal to share with her? Was he thinking about some other woman he'd rather be with? No. If he wanted to be with some other woman, he wouldn't have invited Isabelle to join him today. At least she could take comfort in that.

Minutes later, the lights of Wickenburg appeared on the dark horizon and Isabelle realized she was dreading telling Holt good-night. She didn't want this special day to end, or her time with him to be over.

They had passed through the small town and were nearing Hollister Animal Hospital when Isabelle questioned an earlier plan they'd made to deal with getting the two horses she'd purchased home to Blue Stallion Ranch.

"Now that I think about it, Holt, leaving my horses overnight at the clinic barn isn't such a good idea. They haven't been quarantined. They could pass shipping fever to Chandler's patients and I'd feel very guilty if that happened. Not to mention how angry it would make him. I can drive home, pick up my trailer, and be back in an hour or so to collect them."

His attention remained focused on the highway. "Don't fret about it, Isabelle. We're not leaving your horses or mine at the clinic. I'm going to take all four of them out to your ranch."

She sat straight up and stared at him. "Oh. But I thought—"

He arched a questioning brow in her direction. "The four of them have been trailered together for the past three and half hours. Penning them together tonight won't hurt. I'll leave mine at your place and haul them home to Three Rivers in a few days. That is, if you don't mind."

"Um—no. I don't mind."

That meant Holt would be following her home to Blue Stallion Ranch. After they tended the horses, would he want to stay? Or was he worried that if he let her get too close, she might try to throw a lariat on him?

The notion of any woman trying to tie Holt down was ridiculous. He was a maverick. But even mavericks needed love sometimes, she mentally argued. And tonight he just might decide he needed her.

Chapter Nine

During the twenty-minute drive to Isabelle's ranch, Holt tried not to think past getting the mares comfortably settled, but he knew the smart thing to do would be to kiss her and tell her goodbye. But the kiss would have to be on the cheek, not her lips. Otherwise, he'd be totally and completely lost to her.

And what would be wrong with that, Holt? This day with Isabelle has been more than special for you. It's been a game changer. She's no longer just a sexy female you want to bed. You want much more from her. Like her company and friendship and—

Muttering a curse, he reached over and turned up the volume on the radio in an effort to drown out the voice in his head. Tonight wasn't the time to let his heart do his thinking for him. If Isabelle was ready to invite him into her bed, he'd be a fool to turn her down. It was that simple.

When he braked the truck to a stop near Isabelle's barn, she, along with Ollie and Sol, were waiting to help. With the four of them working together, it took only a few short minutes to have the mares settled into a sheltered pen with plenty of alfalfa and water.

As Ollie and Sol headed back to the bunkhouse, Holt turned to Isabelle. "Now that we've finished that chore, how about you and me having coffee?"

Her smile flashed in the darkness. "I can probably come up with a cup of coffee."

"Only one cup?"

Her laugh was suggestive and Holt couldn't stop his thoughts from heading straight to her bedroom. But what kind of consequences would that produce? After learning his father might have been involved with another woman, Holt had been pondering on his own past. Before, he'd never really wondered if his playing the field had ever caused anyone to suffer. Now it bothered him to think that what he'd considered fun and games might have actually hurt another person.

He was getting soft, he thought sickly. He was getting all messed up in the head, and why? Because he thought his father might have been an adulterer, or because Isabelle was transforming him into a different man? Either way, Holt felt like everything around him was rapidly changing. And he was helpless to stop any of it.

"If you mind your manners, you might get two cups," Isabelle said, breaking into his thoughts. "I might even give you a brownie to go with the coffee."

"I can't wait." He curled his arm around her waist and kept it there as they walked the remaining distance to the house.

Inside the mudroom, they both shed their jackets

and hung them on a hall tree. Holt added his black hat to one of the wooden arms, then followed Isabelle into the warm kitchen.

While she went to work putting the coffee makings together, Holt stood to one side, watching her graceful movements. All day long, he'd had to fight with himself to keep his eyes off the way the soft pink sweater outlined the shape of her breasts and the way her jeans cupped her pert little bottom.

Now that the two of them were completely alone, the urge to stare was turning into a need to touch. By the time she handed him a steaming cup of coffee and a brownie wrapped in a piece of wax paper, he didn't want either one. All Holt wanted was her in his arms.

"Do you want to go out to the living room?" she asked. "There's no crackling fire waiting for us, but the furniture is more comfortable."

"I can build a fire—if you'd like," he suggested.

She paused for a second, then reached for her cup. "No. That's too much trouble. And you'll be leaving soon."

Her gaze lifted to meet his and the flicker of yearning Holt spotted in the soft blue of her eyes caused his heart to do a crazy flip.

"I will?" he asked softly.

Her rose-colored lips formed a surprised O. "Uh—I thought that's what you wanted," she said, huskily. "You said you needed time to think about you and me and—"

Holt couldn't stand anymore. He placed the brownie and the cup onto the cabinet counter and reached for her. As he circled his arms around her, he murmured, "These past few days I've done a hell of a lot of thinking, Isabelle. About that kiss that blew me away—about those strings that neither of us want. And the more I think, the more everything comes down to this."

He lowered his head and covered her lips with a kiss that was just long enough to fill his loins with heat, yet short enough to keep him from losing his breath.

"Holt, I—"

"You want me. I can hear it in your voice. Taste it in your lips."

There was no indecision in her eyes as her hands came up to curl over the tops of his shoulders.

"Yes," she murmured huskily. "I do—want you— very much."

He brought his lips back to hers and she groaned as his lips moved over hers in a rough, consuming kiss. She matched the hungry movements of his mouth and in a matter of a few short seconds, Holt was out of his mind with need to have her closer.

When he finally found enough willpower to tear his mouth from hers, he could see a dazed cloud in her eyes. He was equally stunned by the passion exploding between them, and his rattled state must have flickered in his eyes.

"You're not thinking about leaving, are you?"

Tightening the circle of his arms, he said, "I couldn't leave you now even if Ollie and Sol started yelling the barn was on fire."

Her laugh was low and sexy and the erotic sound was like fingertips walking across his skin.

"I think the coffee can wait." She took his hand and led him out of the kitchen and down a long hallway to her bedroom.

There was no light on inside, but like the rest of the house, the windows were bare of curtains and the silver glow from a crescent moon was enough to illuminate a path to a queen-size bed covered with a patchwork quilt.

As soon as they reached the side of the mattress, she released her hold on his hand and slid her arms around his waist. Holt dropped his head and found her lips once again. This time he tried to keep the kiss slow and controlled, but that plan was waylaid the moment her lips began to respond to his. Like a flash fire, their embrace turned hot and out of control.

"This is going too fast, Isabelle. But I—"

Frantically, she whispered, "I don't want you to slow down." She planted quick little kisses against his jaw and throat. "I can't bear the waiting. We'll go slower the next time."

The next time. Just the idea of a second time with this woman was enough to lift the hair off his scalp.

"I can't bear the waiting either." His voice sounded like he'd been eating gravel and his hands were shaking as they skimmed down her back and onto her hips.

Having sex with Isabelle. That's all he was doing, Holt silently shouted at himself. This wasn't anything to fear. It wasn't going to change him. All it was going to do was give him pleasure. Hot, delicious pleasure.

He recognized her hands were on the front of his shirt, jerking at the pearl snaps. When the fabric parted and her palms flattened against the bare skin of his chest, he was already hard, his body aching for release.

"I, uh, better do this, Isabelle—or—we might never make it onto the bed."

With the smile of a tempting siren, she stepped aside and began to undress. Next to her, Holt hastily jerked off his boots and jeans, then added his shirt to the pile. From the corner of his eye, he saw a circle of denim pool around her bare feet. Before she could step out of it, he planted his hands on either side of her waist and lifted her backward and onto the bed.

The jeans dangled from her toes and she laughingly kicked them off as she waited for him to join her.

"You're still dressed," Holt said.

She glanced down at the black scraps of lace covering her breasts and the V between her thighs. "You should be able to handle these little ole things."

He joined her on the bed and allowed his gaze to take in the glorious sight of her nearly naked body.

"It'll be my pleasure." Propping his head up on one elbow, he used his other hand to slip over the mound of one breast, then onto the concave of her belly. "The moonlight makes you look like a silver goddess. I'm not sure that you're real. I should kiss you just to make sure."

She rolled eagerly toward him. "I'm real, Holt, and at this moment I wouldn't want to be anywhere else, except here with you."

Holt wasn't expecting her little confession to smack him in the chest, but then nothing about this time with her was how he'd thought it might be. She was making him feel vulnerable and insecure. It was crazy. Even laughable. Yet he couldn't laugh. He was too busy worrying that he was going to disappoint her.

"Isabelle." Her name came out on a whisper as he thrust his hand into her hair and allowed the white-blond strands to slide through his fingers. "I've imagined you—us—like this so many times. But I—wasn't sure it would ever happen."

"I wasn't sure I wanted it to happen."

"And now?"

Sighing, she echoed his earlier words. "I couldn't leave you if Ollie and Sol yelled the barn was on fire."

He leaned over and kissed the lids of her eyes, then moved his lips down her nose and finally onto her mouth. Her arm slipped around his waist and she tugged herself forward, until the front of her body was pressed tightly against his. The sensation of having her warm skin and soft curves next to his bare body very nearly shattered the fragile grip he held on his self-control.

He broke the kiss and scattered a trail of kisses beneath her ear and down the side of her neck until he reached the spot where pulse thumped against the soft skin. His lips lingered there, savoring the taste, before he finally claimed her mouth in another hungry search.

After that, his brain became too fuzzy to clearly perceive what the rest of his body was doing. He remembered slipping away her lingerie and his boxers, recalled her reassuring him that she was on birth control. Then the next thing he knew, his hands were cupped around her breasts and he was entering her with one urgent thrust.

Her soft cry of pleasure jolted his rattled senses and he looked down to see her face bathed in moonlight. The delicate features were almost ethereal, making him wonder if he was going to suddenly wake and discover this was an incredible dream.

But then her hips suddenly arched toward his and the reality of the moment hit him. Slowly and surely he began to move inside her and as he did, he realized his greatest fear about making love to Isabelle had happened. After this night, he'd never be the same.

This was not what Isabelle had imagined. Making love to Holt wasn't supposed to be turning the room upside down. His kisses, his touches weren't supposed to be slinging her senses to some far-off galaxy. But that was exactly what was happening.

His hands were racing over her bare skin, lighting a fire wherever his fingers dared to touch. His lips were consuming hers, while his tongue probed the sensitive area beyond her teeth. She welcomed his dominating kiss and reveled in the fact that it was melting every bone in her body.

Over and over, he thrust into her and the feeling was all so glorious, so incredible, that the pleasure was almost too intense for her to bear. And when she began to writhe frantically beneath him, he must have recognized her agony.

He tore his mouth from hers and buried his face in her tumbled hair. "Hold on, my sweet," he whispered urgently. "Just a—moment longer. A moment more—so I can give you—everything. Everything!"

With her legs wrapped around his hips, she gripped his shoulders and tried to hang on, but it was impossible to stop the white-hot tide of pleasure from washing her away.

Through the whirling haze, she heard him cry her name and felt his final thrust. She tried to breathe, but her lungs had ceased to function. And then breathing suddenly seemed superfluous as the room turned to velvety space and the both of them were drifting through an endless universe.

When Isabelle finally regained awareness, her cheek was pinned between the mattress and Holt's shoulder. With most of his weight draped over her, the pressure on her lungs made breathing even more difficult. Even so, she didn't want him to move. She wanted to hold him close for as long as he would stay.

"Sorry, Isabelle. I'm squashing you." He rolled to one side and pulled her into the curve of his warm body.

Sighing, Isabelle pillowed her head on his shoulder and closed her eyes. Neither of them spoke, but the silence was far from awkward. She was enjoying the precious sound of his breathing, the night wind blowing against the window and the faint whinnies of the mares as they accustomed themselves to their new home.

This was everything she'd ever wanted, Isabelle thought drowsily. Her ranch and a man who filled her heart to the very brim.

"I hear the mares," Holt murmured. "They've been through some changes today. They're not sure what's going to happen to them now."

Isabelle could empathize with the horses. Her life had taken a drastic change tonight, too. And she had no idea what it might do to her future or her happiness. She wanted to think that Holt might want them to remain together. Not just for a few weeks or months, but for always. And yet, she recognized that wasn't likely to happen.

Resting her palm upon his chest, she said, "They'll soon realize that they're safe."

His fingers absently played with her hair. "I've been thinking about those two mares I bought today. Do you like them?"

She slid her hand across his warm muscles until she felt the quick thump of his heart. "I love them. Next to blue roan, my favorite color is plain brown with no markings. They're almost as hard to find as the blues and today you happened to latch onto two of them. You're a lucky man, Holt."

"Yeah, like latching onto you." He pressed a kiss to the top of her head. "Now, about the mares—what would you say about keeping them here at Blue Stallion for a while? Since they're already bred, there's no need for me to put my stud on them. Maybe we could go partners on them?"

She snatched the sheet against her naked breasts and sat straight up. "Partners? Really?"

A lopsided grin spread over his face. "Yes. Really."

The grin coupled with the dark hair tousled across his forehead, along with the five o'clock shadow on his jaw, was enough to shred her focus. The subject of the mares completely left her mind as she leaned down and kissed him softly on the lips.

"Mmm. That's so nice," she said.

His hand came to rest against the back of her head and he held her there, kissing her again, until desire began to flicker and glow deep within her.

"My suggestion about the mares? Or the kiss?" he wanted to know.

She smiled against his lips. "The kiss. And the mares. I'd love to keep them here with me."

And keep you here, too, she wanted to add. But bit back the words before they could slip out. For tonight it was enough to be in his arms.

He said, "That's what I wanted to hear."

She cupped her hands around his face. "I thought you wanted to hear it was time to finally eat those brownies we left on the counter."

A chuckle fanned her lips, and he pressed her shoulders backward until she was lying on the mattress and he was hovering over her.

"What brownies?"

Her soft laugh was instantly blotted out with a kiss.

"Wake up, sleepyhead. You're burning daylight."

The sound of Isabelle's voice caused Holt's eyes to

pop open and he blinked several times before he managed to focus on her image standing at the side of the bed.

She was already dressed in jeans and boots and a blue shirt that matched her eyes. One hand was holding a cup of steaming coffee.

"Is that coffee for me?"

The smile on her face was as bright as the morning sunlight streaming through the windows.

"It is. How do you want your eggs? Fried, scrambled, or in an omelet?"

He didn't have time for eggs! He shouldn't even be here! What had he been thinking last night?

He hadn't been thinking, that's what. Making love to Isabelle and lying next to her warm body had lulled him into a quiet sense of contentment. Instead of getting up and going home, he'd fallen asleep.

He took the cup from her and swallowed several hurried gulps before he swung his legs over the side of the bed.

"I really shouldn't take time to eat, Isabelle. If I don't get home, I—my family is going to send the law out looking for me."

Her brows shot up. "Really? Aren't they used to you being out all night?"

His face hot, he purposely set the coffee aside and reached for his clothing. "Not like this. Not overnight."

"Oh."

He pulled on his boxers and jeans before he glanced at her. She looked confused and skeptical, which made him even more frustrated with himself. Holt had always made special rules for himself regarding women. And he'd always followed them. Until now.

Standing, he zipped and buttoned his jeans. "That doesn't ring true with you, does it?"

"I didn't say that." She moved close enough to rest her hand on his forearm. "And frankly, it doesn't matter. That was then, this is now. Anyway, we agreed there'd be no strings. Remember?"

Hell, was she going to keep bringing that up? He was getting tired of hearing it.

That's the way it has to be, Holt. Keeping things casual is the best way for both of you. She won't get hurt when your eye starts to stray elsewhere. And you won't give it a second thought when she finds herself another man.

The mocking voice in his ears made his head throb and he reached for the coffee cup. Caffeine was all he needed right now, he assured himself. That and a plate of food. The rest would fix itself once he got home to Three Rivers.

After several more sips of the hot liquid, the bitter taste in his mouth eased enough for him to speak. "Yeah, I remember."

She studied his face for a long moment, then stepped closer. "Holt, are you regretting last night?"

The confusion on her face suddenly wiped away the turmoil going on inside him. He placed the coffee back on the nightstand and wrapped his arms around her. "Oh, no, Isabelle. Last night was incredible."

She tilted her face upward until their gazes locked. "It was that way for me, too," she said softly.

Everything about her was warming him, touching him in ways that tilted his common sense and went straight to his heart.

You don't have a heart, Holt. You have lust and pride and a man's ego, but when it comes to women, you're lacking a heart.

Shoving aside the brittle voice in his head, he smiled

and rested his forehead against hers. "You know, those eggs sound mighty good."

"What about your family calling out the law to search for you?" she teased.

He pressed a tiny kiss between her brows. "My family might as well get used to me being gone. 'Cause the two of us are just getting started."

Chapter Ten

February arrived with a wallop. Only this morning, Isabelle had spotted a few bits of snow flying on the north wind. After living in Albuquerque for two and half years, she'd gotten used to the cold winters and the heavy snowfall. But that didn't mean she liked it any more than Ollie and Sol did. Both men had shown up at feeding time dressed in heavy coveralls. Now, as Isabelle entered the cozy, warm interior of Conchita's coffee shop, she was grateful to be out of the bitter wind.

The clang of the cowbell over the door brought Emily-Ann up from behind the counter, where she'd been placing a tray of fresh pastries in the glass case. The moment she spotted Isabelle, her face creased into a smile.

"Well, I finally get a customer on this freezing morning and it happens to be one of my favorites," she said. "Hello, Isabelle. What are you doing out in this weather?"

Isabelle yanked off her mittens as she walked up to the glass counter. "A rancher's work never takes a holiday, even during bad weather. I had to come to town for a load of feed."

"I thought you had two ranch hands to do all that stuff for you."

"I still have them," Isabelle told her. "But I had a few more personal errands to run."

She pointed to a cake doughnut covered with white icing and chopped peanuts. "Give me one of those and a regular coffee with cream."

Emily-Ann looked surprised. "That's all? No apple fritter, or maple long john?"

Isabelle laughed. "Okay. Give me a cinnamon roll, too. The one with the raisins. That will be my attempt at a healthy diet today."

While Emily-Ann gathered her order, Isabelle walked over to one of the two small tables in the room and hung her puffy red coat on the back of one of the chairs.

"Good thing you're not busy," Isabelle commented as she took a seat. "I'd hate to have to eat outside in this weather."

Emily-Ann carried the coffee and pastries over to Isabelle and sat down across from her.

"I'm hoping this cold will blow out before Thursday. The Gold Rush Days celebration will be kicking off then."

Isabelle munched on the doughnut. "When I first drove into town, I noticed the banners crossing the street. Just what is this celebration?"

Emily-Ann's eyes sparkled. "Oh, it's such fun. There's a carnival, plus all kinds of street vendors and entertainment. And then, of course, there's a big rodeo, too. This one will be the seventy-first annual celebration. It's been going on for a long time."

"Exactly what is being celebrated?" Isabelle asked.

Emily-Ann made a palms-up gesture. "I'm not much of a town historian, but it's to celebrate how the ranchers and miners first got the town going. Which was back in 1863—even a few years before the big city of Phoenix came into existence."

"That's interesting. So do very many people show up for Gold Rush Days?"

"Thousands and that is no exaggeration. It's always a busy time for everyone in town. Even with this street being off the beaten path, I get lots of extra customers. You should come join the fun. There's even a gold panning event. Who knows, you might get lucky and find a nugget." She cast Isabelle a clever look. "But from what I'm hearing, you've already found your nugget."

The doughnut in Isabelle's hand paused halfway to her mouth. "Me? I haven't been panning for gold. Even though Ollie and Sol tell me there might be some on my property. From what they say, one of the richest gold mines ever was somewhere in this area." She shrugged. "But I don't have time to chase after a fortune in yellow mineral. My dream is pastures filled with horses."

"Hmm. I thought since you started seeing Holt, your dreams might include a husband and children."

Isabelle stared at her. "Where did you hear that Holt and I were—seeing each other?"

Emily-Ann giggled. "Holt's sister Camille told me. We've been best friends since kindergarten. Her mother and sister keep her caught up on family happenings. Have you met all the Hollisters yet?"

Holt had been coming over to Blue Stallion Ranch to be with her almost every night, but so far he'd not invited her to Three Rivers or suggested she meet his family. Isabelle had been telling herself that none of that was important. The two of them hadn't been together for that long. They needed to focus on each other first before his family or her mother were involved.

Isabelle said, "The subject of meeting his family hasn't come up."

"Well, I figure it will. From what Camille says, the whole family believes he's besotted with you."

Isabelle made a scoffing noise. "Then they're overblowing the whole situation. Holt isn't falling for me. We're just—enjoying each other's company—for now."

Emily-Ann shook her head. "It's exciting to think of you and Holt together, but I'm kinda glad you're saying it's not serious with you two. Holt is gorgeous and sexy, but it would be heartbreaking to end up being just a notch on his belt. I'd rather have a simple man who loves me for real. Wouldn't you?"

Real love. That's what Isabelle wanted more than anything. And sometimes when she was in Holt's arms, when he was kissing her, touching her, she thought she felt love in the touch of his fingers, the taste of his lips. But she was afraid to believe or hope his feelings were the real thing.

"You couldn't have said it better." Isabelle reached across the table and patted her friend's hand. "What about you? Have you found anything close to that 'simple man'?"

"Me?" Her short laugh was scornful. "I've quit looking. There's something about me that turns men off. My red hair and freckles, I guess. Or I'm too big and gawky, or maybe I talk too much, I don't know. Anyway, most of the guys around here I've been acquainted with all my life. And they know about—"

Isabelle noted the somber expression on her friend's face. "About what? Or would you rather not tell me?"

Emily-Ann's gaze dropped to the tabletop. "It's hardly a secret. I'm from the wrong side of the track, I guess you'd say. My real father left town right after I was born. He never married my mother. She was from a poor background and his folks would've never stood for their son to marry a girl like my mom. Even though she was pretty and hardworking and honest—that wasn't enough. You know the kind."

Isabelle nodded. "Unfortunately those kind of snobbish people are very easy to find."

"Well, anyway, my grandparents kicked my mom out of the house. They never could forgive her for having a child out of wedlock. And just between you and me, I don't think they wanted to spend any money to help support us. But somehow Mom managed on her own to care for the both of us. Until she finally married a salesman who showed up one day in Wickenburg. He filled my mother's head with all sorts of big dreams. But he was nothing but a blowhard. None of the promises he made ever materialized. But the old saying about love being blind must be true. Mom believed every word he said. When she died, she was still waiting for the nice house and all the things that would've made her life easier."

"I'm sorry your mother is gone. And sorry that her dreams didn't come true," Isabelle said gently. "Does your stepfather still live here in Wickenburg?"

"No. Shortly after Mom died, he left and no one has seen or heard from him since. That's been ten or more years ago." She let out a long sigh. "So you see, I'm not exactly the sort of gal a guy takes home to meet Mama."

Isabelle grimaced. "That's ridiculous. You had nothing to do with your mother's decisions, or the way her family treated her."

"Isabelle, it's just like spilling something. The stain keeps spreading and spreading. That's how it is with me. The past spilled over and I can't outrun it or wash it off."

"Well, you shouldn't be trying to outrun or wash anything," Isabelle gently scolded. "And you know what I think? Some really nice guy is going to show up in your life and he's going to make you see just how special you are."

Emily-Ann's eyes grew misty as she gave Isabelle a grateful smile. "I'm so happy you came to live here, Isabelle."

"You know what, I'm pretty happy about it, too."

Blue Stallion Ranch was a beautiful piece of Arizona. The rugged hills and desert floors that made up the property were everything she'd been looking for. Given time and work and money, it would be thriving again. And the prospect was exciting.

But this past week and a half since she'd welcomed Holt into her bed, she'd come to realize that her dream of a horse ranch wasn't enough to give her complete happiness. Nothing would mean anything without him at her side.

She'd tried to gloss it all over with Emily-Ann and pretend that what she felt for Holt wasn't serious. But she couldn't delude herself. She was falling for the cowboy in the worst kind of way. Now she could only pray she wouldn't end up being just another name in his little black book.

When Holt unsaddled the two-year-old and started toward the ranch house, it was already dark. Any other time, he would've been feeling the fatigue of being in the saddle for the past five hours, but this evening he actually had a spring in his step. He was going to see Isabelle. He was going to talk to her and listen to her talk to him. He was going to eat with her, sleep with her, and make slow, delicious love with her. In short, being with Isabelle was like stepping into paradise. Just the thought was enough to push the tiredness from his body.

As soon as he entered the back of the house and let himself into the kitchen, he knew something out of the ordinary was going on. The room was full of women-folk scurrying from one task to the next, including his sister Vivian.

She was standing at the cabinet counter, placing tiny appetizers on a silver tray. Wearing a vivid green dress that flowed over her pregnant waistline, she looked like she was dressed for a party.

"Sis, what are you doing here?"

She looked up and, with a huge smile, walked straight into his arms. "Hello, my naughty little brother!" Considering the girth of her belly, she gave him the best bear hug she could manage. "I thought I was going to have to go drag you out of the saddle to get you up here to the house!"

He dropped a kiss on the top of her red head. "If I'd known you were here, I would've shown up sooner. What's going on anyway? Is it someone's birthday?"

She laughed and not for the first time Holt thought how beautiful she looked now that she was carrying her and Sawyer's twins. Her face glowed and there was a shine in her eyes that mirrored her happiness.

"Have you been hiding under a rock? Gold Rush Days are starting Thursday and Mom always throws a little party beforehand."

Oh, Lord, none of that had entered his mind. "Uh—

yeah. It—just slipped my mind." He glanced quickly around the room. "Is Sawyer here? And Savannah?"

"They wouldn't have missed it for anything. Onida came, too." She winked slyly. "I think she didn't want to miss the opportunity of seeing Sam. She thinks he's a real gentleman."

Sam was the crusty old cowboy who worked as foreman for Tessa and Joseph's ranch, the Bar X. So if Sam was here, that meant Tessa and Joseph and Little Joe were here, also. Everyone would expect Holt to join in on the fun. Especially his mother, he thought with a pang of guilt.

"I've never been able to figure out what that old man has, but whatever it is, the women seem to like it. I think he's an older version of Holt Hollister," Vivian added with a cunning laugh.

Holt grunted with amusement. "I always did want to be like Sam."

She tapped a forefinger against his unshaven chin. "There's only one Sam and only one you. Thank God."

Holt patted the front of her protruding belly. "How're my little nephews? Isn't it about time for them to show their faces?"

"Not yet. And the boys or girls are doing fine. Just because you guessed the gender of baby Evelyn correctly doesn't mean you'll get lucky this time."

"It's a pair of boys. They'll probably look just like Sawyer and grow up to break dozens of hearts."

She laughed. "Possibly. But your son, whenever you finally have one, will be the real heartbreaker."

Holt noticed Vivian said when, not if, he had a son. Marriage had really messed with her mind, he thought.

"You're dreaming, sis."

Vivian was about to reply when Reeva practically

yelled from across the room. "Holt! What are you doing in my kitchen with those dirty chaps and spurs on? I don't want horsehair flying all over my food! Get out of here!"

"Excuse me, sis, I've got to go charm the cook."

He sauntered over to where Reeva was taking a pan of crescent rolls from the oven. "Reeva, why do you want to be mean to a hardworking man like me? All I want is a little love."

"Ha! Just like you don't get enough of that already." The cook playfully swatted a hand against his arm, which caused a puff of dust to billow out from his shirt-sleeve. "Get out of here and see if you can find some soap and water. We'll be eating in twenty minutes."

"Can't eat," he told her. "I have a date tonight."

She was stabbing him with a stern look when Maureen walked up behind him.

"Holt, did I hear you say you have a date tonight?"

He turned from Reeva's reprimanding frown to his mother's unsmiling face.

"You heard right," he told her. "I do have a date with Isabelle. Sorry, Mom. I didn't know about the party."

She rolled her eyes. "I've been having a Gold Rush Days party since before you were born. Every year at this same time. Where the heck have you been living, Holt, besides the horse barn?"

Normally he would've laughed at Maureen's scolding sarcasm, but not tonight. He worked his butt off and then some for Three Rivers and there were times, like this one, when he felt his mother took him for granted.

"In case you haven't noticed, Mom, someone has to keep the ranch's remuda going," he retorted.

"Holt! You don't have to be so snippy," Vivian chided as she came to stand at his side. "This party is important to her and so is your being here. That's all she's trying to say."

"I have a life outside of this ranch and this family! And it's important to me!" He reached to the back of his leg and started unhooking the latches on his chaps. "I'll go have a drink with the men and then I'll be leaving."

He started out of the kitchen with the three women staring after him. He was almost into the hallway, when his mother's hand came down on his arm.

"Holt, just a minute," she ordered.

He turned to her and for an instant, as he took in her troubled face, he wanted to grab her into a tight hug. He wanted to rest his face against her shoulder as he had as a boy, feel her comforting hand stroke the top of his head, and hear her say that everything was going to be all right. But those days of his childhood were over and though he hated to admit it, his life, and the whole Hollister family, were changing.

"Mom, I apologize. I didn't mean to sound so short."

"I'm sorry, too," she said ruefully. "Nothing I said came out right. That's been happening too much with me here lately."

He shook his head, while feeling guiltier by the minute. His mother had an enormous workload on her shoulders. She didn't need any of her sons adding to her stress.

"I wasn't exactly Mr. Charming either," he admitted. "Look, Mom, if you want me to hang around for the party that badly, I can call Isabelle and cancel our date for tonight."

"No! That isn't what I want at all. You deserve time for yourself. I only—" She grimaced as she seemed to search for the right words. "You've been seeing Isabelle for a while now. I wish that you cared enough to have her over here to Three Rivers."

Did he care about Isabelle? Yes, he could admit that he cared for her. A lot. But he couldn't go so far as to say he loved her. No. That was for men like Blake and Chandler and Joseph. Not him. His mother should know that.

"I'll have her over," he promised. "Sometime. Whenever it's right."

Maureen knew he was hedging. Just like Holt knew it. But thankfully, she wasn't going to hound him about it tonight.

"I'll look forward to that day, son." She motioned on down the hallway to where his bedroom was located. "You go on and clean up. I'll tell Jazelle to make you a bourbon and cola. The good stuff that Sam gets," she added with a wink.

"Thanks, Mom."

She patted his check, then turned and headed back to the kitchen. Holt trotted on to his bedroom and after texting Isabelle a quick message to let her know he'd be running late, he jumped into the shower.

Short minutes later, he was buttoning his shirt when a light knock sounded on the door. Figuring it was Jazelle with his drink, he went over and opened it. But instead of Jazelle, it was Vivian.

"Here's your bourbon." She handed him a short tumbler. "Everyone else is going in for dinner. May I come in?"

"Sure. I'm just about finished here anyway." He tucked the tails of his shirt into his jeans, then walked over to the dresser and picked up a hairbrush. "But you should go on to dinner. You don't want to be late to join the others."

"It's okay. Sawyer is going to fill my plate for me.

Double everything. To feed two babies. Or so he says. I think he just wants me plump." She eased onto the edge of his bed and looked at him. "I wanted to talk to you for a minute. We don't get to do much of that since I moved to the reservation. I miss you."

His throat tightened. Even though she was his sister, Vivian had been his best buddy since he was old enough to have a memory. Through good and bad, they'd stuck together. And even now, with her living some ninety miles away, he didn't have to wonder if she still loved him, or if she'd run to his side if he needed her. She'd be there in a heartbeat.

"I miss you, too, sissy. But you're happy with Sawyer and that's what counts."

"Happiness, I want that for you, too, Holt."

He cast a droll look at her. "Listen, I apologized to Mom for that outburst in the kitchen. And she apologized to me. We grate on each other's nerves sometimes. That's all. See, I'm so happy I can hardly stand myself."

She left her seat on the mattress and came to stand in front of him. "Right now, I'm finding it very hard to stand you myself."

Seeing that she really meant it, he was taken aback. "What is that supposed to mean? You just said you missed me."

"I do miss you. In more ways than one. Because of the miles between us, yes. But I miss the old Holt, the adorable Holt, the one who wasn't trying to hide his feelings."

He tossed the hairbrush back onto the dresser top. "Carrying twins is affecting your eyesight, sis. I'm not trying to hide anything." Except that their father might've been an adulterer. And he was getting far more attached to Isabelle than he'd ever planned to be.

"Liar, liar, pants on fire. You know better than to try to fool me, Holt. You're getting in deep with this Isabelle, aren't you?"

He rubbed a hand against his forehead, then glanced at his watch. "As much as I love spending time with you, sis, I've got to run."

She threw up her hands. "Okay. Go ahead and run off. You just answered my question anyway. You've fallen for Isabelle Townsend."

"And what if I have?" He tossed the question at her. "What's the problem? You and everybody else in this family has always wanted me to find *the* woman."

"I'll tell you the problem. If you can't even admit to me that your feelings are serious, then how do you expect things to work with her?"

Holt grabbed his jacket from the closet and shouldered it on. "I don't expect it to work forever. Not like you and Sawyer will. I'm not built that way. But I love you for caring about me." He kissed her forehead. "Now go join everybody for dinner. And I'll talk to you soon."

Over on Blue Stallion Ranch, Isabelle glanced at the small clock on the end table. Nearly two hours ago, she'd gotten Holt's text explaining he'd be a little late. Just how late did he consider a little? At this rate, they'd be eating supper at midnight.

That first day Isabelle had walked up on Holt in the horse barn, she'd been struck by his rugged good looks, but she'd not missed the fact that he'd looked like he'd been running on empty for too many miles. After that initial meeting, she'd quickly learned that in a day's time he usually accomplished the work of two men.

Only yesterday he'd told her that the bulk of his mares had already foaled, so he'd been spending his time in the training pen, breaking two-year-old colts. It was a slow, painstaking job, along with being extremely dangerous. Holt's text message earlier this evening hadn't explained why he would be late. Now as time ticked on, without him showing up, she was beginning to worry that something had happened with one of his horses or, God forbid, to him.

The fire in the fireplace had turned to little more than a pile of burning coals, so she got up from the couch to add another log. She was finishing the chore when a sweep of headlights passed in front of the living room windows.

Relieved, she put away the poker and hurried out to meet him. As soon as he stepped down from the truck, she hugged him tight.

"I was beginning to think you weren't going to show," she said.

He kissed her cheek. "You got my text, didn't you?"

"Yes, but it's getting so late I was afraid there might've been some sort of accident."

"No. Just lots of company at the house." He wrapped his arm around the back of her shoulders. "Let's go in and I'll tell you about it. Got anything to eat?"

"Peanut butter and jelly sandwiches," she said, loving the warmth of his arm around her. "The pork chops and scalloped potatoes are ruined. Oh, but if you don't want the peanut butter and jelly, you can have bologna. I know you like that."

"Are you serious?"

The deflated look on his face had her laughing. "Yes. I'm kidding. I have the chops and everything to go with them in the warmer."

He playfully pinched the end of her nose. "You little teaser. I'm going to get you for that."

She let out a sultry laugh. "I'll just bet you will."

They entered the house and the first thing he noticed was the fire. "Wow, you built a fire for me? I feel special."

"That was my intention," she said, then tugged his head down so that she could kiss his lips.

"Mmm. You keep that up and those chops will have to stay in the warmer a little longer," he murmured, then kissed her twice more before she grabbed both his hands and tugged him into the kitchen.

"We'd better eat," she said. "You look famished and I'm starving. Let's fill our plates off the stove and carry them to the dining room. It'll be quicker."

"Sounds good to me."

Minutes later, they were eating at the long table, where Isabelle had lit a pair of candles and poured blackberry wine. Beyond the row of arched windows in front of them, the starlit sky shone down on the quiet ranch yard. The view was always beautiful to Isabelle but having Holt sitting across from her made it perfect.

As their conversation naturally turned to work, he asked, "How's the fence building coming along?"

"Good. We're making progress. And since we've moved farther away from the ranch yard, I'm finding more good grazing land. There's one little valley where Mr. Landry used to grow hay. I'm thinking I might like to try my hand at that. Ollie and Sol seemed to know a bit about it. And they believe they can get the irrigation system going again."

He said, "Sounds like you've turned Ollie and Sol into big dreamers, too."

She pulled a face at him. "Ollie and Sol believe in themselves and me. The three of us plan to get all sorts of things accomplished—together. And to grow my own hay would be a big savings. Especially when my herd gets a lot larger."

He smiled. "You really love this place, don't you?"

"I do love it. Very much. It makes me feel—well, like I'm home. Really home. Do you understand what I mean?" she asked, then shook her head. "That's a stupid question. Of course, you understand. Three Rivers is undoubtedly in your blood the way Blue Stallion is in mine."

His fork hovered above his plate, while his green eyes made a slow survey of her face. "Is there anything that could make you move away from here?"

The question surprised her. Not only because he'd asked it, but because it was so easy to answer.

"No. I'm here to stay. Like I told you before, my parents were free spirits. While they were together, we moved around. Mostly to follow Dad's gigs, but sometimes just because my parents wanted something different. As a kid, I didn't know what it was like to put down roots. Later, Mom and I settled in San Diego, but city life wasn't for me. Then I thought I'd found a home in Albuquerque with Trevor. But that place was never really where I was meant to be." She gestured toward the window. "This is my land, my home. It's where I want my children to be raised. Where I want to live out my life."

"I figured that's what you'd say."

She wasn't going to ask him to explain what had prompted his question. She didn't know why, but she had the uneasy feeling she might not like his answer.

Picking up her fork, she began to tackle the mound of scalloped potatoes on her plate. "You haven't told me about the company at Three Rivers tonight."

"Every year my mother throws a little family party

in honor of Gold Rush Days. My whole family was there. Plus Matthew, our foreman, and Sam, the Bar X foreman. I think they were all a little peeved at me because I didn't stay."

A family party. Isabelle supposed she should feel honored that Holt had chosen to spend the evening with her. And yet, a part of her felt dejected because he'd not invited her to attend the party. With everyone there, it would have been the perfect time for him to introduce his new girlfriend.

But Holt might not think of her as his girlfriend, Isabelle pondered. In his eyes, she might just be a woman he had sex with and that's all she'd ever be.

Stop it, Isabelle! Quit feeling wronged or sorry for yourself! You went into this thing with Holt knowing who he was and what he was. You even told him there'd be no strings, so don't go thinking he's going to change.

Shutting out the taunting voice, she said, "I'm sorry you're missing the party, Holt. You should've told me. I wouldn't have been annoyed if you'd canceled your time with me."

The frown on his face slowly turned into a wan smile. "That's nice of you, Isabelle. But to be honest, I didn't want to stay for the party. I wanted to be here with you."

His words wrapped around her heart and she reached across the table and folded her fingers over his. "I'm happy you are here with me."

"So am I."

Chapter Eleven

In the past, Holt had never been bothered very much by his conscious. The only time he'd ever regretted his behavior was when he'd believed he'd disappointed his father or mother. Other than that, he was usually the to-hell-with-it sort. He tried to be a decent person, but he wasn't going to break his back trying to please everyone. If he offended or disappointed someone, it was their problem to get over it. Not his.

But tonight as he sat across the table from Isabelle, he suddenly realized he was a bastard. He didn't deserve her, or her sweet, understanding nature. If he had any decency about him at all, he'd put an end to this thing between them. He'd step away and let her find a good man, one who'd love her with all his heart.

Yeah, if he was a decent man, he could do that. But he was selfish and for most of his adult life he'd taken what he wanted and not worried about the consequences. And he wanted Isabelle. Wanted her more than he'd ever wanted anything in his life.

"Are you going to attend any of the Gold Rush Days celebration in town?"

Her question broke into his troubled thoughts and he looked over to see she'd finished the food on her plate.

"I used to go to the rodeo," he said. "But not these days. I have too much work at the ranch."

"I do, too. But it sounds like fun. Emily-Ann tells me Valentine Street is filled with a carnival and all sorts of interesting vendors. She thinks I should try my hand at gold panning." She paused and laughed. "I told her I could do that right here on the ranch."

He swallowed the last bite on his plate and pushed it aside. "You might find a nugget or two. The ranch hands on Three Rivers sometimes find rocks with streaks of gold. And Blake and Joe found a couple of nuggets in the same gulch where they believe, uh, where they found the scraps of Dad's shirt."

A thoughtful look suddenly came over her face. "Holt, did you ever think someone might have been digging around on your property for gold? I know it sounds far-fetched, but think about it. With gold prices what they are nowadays, one nugget would be worth a lot of money. Your father could've run across a trespasser and a fight ensued."

"That's a very logical deduction. But that's not what happened," he said resolutely.

Her brows arched. "How can you say that? You told me that you don't know what actually happened concerning your father's death."

Unable to look her in the eye, he rose to his feet and gathered up his glass and plate. "Trust me. It didn't happen that way!"

He carried his dirty dishes to the kitchen with Isabelle following directly behind him.

As she began to put the leftover food in plastic containers, she said, "I'm sorry I theorized about your father's death, Holt. I realize it's not something you want to talk about."

Holt watched her place the containers in the refrigerator and walk over to the coffee machine. He should've already told her that she looked extra beautiful tonight in a long, blue and green skirt that swished around the tops of her cowboy boots and a matching green sweater tucked in at her tiny waist. It amazed him how she could go from a rough and tumble ranching woman to a soft, feminine siren. But then everything about Isabelle amazed him. That was the problem.

"Would you like coffee and dessert? I have ice cream. Or candy bars. The kind with caramel and nuts."

He walked over to where she stood and wrapped his arms around her. The feel of her soft body next to his was like a sweet balm that filled him with goodness. "I don't want anything—except to hold you. Make love to you."

She tilted her face up to his and he kissed her for long moments before he bent and picked her up in his arms.

With her hands locked at the back of his neck, he carried her to the bedroom and carefully placed her in the middle of the mattress. Then without bothering to remove his clothing or hers, he lay down beside her and gathered her into his arms.

His lips hovering near hers, he said, "I think about you all day. About you. About being inside you. You're making me crazy, Isabelle."

She slipped her arm around his neck. "That's the way it's supposed to be. Crazy good."

With a groan that came from deep within him, he completed the connection of their lips and kissed her deeply, urgently. Her desperate response caused desire to erupt in him, arousing him to an unbearable ache.

Mindlessly, he rolled her onto her back and pushed the hem of her skirt up to her waist. She moaned as he hooked his thumbs beneath her lace panties and peeled the scrap of fabric down around her ankles and over her boots.

The urge to be inside her was pounding in his brain, gripping every cell in his body. There could be no holding back. No waiting.

His hands shaking, he managed to unzip his jeans and release his arousal, but that was as far as he got before she grabbed his hips and pulled him into her.

The hot, frantic connection wiped all thought from his brain, except that Isabelle was beneath him. Her arms were around him and her lips and breaths were merged with his. His thrusts were rapid and each time she rose up to meet him, she took more and more of him. And each time he felt his control slipping.

He was going to die right here in her arms. And he was going to die a happy man. The fateful thought was flashing through his mind just as she cried out.

"Oooh—Holt! Hold me—hold me tight!"

He tried to answer her pleas, but his body wouldn't cooperate. In the next instant he felt everything pouring into her until there was nothing left of him, except a beating heart. And even it wanted to belong to her.

When Holt eventually returned to earth, he felt as if he'd been on a long, long journey and his body was too spent to take another step. As to what had just occurred between them, he couldn't define it, much less understand why this woman made him lose all control.

But he did realize one thing: the whole thing scared him more than anything he'd ever encountered.

He rolled away from her and with a forearm resting against his forehead, fought to regain his breath.

Next to him, Isabelle stirred, then draped her upper body over his.

"That was pretty darned incredible, cowboy," she whispered against his cheek. "Just think how good we might be if we ever get our clothes off."

He chuckled, then silently groaned, as her lips came down on his and the fire in his loins started all over again.

Three days later, on Friday night, Isabelle had been expecting Holt to show up for supper and she'd taken the time out of her busy day to put a roast and vegetables in the oven. But shortly after dark he'd called to inform her that one of his young mares was about to foal and he didn't want to leave Chandler with the job of watching over her.

She'd understood his dilemma, but for the past three nights, he'd called with a reason he couldn't see her. True, they'd all been legitimate reasons. But she was getting the impression there was something else going on with Holt.

Was he getting ready to end things with her? He'd not said anything that hinted at those types of feelings. But then he'd definitely not spoken about how much he needed or loved her. No. Holt would probably never say the *L* word to her. Because, whatever he was, he wasn't a liar. He'd be blunt and painfully honest before he'd lead her on with words he didn't mean.

Oh, well, she thought, as she bit back her disappointment. Tomorrow was another day. And the food wouldn't go to waste. Ollie and Sol would be more than happy to eat it.

With that thought in mind, she donned a coat, placed the roast pan into a cardboard box, and carried it out to the barn.

The door to Ollie and Sol's bunkroom was closed to shut out the cold night air. Isabelle stepped up on the wooden step and started to knock when she caught the sound of the men talking and one of them said her name.

She'd never been one to eavesdrop. A person rarely heard good things said behind his or her back.

With that old adage in mind, she raised her knuckles to the door, then let them drop a second time as Holt's name was spoken by Ollie.

"Have you noticed Holt hasn't been over here in the past few days?"

"Yep, I've noticed," Sol said. "I'd be blind not to."

"Yeah," Ollie said after a moment. "As much as I like the guy, I hope he stays away."

There was a long pause and during the intermission, one of the female barn cats began to weave around Isabelle's legs and meow up at her. No doubt, the cat smelled the roast. Isabelle just hoped the men didn't hear her loud cries and open the door.

Finally, Sol said, "That's bad for you to talk that way about Holt. After all the man has done for us. Why, even now he's paying our way."

Paying their way? What did that mean?

She held her breath and refrained from placing her ear against the wooden panel. If one of them suddenly opened the door, she didn't know how she'd explain herself. She wouldn't be able to. She'd simply have to confess that she'd been listening in on their private conversation.

"That's all well and good," Ollie retorted. "But that doesn't mean we're blind to his ways. We both know if this keeps up, he's going to hurt Isabelle. And I don't mean just hurt her pride. He's gonna break her heart wide-open. I can see it coming."

There was another long stretch of silence and then Sol said, "Well, I'm thinking that she loves him, Ollie. We can't just come out and tell her she needs to stop seeing Holt. We're just a pair of old widowers. Neither one of us have had a wife in years. We don't know anything about the way young folks feel and think nowadays. Besides, she'd probably tell us it's none of our business."

"Don't guess it is," Ollie remarked. "But being her ranch hands sorta makes us her caretakers in a way. And I sure hate to see her heart broken. We both know Holt will never settle down with just one woman. And he'd sooner jump off a cliff before he'd get married."

"Yeah," Sol soberly agreed. "Isabelle's too good for that. She needs a man who'll marry her and help her run this place. Holt is a Hollister through and through. He wouldn't leave Three Rivers for any reason. And sure not for a woman."

After a moment, Ollie said. "Let's talk about something else. Something happier. Are we going to the parade in the morning?"

"We haven't ridden in the Gold Rush Days parade in years. Why would we go now?"

"I don't know. Might be fun if we dug out our fancy chaps and spurs. We might catch the eye of some widow women."

"Hell." Sol snorted. "What would we do with widow women? Invite them out here for a cup of tea?"

"Well, what would be wrong with that? Isabelle drinks coffee with us. She likes it."

"Yeah, but Isabelle is different."

Isabelle had heard more than enough. She blinked back the foolish tears in her eyes and knocked on the door.

Sol opened the door and looked at her with dismay. Hopefully he didn't have a clue she'd been standing on the step for the past five minutes.

"Hey, guys, would you two like some supper?"

"Why, Isabelle," he said. "What are you doing out in the cold and dark?"

She did her best to put on a cheery smile. "I cooked a roast and vegetables for Holt, but he can't come tonight. I thought you two might want to share it."

Ollie's face suddenly appeared over Sol's shoulder. "That's nice of you to think of us, Isabelle. And it sure smells good. You want to come in and eat with us?"

Handing the box to Sol, she said, "Thanks, but I've already eaten and I have some chores in the house to finish before bedtime. You two enjoy it." She started to leave, then on second thought turned back before the men had a chance to shut the door. "Uh, I forgot to mention it earlier this evening, but if you two would like the day off tomorrow to go to Gold Rush Days, it's okay with me."

Sol's solemn face brightened considerably. "Thanks, Isabelle. Are you going to go? Me and Ollie might get in the parade. You could watch us ride down the street."

Ollie elbowed him in the ribs. "Goofy, she sees us on horseback every day. She might want do something else. Like go to the carnival."

Any other time, Isabelle would be laughing at the two men. But tonight she could hardly keep her voice from wobbling. "No. I won't be going to town. I have something else to do," she told them. Something she should have done from the very first day she'd met Holt Hollister.

* * *

Back in the house, she sat down at the kitchen table and picked up her phone. Gabby had been ringing her earlier, but she'd been outside helping finish the evening chores. After that, she'd gotten busy with supper, until she'd gotten Holt's inauspicious call.

Now, as she punched her mother's number, Isabelle wondered what she was going to tell her. What could she tell her? That she was happy? That everything was wonderful? Three days ago, she'd thought everything was great. In fact, the intensity with which Holt had made love to her had almost made her believe he was really beginning to care for her. Perhaps even falling in love with her.

But now her eyes were wide-open. And they were filled with stupid, useless tears.

"Hello, Issy! I gave up on you calling back. I was about to step into the shower."

"Sorry, Mom. Go ahead with your shower. I'll catch you later."

"No! I'm already wrapped up in my bathrobe and taken a comfy seat on the end of the bed. I just wanted to see how things are going and if you'd taken time to call your father."

Isabelle tried to swallow the lump around her throat. Her mother had lived without a loving husband for more than twenty years and she was happy. Isabelle could be happy, too. Just as soon as she got Holt out of her system.

"I called Dad yesterday. He sounded good, but like he was on another planet, as usual. He's been working on some new arrangements," Isabelle explained. "You know how preoccupied he gets."

Gabby laughed knowingly. "Why do you think I'm living alone? Bless his heart, he can't help himself."

Just like Holt couldn't help his fascination for horses and women, she thought sadly. In the very plural sense.

"So how are you and your rancher friend getting on? Holt? Isn't that his name?"

"Forget his name, Mom." Isabelle's throat was so tight she could scarcely speak. "Because I'm definitely going to forget him!"

Gabby went silent for a long stretch. Then she said, "Okay. What's wrong?"

Isabelle explained how she and Holt had been seeing each other on a regular basis until the past three days. Then she went on to relate everything she'd overheard Ollie and Sol discussing.

"Oh, Issy, you're being unreasonable and unfair. You can't make that sort of snap judgment just because your ranch hands think Holt is the wrong man for you. That's crazy thinking!"

"Yes, it would be. But Ollie and Sol know Holt just as well as anyone. They've worked around him for years."

"Yes, but people change, darling. Now that Holt has been dating you, he might be thinking differently."

"When I first mentioned Holt you didn't approve of me seeing another wealthy man, Remember?" Isabelle asked pointedly.

"That's because I spoke before I thought," Gabby said. "Having money or several girlfriends in his past doesn't make him a bad person. Nor does it mean he's the wrong man for you."

Her mother had always had a Pollyanna sort of view on everyone and everything. Isabelle sometimes wished she could be more like Gabby. But where Holt was concerned, she had too much of a realistic streak in her to believe he was a changed man.

"Oh, Mom," she said in a choked voice. "This misery is all self-inflicted. I knew all about Holt before I ever agreed to date him. I kept warning myself, but I couldn't resist him. And now I have to own up to the fact that I've made another mistake with a man."

"You've fallen in love with him, haven't you? I can hear it in your voice. I can hear the tears. Oh, Issy, I think—well, I can step away from the art exhibit for a weekend. I'm going to catch a flight up there!"

"No! No! And no! You've been waiting years for a break like this. You're not going to mess up the exhibit because of me. I'll be fine, Mom. Really."

Gabby was slow about replying and when she finally did, Isabelle was relieved that she sounded reassured.

"All right, honey, if that's the way you want it."

"I do. Now I need to get off the phone. I have laundry to do."

She told her mother goodbye, then hung up and promptly burst into tears.

Early the next morning, Holt was sitting at his desk, trying to sift through a list of hay suppliers, but Isabelle's voice kept drifting through his mind and getting in the way.

To grow my own hay would be a big savings. Especially when my herd gets a lot larger.

She was always so animated when she talked about Blue Stallion. She loved the land and the horses with equal passion. But what about Holt? In lots of ways, she'd showed him that she cared about him. But she'd never said the word *love* to him, or even hinted that she might be falling in love with him.

But you've felt it in her kiss, Holt. You've felt it every time she puts her arms around you. Each time she welcomes you into her bed. That's why you've been finding excuse after excuse to avoid seeing her. You're afraid that you're falling for her, too. And you don't know how to stop it. Other than stop seeing her completely.

To hell with that, he silently shouted back at the arguing voice in his head. He wasn't going to stop seeing Isabelle. She was the only thing that made his life seem worthwhile.

Shaking his head, he tried to refocus his attention on the list in front of him. Burl Iverson, Kern County, California; Walter Williamson, Churchill County, Nevada; Renaldo Ruis, Fresno County, California. The list continued, but Holt's attention was drawn away once again as he caught the sound of a woman's voice just outside the door.

Dear God, he was beginning to hear Isabelle's voice everywhere.

"Thank you, Matthew. You're very kind."

That was her voice! She hadn't said anything about coming here to see him. And at this early hour!

He jumped to his feet just as she was stepping through the open doorway. Her usual smile was nowhere to be seen. In fact, she looked drawn and peaked.

"Isabelle! What are you doing here?"

She carefully shut the door behind her, then walked over and took a seat in one of the chairs in front of his desk.

Not bothering with a greeting, she said, "Don't worry. I'm not here to ask you to introduce me to your family. I'll be gone before they ever know I'm here."

The bitter tone in her voice knocked him off-kilter

for a moment. "I'm not sure what that is supposed to mean. But you meeting my family isn't worrying me."

"I'm sure it isn't. Why would it?"

"I don't know. Why would it?" he repeated inanely.

She crossed her legs and tapped the air with the toe of her cowboy boot. This morning she was wearing a pair the color of butterscotch. Tiny metal studs covered the tops and the slanted heels, and he didn't have to be told they cost a fortune. Clearly she wasn't here to walk through the horse paddock, he thought wryly.

"Why would you worry about something you never intended to do in the first place?" she asked, then shook her head. "Sorry, Holt, I'm going at this all wrong. I didn't come here this morning to be curt or tacky. I wanted to be nice about all this. That's the way two people who've shared the same bed should be to each other, wouldn't you say?"

"Nice. Naturally, I would." He walked around the desk and looked down at her. "I'm not yet sure what this visit is about, but I'm glad to see you."

She swallowed hard and as he watched her features tighten, he realized something was very off with her. This wasn't the Isabelle he knew, the Isabelle he'd spent hours with, the one who made him feel as if he was the only man in the world.

"Are you?" she countered.

"Look, Isabelle, if you're angry because I've not been over—" He broke off as she began to shake her head.

"I'm not angry," she said. "I understand you have more work on your shoulders than any one man should have."

Folding his arms across his chest, he said in a slow, inviting voice, "Okay, so if you're not angry, then why aren't you kissing me? Why aren't you telling me how much you've missed seeing me?"

Her sigh was weary. "Because I'm not going to kiss you anymore. I'm not going to see you anymore. Period."

Her words were like a punch in the jaw and he reached backward to clamp a steadying hand around the edge of the desk. "Isabelle, I'm well aware that you like to tease, but this isn't amusing. Frankly, I don't like it."

Her head dropped and Holt was faced with the shiny crown of her blond hair. The other night when she'd talked about finding gold nuggets, he could have told her he'd found his treasure when she'd come into his life. But he'd kept the thought to himself. He didn't dare utter anything she might take to heart. That was the way a man like him had to be.

"I'm not teasing, Holt. Whatever we had between us is over."

"Who says? You? Isn't that a one-sided decision?"

She looked up at him and Holt was shaken by the emptiness he saw in her blue eyes.

"Probably," she answered. "But I'm sure you've made more than your share of those one-sided decisions before. You understand the drill."

He frowned with confusion. "I'll tell you one thing I don't understand—this—you! Do you think I've been seeing another woman? Is that what this is about?"

"I don't think you're seeing other women. Not now, but you will soon." Shaking her head, she stood up and stepped close enough to place her hand on his arm. "Holt, it's become clear to me that the two of us are headed nowhere. At first I told myself that didn't matter. But I can't keep fooling myself. It does matter. All those evenings I waited and watched for you to come to Blue

Stallion, I asked myself why I was devoting so much time and emotion. Just to have you in my bed? That's not enough, Holt. And it's my fault for ever thinking it could be."

The anger that poured through him was far more potent than a double shot of Sam's bourbon. He wanted to ram his fist into the wall. At least he could think about the pain in his hand, instead of the one that was boring a hole in the middle of his chest.

"Oh, this is perfect, Isabelle. This coming from a woman who insisted she didn't want strings between us. Now you're whining because there are no strings."

Her nostrils flared as two red spots appeared on her cheeks. Dear God, she was so beautiful, he thought, so perfect. What was he doing? Had he lost his mind?

No. He was hanging by his fingernails, he thought. He was desperately trying to hold on to his life the way he'd always lived it. The only way he could live it. Without fences or restraints.

"I'm not whining, Holt. I'm walking out. Because I can see the future that I'm dreaming of is nothing like the one in your mind."

He sneered. "Oh, that's right. I keep forgetting you were born to a couple of dreamers. And you have to be just like them—always carrying around a fantasy. What is it now? Rainbows and unicorns? A fairy tale where some prince appears and makes everything perfect for you? Well, I don't want a dreamer. I want a real flesh-and-blood woman!"

Her teeth snapped together. "Good! Because I don't want a man like you! You're just like Trevor—incapable of giving your heart—your love. And as far as I'm concerned, you can go find yourself a real flesh-and-blood woman. Gold Rush Days has Wickenburg brimming over with people. Today would be the perfect time for you to start looking for one!"

She turned to walk away and he instinctively reached out and caught her forearm. "You're wrong, Isabelle."

Her blue eyes darkened with shadows. "I only wish I were," she said soberly, then quickly added, "Don't worry about your brown mares. I'll have Ollie and Sol bring them to you."

The brown mares. The mares he'd wanted for her and only her. He felt sick to his stomach.

"I don't want the mares! Keep them!"

She pulled her arm from his grasp. "I don't want anything that doesn't belong to me."

There was nothing for him to do now but to watch her walk out the door. But even after she was gone, her soft scent lingered about him, her cutting words continued to wound him.

Holt was still standing in the same spot, trying to compose his fractured emotions, when Blake knocked on the door frame and stepped into the room.

"Was that Isabelle I just saw driving off?"

Holt shoved out a heavy breath and managed to walk around to the back of the desk. As he sank limply into the executive chair, he said, "Yeah. That was her."

Blake poured himself a cup of coffee and took a seat. "Why didn't she hang around? You know how much Mom has been wanting to meet her."

Avoiding the truth would be pointless now, Holt thought miserably. He cleared his throat, but his voice still sounded like he'd been eating chicken scratch. "Mom might as well know that meeting Isabelle isn't going to happen. She just dumped me."

Blake's jaw dropped. "Is this one of your jokes?"

Holt was suddenly furious at himself and the waste

of it all. He'd been stupid to attempt to have anything remotely close to a long-term relationship with a woman. Or to think he could ever have what his brothers had with their wives. "No! It isn't anything to joke about, Blake."

Over the rim of his coffee cup, Blake carefully studied Holt's mutinous face. "Well, well. A woman has finally dumped my little brother. How does it feel?" he asked, then barked out a short laugh. "Forget I asked. Whether you did the dumping or she did, you must be feeling damned relieved."

Holt wasn't relieved. He was angry and sick and crushed. Most of all, he was afraid. Scared to even think of the coming days without Isabelle.

Rising from the chair, Holt tugged on his jacket and plopped his hat onto his head. "As much as I appreciate this brotherly visit, I have things to do," he muttered.

Blake frowned at him. "Go ahead. Run off. But before you do, I'll tell you straight out, I'm glad Isabelle put an end to this."

Holt pierced him with a steely look. "Can you explain that?"

"Easily. You're not equipped to handle a woman like her. And I don't want to see you unhappy."

Blood was suddenly boiling beneath Holt's skull. "You do manage Three Rivers, Blake, but that doesn't mean you manage my life," he practically shouted. "And while we're at it, I'll tell you something. If it turns out that our father was a cheating bastard, then our sisters are going to know about it! You and Chandler and Joe might think you know what's best for everybody else, but I have a say in this, too!"

"Holt! What—"

Holt didn't stay around to hear more. He stalked out

of the office and didn't stop until he reached the mares' paddock. But even though he was a quarter mile away from Blake's know-it-all advice, he found no relief from the anger and pain inside him. The sight of the mares milling around in the small pasture only made it worse.

If Ollie and Sol showed up with the brown mares, he'd send the men right back to Blue Stallion Ranch with their load. The mares were a symbol of the day he'd spent with Isabelle in Tucson and the night they'd first made love. The horses were meant to be on Blue Stallion—with Isabelle.

And him? Well, he was going to get out his little black book and find a woman who'd make him forget.

Nearly two weeks later, on Friday evening, Holt was sitting in the den, having a drink with Chandler. A half hour from now, he needed to head to town, where he was meeting his tenth different date in as many nights. He wasn't looking forward to it. Hell, he'd rather pull out his back molars with a pair of fencing plyers than to go pretend he was having a good time. Pretending that the woman sitting across from him was piquing his interest mentally, or sexually.

So why are you doing this, Holt? Why do you keep going through this long list of ladies, when you know none of them are going to wipe Isabelle from your mind? She's burned into your brain and no matter what you do, she's going to remain there.

The mimicking voice in his head was like a propaganda message being shouted repeatedly over a megaphone. And if it didn't stop soon, he was going to go crazy, Holt thought.

"Well, look who's here! Our beautiful sister," Chandler said, suddenly breaking into Holt's miserable ponderings.

Holt looked around to see Vivian strolling into the den. Since she was still wearing her ranger uniform, it was obvious she'd driven straight here to Three Rivers from her job at Lake Pleasant. He couldn't imagine what she was doing here, but he was more than pleased to see her.

Rising to his feet, Holt said, "Hi, sis. This is a nice surprise."

Chandler rose, too, and both brothers kissed their sister's cheek.

"Did you forget and think you still lived here at Three Rivers?" Chandler teased.

Vivian chuckled. "No. Pregnancy hasn't confused the navigation system in my head. I do still remember east from west."

"Sit down and I'll make you something to drink," Holt told her. "Take the chair by the fire. It's cold out this evening."

"Just a bit of sparkling water or juice," she told him as she sank into the wingback chair. "I can't stay long."

While Holt went to a small bar in the corner of the room to get the drink, Chandler's phone began to buzz.

"You two are going to have to excuse me," he said as he scanned the message. "Roslyn needs me upstairs. Evelyn is throwing one of her fits. The little diva never wants to get out of the bathtub."

"Tell me about it," Vivian said with a laugh. "I have a fourteen-year-old diva."

"Bah!" Holt said as he handed her a small glass of orange juice. "Hannah has never been spoiled. Well, there might've been a few occasions when I spoiled her a little."

"You certainly did—letting her ride those wild two-year-olds when I wasn't looking. It's a wonder she didn't break every bone in her body!"

He eased down in the matching chair across from her and took a long sip of his drink. It was the second one he'd had this evening, and since he'd not eaten anything but a few bites of gooseberry pie early this morning, his stomach was more than empty. Now the bourbon was going straight to his head. Thank God. He didn't want to have to think. Not about anything.

Vivian watched Chandler leave the room, then glanced over at Holt. She didn't appear to be in a happy mood, but he smiled at her anyway.

"That belly of yours is getting enormous," he told her. "Makes you look real pretty."

She eyed his half-full glass. "How much of that bourbon have you had this evening?"

"Not enough," he muttered.

She grimaced. "Aren't you wondering why I'm here?"

He shrugged. "I figured you came to see Mom. She's not made it in yet. She and Blake went up to check out some of the Prescott ranges."

She took a sip of the juice. "I know. She texted me."

"Oh." He darted a glance at her. "Then why are you here?"

"Because Mom and Chandler told me you looked like hell and I wanted to see if they were right."

His jaw tight, he stared into the fire. "Were they?"

"No. They were wrong. You look worse. What are you doing? Trying to commit a slow suicide?"

"I'm not trying to do anything," he lied. "I've just gone back to being good ole Holt. You know, the one that changes women as often as he changes wet saddle blankets."

"Don't try to play cool with me. I may not live in this house anymore, but I hear what goes on. And I hear you've been staying out late every night, dating one woman after another. Are you actually enjoying this marathon you're putting yourself through?"

He rose from the chair and stood on the hearth with his back to the fire. After swigging down a good portion of his drink, he said, "It's nice that you've always thought of yourself as my little mother, Viv. But in this case, I don't need your mothering. There's nothing wrong."

She snorted. "Don't try to give me any of your bologna. It won't work. And you might as well down the rest of that drink. Because you're going to need it after you hear what I have to say!"

He frowned at her. "I have a date tonight. In fact, I should be getting ready to leave right now. I don't have time for a lecture from my big sister."

"Cancel the date. You're not going anywhere."

The stern resolution on her pretty face got to him more than anything she'd said and he suddenly bent his head and closed his eyes against the onslaught of pain hitting his from every direction. Of the whole Hollister family, Vivian had always loved him the most. Just as Isabelle had loved him.

Oh, yes, he could admit that to himself now. Even if she hadn't so much as spoken the words to him, he'd known it and felt it in his heart. He'd just not wanted to acknowledge her feelings or think about what any of it meant to him. Now he could only wonder if he'd thrown away the most precious gift he could've ever been given.

Vivian's hand suddenly rested on his arm and he looked up to see she'd joined him on the hearth.

"Why did you let this breakup with Isabelle happen? And don't try to tell me your relationship with her was nothing. I can see how much you're hurting."

He groaned. "I didn't let it happen, Viv. She's the one who ended things."

"No. You did. Because you couldn't be honest with her. You couldn't tell her that you loved her or wanted to be with her for the rest of your life. No, that would have taken some guts. Courage that you don't seem to have."

He scowled at her. "What do you know about it?"

"Ha! You ask me that after all I've been through? Think about it, Holt. Before I met Sawyer, he was a known ladies' man. I didn't trust him any farther than I could throw him. Plus, he was just like you. He didn't believe he could ever be a husband or father."

Holt looked at her as he remembered back to those days when Vivian had been agonizing over falling in love with the wrong man, or so she'd believed. "I called you a 'fraidy cat back then," he recalled. "I told you that if you really loved Sawyer you needed to hold on to him and never let go."

She smiled. "That's right. Imagine me taking love advice from my tomcat brother. But I did. And because I did, I learned real love has a way of taking away all those doubts and fears we have. If you let yourself grab hold of Isabelle and never let go, you'll learn that, too."

He scrubbed a hand over his haggard face. He had to find the guts to face Isabelle again, to tell her exactly how he felt about her. Otherwise, his life was going to be a big black hole. "She doesn't want me in her life. Not now."

"Since when would you let something like that stop you? Don't you think you can change her mind?"

"I don't know," he mumbled. "Maybe Holt Hollister has lost his mojo."

Laughing now, Vivian leaned over and kissed his cheek. "You'll never lose that, little brother."

The next morning, Isabelle tethered the brown mares beneath the tin overhang of the barn and began the chore of grooming them. Since there'd been a sprinkle of rain sometime during the night, the horses had enjoyed a roll in the damp dirt. Now dust flew as Isabelle moved the brush over the mare's back.

She'd never intended to keep the pair. She'd even loaded them in the trailer and had Ollie and Sol drive them over to Three Rivers Ranch. But they'd come back with the two mares and told her that Holt had refused to take them. After that, Isabelle had decided not to worry about the matter. If he wanted the mares, he knew where they were. He could send some of his hands to collect them.

"Need some help?"

Isabelle looked around to see Ollie walking up near the mare's hip. Sol was a step behind him.

"No. I got this." She continued to brush down the horse's shoulder. "It's Saturday. Aren't you guys going into town for coffee at the Broken Spur? There might be some single women hanging around just waiting to join you."

"We're going." Sol spoke up. "But we don't expect to see any women."

"Don't ever say never, Sol," Ollie told his buddy. "We might get lucky one of these days."

Isabelle glanced up just in time to see Sol frowning at Ollie and making a motion toward her. From the sheepish looks on their faces, she decided they wanted to discuss something with her but felt awkward about it.

"What's up, you two? Is there something you want to talk to me about? Are you needing a raise in salary?"

"Oh, no, Isabelle. We're making more than enough money," Sol was quick to answer.

"We don't need money," Ollie added. "You just forget about that, Isabelle."

She didn't see how the men could consider the meager amount of salary she paid them as plenty, but for now it was the best she could do. Later, when the ranch began to actually take in money, she'd do her best to give them a substantial raise. "Okay. Then what's on your mind?"

"We're wondering about Holt," Ollie answered. "He hasn't been here for a while. And when we hauled the mares over to Three Rivers, he wasn't exactly a happy camper. Did you two have a falling-out or something?"

Isabelle bit down on her bottom lip to stem the tears that burned her eyes. "Uh—I guess you could put it that way. I'm not seeing Holt anymore. I decided he—wasn't the right guy for me."

Sol exchanged a guarded look with Ollie. "We thought— To be honest, we didn't much think Holt was the right guy for you. But you were happy when he was coming around. You're not happy now."

It was all Isabelle could do to keep from bursting into tears. These past two weeks since she'd parted ways with Holt, she'd never hurt so badly or felt so empty inside.

"For a while there I was mixed up. I thought Holt was the right guy for me. But you two know Holt. He's not the marrying kind. And I want—well, I want more than just a boyfriend."

Ollie said, "Isabelle, if you're letting gossip about Holt sway your thinking, then you're messing up. Sure, he's been a bachelor for a long time, but he's a good man. Better than you probably even know."

Sol cleared his throat and frowned at Ollie. "It might take some doing, but me and Ollie figure if anybody can settle his roaming ways, it'd be you."

"That's right," Ollie added with a nod of his head. "If you care anything about him, you ought to go after him. You don't want some undeserving gal to snatch him up."

Isabelle pulled a tissue from the pocket on her jacket and dabbed her misty eyes. "Oh, guys, this doesn't have anything to do with gossip. I've been married once and that man didn't love me. I, uh, don't want to get into that again."

Ollie gave her a kindly smile while Sol patted her shoulder.

"We just want you to be happy," Ollie said.

"Yeah, that's what we want," Sol added. "So you think about what we said, Isabelle."

The two men must have decided they'd talked enough. Sol mumbled that they'd see her later and the two of them walked off. Moments later, she heard them climb into their truck and drive away.

Isabelle thoughtfully went back to grooming the mares, but all the while she brushed and curried, her mind was replaying everything she'd said to Holt and everything he'd said to her that last day she'd seen him at Three Rivers. The whole scene was like watching the world crumble around her.

He'd accused her of living with her head in the clouds, of fantasizing of a prince coming to make her life perfect. Was Holt right? Was she guilty of wanting too much from him? Expecting too much from the brief time they'd been together?

With Trevor, she'd waited for more than two years, hoping his feelings for her would turn into real love. It hadn't happened. She'd accused Holt of being just like her ex, incapable of giving his heart. But she'd flung those words at him out of hurt and frustration.

Holt wasn't like Trevor. He wasn't like any man she'd ever known. He was incredibly special. He was everything she'd ever wanted and she loved him. Now that she'd found him, she couldn't give up and let him slip away.

But would he be willing to try again? She wouldn't know the answer to that until she faced him and laid her heart out for him to see.

Determination fueling her, Isabelle quickly finished the grooming chore, then released the mares into a nearby paddock. As she hurried to the house, she decided not to text or call him. No. Better to catch him off guard, she thought, than to give him a chance to run from her.

Inside the house, she went straight to her bedroom closet and began searching through the hangered clothes for something suitable to wear. She needed something feminine. Something that would make her look irresistible to him.

No, she thought suddenly. She shut the closet door and walked over to the dresser mirror. The image staring back at her was a woman dressed for the job she loved. This Isabelle, in her jeans, yellow shirt, and dusty boots, was the essence of who she was and what she wanted. If Holt couldn't love her like this, then she truly needed to put him behind her once and for all.

With that decision made, she went back to the kitchen to collect her handbag and truck keys.

And then she heard it. The rattling sound of a stock trailer coming down the long driveway.

Who on earth could that be? Ollie and Sol hadn't taken a trailer with them. And it couldn't be a horse buyer. It would be a year or more before she began advertising Blue Stallion Ranch.

Deciding someone had taken the wrong backroad and was lost, she exited the front of the house and from the edge of the porch, peered out at the vehicle that was rolling to a gentle stop.

Oh! Oh, my! It was Holt's truck and an expensive-looking horse van hooked to it.

Her heart racing wildly, she watched him climb down from the cab and start toward the house. The moment he spotted her, he paused briefly, then continued striding toward her.

Fearful and hopeful at the same time, Isabelle stepped off the porch and began walking toward him, until the two of them met just inside the yard gate.

"Hello, Holt," she said, relieved that she'd managed to squeeze the words past her tight throat. "Are you here to collect your brown mares?"

The expression on his face was unlike anything she'd seen on him before. It was rueful and pleading and so raw that it made her ache just to look at him.

"Those aren't my mares," he said huskily. "Those are yours and ours—together. Remember? We're partners."

Tears filled her eyes and spilled onto her cheeks. "Are we?"

Groaning, he reached for her and Isabelle fell willingly into his arms. His face buried itself in the curve of her neck and she wrapped her arms tightly around him.

"Isabelle. My darling, Isabelle," he said hoarsely. "Will you forgive me for being a blind, stubborn fool?"

She let out a sob of joy. "I'm the one who should be asking for forgiveness. I'm the one who broke us apart. But only because—"

He eased his head back and looked deeply into her eyes. "We both know that everything you said that day in my office was true. That's why it made me so angry. For years, my family warned me that one day I'd find my match and fall in love. I didn't believe them. Until you forced me to see how empty my life would be without you. I love you, Isabelle. More than you can ever know."

Holt didn't just want her. He loved her! The knowledge caused something to burst inside her and send sweet, warm contentment flowing into her heart.

"Oh, Holt, I love you so much. But I was afraid to tell you. Afraid you didn't want to hear it."

"I didn't want to hear it," he admitted, "because it would've forced me to examine my own feelings." Smiling, he pressed his cheek against hers. "But I want to hear it now, Isabelle. Every day. For the rest of our lives."

She was trying to take in the wonder of those words when, a few feet behind them, a loud whinny sounded from inside the horse trailer. Across the way, the freshly groomed brown mares answered the call.

Isabelle eased out of his arms and looked at the horse van. The side windows were closed, blocking any view of the interior, but the subtle rocking movements told her a horse was inside.

Her gaze slipped back to Holt. "You brought a horse with you?"

Grinning, he caught her by the hand and led her out

to the truck and trailer. "Not just any horse," he said, then with a hand on her arm, carefully guided her to a safe spot. "Let me show you."

A minute later, Isabelle stared in stunned disbelief as he backed the blue roan stallion down the loading ramp and onto the ground. "That's Blue Midnight! What is he doing here?"

His expression full of love and tenderness, Holt handed the horse's lead rope over to Isabelle. "He's yours now. He's going to make Blue Stallion Ranch more than just your dream, Isabelle. He's going to help turn this place into a prosperous horse farm for you— for us. That is, if you want me here with you."

"As my partner?" she asked.

"Your partner, lover, husband, and father of your children. Anything you want me to be," he told her, then with a big grin, added, "As long as I don't have to sleep in the bunkroom with Ollie and Sol."

"You want us to be married? But what about those strings you never wanted? What about your job at Three Rivers?"

She barely got the question out when Blue Midnight nudged her in the back and propelled her right into Holt's loving arms.

His hands cupped her face. "You can throw a lariat on me if you want—just as long as we're together. As for my managing the horse division at Three Rivers, I can still do that and help you, too. My family has been telling me to hire more trainers to ease my workload. The time has come for me to follow their advice." He brought his lips next to hers. "I want Blue Stallion Ranch to be my home—our home. Together."

"Oh, Holt, I'm so glad you've come home to Blue Stallion Ranch."

He closed the tiny distance between their lips and as he gave her a kiss full of promises, Blue Midnight looked over at the brown mares and whinnied a promise of his own.

Epilogue

"**Y**ou know, roses are delicate and romantic. Most women like having a garden of roses in their backyard," Holt said as he peered down at Isabelle who was on her hands and knees, carefully planting a large barrel cactus. "But no, you want a garden of tough, thorny cacti."

Tilting her head back, she pulled a playful face at him. "That's right. How long do you think a rose would last in this blistering heat? Besides, cacti have beautiful blooms," she argued.

"They grow at glacier speed and you're lucky if they bloom once a year," he pointed out.

She stood up and brushed her gloved hands on the seat of her jeans. "You want instant gratification. That's your problem," she joked and poked a finger into his hard abs. "I honestly don't know how you bear to wait eleven months and twenty days for a foal to be born."

"Patience, my beautiful Isabelle. I'm brimming over

with it. That's why I waited until I was thirty-three to find the perfect wife for me."

"Ha! You mean you waited until I chased you down. Or did you chase me?" She laughed and curled an arm around his lean waist. "It doesn't matter, does it? We caught each other."

A little more than six months ago, she and Holt had been married in a simple ceremony here on Blue Stallion Ranch. All of the Hollister family and a few of their close friends had attended, along with Isabelle's mother and father. Emily-Ann had acted as Isabelle's maid of honor, while Chandler had stood next to Holt as his best man.

Isabelle's dreams had come true that day as she and Holt had spoken their vows of love to each other. And since then, she could truthfully say she was happier than she could have ever imagined.

Holt nudged her toward the back door of the house. "The sun is going down. We'd better go in and get ready. If I know Reeva, she'll have Jazelle passing out drinks and appetizers two hours before dinner."

Tonight they were going to Three Rivers Ranch to attend Blake's fortieth birthday party. From past visits to the big ranch house, Isabelle knew there would be piles of delicious foods and all sorts of drinks, along with plenty of conversation and laughter.

"I'm going to miss seeing your mother tonight," Isabelle remarked. "Do you have any idea when she might be coming home?"

A little more than two weeks ago, Maureen had packed up and driven down to Red Bluff to visit her youngest daughter, Camille. Her decision to make the trip had been rather sudden and Isabelle knew the rest of the family didn't quite know what to make of Maureen's unexpected departure. All of them wondered if she'd gone down there with intentions of bringing Camille back to Three Rivers, or if she'd made the trip just as a way to escape whatever was gnawing at her.

"Blake heard from her last night. He said she sounded cheerful enough, but he couldn't pin her down as to when she might be coming home." He shook his head. "This isn't like her at all, Isabelle. Normally, she's content to be working around the branding fire or herding cattle."

"Well, you do you have a few cowboys working the ranch down there. Could be she's keeping busy helping them," Isabelle reasoned. "Or it could be that she simply wants to be with her daughter."

Holt nodded. "That's true. Camille has been gone for a couple of years now. I know Mom misses her." He wrapped an arm against her back and urged her into the house. "Come on, we can't let any of this dampen the party."

Inside the house, they walked through the kitchen and started down the long hallway to the bedroom. As they passed the open door to the guest bedroom, Holt said, "Speaking of mothers, where is yours? Isn't she going to the party with us?"

A month ago, Gabby had flown up from San Diego for an extended visit. So far, her mother had been having a blast getting to know the Hollisters and exploring Wickenburg and the surrounding areas. Isabelle loved having her mother's company and Holt seemed to enjoy her offbeat personality. Thankfully she made it a point not to intrude on their privacy.

"Yes. Mom's going to the party. But not from here. She's over at the Bar X with Sam. They'll be leaving for the party from there."

Holt paused to shoot her a comical look. "Gabby is with Sam?"

Isabelle laughed. "I know. It's hard to figure. She took one look at the old cowboy and flipped. Now she's talked him into sitting still long enough to let her paint his portrait."

Chuckling, Holt shook his head in amazement. "Do you really think she's attracted to him? In a romantic way?"

Isabelle made a palms-up gesture. "Who knows? I thought she was falling for the guy who exhibited her artwork. But she's obviously forgotten all about him."

They entered the bedroom and while Holt showered, Isabelle began to lay out the clothing she was planning to wear for the party.

"Isabelle? Are you sure you don't mind going tonight?" Holt called to her over the sound of the running shower. "I know it must feel like we go over to Three Rivers for some reason all the time."

She walked over to the open doorway of the bathroom to answer. "I love visiting with your family. Gives me a chance to see all the new babies. Vivian and Sawyer's twin boys, Jacob and Johnny, and Tessa and Joe's new daughter, Spring. And just think, it won't be long before Chandler and Roslyn have their second baby to go with little Evelyn. I think her due date is sometime before Halloween."

The shower turned off and Holt stepped out of the glass enclosure and wrapped a towel around his waist. The sight of his hard, muscled body never failed to excite her and just for a moment she considered stepping into the bathroom and pulling the towel away.

Grinning slyly, his wet hair tousled around his head, he walked over to her. "Are you sure you don't have something to tell me? Like the smell of breakfast is making you sick?"

She tried not to smile. "Actually breakfast has been tasting better than ever."

"Damn."

Her smile grew coy. "Could be I'm eating for two."

His eyes grew wide. "Is that what I think it means?"

The eager hope in his voice told her how very much he wanted to be a father.

She nodded. "I made a doctor's appointment today. We'll find out for certain tomorrow."

"Oh, Isabelle, honey!" He pulled her into his arms and she laughed as she wrapped her arms around his wet torso. "This is fantastic! I'm going to be a father! Let's tell the family tonight. While everybody is there."

She leaned back far enough to look at him. "But, Holt, we don't know for certain yet."

He gently touched his fingertips to her cheek. "I'm certain. You have a glow in your eyes."

"That's because I'm looking at the man I love." She kissed him, then added slyly, "By the way, I thought you might want to know that Ollie and Sol made a confession today."

His brows arched. "That's good to hear. I'll bet the priest was exhausted before they ever finished."

She pinched his arm. "Not that kind of confession! They ratted on you. About how you paid them an extra salary long before we got married. Why did you do that?"

Pulling her close, he rested his cheek against hers. "Can't you guess? That was just my way of saying I love you, darling."

* * * * *

COMING SOON!

We really hope you enjoyed reading this book. If you're looking for more romance, be sure to head to the shops when new books are available on

Thursday 5th September

To see which titles are coming soon, please visit

millsandboon.co.uk/nextmonth

MILLS & BOON

Coming next month

CINDERELLA'S PRINCE UNDER THE MISTLETOE
Cara Colter

Imogen could tell Luca's experience with snowballs was limited. The ball was misshapen and did not look like it would survive a flight through the air.

"Yes, Your Highness," she said with pretended meekness, "please remember I'm injured." Then she swatted his snowball out of his hand. Before he could recover himself, ignoring the pain in her foot, she plowed through a drift of heavy, wet snow. She snatched up a handful of it, shaped a missile, turned back and let fly.

It hit him smack dab in the middle of his face.

She chortled with glee at his stunned expression. He reached up and brushed the snow away. But her laughter only lasted a moment. His scowl was ferocious. And he was coming after her!

She tried to run, but her foot hurt, and her legs were so much shorter than his in the deep snow. He caught her with incredible swiftness, spun her around into his chest.

"Oh, dear," she breathed.

"What would an ordinary guy do?" he growled.

Kiss me. She stared up at him. The tension hissed between them.

"Cat got your tongue?"

She stuck it out at him. "Apparently not." Then she wriggled free of his grasp, turned and ran again. And she suspected her heart beating so hard had very little to do with the exertion of running through the snow and what felt like it was a near miss of a kiss!

With the carefree hearts of children, the air was soon filled with flying snowballs – most of which missed their targets by wide margins – and their laughter. They played until they were both breathless. Imogen finally had to stop as her foot could not take another second of this. Though with her hands on knees, breathing heavily, she decided it was well worth a little pain.

He took advantage of her vulnerability, pelting her with snowballs, until she collapsed in the snow, laughing so hard her legs would not hold her anymore.

"I surrender," she gasped. "You win."

He collapsed in the snow beside her and a comfortable silence drifted over them as the huge snowflakes fluttered down and landed on their upturned faces.

Finally, he found his feet, and held out his hand to her.

"We're both wet, we better get at that snowman."

She took his hand. "Before the dreaded hypothermia sets in."

He tugged and she found her feet and stumbled into him. His hand went around her waist to steady her, and he pulled her closer. She could feel a lovely warmth radiating through the wetness of his jacket. She could feel the strong, sure beat of his heart. His scent filled her nostrils, as heady as the mountain sweet crispness of the air around them.

She looked up at him: the whisker-roughness of his chin and cheeks, the perfection of his features, the steadiness in the velvet-brown warmth of his eyes.

They were back at that question: what would an ordinary guy do?

But despite his clothing, he was not an ordinary guy. A prince! She was chasing through this mountain meadow with a prince.

Would kissing him enhance the sense of enchantment or destroy it

Continue reading
CINDERELLA'S PRINCE UNDER THE MISTLETOE
Cara Colter

Available next month
www.millsandboon.co.uk

LET'S TALK
Romance

For exclusive extracts, competitions
and special offers, find us online:

 facebook.com/millsandboon

 @MillsandBoon

 @MillsandBoonUK

Get in touch on 01413 063232

For all the latest titles coming soon, visit
millsandboon.co.uk/nextmonth

MILLS & BOON
MEDICAL
Pulse-Racing Passion

Set your pulse racing with dedicated, delectable doctors in the high-pressure world of medicine, where emotions run high and passion, comfort and love are the best medicine.

MILLS & BOON

MODERN

Power and Passion

Prepare to be swept off your feet by sophisticated, sexy and seductive heroes, in some of the world's most glamourous and romantic locations, where power and passion collide.

Julia James
Heiress's
PREGNANCY SCANDAL

MILLS & BOON
MODERN

Jennie Lucas
Chosen as the
SHEIKH'S ROYAL BRIDE

MILLS & BOON
MODERN

Kim Lawrence
A WEDDING at the
ITALIAN'S DEMAND

MILLS

Sharon Kendrick
The
SHEIKH'S SECRET BABY

MILLS & BOON
MODERN

MILLS & BOON

HISTORICAL

Awaken the romance of the past

Escape with historical heroes from time gone by. Whether your passion is for wicked Regency Rakes, muscled Viking warriors or rugged Highlanders, indulge your fantasies and awaken the romance of the past.